BEFORE MARS

A PLANETFALL NOVEL

EMMA NEWMAN

This edition first published in Great Britain in 2019 by Gollancz

First published in Great Britain in 2018 by Gollancz
an imprint of the Orion Publishing Group Ltd
Carmelite House, 50 Victoria Embankment
London EC4Y 0DZ

An Hachette UK Company

1 3 5 7 9 10 8 6 4 2

A CIP catalogue record for this book is
available from the British Library.

ISBN 978 1 473 22390 5

Printed and bound in Great Britain
by Clays Ltd, Elcograf S.p.A.

MIX
Paper from
responsible sources
FSC® C104740

www.enewman.co.uk

For Peter,
who understands the places this book came from
and loves me nevertheless

1

I AM NOT on this beach. I see the waves and hear them smashing against the shore. I can even taste the salt on my lips and feel the grains of sand between my toes. I breathe in deep and for a few moments even believe that the crisp, fresh air is filling my lungs. I close my eyes and tilt my head back like a sunflower to the sky, letting the sun's heat soak into my skin and turn the darkness into the deep pink of my eyelids.

But I'm not choosing to do any of this. I'm just going through the motions now. And it's not enough.

There's the dog barking, right on cue, the sound of his panting getting louder as he closes in. The first time this happened, I thought Basalt was going to crash into me, but now I know he is racing past. As I open my eyes again I see him, all wet fur and exuberance as he plunges into the surf and barks. Stupid dog, I think affectionately yet again. But unlike the first time, when he stank the car out on the way home, I feel a terrible longing to be with him.

"Mama!"

I turn to face my daughter, her chubby legs paddling in the shallows, arms stretched up so her little hands can hold on to her father's thumbs. "Are you paddling, Mia?"

"Mama!"

I can't see her face beneath the ridiculous sun hat's frills. But I can see Charlie's face already going pink, despite the sun cream. His ginger hair is already bleached white-blond in places and the freckles across his nose are a deeper browny orange than they were a month ago. He's watching Mia, smiling at her staccato steps and the way her legs jerk up, forward and down, the walking too new to be smoothed into an easy gait.

"We should have come here before!" he says. "Mia loves it!"

I look away, seeking the horizon. We couldn't come before but I won't say it. And the reason we're here isn't as pure as he thinks it is. It's not for Mia. It's for me. Selfish as ever, I wanted to come to this beach and make the recording to capture something precious. Something to take with me.

"Anna?"

Charlie looks at me and I smile like everything is fine. I can see him searching my face for any signs of brittleness. We are reduced to this; even when I smile, he worries.

"We should go," I say. "You're starting to burn."

"I'll put on my hat." He lifts Mia out of the surf and earns a squeal of delight as he swings her across the sand ahead of him while taking giant strides. I watch them go back to the towel and the remains of the picnic, and listen to the babbles that Mia makes as they go.

I crouch, scooping up a palmful of sand so I can examine the grains and tiny shells. It's easier than watching my family. I know the first time I did this I was wondering when to tell them. How Charlie would take the news that I was leaving. I was lining up the arguments, ready to fling back at his inevitable anger and distress. Those thoughts weren't recorded though. Just what I saw and smelled and touched and heard.

Using my lenses to zoom in on the sand grains, I study the tiny shapes and colors that only magnification can reveal. I let most of the sand fall through my fingers and zoom in again on the specks left stuck to my skin. They resolve into the calcified shells of organisms that once lived in the sea, chips of coral and a peach-colored fragment of shell. Minuscule lumps of olivine have been tumbled smooth by the violence of the ocean, along with a few specks of quartz.

Even as I studied the microscopic world in my palm, I knew I should have gone over to Mia and Charlie. But I tried recording them close up during the picnic and I kept wanting to cry. I don't want to spoil today. I've done that too many times. *Did*; I did that too many times. I didn't want to spoil that day on the beach. It was supposed to be perfect.

But it is not enough.

I brush the last grains of sand from my hands, just like all the other times, and look down the coastline. I cannot help but identify the different strata of rock exposed in the cliffs. It's impossible to ignore the booming sound of the sea in a nearby cave that's been carved out by so many thousand years of relentless energy from the waves. Farther down the coastline, I see a stack of rock left standing in the sea, now looking like it was never once part of the cliff. Shading my eyes, I stare at it, imagining the way the sea beat against its former connection to the headland, how it bludgeoned the softer rock and made it crumble. I picture a rugged hole between it and the rest of the cliff, a gaping wound where the sea has smashed space between the stack and its source, a thin bridge of rock all that's left joining it to the land. Then I imagine that last connection collapsing, the roar of the rock plummeting into the sea, the stack left stranded out on its own.

"Anna," Charlie calls. "Come and have a drink."

I look at him and Mia, the stretch of sand between us, and feel as if my legs are rooted in place. I simply cannot cross the distance between us. "I'm fine, thanks," I call and turn back to the ocean.

Like all mersives, even full-sensory memory recordings get stale. I have echoes of the feelings that flooded me when I recorded this day, triggered by the associated neural pathways being lit up by my chip's playback, but weaker than when I first came back and sank into this recording. Those pathways have been distorted by all the other emotions experienced in the months since—not just diluted, but fundamentally changed, like those chips of olivine. The playback of this day on the beach has been tumbled by the wash of my thoughts and emotions, its sharp edges smoothed, its original raw shape softened. And now there is a new emotion being added to the churn, one I am trying my best to ignore.

I am afraid.

As soon as I acknowledge the fear, I try to suppress it. In some bizarre way I am surprised nothing is altering the force of the sunlight here. If this were a dream, a thunderhead would be blooming in the sky behind me. Its shadow would stretch across the sand, swallowing my own, whipping the gentle breeze into squally gusts and adding white crests to the waves. Mia and Charlie would look up at the gathering storm; she would probably start to cry, and he would hurriedly pack away the picnic as the sand stings his legs. We would all know something terrible is coming, something destructive that will end this fragile warmth and shift this haven of natural beauty into something that wants to scrub us from its presence with waves and rain.

But the sky remains blue and the cloud is nothing but an echo in my imagination, reverberating through mental corridors to where I am now, a long way away from its cause.

Yes, I am on this beach and the sun is shining and my family are safe and happy. All is well.

Perhaps I could just stay here. Forever. Knowing my family are just over there, happy, better off without my being right there. Yes, better that I am over here, the water just a few steps away.

"Dr. Kubrin?"

The woman's voice makes me jolt. This isn't part of the recording!

"Dr. Kubrin, the connection has been made now. You need to end immersion and disembark."

Stupidly, I look around for the source of the voice. Connection? What is she talking about?

"You need to end immersion now, Dr. Kubrin, or I'll take steps to do that myself. It's time for you to disembark. You've arrived."

"Arrived?" I look around the beach. I've been here forever, haven't I?

"Yes, Dr. Kubrin. You're disoriented due to immersion, prolonged solitude from the trip and being in a low-g environment. There's nothing to worry about."

"Arrived where?" I ask.

There's a pause. "On Mars, Dr. Kubrin. You've arrived on Mars."

"END immersion."

The waves pause, impossibly, and the sound of the sea ends with an awful, swift finality that feels frightening on a deep level. I go to turn around, to take one last look at Charlie and Mia before I leave the beach, but of course, I can't. This is a recording, not a fully rendered virtual environment.

There is a moment of total darkness, and then I see the

interior of the craft that's been my home for the past six months. I look down at my body, encased in the flight suit I cannot wait to take off (and burn, if I had my way) instead of the blue summer dress from the mersive. I'm a stone lighter than I was when it was recorded, fitter than I've ever been in my life, even taking into account the inevitable decline caused by the journey here. I throw a glance at the door to the mini-centrifuge. I'd burn that whole section of the craft too, if I could.

It's nothing like the spacecraft in the mersives I played when my chip was first implanted, and even just calling it that seems wrong. There's no consideration of a pleasing aesthetic in the design, no smooth lines or sleek panels hiding all the tech behind them. Practically every inch is filled with equipment designed to keep me alive and, where possible, comfortable. There's just enough space for me to stretch out my entire body in the main section, positioned right behind the seat I'm in now, but that's it. The rest of the craft—little more than a glorified rocket—is filled with cargo and the pod that's designed to keep my body working properly on the journey over. I'm just the sort of cargo that has more demanding needs.

The large screen in front of me is filled with the communication between my rocket's AI and the Mars Principia base. I scan it, catching up on what's happened since I immersed, in an effort to convince my brain that I am actually in the cockpit of a rocket recently landed on Mars and not on a beach on Earth.

Most of the "conversation" between the two AIs relates to a problem with the connecting corridor between the base and my craft—the connection that woman mentioned—which has been resolved. I've got a green light to disembark. It's all I've wanted to do since I climbed into this bloody tin can, and now, strangely, I find myself reluctant. For a moment I consider looking through the external cams but decide against it.

I've seen enough of Mars through a camera lens. The next time I look at it, I want it to be with my own eyes, with only the plasglass of my helmet between me and the view.

An icon flashes on the screen, indicating an incoming call. I'm confused by the lack of a corresponding ping from my neural chip's Artificial Personal Assistant before realizing I must have disabled that feature. I haven't needed it for months. I answer the call with a two-second-long stare at the icon and the screen shifts to show the face of a woman I recognize from my briefing. It's Dr. Arnolfi, neurophysiologist and psychiatrist. Her hair is a sandy brown, her large eyes blue with long lashes. She looks older than I expected though, in her early sixties at least and tired enough that her face borders on haggard. I wonder how long ago the picture of her included in the briefing files was taken. Probably before she went to Mars. That was only a year or so ago and she looks at least ten years older. Shit, is this what this assignment will do to my face? Perhaps she was too vain to have a more up-to-date picture taken.

She smiles and I force myself to return it. I'm out of practice. "Welcome to Mars, Dr. Kubrin. I'm very sorry about the delay. Some dust interfered with one of the instruments, giving us a false reading so the umbilical corridor wouldn't attach and form an airtight seal. It's been resolved now."

I nod. Then I remember I should reply straightaway. "I see. Good. Thank you."

"It's very common for new arrivals to feel a reluctance to disembark," Arnolfi says, "no matter how much they've looked forward to leaving the ship. Leaving a place that has become familiar in a time of upheaval can be difficult. It's perfectly normal to feel a variety of emotions that may seem contradictory."

I frown, bristling at the way she has decided how I feel and commented on it as if I asked for a diagnosis. Bloody psychiatrists. They're all the same. "I'll be out in a couple of minutes. I just want to check a couple of things first." I'll leave when I'm ready.

She nods, but I can tell she doesn't believe my excuse. "These will be a challenging few days for you, with a huge amount of new information to assimilate. We're all looking forward to meeting you properly and will do anything we can to make your stay here rewarding and comfortable." There's a sense of her managing me, a firmness to her suggestions, probably to challenge my inertia. Her confidence and professional manner are impressive but they don't make me warm to her.

"Thank you," I say.

I don't like her. I end the call and stare at the blank screen, trying to work out why I've made such a snap judgment. She seems friendly enough. Polite. I want to put it down to the fact that she's the first person I've interacted with in real time for six months, but I know the truth. It's because she's responsible for my mental health here. She'll have read my file. She knows me far better than I know her, and that sticks in my craw.

The hatch lock is displaying a green light for the first time since it was closed, indicating it is safe to unlock and open the door. I release the harness that holds me snugly in the seat and feel a small thrill at the fact that I don't immediately start to float off. My head aches and I'm already tired, even with the weaker Mars gravity. I dread to think what I'll feel like when I return to Earth and back to feeling gravity three times stronger. There's a doctor here though, and I'll be checked over right away. That, I'm not looking forward to.

Before I unlock the hatch I grab the tiny case I was allowed to bring with me into this section of the craft and check that everything is inside. I pull out the tiny plaited ginger and blond locks of Mia and Charlie's hair, tied with a pale blue ribbon, and kiss it tenderly. "Well, I got here," I whisper to it. "I didn't die or anything."

I want to go home. I'm not supposed to be here. I press the plait against my lips, squeezing my eyes shut. It doesn't smell of them anymore. I've handled it too much over the past few months. Putting it back in the case, I look up until the urge to cry passes and then make my way to the hatch to press my palm against the lock display. It reads my identity and confirms that it is safe to leave, and with a hiss, the locks disengage. Gathering up every mote of courage I have left in me, I push on the hatch and it swings open, revealing a short temporary corridor linking the rocket's life pod to the base. Its retractable segments are visible even when locked into position, and while it looks sturdy enough, I don't stride out confidently. I'm feeling dizzy and strangely aware of all of my limbs. Then I recall how in the first few hours of flight I kept checking to see if my arms and legs were still there. This overawareness must be an effect of feeling gravity again.

The corridor is about five meters long and at the far end there's a metal door that looks like the elevator. It opens and Dr. Arnolfi comes out with a man who has an empty wheelchair. I recognize him as the base doctor—though he's trained in several disciplines, that's his primary role. He has light brown skin, dark brown eyes and black hair. Dr. Asil Elvan smiles at me and I find it easier to return one to him. He pushes the chair down the corridor as Arnolfi hangs back in the elevator.

"Here's your welcome-to-Mars wheelchair," Dr. Elvan says, extending his hand. "Even if you feel fine, please accept the help. You need it just until I complete your physical assessment and get some things sorted out from the journey over."

The handshake is brief and my hand tingles afterward at the first human contact since I left Earth. He notices me staring at my hand as he takes my case, slots it behind the chair back and straps it into place. "Need a hug?"

Amazed at myself, I nod and he embraces me. He's warm and real and smells faintly of antiseptic soap. It is extraordinarily comforting. "This is your welcome-to-Mars hug," he says quietly. "It's going to be fine."

I sag a little, with relief and fatigue, and he releases me to steer me into the chair. I plop down and let him put my feet into the rests. "Please keep your arms inside the vehicle at all times," he says cheerily as he pushes me toward the elevator.

Arnolfi extends a hand when I get to her and I shake it. "It's good to meet you at last." She smiles. "Once you've had the all clear from Dr. Elvan and recovered a little more, I'll speak with you about the trip over and settling in here. If you have any questions, don't hesitate to ask."

"I won't bother you with them," I say. "The base AI must be . . ." I pause. There's been no virtual handshake. I ping my APA and find that I haven't put it back into active mode since the trip, even though I realized that when it didn't alert me to the incoming call earlier. Damn, I'm more out of it than I realized. I activate it with a simple thought command and the handshake with the Mars Principia AI is confirmed right away. The familiar icons appear down the right-hand side of my vision: messages, notes, media and a new one for Mars Principia. I recall from the briefing that it's the name of both the base and the AI that runs it. "That's better," I say as Dr. Elvan pushes my chair into the elevator, Arnolfi pressed into a corner as a result. "I'm fully online now."

A new message arrives via the base AI as Elvan pushes the button to descend. It's from Charlie. I want to open it instantly, but it's a video file and I can't give it the attention it deserves right now.

The elevator interior is plain and functional. The structure is exposed and the cable mechanism is visible behind a clear plasglass ceiling panel, to make access for repairs easy, I suppose. I marvel at my initial disappointment. What did I expect, Martian decor? A plush carpet the same color as its dust?

"How did you find the self-care regime on the way over?" Elvan asks. "I know there were some new meds you were testing out. Did it make the centrifuge easier to deal with?"

"I don't know about easier," I say. "I don't have a basis of comparison. It didn't make me sick though; I know that was a problem for some people." I don't moan about the centrifuge and having to spend a couple of hours in it a day so my body could be subjected to artificially created gravity. He would have gone through the same regime on his flight over, and I don't want to form a bad impression. And better to be spun every day than go through six weeks of recovery time once I'm here. "I was kind of hoping I'd feel better than I do right now though."

He nods. "It's always a bit of a shock, but you could be much worse. By the look of you, and the fact you can walk, I reckon your bones and muscles aren't too bad. Your brain and your eyes need to get used to this little bit of constant gravity again though; that's why you feel dizzy. It won't be too bad. I'll get you back on your feet in no time—don't you worry."

I think back to the preflight training and the barrage of information about what six months of space travel would do to my body. The rocket was insulated well enough to shield me from the radiation and anything except the most extraordinary solar flare events, so no one was very worried about that sort of exposure. It was the weightlessness that was the real problem. I had no idea how much the human body was dependent on gravity to function well. I left that first training session in a complete mess and almost called it all off. Sod Gabor and his "wonderful idea"—he wasn't the one putting his body through hell. I couldn't muster the courage to say that to my multibillionaire boss in person though, so I went back the next day and learned more about how advances in medicine over the past ten years of people being flown to and from Mars were making it easier to protect people against long-term effects. It calmed me down. As one of the trainers pointed out, "If Gabor is going to spend all this money to send you to Mars, he's going to want you in a fit state when you arrive, isn't he?" It didn't escape my notice that they told me all the horrors first, before explaining that the mini-centrifuge would protect me from most of them. I suppose they were just making sure that I would follow the daily regime.

The elevator reaches the bottom and the door opens. A corridor stretches ahead, lined with the same functional printed moldings that can be seen in any underground car park in London. The only difference is the color; instead of the ubiquitous gray of normal concrete moldings, these are a warm rusty red, thanks to being made from Martian concrete, using materials harvested on Mars and re-formed into building materials.

This base doesn't look like anything in the gaming mersives. There are no panoramic views of the Martian landscape and there won't be until I go outside; most of the base is built underground as the cheapest and safest way to protect the inhabitants from dust storms and the radiation that gets through the thin atmosphere. The most dangerous dust storms are fairly rare, but when they happen no one wants to be on the surface.

Even though it's nothing much to look at, there is still a thrill. I've been watching the show they make here for years and when we start walking down the corridor it's just like all the times I imagined being here, being one of the presenters, leading the viewer to see another aspect of life in Mars Principia. That was way before actually coming here was a possibility, when it had the fuzzy glow of a favorite daydream. Since then, I've walked around this base in virtual simulations so many times I know where everything is, and it feels odd to actually be here now. There's a temptation to instruct my APA to end immersion, just in case I'm still on Earth and able to go home this evening. The thought that I can't do that makes me crumple a little. Why did I say yes to this ridiculous scheme?

"You might be feeling overly aware of your limbs?" At my nod, Elvan says, "All normal. There are a few things we can do with your APA to help your brain remember how to process proprioception within a constant-gravity environment." Perhaps he's mistaken my silence for worry. "Did you keep up with the virtual program too?"

"Yes, I did all of it." I don't mention the days when I really didn't want to. There were a couple, early on, but then MyPhys identified the early stages of depression, ran a neurochemical analysis without my permission and had the printer make me some meds. When I couldn't muster the desire to take them, the printer included them in my food.

"Good. You'll be on your feet in twenty-four hours, then. I'm not saying you'll be able to run a marathon then, but I'll be able to sign you off for trips in the rover in three to four days, if you follow all my advice."

We get to the end of the corridor and through a set of double doors into the central hub of the base, from which all the different areas can be reached. There are several large screens (which puzzles me, considering we're all chipped), chairs and shelves of equipment, which mostly looks like it's all to do with exploration and surveying. It's well lit and functional, rather than comfortable. Through the doorways off this room there are labs, as good as the ones back home, along with quarters for the team, of which I am now the fifth. Elvan starts steering me toward the medbay and fitness suite. I know Arnolfi has a lab in that area too.

"I'm going to make sure your personal belongings and cargo are put in your quarters," Arnolfi says. "Then when you're finished with the good doctor, you'll have everything you need to settle in."

"Thanks," I say. "Where are the others?"

"Banks and Petranek are on an expedition. I was hoping they'd be back by now but they were delayed. They should be back soon."

Hiding my disappointment at not getting to meet Banks yet, I watch Arnolfi leave, unable to shake my initial gut feeling, even though she's been nothing but polite and welcoming. "Do you get along with her?" I ask Elvan as we head to the medbay.

"Arnolfi? Yes, she's very easy to get along with. We all are. That was one of the recruitment criteria."

It wasn't for me, I think, but neither of us raises that point. I wasn't subject to the same requirements as them and didn't fight several thousand other candidates for the privilege to be here. Even though everyone in this base—on this planet!—is an employee of Gabor's corporation, they still had to compete to earn their place here. I'll be sharing this base with four of the brightest, fittest and most remarkable people in the corporation. Yet again, I question why I am here. Why did Gabor send me, and not one of the thousands of better-qualified people? There are better geologists and better artists than I. The string of events that led to my being here seems just as unlikely as it ever did. Some would say that having one's art come to the attention of one of the richest men on Earth was good fortune. I am yet to be convinced.

The medlab is similar to the ones on Earth, thanks to it all being GaborCorp kit, and the concrete walls have been covered with turquoise blue panels that are easy to keep clean. The change in color is pleasant after the red corridors, and the examination bed is comfortable enough that I can rest while various test results come back. My bone density and muscle tone are pretty damn good and Elvan talks excitedly about the difference the new meds regime has made and how excellent my results are. He sends a recovery program to my APA and after overseeing a couple of hours of my trying the exercises out—all designed to help my brain recalibrate—he lets me walk around unaided.

"Okay, you can go and settle in, get a bit of rest, but then I want you in the gym at nineteen hundred hours so I can do a baseline physical. And nothing strenuous, no fast movements or attempts to work any machinery or lab equipment, got it?"

"Got it."

He watches me as I shuffle to the door. I don't feel too bad; I'm just being careful, but I am still thinking far more about which way is actually up and how my body is moving than I would normally.

When I leave the room and am alone again, I almost turn around and ask if I can stay a bit longer. I've been alone for six months, and the thought of going to my quarters to be alone there instead fills me with the same dread that I felt each day I woke up in the craft on the way over, facing another day of solitude. But I should see where I'm going to sleep and check that everything is there. Maybe if I can just put up a couple of pictures, I'll feel like I've actually arrived. Maybe if I say that to myself a few more times, I'll even believe it.

It's strange walking to the sleeping-quarters section. It's so familiar, even though this is the first time I've been here. It helps in some ways; I hate the feeling of being lost, but to have it replaced by this curious duality is unnerving. There are conflicting sensations of being newly arrived and yet so well rehearsed that I don't know how to feel. It's almost a relief to find my room, thanks to guidance from the Mars

Principia AI, and I look upon it with the genuinely hungry eyes of a new arrival seeking comfort.

It's basic but nice enough and the bed's memory foam feels good when I sit on it experimentally. There are no wipe-clean panels on the walls in here, and three of them are dull red Martian concrete. The fourth wall is displaying a forest and there's the faint sound of birdsong being piped through speakers somewhere. Did Arnolfi think that would make me feel less homesick for Earth? As I stare at it, my APA pops up a dialog box with options to change what's displayed. All the usual things are there: seascapes, meadows, deserts that can be enjoyed without the dangerous heat. None of them seem right. I scroll down with a flick of my eyes and see a Mars option that makes me laugh. Discarding my previous decision to see it through my own eyes, I select it, and the pines of a Noropean forest are replaced by the brutally barren Mars landscape. With a thrill, I see a small plume of dust kicked up by the wind and I realize it's a live feed from one of the external cameras.

I have arrived on Mars.

My little case rests at the foot of the bed and the crate that was stored in the cargo hold for the trip stands in the corner. Arnolfi must have used a drone to bring it here; it's so heavy. I go into the tiny bathroom area and see everything I might need already there. A notice displayed next to the shower details the time limit and water-flow limitations, to ensure no one depletes the water supply faster than it can be replenished. I use the toilet, grinning at the simple pleasure of doing it the old-fashioned way, and wash my hands with the same delight.

I open the case and pull out the photo I printed of Mia and Charlie, taken a week before I left. She is sitting on his knee, pointing at a page in a storybook passed down from my great-grandmother, her little mouth in a perfect O shape.

Charlie's expression mirrors hers as he echoes her reaction, and it still makes the breath catch in my throat. As soon as I've unpacked, I'll watch the message, have the inevitable cry that follows and then record a reply.

There's a narrow ridge that runs around the room at about waist height, standing out from the wall by just a centimeter or two, presumably just the join between concrete moldings. I decide to prop my photo on it, in line with my pillow, while I look for something to use to stick it to the wall. I look away for just a moment and hear it slide down behind the bed.

"Shit." I kneel on the bed to slip my hand down the side of the mattress and pluck it out. I find the edge of it with my fingertips and pull it up, only to find it's not the photo, but a scrap of paper. I can't imagine that anyone else here has this kind of paper; it's too thick for notes, and anyway, hardly anyone uses disposable paper anymore. I can tell from the way it feels that it's the real stuff, not printed. Charlie could never tell the difference, but I could. I cannot see how else this paper came to be here unless it came with me.

But I haven't unpacked my cargo crate yet. Confused, I turn the paper over, wondering if it's something a previous inhabitant lost and left behind. There are words painted on the thick stock, swirling like informal calligraphy.

DON'T TRUST ARNOLFI! the message reads, and my heart stops in my chest at the sight of the familiar style.

Even though they're just words on a plain background, and not the usual landscapes that I paint, I know my own style too well. I painted this myself.

2

I STARE AT the scrap of paper, the dizziness returning as I pay less attention to the room and how I am standing. I sit on the bed, staring at the brushstrokes, certain it's my own style. Slowly, my spinning thoughts settle enough to try to fathom this. I can see several possibilities and the first one that leaps to mind is so frightening that I immediately push it away. Instead, I fixate on an alternative: that someone on this base is trying to play some sort of sick joke. But I've only just met these people. Why would they want to do that?

Another possibility is that I have been here before, left that note for myself to find by pure chance and then somehow forgot all about it.

Just the simple thought that I might have been in this room before—the only place that seemed unfamiliar on the base—sends a shiver down my back. That seems like the first stage of immersion psychosis and I know I'm at high risk for that. Covering my eyes with my hands, I feel sweat on my upper lip even as I try to fool myself into thinking I'm not afraid. But I can't shake that thought, so I open the calendar via my APA to review my activities for the past six months. It's all there: the date I left Earth, all the minutiae of my self-care regime during the flight, the media I consumed, the messages I received in transit and the replies I sent.

Of course, it could all be false data. But then, I remember it all. Not every single moment, but I recall it as well as any other six months I've ever lived through. Well, most of them anyway.

Even if those memories are real, I could still be on Earth and could have spent those six months in a fully rendered virtual environment. It makes a perverse sense; surely it would be cheaper to trick me into thinking I'm here than to actually send me?

I call up my v-keyboard and type, "End immersion."

"No immersion in progress." My APA flashes up a message in the lower half of my visual field.

It could be reporting that as part of the scheme to trick me into think—

No.

No. No. No. I am not going to fall into that spiral. That way lies madness, and I am not going to let a slip of paper make me lose my grip on reality. There has to be a more plausible explanation. Gabor wanted the real deal; he made that perfectly clear to me. Nothing short of my physically coming to Mars and doing his bidding was going to satisfy him. It's not like the man couldn't afford to send me here.

Instead of trying to work out whether the last six months actually happened the way I remember, I focus on the paper, and the first, terrifying explanation that occurred to me returns to mind. I have to face it rather than push it away; I know that.

What if this piece of paper isn't even real? What if I think it's there, but it isn't? Seeing something that definitely isn't real would be a step further than immersion psychosis, and I slide deeper into an old fear that has dogged me for most of my life. I breathe in deep and release the air slowly, calming myself, to avoid having an elevated heart rate reported to Dr. Elvan. I run my fingertip around the edge of the paper carefully, so I don't cut myself, studying its dimensions and the way it feels in my hand. I zoom in, looking at the fibers. It is really there. This isn't what happened to my father. I am in control and I know what is real. "I know what is real," I whisper to myself. "This piece of paper is real." The fear subsides.

The paper is the same weight and texture as that of my preferred sketch pads, four of which should be in the cargo box in the corner. A quick glance at the touch pad on the side of the box confirms that it remains sealed and locked. Only I can open it, and the lock date matches the day before I left Earth, so I couldn't have taken the paper from this crate and neither could anyone else. I unlock it. The blank canvases are wrapped and packed in protective foam; my boxes of paints and pencils are strapped into place. After some effort, I move enough out of the way to find the smaller container that holds the sketch pads.

There are only three inside. That can't be right. I'm sure I brought one more.

A quick check of the flight manifest, and the form I filled in listing all my materials, confirms I packed only three. I was warned this would happen: disorientation and loss of details due to the long period of isolation and probably far too much immersion. I scan down the list and note that there are also four fewer canvases than I thought I'd planned to bring. Shit.

Could this form and the flight manifest have been doctored?

Arnolfi said she was going to make sure my belongings were brought to my room. I type a request to my APA, asking it to check Principia's drone records and see if it really was Arnolfi who arranged for the cargo crate to be brought here. In moments I receive confirmation that it was she. She could have followed the drones in, cracked the lock somehow, stolen the—

"Stop it," I say to myself out loud. I don't like the woman, but I know that's my problem with psych professionals more than anything else. How could it be because of anything else when I've only just met her? And anyway, if she went to all this trouble to screw with my brain, why the hell would she want to seed even more distrust between us? It makes no sense.

She could be fishing for more work, a pernicious little voice whispers at the back of my mind. She could be deliberately sending me over the edge so she has something to do. All these perfect, balanced people here must make life as a shrink so dull. She's—

I rest a hand on my chest and focus for a few moments on the breath filling my lungs and then leaving them, consciously pushing those thoughts away. I have to keep it together. I can't screw this up on my first bloody day!

"Just because something is possible, it doesn't make it plausible," I say to myself. "What is the most plausible explanation here?"

I packed that crate months ago; it's more than plausible that I misremembered a couple of tiny details. I was so nervous when I packed, and when I filled out that form, that it's no wonder I've gotten confused.

I rub my thumb over the scrap of paper again. Am I really certain it's the proper stuff? I could take a look at it in the lab when I'm able to use the equipment and then do an analysis of the paint too. That will confirm whether it's from my supplies—or at least the same brand.

But leaving aside human error and the preservation of healthy, scientific doubt, this note is still here and still doesn't make sense. If I don't want to spiral off into some endless fractal of self-doubt, I have to assume I didn't paint this—I have no memory of doing so, nor have I had the time to do so since my arrival, after all—so someone else did. That person could have hacked the lock and forged the opening date. The thought that someone here is screwing with me slithers back. Not Arnolfi—that would make no sense—and I can't believe that Dr. Elvan would either, though I barely know the man. Besides, I was with him from the moment I disembarked and came to this room. The person who had this room before me left for Earth months before Mars Principia was told I was coming. Hell, before I even knew I was coming. That leaves Banks and Petranek as the only other candidates.

I know the decision to send me here was controversial—not just in my home but also here in Mars Principia—but this just seems . . . childish. Why would anyone here want to freak me out like this? And to take the time to find an example of my art, and then create such a good forgery of my style . . . it seems ludicrous. Almost as ludicrous as my having painted it myself and planted it behind the bed. It could have sat there for the entirety of my stay without being discovered.

The implausibility of either explanation frustrates me. I toss the scrap onto the bed, uncertain of what to believe about it. Strange that it resonates with my dislike of Arnolfi though . . .

I snatch it back up and stuff it down the side of the bed, as if putting it back where I found it can make it go away. I don't want to think about it anymore. I need to settle in, find a sense of normality, before I start poking at that puzzle again. I find the photo that slipped down in the first place and prop it up on the small desk on the opposite side of the room.

Once I've unpacked the handful of personal belongings, showered and dressed in a set of the superlight clothes I packed in the cargo box, I stuff the flight suit into the chute for dirty clothes with no small amount of satisfaction. I'd recycle the damn thing if I didn't have to wear it again.

Lying on the bed, I open the message from Charlie and have it played on the screen. His face looms out, huge, from where the Martian landscape was just moments before. He looks tired.

"Hi," he says into the camera, running a hand through his hair. It's longer than he normally wears it. I suppose I'm not there to remind him to get it cut. "So, I guess you'll either be just about to land or just arrived. I'm hoping to get a confirmation that all is well any minute now, and it's making me worry, so I thought I'd message you. It's . . . just after three in the morning. Mia was up earlier and I just couldn't get back to sleep.

"Your mum says hello, by the way. I keep telling her she can send you messages but she said that every time she tries, she starts crying, so . . ." He shrugs. "It's like you died or something. Maybe you should send her a message? Just to tell her you aren't dead? She doesn't seem to believe me.

"What else . . . well, work is stupid at the moment, with all the capsule bollocks going on." It takes me a moment to remember what he's talking about, as I stopped reading the news feeds about halfway through the journey. The capsule was one of the reasons I stopped, as the endless speculation about what was inside was getting boring. The fascination with it is understandable though; when a genius claims to know where to find God, builds a spaceship to go there and leaves behind a locked time capsule to open forty years later, it's natural to be excited about what could be in it. I remember the bet I had with my neighbor and wonder if he'll honor it if I win, seeing as I'll be on Mars when it's scheduled to open. He's convinced it will contain the blueprints of Atlas, the ship the "Pathfinder" built, whereas I think it will just be a collection of her memoirs. Charlie was so fed up with it all he refused to join in. That's what he said, at least. I had the feeling he didn't like finding me out in the hallway talking about it. Not that I ever said that to him.

"We keep getting customers asking if the prices are going to change when it gets opened," the message continues. "It's just batshit crazy. The AI hasn't had a clue about how to respond to the calls, so I'm having to teach it how to handle this sort of speculation. It means I get to listen to all these weird calls, which is kinda fun actually. There was this one bloke who called and I listened in live. He said, 'If the Pathfinder left coordinates for where Atlas went to, will you be relocating to that planet?' I mean, what the fuck? Even if we did get the coordinates and another Atlas was built and was sent off to follow the Pathfinder, I doubt an insurance brokerage service would be relocating there. So the AI said that it was a highly unlikely scenario and this guy was like, 'But why not? It could be a very lucrative opportunity for your business.' And the AI was like, 'Okay, sir, thank you for your suggestion. I'll pass that on to my manager.' The whole time I just wanted to jump in on the call and make some comment about the most intelligent people having left on the first Atlas, but then I figured that wouldn't reflect very well on our parents, so . . ."

His shrug and lopsided smile make me yearn to reach over and touch him. He looks so tired, so drained, I want to hold him and tell him I'm sorry I had that conversation at the stupid dinner party, sorry that I was forced to host it and that I wasn't strong enough to refuse. I want to tell him that if I could start over, I'd take down the paintings in the flat and replace them with the ones that used to be there, foul as they were. But I can't.

"Mia's fine," he continues. "Walking is nothing; now it's running. Everywhere. And she worked out the manual controls for the printer, which I only discovered when I came back from the bathroom and found her covered in ice cream that she'd printed and then tipped over herself. I freaked out a bit, I have to admit. What if she'd said stew? JeeMuh. She could've been burned! Anyway, I've disabled the manual controls now and it all goes through my APA, which she isn't happy about. I haven't told my mum about it; she'd do her nut. She's getting on my tits actually. Nothing I do is good enough at the moment. It's like being a fucking teenager all over again."

That's my fault. In my absence, my mother-in-law has taken it upon herself to step into the breach, even though Charlie was the primary caregiver when I was on Earth. We got along fine even when I was at the lab all hours and generally absent for the rest. She was furious with me when we told her I was coming to Mars. I didn't even get a chance to explain how it all happened. She judged, she found another reason to condemn me as a terrible mother—which she has had good reason to do, in fairness—and I haven't heard anything from her since. Not that it bothers me. That sour old bag is probably responsible for all the bits of Charlie that I could do without. I'd never say that to either of them though.

"I can't believe how far away you are," Charlie says, looking down so all I can see is the top of his head. In the darkness of the living room, the lights of the city behind him are bright through the window and the glow from the screen plays over his hair. "I keep trying to get it straight in my head, you know? I looked for Mars through the telescope your mum lent me and I couldn't see a bloody thing with all the light pollution, but even when I was trying to find it, I couldn't really believe I was looking for where you are." There's a long pause and he sucks in a breath and I realize he's crying. "I miss you, Anna. It's . . . it feels like you're dead. I know that's total shit and it's just that it's like three in the fucking morning and I'm knackered, but that's what it feels like. I've stopped waiting for you to come through the door at the end of the day. I've stopped wondering where you are when I wake up. This is . . . it's just shit, you know? And I'm trying not to be a total dick about this, and I know why you're doing this but . . . fuck. It's really hard doing this without you." He wipes his face, still hidden from view, and looks back up at the camera. "Just send me a message when you get there, okay? I know Mars Principia will ping to let me know you're there, but I need to see your face, okay? Okay. Bye, then."

The message ends and I find myself wiping tears from my own face. I knew this was going to be hard—we both did—but that doesn't offer any comfort now.

"Oh, come on," I say to myself. "Get a grip, woman. Just a few months; then you can go home and it will be done and everything will be so much better."

I don't let myself dwell upon the dread that flickers to life at the thought of returning to that flat. Nor do I allow myself to question the real reason behind those tears I saw on his cheeks. I need to be careful. Stay positive. Be what I need to be here. Who I need to be.

And I can't forget how lucky I am. I didn't exactly choose this, but so many would do anything for the same opportunity. I'm on Mars! That's amazing! I have to focus on the adventure, on the potential. Otherwise I'll never make anything good and I need to not fuck this up. "Just once, Anna," I whisper. "Just once in your life don't fuck this up."

I pat down my hair, still fluffy from the shower, check that I don't look blotchy from crying—I don't want Charlie to see that I've been upset—and instruct my APA to record a message. A prerecording icon flashes up on the screen and invites me to select the amount of the room that I want included in the shot. I expand the boundary to its farthest edges, sit on the edge of the bed and tap the record icon.

"Hi, Charlie. I'm here! This is my new room. Nicer than the rocket and it's got a proper loo. It's the stupidest things you miss in space. I'm not saying that missing you is . . . Ah, shit." I stop the recording and tap the delete option floating in the lower-right quadrant of my visual field. After a moment to think through what I'm going to say, I tap the record button again. "Hi, Charlie. I'm here! This is my new room on the base and I'm really pleased with it. I just had a shower, which was amazing. I got your message. I really wish I could hold you right now. I'm so sorry things are tough. Tell your mum to bugger off if she's giving you a hard time.

"So, I've only met two of the base crew, Dr. Arnolfi and Dr. Elvan. They're nice enough. Remember me moaning about the spinner? I take it all back; it really was worth it.

"Mia is still into the ice cream, then? Ummm . . . I'll record a separate message for her. Later on. I have to go to the gym and have my baseline physical tests done. Another couple of days and they'll let me out in one of the rovers. Then I'll start painting, obviously, but I'm most excited about being able to go out to the Gale crater. I'm gonna take a selfie with Curiosity. Poor old lump. If there was a museum on Mars it would be pride of place, but I think they're just going to leave it there to fall apart. I'll finally be able to get some decent samples that haven't been dug up by some fucking drone. I cannot wait to get cracking on all that. And don't worry—I'll be painting too, obviously. I just . . . I just . . . I guess what I'm saying is that I'm excited about being here and I feel bad about that, because I know it's tough on you. It's been tough for me too, but I'm so close to being out there, on the surface, after all these years of blathering on about it!" I pause, wondering if I should delete that. "I don't know whether to send this to you now. I don't know whether it'll make you angry, seeing me happy to be here. I hope not. I . . . I know I wasn't happy when I was home and . . . that was nothing to do with you. I mean, it wasn't because of us. It was . . . shit. Look, I'm still a bit knackered from the flight so I'm gonna sign off, okay? Tell Mum I'm not dead and I'll message her in the morning. I love you. Bye."

I end the recording and send it without reviewing it; otherwise, I'll never send the damn thing. I check the time and there's still more than an hour until I need to be in the gym. I have time to record for Mia, and in all honesty, I knew that when I lied in the message. I shake my head at myself and print a hot chocolate.

Left without distraction, I become aware of my nervous excitement about meeting Dr. Banks. I'm not ashamed to admit to myself that I've had a bit of a crush on him for ages. I've watched what must be hundreds of hours of him presenting the show over the past seven years, and I'm worried I'll be all starstruck when we finally meet. I remind myself that he probably won't be anything like he is as the presenter, but it doesn't stop the anticipation from building.

Banks is the backbone of the show, having been here for so long the crew changes around him. They get far less screen time, probably because they're not natural presenters like he is. Charming, eloquent and often funny, he's easy on the eye and has the most gorgeous voice.

I try to work out what I'll say to him when we meet. I don't want to just gush and be all fannish at him; he'll write me off as one of the thousands who send him love emails every week. I want him to respect me as a professional. An equal. Maybe not that . . . oh shit, I'm getting really nervous now.

Perhaps I could make some witty allusion to one of the latest season's episodes, just enough to signal that I watch it but not so full-on that he'll think I'm a stalker. I scan through the list of episodes I watched most recently and find the one where he's gone outside to watch one of the dust devils passing near the base.

Skimming through the frames, I find the part where we are seeing exactly the same view as he does through his chip as he walks closer to the swirling tower of dust.

"Principia is giving me various warnings now, but this isn't a very powerful one. The winds aren't strong enough to blow me off my feet or anything, so I'm going to go closer. The strongest devils can be a real problem here, but Principia was built in a region that is relatively stable and— Oh for the love of . . . Principia, will you just shut up? Honestly, it's freaking out at me about the moving dust. It's acting like a nervous mother watching her child about to walk off a cliff. There's more risk that this AI will drive me mad than there is in anything that could happen to me here. Right, that's it!"

The stable view of the dust devil starts moving as Banks runs toward it. I remember holding my breath when I first watched this, thinking that as he got closer, it looked far more dangerous than it had farther back. But he runs right into the center of it, filling the screen with a messy soup of fast-moving dust that obscures the view of the surrounding red landscape. He laughs, then cheers until a few moments later the dust devil moves on.

"And that is a Martian dust devil," he says, breathless with excitement. The view switches to that of a cam drone, showing his suit and helmet covered in fine red dust. With that dazzling smile of his, he adds, "And remember, kids: don't try this at home."

As I smile, there's a flash of the messages icon, superimposed over his shoulder, indicating an incoming call. It's Arnolfi. I end the mersive and accept voice contact. "Sorry to disturb you, Dr. Kubrin, but I thought you might like to meet Drs. Banks and Petranek. They're back in the base and will be in the communal area shortly."

"Great, thanks. I'll come and say hello."

I end the call and finish the drink, trying to still the flutter of excitement in my chest. Above all else, I mustn't gush at him. I wonder whether I should put my wedding ring back on. It's still in the small velvet box it traveled in, as jewelry wasn't permitted for the flight. Just as I'm about to put it on, a ping comes through my APA, signaling that everyone else is in the communal area.

A brief check in the mirror confirms that I still look horribly pale and tired and that my hair is still a fluffy blond mess from the shower. I head out, hearing the murmur of conversation and occasional bursts of laughter from the room at the end of the corridor. I pause, taking a moment to gather my wits before I meet Dr. Banks. What if he doesn't like me? What if I've forgotten how to be sociable? I shrug off the concerns. I don't want to be that person, the one I was before Manchester and Charlie and the corporate life. Being sociable has never come naturally to me, but I've learned how to do this before, on Earth. It will come back to me.

On the other side of the doors in the central-hub room I find Dr. Elvan and Dr. Arnolfi with the last two people I need to meet. Dr. Banks, thinner than he looks in the show, is a tall multiracial man with both European and Chinese heritage. His primary specialism is corporate law, with a second in UX design, and if it were possible, he'd have substantial qualifications in being a media darling. He holds the record for the longest-serving member of the base, and also the longest single period a human being has lived on Mars. He hasn't been back to Earth in more than three years now.

Standing next to him is Dr. Petranek, nonbinary, in hir mid-thirties with the broad cheekbones of Eastern European heritage and curly brown hair. Ze, too, is tall and confident, standing with hir thumbs hooked into hir belt loops and laughing heartily at something Banks has said. Dr. Petranek is one of the best Noropean engineers of hir generation and the designer of several systems used to keep us alive here, I recall from the show. Secondary specializations in synthetic biology and human biology.

"Hello," I say, taking a step farther into the room. "I'm Anna. Pleased to meet you."

Petranek's smile doesn't falter. "Hi," ze says brightly. "Welcome to Mars."

Banks turns to look at me, the cheerfulness dropping from his face. "Oh, the artist," he finally says. "Just who we needed," he adds beneath his breath, but my augmented hearing picks it up.

It feels like a physical shove to my chest and I'm momentarily off-balance. "The *geologist*," I say. "That's my primary specialty. The painting is just a hobby."

The snort adds punch to the derisory smirk on Banks's face. "Oh yes, my mistake. Well, I'm sure you'll make such a crucial contribution to the—"

"Don't be such a dick, Kim," Petranek says.

"Anna has excellent references and has been working on the samples sent back from Mars Principia for the past five years," Elvan adds. "She—"

"Thanks, but I don't need you to defend me," I say, closing the distance between me and the group. "There hasn't been a resident geologist here for the past four years and it's long overdue. Why do you have a problem with me being here?"

Banks faces me fully now, arms folding over his chest. "Don't try to pass off your jaunt over here as something for the greater good, or even just for the corporate advancement of scientific knowledge. We all know that Gabor wants you here to paint pictures for him and his rich friends. You're just benefiting from his lack of taste in art."

"That's enough, Banks," Arnolfi says, stepping forward from the shadows. "We all make multiple contributions to the profitability of Mars Principia. You have a problem with the decision to bring Dr. Kubrin here, that's for you and me to discuss in session. It's not appropriate for you to treat anyone in this team with anything less than the utmost respect, regardless of what you might think you know about the reasons they're here."

Banks looks away, an eyebrow twitching as he thinks it through.

"I have as much right to be here as anyone else," I say. "I passed the tests and I—"

"And you will make a fuck ton of money when you go back home after your jaunt," Banks says, rounding on me again. "Don't try to pass yourself off as the noble scientist. You're here to make a quick buck and to give Gabor and his cronies something to wank over at dinner parties."

"Okay, Banks, my office. Now," Arnolfi says sternly. To my surprise, Banks obeys without question. Is Arnolfi in charge here? The briefing said that there wasn't a commanding officer but that as the expert in corporate law and with the highest corporate pay grade, Banks would be deferred to in critical decisions that couldn't reach a consensus.

Arnolfi rests a hand on my shoulder briefly, then follows Banks out. I feel bad for making such a negative snap judgment about her. Perhaps she really isn't as bad as I thought.

Petranek rolls back and forth on the balls of hir feet, obviously embarrassed. "Shit," ze finally says. "He isn't normally like that. Really. Um . . . sorry. For what it's worth, I think it's cool you're an artist. Makes a change from all the bloody scientists here. Not that you're not a scientist," ze hastily adds, reddening. "I mean—"

"It's okay," I say, and ze nods and heads off toward the sleeping quarters.

Deflated, I lean against one of the chairs, feeling like Banks really did punch me in the guts. I jolt at the touch of a hand on my back and realize Dr. Elvan is still here. "That was totally out of order," he says softly. "I think something about the latest trip out pissed him off."

"It didn't sound like he was pissed off before I came in," I say. "You don't need to make excuses for him."

"I don't want you to feel unwelcome here. We're a long way from home. Whatever Banks might think about why you're here, it doesn't mean he gets to treat you that way."

His hand is still on my back and I can feel its warmth through the fabric. I turn to face him, to thank him for being kind and caring about a stranger, when his hand slides round to my waist and we both lean in to kiss each other like it's the most natural thing in the world.

Before our lips touch we both pull back sharply. What the fuck was that? I feel like I missed out on the huge chunk that goes between "new friend being comforting" and "leaning in perfectly naturally to kiss a lover," and it's obvious that he feels the same way. He steps back, hands in the air as if he's been caught stealing. "I'm really sorry. That was . . . that was kind of weird. Sorry. I don't want you to think that I'm like that. I'm not. Seriously. I wouldn't even dream of . . ."

"It's okay," I say, when it most definitely isn't. It's not his fault, even though he initiated the contact. It didn't feel like a come-on, or any sort of low-key sexual harassment. It felt like falling into an old habit. "I'm going to get some rest before the baseline physical, okay?"

He nods, not able to meet my eyes, and I go back to my room. I'm still shaking from my encounter with Banks, half from anger, half from the sheer upset of being made to feel like a corporate sellout. Which we all are, whether we like it or not. He can get off his fucking high horse.

I get the velvet box from the crate and open it up. The

gold band sparkles against the black fabric it sits within and I think back to our wedding day. How happy we were. I pull it free and tip it on its side to read the engraving on the inside of the band. With horror, I find it's blank.

This isn't my wedding ring.

3

I DROP THE ring back into the box, not bothering to squeeze it back into the slot, and snap it shut. I toss the box onto the bed with the same panicked horror as if I'd just caught a black widow in it and back away, hitting the desk behind me.

A MyPhys dialog box flashes up in my vision. When I don't select it, my APA speaks to me—even though I thought I'd disabled the voice interface. "Elevated levels of adrenaline and cortisol have been detected, along with abnormally high heart rate," the calm gender-neutral voice reports.

"Fuck off!" I say.

"Would you like to modify your MyPhys interface settings?"

"I switched you off!" I say, feeling sweat bursting out on my forehead. I swipe it away with my sleeve. "You're not supposed to speak to me!"

"Voice notification settings have been set to default. In the event of abnormal readings from MyPhys, I am obligated to inform you via speech if the visual prompt is not activated."

"What? Why? When did I set you to default? I spent bloody ages sorting you out on the trip over."

A pause. Then a text dialog box pops up. "Apologies for the misunderstanding. Your personal interface settings have been restored."

I drop into the chair, spin round to rest my elbows on the desk and prop my head up with shaking hands as I try to breathe slowly and restore my hormones to normal levels. I thought this bloody APA was supposed to be state-of-the-art. That's what they told me. "We can't send you to Mars with that old piece of crap in your skull!" the specialist had said at my first physical exam.

"I like this old piece of crap," I said, gripping the sides of the examination couch.

"It's at least ten iterations out of date and doesn't support the latest advancements in APA technology. Don't worry—we can upgrade without having to operate. Just a local injection, under a mild sedative, a short course of medication and then we'll train you up in how to use it. It's much less invasive than when you had that implanted."

"Thanks, but I don't want to—"

"Dr. Kubrin, I'm afraid this isn't an opt-in-or-out situation. Would you like me to show you the relevant clause of your employment contract?"

I squeezed my eyes shut, trying to breathe through the anger. "That won't be necessary," I said and opened my eyes again, ready to smile in the right place to make it all seem okay.

He patted my hand, like I was being a good little girl who'd agreed to eat the vegetables on her plate without a fuss. I wanted to hit him. But I smiled. Just like I did when Gabor had his wonderful idea. I smiled and I thanked him because I am a coward.

How many times have I smiled at someone while hating them?

"Did you have a bad experience with an early chip?" the consultant asked. "I can't find anything in your history to suggest that."

"It's nothing," I said. "So, tell me all about these latest advancements. They sound exciting!" Another deflecting smile and he was off, happy to gush about it, happier to hear the sound of his own voice.

Where is my wedding ring?

I open the settings for my APA, needing to focus on something I can actually fix. The voice interface is definitely off. I can't turn off MyPhys, but I can reduce the number of notifications. There's no option to stop the data from flowing straight to the Mars Principia AI. I try not to think about it.

As I'm reviewing the list, a dialog box pops up from Mars Principia, asking if I'd like to review my communication options. For a moment I think it means communication with Earth, then realize it's asking me how I would prefer to talk to it. I struggle to find an option that expresses what I want and the delay prompts it to say, "Simply state your requirement verbally."

I sigh and start nibbling at my thumbnail. I'll talk to it once. Just once and then I won't have to again. "Mars Principia?"

"Hello, Dr. Kubrin." The same calm voice as my APA. I know it's the GaborCorp default and I know it's because Gabor himself decided that it sounds soothing, but it still makes all the muscles in my back knot up. "Welcome to Mars Principia. Would you like me to give you a tour of the most commonly used interface options for your stay with us?"

It makes it sound like I'm staying in a hotel. "I just want you to take the interface settings I have for my APA and apply them to you."

"I'm sorry, Dr. Kubrin. I cannot comply."

"Why not?"

"An audio interface may need to be used when you leave the base, due to restricted dexterity caused by the environmental suit impeding the use of a v-keyboard. I can apply those preferences to the times you are in the base, however. Would you like me—"

"Yes. Fine. Now go away."

Silence. Then I become aware of the soft whir of the air-conditioning and the background hum of all the environmental systems working to keep us alive. I left one tightly controlled box to enter another just as tightly controlled and just as critical for my survival. And of course, I am filled with a sudden and intense craving to run outside.

"This is normal," I say to myself. "This is all perfectly normal."

My eyes are pulled to the black velvet box. I get up to grab it from the bed but pitch over, losing my balance as the room spins. I land on my knees, hands braced against the bed. Shit. I need to move more carefully. I need to make sure I don't injure myself; otherwise, Dr. Elvan won't sign me off for a trip outside.

With far more care, I reach over, take the box and chuck it back into the cargo crate. I can't look at that now. I can't think about it. Not with my debriefing looming. I don't want that psych to review my first hour on Mars and see all this physiological drama on my hormone charts.

I pull myself up to sit on the bed. I can't go outside yet. I can't use lab equipment if I fall over when I'm not concentrating. I should probably record a message for Mia. My stomach clenches. No. Not yet. I need to settle in a bit more first. Feel a bit stronger.

Where is my wedding ring?

I start to rifle through the crate, but I get too dizzy again and have to stop. Besides, I can't imagine that the real one will be in there, given that the fake one was in the box. There's nowhere else to look, leaving the question hanging without the possibility of a resolution. If it hadn't been locked in the crate, my suspicion would be that someone lost it and thought they could pass off a replica as the original, to avoid getting into trouble. But given the circumstances, I'm beginning to wonder why someone in Gabor's company went through my personal effects and tampered with them before they were loaded into the rocket. My thoughts return to the scrap of paper. Even if someone replaced my wedding ring before the flight was over, it didn't explain how that note ended up stuffed behind my bed here on Mars. I'm reduced to circular thinking that does nothing but frustrate me. I mustn't conclude anything before I have more data. Yes, that's it. I'll keep alert for any other signs of tampering and see if, collectively, they reveal a pattern.

Mercifully there are messages in my in-box to distract me. It looks like friends and colleagues have received the confirmation that I've landed safely, but there's nothing new from Charlie or anyone else in my family. I skim through messages of relief and excitement, along with reminders to send pictures as soon as I can. My old boss asks me for first impressions. I open my virtual keyboard and start typing a reply.

Hi Drew,

So, Principia looks just like it does in the mersives, but it turns out that Banks is a total arsehole who hates me already, the psych gives me the creeps and someone has stolen my stuff and is trying to make me go mad. I've been here less than two hours. Brilliant. So my first impression of Mars is: this is the place in which I will finally go insane.

How are the kids?

Also I will never forgive you for making me host that dinner party. Fuck you very much.

Anna

I read it over. Then I delete it and close my mail. I'm in no state to reply to anything.

Did Banks take the ring and replace it with a fake? He would have had to find out the right size and then print it, and that seems like a lot of effort to go to. Did he paint that note that I found? Had he decided he hated me before I even left my medical exam, rifled through my stuff and pulled all that off, just to fuck with me? It seems too ridiculous to even be a possibility, but short of either Petranek or Arnolfi doing it instead, I can't think of any sane explanation.

I knead my temples with my knuckles. I am not going mad. This is not immersion psychosis. There is a perfectly reasonable explanation for all of this.

At least I know I can trust Dr. Elvan. He was with me the times I wasn't in my room, so he couldn't have tampered with any of my belongings. But then the memory of the almost-kiss returns and I wince. Thinking of Charlie, I recall what he said about Mum being upset. I need to record her a message.

I put the fake wedding ring on—otherwise she'll only notice it's missing and then get worried about it. After several aborted starts and a cup of coffee I try again.

"Hi, Mum." I wave at the cam. "So I'm here and this is my room and everything is fine." Do I sound convincing enough? "I'm very not dead, as you can see. I'm a bit tired and adjusting to gravity again but the doctor here is really nice and . . ." Shit, don't pause too long—she'll suspect something! "Well, he said that I was in really good shape.

Considering how long I was in zero g, I mean. Are you okay? How's everything back home? Have you heard from Geena? I . . . I haven't heard from her. I thought that maybe she would have seen something on a feed somewhere about me coming here and gotten in touch."

I don't ask the question that naturally follows. Don't think about it. Don't think about *him* either.

"So, send me a message when you can so I know you're okay. Love you. Bye!"

I end the recording, wondering if she is awake now. I send it, knowing it will take more than twenty minutes to get there. She'll cry for at least ten; then, even if she records right away, it will be at least an hour before I get the reply. JeeMuh, that's an age.

With frequent breaks I unpack the crate, checking that all the paints and supplies are intact, before lying down again. Gabor insisted I bring them all with me, rather than printing here, along with the sketch pads and canvases. I can't even begin to calculate how much it must have cost to do that. It's absurd.

With a smirk, I realize that's exactly what Charlie had said when I came home after the emergency meeting at the lab and told him Drew's plan.

"Is this some sort of joke?" he asked, with Mia on one knee. She was still tiny then.

I sat down, dumping my bag at my feet, exhausted. "That's exactly what I said. But Drew thinks it could work. Apparently Gabor has done this in the past."

"What, the king visiting the peasants? Does he disguise himself before he walks among us, trying to find out what we really think of him?"

"You and I both know he doesn't need to do that."

Mia belched as loudly as a king after a feast and Charlie cheered. "Good girl!" he said, twisting her round to nestle against his chest. He rubbed her back gently, staring at me. "Do you want to hold her?" he eventually asked.

"I need to get changed first," I said. "Look, if Drew manages to pull this off, would you be willing?"

"I don't believe he'll agree to a dinner party with the peasants. And anyway, even if he did, Drew should host it, not us. I'm not a chef. I'm . . . an enthusiastic amateur. Gabor eats in all the swanky places. Real meat. Real veg. I just . . . I can't compete. And we can't afford the ingredients."

"Drew said she will help."

"Oh, so she can find the money to fund this but not your job?"

"This is the whole reason she wants to do this! Drew doesn't want to close the project, but if she can't persuade Gabor that what we do has value, there's nothing to be done."

Charlie shook his head. "A fucking dinner party is not going to change anything." He repositioned Mia until she was looking over his shoulder so she could see the city lights through the window.

"It has for other people. Everyone knows they nearly pulled the funding on Renata Ghali's early bioprinting work until he was persuaded personally at a dinner party to continue funding it."

"Who's Renata Ghali?"

"The Pathfinder's best friend. Remember?"

He shrugged. "Sounds like an urban myth to me. And anyway, that must have been . . . what, over thirty years ago! More than that. Drew is full of—" Another wet belch came from Mia and Charlie wrinkled his nose, twisting to look at his shoulder. "Shit. She just threw half of her feed up." He stood. "Come on, monster. Let's get us both cleaned up. And Mummy can get changed too," he added in his singsong baby voice. "And then Mummy can hold you and Daddy can have a rest. Right, Mummy?"

"End immersion," I say with a sigh.

"No immersion in progress." My APA flashes up the same message as before and I jolt. I've relived that conversation too many times on the way over. I must have been dozing off, confusing the memory with the recording.

An incoming call notification makes the relevant icon pulse. I tap the air in front of me and see Arnolfi's picture. Shit. I take a deep breath and tap it again.

"Dr. Kubrin, I hope I'm not disturbing you."

"Not at all."

"I was wondering if you'd be amenable to coming to my office for a chat?"

A chat? How could such a small word hold so much dread?

"Of course. I'm on my way."

I wash my face, run my fingers through my hair. It's still too short to need a proper brush. Strange to think that the long locks they cut off for the trip are in a box on Earth. Hair that grew from my head is now on another planet. I roll my eyes at my reflection. Get over yourself, Anna.

The office is easy to find, thanks to the mersives, and knocking on the door makes me feel like I'm in one of the shows, about to be interviewed by Dr. Banks. I glance over my shoulder, feeling as though there should be a cam drone floating there, but there's nothing behind me except the red Martian concrete.

"Come in."

The office is just as Spartan as it is on the show. There are five large chairs, three of which have been pushed into the corner along with a low table. One of the walls displays a generic woodland. Arnolfi is standing in the center of the room next to one of the two chairs that have been positioned in front of each other. "Still getting used to all the screens?"

I look away from it, hating that she noticed. "I suppose so."

She nods. "It's a safety requirement. If there's a problem with the connection between a chip and the prince, it means alerts and information can be broadcast throughout the base."

"The prince?"

She smiles. "The Mars Principia AI. Of course, you wouldn't know." She gestures to the chair opposite hers as she sits down. "It's what we call the base AI. The show scripts don't call it that."

I hadn't even realized the shows were scripted and immediately feel stupid for thinking that Banks could just effortlessly describe a particular project or aspect of life on Mars off the top of his head with perfect delivery.

"Now, how are you settling in? Do you have everything you need? Are you happy with your room?"

"Everything's fine. Great!" I add with one of my fake smiles. "Everything's great. Thanks. Thank you. Yes."

I'm screwing this up and she's looking at me like they all do. Trying to crack the nut. "I want to apologize for what happened earlier, with Banks."

"Shouldn't he be the one doing that?"

She nods. "He will. But I should have seen it coming and handled it better. If you have any more problems with him, let me know."

I try to remember how she defended me, but sitting here in her office, with her looking at me that way that all therapists do, the distrust overpowers any positive opinion that might have flourished. "Thanks. I will," I lie. She's the last person I'll go to. "So, was there anything else you needed to see me about?"

Arnolfi leans back in her chair. She looks tired. "I reviewed your file."

The words hang between us. What am I supposed to say? "Okay . . ." I close my mouth, resisting the urge to say any more until I understand her angle. She's using the age-old technique designed to implicitly pressure me into saying more. I can handle this silence, lady. I can handle silence better than most people.

"I know we've only just met, and that this is a very unusual situation, but I'd like to open a . . . candid dialog with you. There were several items of interest in your file that I'd like to discuss with you. They could have an impact on you here."

"Items of interest?"

She crosses one leg over the other. The trousers she's wearing look baggy on her. "You don't like therapists, do you?"

I fold my arms; then I unfold them, so I don't look like I'm being defensive. Now I don't know what to do with them. Shit.

Trying so hard to appear friendly and approachable, she spreads her hands, open to me. "I'm a neurophysiologist and I'm a qualified psychiatrist but I don't practice therapy here. It wouldn't be appropriate, considering the way we live in close proximity." What she doesn't say is that none of the people here need therapy. They're all perfect, having worked through their demons long before they were signed off to come to Mars. "My primary role is to study the long-term impact on the brain of living in a low-g environment and the interaction between the prince and the human team. My secondary role is to ensure that the inhabitants of this base are in peak mental health. That's it."

I raise an eyebrow. "But you're the first point of contact should any problems be flagged up."

"Along with Dr. Elvan, yes. But what I'm trying to say is that I'm not here to analyze you. I'm . . . a safety net. And there are items in your file which make me think you might need a little help while you're here, that's all."

Mirroring her, I cross my legs too and only then do I notice my arms are folded once more. I want to tell her to piss off. That I hate the fact she's read the parts of my file that I wouldn't even show to my husband. But I can't appear to be antagonistic. I have to try to make this work. She's just doing her job. "Thanks. I'll bear that in mind."

There's a long pause as she looks at me. She's trying to work out another way in. She probably thought that if she mentioned these "items of interest," I'd bring one up voluntarily. I do all I can to appear calm.

"I understand there were some logistical issues which meant you had to travel alone," Arnolfi says.

"Mr. Gabor was very keen that I come as soon as possible. He didn't want to wait for the next crew exchange, even though it meant the trip took longer."

"I understand there were some complaints lodged by the Noropean gov-corp?"

"I think I became a bit of a political football for a couple of days, that's all. I'm an employee of GaborCorp and my contract supersedes that of my residency in England. Gabor's lawyers reminded them of that soon enough."

"Well, I wouldn't have recommended it. That was a long time to be alone and it's perfectly natural that you depended on mersives to get you through it. And because of the extraordinary amount of time spent in full immersion, you may experience some side effects. You're at high risk of immersion psychosis too. Don't be afraid to come to me if you have any problems."

"What are the symptoms?" I don't want her to think I know them already.

"Early signs are dissociation, loss of concentration and questioning whether you are still immersed. Of course, you've never been here before, so it's less likely to manifest as severely as it could if you'd been immersed in recordings made in your current environment, but you must have trained with mersives of this place?" At my nod, she continues. "The sense of familiarity with the base may well complicate your adjustment period. You may well experience lots of déjà vu and moments of confusion about having done something here before, but that's perfectly natural. It might be a good idea to keep track of them with your APA so we can review them together if you have any concerns."

Don't trust Arnolfi. The note hasn't been far from my thoughts since I saw the damn thing, but now I can't stop thinking about it. "Good idea," I say. "Thanks for looking out for me. I'm sure I'll be fine. I'm keen to get out there and start work, so I'm going to go to the gym now and get my baseline fitness measured."

She holds up a hand. "There's no rush, Dr. Kubrin. May I call you Anna?"

I nod, sinking back in my chair.

"There are numerous risk factors that I'm sure you're aware of, regarding your stay here. The circumstances are . . . very unusual. Integrating you with the team is a top priority, so we can avoid a repeat of that outburst from Banks earlier. Would you be amenable to sharing some of your art and discussing your plans with the team over dinner? We try to eat one meal a day together communally. I think it would be a good opportunity."

"Yes, all right. I can do that." Right now, I'll agree to anything. I want to end this conversation before she—

"And with regards to your father . . ."

Fuck. Too late. "I don't want to talk about him."

"But—"

"I don't see how it's relevant. And this isn't a therapy session. Why dredge up—" I stop myself to draw in a deep breath. "Am I obligated to discuss it with you?"

That stare again. I want to put her through that screen. "No," she says finally. "One last thing, before you go. I review all of the MyPhys data for the team on a daily basis as part of my work, and any alerts are flagged up to me. Your stress indicators spiked earlier, when you were in your room."

"That was Banks."

"No, the one after you calmed down from that. And there have been a couple of others since your arrival. Is there anything you want to discuss?"

I fix the fake smile back in place. "No, thank you. Nothing at all."

"Well, I'm here if you need me," she says, voice light, ending on an up note, no doubt to make me feel happy to come back.

I won't.

4

THE BASELINE FITNESS test is easier than I thought. It seems that trying not to look at the professional conducting the test is a really good motivator. Elvan and I haven't made eye contact since that weird moment. Perhaps we never will again.

That's probably for the best.

I have enough time to clean myself up and get changed and then it's time for dinner. There's no kitchen in the base, just food and drink printers in various rooms, and no dining room either. However, the large central-hub room has enough space for everyone to sit around one of the tables that's been cleared for dinner. While I'm nervous about Banks, I'm actually looking forward to this. It's been months since I ate in company. Simply seeing everyone gathering around the table with their trays of food makes me feel like I really have arrived.

I watch them as my meal is printed. They're all so comfortable with one another. There are two conversations running in parallel. One is between Banks and Petranek, talking about the maintenance trip they went on earlier to check on one of the nearby weather stations. The other, between Elvan and Arnolfi, is harder to hear; they're sitting close together, voices lowered. I worry that they are talking about me, seeing as both of them have been more involved in my arrival, but then I quash that narcissistic impulse. They probably have dozens of things to discuss.

A chair has been set aside for me and everyone breaks their conversations as I arrive.

"What are you having?" Petranek asks, peering at my tray. "Is that some kind of curry?"

"Beef bourguignon," I reply.

"With rice?" Banks raises an eyebrow.

With a shrug, I take my place between Petranek and Arnolfi. "I prefer it with rice."

"Soaks up the sauce." Petranek nods, grinning. "Though top tip for you: use the printer outside the gym to print meals with a high meat content. It reproduces it better than the one in here."

Banks rolls his eyes. "Take no notice," he says, nudging Petranek with his elbow good-naturedly. "They're all the same model and print with exactly the same base ingredients."

"Come on, Elvan—back me up!" Petranek appeals.

Elvan holds up his hands, knife and fork pinched between his fingers. "I can't offer any data. I only use the one in here," he says and Petranek groans.

"Coward," ze declares and looks back at me. "The one in here does desserts better." That earns another jab in the ribs from Banks and ze laughs. "Whatever. So, how are you settling in?"

I take a sip of orange juice—appreciating for a moment just how good the printer is at tricking me into thinking this liquid has come from an orange—and set the glass down again. "Fine."

"Any questions?"

"I do have one . . ." I pause, trying to decide if it's a stupid one. "Do you all call each other by your surnames, like, all the time?"

Petranek grins. "Yeah, it's a habit we got into when there were three Johanns here at one point."

"It worked great until we had two Chans," Elvan says. "But it usually works. When I went home the last time, I couldn't get used to being Asil again. Even my brothers started calling me Elvan."

"You'll get used to it, Kubrin. I don't even know what your first name is anymore," Petranek says to Banks, earning another jab in the ribs. Ze laughs. "Have you apologized yet?" ze says to him. Banks frowns to himself. "Come on."

"I am sorry for earlier," he says. "It won't happen again."

The way he says it is so familiar. I say things like that too, when I'm trying to remind myself of a boundary I need to draw inside myself, closing off a set of thoughts from ever being publicly expressed. He'll still feel the same way about me. He's just committing to not showing it again.

"You were right about some of it," I say, eager to smooth the waters. I'm not quite ready to let go of the fantasy of becoming his friend. At least, friends with the man I thought he was. "I am only here because Gabor insisted upon it. But I really am a geologist above anything else." My husband would agree, even above being a wife and a good mother.

"In the briefing we got about you," Elvan says, in an effort to distract me from Banks's glower, "it said you're an artist and that we need to support your trips outside. What kind of things should we expect to help you with, other than getting to grips with the suit and safety protocols?"

"I want to go outside as much as possible in the first few weeks. I need to collect samples and make observations."

"Is that for the art or for the geology?" Banks asks with a slight sneer.

"Both," I reply, ignoring it.

"Were you briefed on why the need for a team geologist was downgraded?" he asks.

"Banks . . ." Petranek frowns at him.

"I'm not being a dick about it," Banks says and looks back at me. "It's a genuine question."

"I actually spoke to the last one posted here," I reply, "shortly after she got back to Earth. She said there was still such a lot to be done and couldn't understand why the decision had been made."

"She didn't mention the fact that we've discovered enough water deposits to sustain the base for over thirty years?"

"Is that all you think a geologist is good for? Finding water?" I'm trying so hard not to sound annoyed, but having had the same argument with the managers at varying levels between Drew and Gabor, it's difficult. "There's so much left to understand here. So much history. And if there are any plans to extend the human footprint on Mars, we need to understand so much more."

"So little of that actually improves the bottom line though," Banks says, stabbing his fork into what looks like mashed potatoes.

"Oh JeeMuh, we're not seriously going to have an argument about whether scientific discovery only has merit if it increases corporate profits, are we? Because believe me, I've spent my entire career arguing with people about different forms of merit and I thought I'd left all that bullshit behind on Earth."

Banks's eyes flash with something akin to excitement.

"Oh, I can assure you that some of that bullshit has landed on Mars too. I can smell it right now."

"What is your problem?"

"I just want you to be honest, for fuck's sake!" He slams his cutlery down. "I want you to stop pretending you're here for any reason other than making Gabor even more fucking rich!"

My body is rigid, frozen by the violent clang of the metal hitting the table. I keep my eyes on his hands, ready for the moment they move toward me, already planning where I will run when he—

I blink. I am not a child anymore. I am not on Earth and he is not my father. I still can't move though.

"Banks," Arnolfi says quietly. "You need to remember the conversation we had earlier."

As Banks glares at Arnolfi instead of me, I am able to take a breath once more, released from the fear that he'll attack me. There are other people here and they won't let him hurt me. Slowly the logic seeps into the instinctual terror, like rain into rock crevices, finding its weak spots and splitting it open until it no longer grips me. I notice how uncomfortable Elvan and Petranek are and wonder if there's ever been any conflict here before I arrived. Probably not. They will have been selected because they work well in a team and aren't the sort of people who pick fights. Petranek is looking at Banks like he's sprouted horns. Like ze doesn't know him.

"I don't want to cause any trouble here," I say, eager to defuse the awful tension and to remind myself that I am an adult now and everything is different. I look at Banks. "Let's face it—we're all here to make Gabor richer. That's how it works. I happen to have been sent here to create some art that will do that. You make a mersive that brings in millions of dollars a year. I am also a geologist. I want to do that work here too. Just as you carry out experiments alongside being a media star. Can you explain to me what the difference is? Because I'm missing something here, and I don't want to live in this base with you attacking me all the time just because I don't understand it."

He blinks at me and then sags slightly. "You're right. Of course. There is no difference. I'm sorry."

"Did you get your heart broken by an artist once or something?" Petranek asks. There's just enough humor in hir tone to stop it from being more fuel for the fire.

Banks waves his hand dismissively. "I was out of order. I'm sorry."

The last of the tension drains from my shoulders and I feel suddenly tired.

"How did you juggle the art and the geology back home?" Elvan asks, and I am grateful for something to answer.

"The art is purely a hobby. Well, it was." I shrug. "It was sheer luck that my work came to Gabor's attention. And once he gets an idea in his head, there's no stopping him."

"So you didn't get this through a proposal process?" Petranek asks. "There wasn't anything in the briefing about you."

The question makes me wonder what GaborCorp told them. Back on Earth, there was a strict media blackout over the art angle. As far as those who monitored GaborCorp's Mars activities were concerned, I was just a geologist. There was one news feed speculating about why there was such a rush to send me, but Gabor's lawyers soon quashed that. I asked about it when I went for my media-training module and the tutor said it was all to do with building excitement about the art to peak at the right moment. These paintings I'm contracted to produce are being sold to the super-rich. Gabor has no interest in stirring up a media furor among the masses in the vast majority of pay grades. Doing any publicity before I left Earth would have meant the story was stale before I'd even put brush to canvas. In a couple of months I'm supposed to start taking part in some of the mersive episodes, and a cam drone will be filming me as I paint, but I'm used to that.

"Not a proposal process, no," I reply, feeling reluctant to tell them the story of how all this came about. It feels . . . sordid somehow, especially given Banks's earlier outburst. "Ironically enough, I applied to come here as a geologist over ten times. I got to the final round of the proposal process one of those times, in fact. So I guess that's why I'm keen to push the geology part," I say to Banks, hoping for a moment of conciliation. He's too busy working on his meal.

"You probably got turned down because the previous geologists did their job so well," Petranek says. "The corp wanted water sustainability guaranteed for ten years and they achieved that sooner than predicted. Bad luck for you though!"

"Yeah, just bad luck," I say, even though I know the real reason I was turned down. Arnolfi must know it too, having read the whole file on me. Is that why she wanted me to talk about my father?

"So, did Gabor see your work in a gallery or something?" Petranek asks.

I wave a hand at my full mouth, taking my time to chew and draw out the excuse for not replying as long as possible. "Do you want to see some of it?" I ask, counting on curiosity to help with the deflection. "I used to have a feed but my contract stipulated that I had to take it down." The thought occurs to me that the lack of publicly accessible examples of my art would make it difficult for whoever the note forger could be. Would there be examples in my personnel file? Could Arnolfi have seen them and used them to copy my style and forge the note? No, that still seems ridiculous, and this isn't the time to dwell upon it anyway.

There are several enthusiastic nods. "So that's why we couldn't find it online," Elvan says, as if it's been bugging him for some time.

I nod. "It was all pulled."

The day they did that, I felt like I had been erased. Of course, I was still all over the Internet, but only as a geologist and a wife and a mother. I felt sick, searching obsessively for just one mention of my art feed, some little nook of the Web the seek-and-destroy bots had missed. Charlie had found me hunched over, weeping and staring into space in the dark living room. He'd freaked out, put Mia in her cot to play with her special bear, and run back, put the lights on and shook me until I blinked out of the interface.

"What's happened?" he asked.

"All my art is gone. They did it today. I can't find it anywhere online. Not even a mention of it."

He'd flopped back and groaned. "JeeMuh, I thought it was something terrible."

"This is terrible!" I yelled. "It feels like I've died again!"

"Again?"

I bit my lip, staying silent, knowing he wouldn't understand.

"The paintings are right there." He pointed at the canvases crammed onto the walls.

"It's not the same. That's only part of it, the end of the process. That's what's gone."

"Sweetling, it's all still in your private cloud. It hasn't been destroyed. And I bet it's out there somewhere."

"You find it, then!" I hated his tone, that way he had of making me feel like I was totally overreacting.

With a sigh, he tried to find some himself. I watched as his slump shifted into sitting up, knowing he was challenging himself to find some scrap online to prove to me that it wasn't so bad. When Mia cried, I went to change her, cuddled her a bit and put her back, returning to find him on his feet, working hard with virtual tools he was barely familiar with. I printed dinner, called him and then ate mine when he didn't respond.

"Fuck," he finally whispered, coming over to sit next to me.

"Want me to print you another meal?"

"I didn't think they could actually do that," he said, staring past his dinner, long gone cold. "I mean, I'd heard of it, but . . . fuck. I thought that was all just conspiracy theory bollocks, you know? What else have they scrubbed from the Web?"

"Careful," I said. "You'll end up like my mum."

He visibly shuddered and went to the printer. I could see him pushing the fear to the back of his mind, almost hear his voice in his head: Don't think about it. There's nothing you can do about it. It's just the way the world works.

Seated at this table now, with them all watching, I feel self-conscious using my v-keyboard and tapping icons to send the images from my private space to the communal screens, but I'm faster at it than most people are these days, and soon enough, one of my paintings is displayed.

Like all of the pieces I feel happy to share with other people, it depicts a Martian landscape. The sky is a dull gray-blue; the land is painted in the iconic shades of rusty red that everyone associates with Mars. Other than the rocks in the foreground, which are sharply defined, it's mostly a bleak, sweeping vista of dust and sky.

"That's actually really good," Banks says.

"You sound surprised," I say, biting back something more cutting, and his lips twitch.

"I suppose I am," he admits and looks at me properly. "You're very talented."

His compliment makes me feel like an eager child, hanging off the words of her favorite teacher. I suppress the urge to say, "You really think so?" and give him a small smile. "Thanks."

"So, Gabor saw these and decided you should come and paint in situ?" Elvan asks and I nod.

"More or less. This image doesn't really show the texture. If you want, I can put the scans into the communal files, so you can look at them in 3-D at your leisure. I try to build the sense of depth with the oils. Gabor wants me to experiment with texture using actual dust and rocks from here. It's a gimmick, if you ask me, but that's what he wants. The first art painted of Mars, on Mars, using Martian materials."

"Do you have any others?" Petranek asks and I display the rest on a slow-changing cycle.

It's not the same as seeing the actual canvases. Up close, the texturing is built up enough to cast shadows on other parts of the painting, moving as the viewer moves. That was the feature that had made Travis, Gabor's husband, so excited that night at the dinner party.

Charlie and I had argued about whether to take the canvases down. I wanted to; they made our tiny flat seem smaller and I didn't want anyone to think I was showing them off to the VIP guests. Once I finished each one, the canvases were to be enjoyed in private, something separate from the digital images of them all over the Internet. But Charlie said it would be good to show my passion for Mars and how it went beyond the work we did at the lab. "And it will give us something to talk about," he said as he chewed on a fingernail. "It might distract them from the food."

He was even more nervous than I was. We sent Mia to his mother's for the night, not wanting to worry about nappy changes and feedings at the same time as entertaining the man who famously disliked children. Once Mia had gone, we packed her cot away, clearing a space in our bedroom so we could store the sofa in there, making enough room in the living room for a table large enough to sit five. We'd spent the morning making it out of our small table, plus another small table, with a large board over the top that we'd borrowed from our neighbor. Once the tablecloth was on, it looked fine.

"The chairs don't match," Charlie said.

"Even if I went and found matching chairs, they'd still be roughing it," I'd said, long past the point of caring about whether it was good enough for the Gabors. None of it would be. Stefan Gabor earned thousands of times what I did each year. Our entire flat was probably the size of one of their guest bathrooms. No, smaller than that; the Gabors probably still had baths installed in them. Enough wealth to fill a whole bath with water just to sit in it until it went cold. While the thought appalled and angered me, it made me feel less uncomfortable about asking for more funding. The amount we needed to secure the lab for the next five years was probably what they spent on bloody toilet paper.

Drew arrived an hour early to "help," as she put it, revealing a surprising talent for laying out a table nicely for dinner. It was so rare we ate formally, I was grateful for the guidance. Then before we knew it, security staff were at the door to sweep the flat before the Gabors arrived as a lawyer looked on. When they asked Charlie to step out of the kitchen, I worried that he was going to throw them out. The stress of cooking the meal was making his skin blotchy and lips white.

I felt awful and could tell that Drew felt guilty too, offering to help Charlie just the once before being sent away with short shrift.

Watching the security staff, and the drone that followed them, I realized that must have been what my mother felt like, all those years ago. I pushed it from my mind and tried to look relaxed. I probably ended up looking more guilty as a result.

Once they were done, the lawyer stepped forward. He was a short man who seemed to be in a dreadful hurry to leave as soon as he'd arrived. "As per the contract you have all signed pertaining to this meeting, we'll be blocking your APAs' connections to the Internet while Mr. and Mr. Gabor are here. Do you have any business that needs to be concluded online before we do that?"

Charlie made a swift call to his mother, warning her we'd be incommunicado for a few hours, and then we were cut off.

"And of course, as per clause twelve of that contract, we'll also be shutting down your APAs. I'd like to remind you that any online mention of this meeting"—he paused, taking in the table for the first time—"this . . . er . . . dinner party, after the event, will be considered a breach of contract and you would be prosecuted accordingly. Any questions or concerns?"

"Does Mr. Gabor like garlic?" Charlie asked and the lawyer blinked at him.

"I have no idea," he finally answered. "It isn't a listed allergen."

"It was just a joke," Charlie muttered. He frowned at the way the lawyer was staring at the pan on the hob. "I got the menu signed off and all the ingredients were bought through approved suppliers," he said defensively.

"Oh, I know. I beg your pardon," he said. "It's just that I haven't seen someone cooking on a hob since I visited my grandparents as a child. The smell is quite extraordinary. Is that . . . black currant?"

Charlie dipped a teaspoon into the sauce and gave it to the lawyer, whose eyes sparkled with delight. It was as if the years of bearing legal burdens were shrugged off him and he was a child again, accepting a spoon covered in uncooked cake mixture from a grandmother in some nostalgic mersive. He licked the sauce off the spoon and visibly shuddered with delight. "Lovely. Just lovely," he said, handing the spoon back. "I do hope it goes well." He headed for the door, following the security staff, but paused to look back at Charlie before he went through it. "With Mr. Gabor, I've found that being direct is always the best option. He knows this isn't just a social visit. Get to the point quickly, get it out of the way, and then entertain him. And if his husband likes you, you have nothing to worry about."

He closed the door behind him, leaving the three of us in silence.

"Well," Drew said, "I don't think you have to worry about the sauce anymore, Charlie."

The icons disappeared from my visual field, sending Charlie into a panic as he realized he couldn't access the recipe he'd been following anymore, before realizing he'd done it all anyway. Five minutes of frantic last-minute checks and then came the knock on the door.

Stefan Gabor was bigger than I thought he'd be, in every sense. He was overweight, but so tall his large belly looked merely proportionate. He filled the room and made me want to retreat into the corner. His handshake made me feel tiny and I could see how intimidated Charlie was when that blast of wealth and epic confidence was fired at him. "Call me Stefan, please," he boomed, as if any of us would dream of it.

I didn't notice his husband, Travis, enter. Eclipsed as he was by his spouse, it was only when there was a loud, theatrical gasp that I even realized he was there. Charlie and I, alert for any signs of unhappiness in our guests, froze, waiting to see what had made Travis so shocked. Was it the tablecloth? The mismatched chairs? The comparable poverty?

"It *is* you!" he said, but he was staring at one of the canvases. "I hoped it was but I couldn't be sure and I am so *thrilled*!"

Travis Gabor was more handsome in person, his auburn

hair so perfectly coiffed and face so beautiful that I wanted to run out of the flat and go find someone else's body to wear instead of my own. He dodged past his husband and headed straight for me, throwing his arms around me as if I were some long-lost sister. He let me go to stand by my side, arm around me. "Darling," he said to Stefan. "This is ArtyGeo359!"

The flush that spread up my neck and into my cheeks was hot enough to flambé one of Charlie's dishes. When Stefan frowned in confusion, Travis sighed as if the weight of the world was upon his perfect shoulders. "I told you about the feed last week, darling. This is the lady who teaches the world how to paint!"

"It's not anything so grand," I stammer. "I just film while I'm painting and talk people through how—"

"Don't be all small about this!" Travis said. "I watched every single one and I swear I am going to die from how exciting this is. And look! There's my favorite, right there, with little Curiosity in the corner there. Do you see it, darling?" He released me to go and point out the detail to his husband. "Oh, it's so much more than I thought. The texture! Oh . . . and look, when you move from left to right, there are the tiniest shadows here and . . ."

"He wants me to buy it," Stefan said, as if this was something that often happened.

"It's not for sale," I said, and Stefan laughed as if I'd made the funniest joke he'd ever heard. But I meant it. And I wanted, in that moment, for him to feel like he couldn't just walk into any room, anywhere in the world, and buy whatever he saw there.

"Let's eat," he said. "Then you can tell me how much you want for it."

"I want five years' worth of funding for our lab," I said. "And if you give us the full five years in a cast-iron contract, I'll throw in another couple of paintings for free."

Charlie's mouth hung open as he peered past Stefan's shoulder, staring at me in horror. Drew's eyes had taken on the intense gaze of a person watching another play Russian roulette.

The moment stretched ever more taut until Stefan gave a hearty laugh and clapped his hands down on my shoulders. "Deal. Do I smell garlic?"

Drew and I exchanged a grin and sat down as Charlie talked the Gabors through the menu. I felt light-headed with relief and poured the wine Travis had brought with them; I drank half a glass before they even sat down. Real wine, made from real grapes! And despite what people say, it really did taste different.

"End immersion," I say, but even as the words leave my lips I realize I've made a mistake. That was just a memory. I've been sitting at this table on Mars the whole time. I can see Dr. Elvan's concerned frown as I blink myself back into fully appreciating my surroundings. "No, wait. I didn't mean that," I say and force a laugh, but it's too late.

Dr. Arnolfi stands. "I think you need to get some rest, Dr. Kubrin."

5

I SLEEP HEAVILY, thanks to the sedative Dr. Elvan gives me in an effort to help me adjust my cycle to base time. I tried to do that on the journey over, but it clearly didn't work. He said nothing about my mistake at the dinner table and I didn't raise it either. I didn't want to invite a discussion; I just wanted to rest and be fresh the next day to pass the next physical and be signed off for my first trip outside.

There's a message from my mother waiting when I wake, and one from Charlie too, and I realize with a jolt that I didn't record a message for Mia. I brace myself for the guilt trip and play Charlie's message first.

He looks tired, which is unsurprising, seeing as his last message demonstrated how little sleep he's been getting, but he looks a bit more composed than before. He's sitting in the living room, recording with our cam drone by the look of it, and I can hear Mia's babble coming from off screen.

Through the window I can see that it's raining in Manchester, which is nothing new, but I can't pull my eyes from it. How many times have I cursed that weather, only to find myself craving it now? There's a temptation to go back to the mersive I recorded of the storm we were caught in about a week before I left, but I resist it. Messages first. Then breakfast. Then storm.

"Hi, love," Charlie says with a wave. "I was so relieved to get your message. Thanks. The room doesn't look too bad. Are you going to put some pictures up? It's a bit impersonal." He keeps looking away from the cam, keeping an eye on Mia, I suppose. "Anna, I don't resent you being happy. Why did you say that? I can't stop thinking about it. Is that how you felt here, at home?" He sighs and rubs his forehead in the way he does when he's got a headache. No doubt he'll print something for it once he's finished the message. I can see him shrug off the moment of self-pity, rallying himself to be the cheerful one, the counterbalance. The familiarity of it pains me. "I got a parcel from the Gabors today." He gets up and the cam moves with him, keeping his face fully in shot as he walks. I catch glimpses of the flat. The gaps left by the missing canvases haven't been filled. I suspect he's glad of the space. They need to be rearranged, positioned so that the white space looks designed rather than like an aftershock of things disappearing. It irritates me. Probably because I can't do anything about it.

Is he leaving those gaps there deliberately? Is it some sort of statement? No, Charlie isn't that calculating.

He's crossed to the kitchen corner of the room and I can see dust on the hob, unused since the dinner party. Mia must be in her cot; I can't see her anywhere. On the table there's a basket with a lid, which looks like something out of a period-drama mersive, the sort of thing that rich Edwardians used to take on picnics, if the one I played in was to be believed. I didn't realize that they were still being made in the real world. It looks like it's been woven out of thin sticks, and the imperfections in the weave scream out the fact that it's been made by hand rather than printed.

"Look at this," he says, flipping the lid open. "Champagne, caviar, chili jam—whatever that is—and this stuff." He pulls out a package made of food-safe biopackaging containing pale brown cubes. I've seen something like that before but can't place it. "This is called fudge," he says, opening it up. "Seriously, love, this stuff is . . ." He leans closer to the cam, lowering his voice to a level outside of Mia's hearing range. "This stuff is so fucking good. It's made from . . . cream, butter, milk and sugar and . . . shit, is that it? I've never tasted anything like it. Honestly, it's like someone made cubes of D-liite and made it taste like an orgasm."

I chuckle. He's never taken drugs, certainly not D-liite, which is banned pretty much everywhere, but I get the idea. He puts a chunk in his mouth and his eyes roll upward before he closes them. He gives a long, drawn-out sigh. "Seriously," he says around the mouthful, "it's like . . . there's just so much stuff going on in the pleasure centers of my brain right now, that MyPhys is flagging up an alert, asking if I've taken an illegal substance."

He laughs and I laugh too and then I suddenly miss him, painfully, an actual physical pain in my chest. I take a couple of deep breaths until it passes, trying to resist the tears that threaten to spill. He finishes the piece of fudge and rummages in the basket again.

"There's chocolate in here too, but I'm saving that. I would say that I'm saving that until you come home, but I'm not that strong." He grins at the cam. "And, you know, if this is the hamper we get when you land on Mars, imagine what we'll get when you come back to Earth! That's what this is called, apparently. There was a leaflet inside." He rifles through the contents and swears beneath his breath. "I don't know where it is, but it said something like 'A hamper for connoisseurs of . . .' something or other. And it had this thing about how in the twentieth century sending a hamper filled with luxury goods was something people did all the time. Weird. And get a load of this basket. Handmade from wicker, whatever that is. They're being sold online for a small fortune, just in case we wanted to get a new sofa at some point. I thought you could keep your brushes and stuff in it, so I won't sell it until you've seen it."

He closes up the bag of fudge and puts it back in the hamper, buckling the cover closed. "These buckles are made from real leather. I mean, it's just . . ." He shrugs. "I don't really know what to make of it, you know? Gabor's real-life personal assistant probably just sent this automatically through an APA. I mean, no real thought has gone into this I reckon, but still . . . it makes me feel weird. Like . . . why are they sending me a hamper? Is it like, 'Sorry we sent your wife to another planet. Here are some "luxury comestibles" to ease the pain'? That was it! Luxury comestibles! That leaflet said it's 'a hamper for connoisseurs of luxury comestibles.'" He smirks, shaking his head. "They live on another planet. Whoa. You are literally living on another planet now."

"Ream?" Mia's little voice sounds much closer all of a sudden, accompanied by the sound of plastic tapping on a surface.

Charlie turns around and the cam swoops round to keep his face in shot, giving me a glimpse of Mia standing beneath the food printer's slot in the wall, tapping it with a plastic bowl from her picnic set.

"No, no ice cream, Mia. We've just had breakfast!"

"Ream now!"

"No, no ice cream. Hey, want to send Momma a message?" He crouches down next to her and there she is, pink cheeked and still baby plump, wearing an all-in-one fluffy suit with orange fur and black stripes. She still likes tigers, then. Charlie points at the cam. "Say hello to Momma!"

She looks past the cam, confused. "Momma?" she calls. Then she points to the wall we project her games and shows onto, and where the projector displays me when I call her from work. "Momma?"

"No, sweetling, Momma isn't at the lab; we need to send her a message."

Mia gives the cam drone a cursory glance, then bangs the bowl on the wall again, looking at Charlie. "Ream, Dada. Ream now!"

With a sigh he picks her up. "Sorry, love," he says to the cam. "She just doesn't understand recording messages yet. I'll film her when you send your first message to her. That wasn't a dig at you, by the way. I understand there must be tons of new stuff to come to grips with there. Just, when you have a moment, you know."

Mia drops the bowl and starts playing with his ear and then one of the curls that have grown above it. Then she wraps her arms around his head, covering his eyes, and kisses him right on the ear. He turns and kisses her back, then blows a raspberry on her neck, making a loud, gurgling giggle erupt from her.

I smile, but the old ache returns, the bittersweet witnessing of their ease with each other. I am, once more, an observer rather than a participant. At least this time there is a more acceptable reason for feeling this way.

A flare of anger at myself chases the heels of the sadness. Why am I this way? What is missing inside me?

Charlie puts her down and as she runs off to the bedroom, he rubs his ear, his nose wrinkling at the dampness her kiss left behind. "I'd better go now; I want to get some work done before Mum comes over later." There's a long pause as he stares at the floor. "She sends her love, by the way," he adds and I know he's lying. I hate that woman and it's entirely mutual. She probably threw a party the day I left Earth.

I have the feeling there's something else he wants to say, but whatever it is, he isn't ready to share it. He smiles into the cam, doing his best to make it seem natural, but it's not the same smile I see in the mersives I recorded myself, when he was looking into my eyes. The distance between us seems insurmountable. The message ends.

I sit for a while, weighing up whether to find an old recording to see that real smile again. How far back would I have to look? How many fake smiles would I have to pan to find gold? I decide against it. I have things to do and I don't want Principia to report to Arnolfi that I haven't been able to get through an hour without going back into a mersive. I call up the message from my mother instead.

The message begins with a pink blur that fills the screen, along with the muffled noise of something scraping against a microphone. "Bloody thing," my mother mutters, and then the pink blur disappears as she releases her cam drone and steps back until I can see her nose and chin. "Hello, Sprout! I think this thing is working now. It wasn't playing nicely with my tablet but I got there in the end. Oh, why is it beeping now?" She glances over at what I assume is the tablet screen and then takes another couple of steps back until I can see her whole face. It fills the screen. She looks tired and her eyes are still a little bit puffy, but her broad smile is the same as ever. "There! I think you can see me properly now. I thought it was supposed to do all the face-distance thing automatically. They make these things without considering people who use tablets, just like every bloody thing ever I suppose. It's discrimination, dammit. Sorry. Hello, Sprout. I am so glad you arrived safely. I remember putting you on the train to Paris when you were fifteen and staying up all night worrying about you arriving, but that was nothing compared to this!"

Her face is so close to the cam I can't see where she is exactly, but then there's a loud yowl and I realize she's at home, confirmed when she bends down to pick up the cat and goes out of shot. There are the rough walls of the house we all built together and she's standing right by the bit where all of our handprints are pressed into the cob. Of course she is. She wants to remind me of what we all built together. She wants me to see four sets of handprints. To remind me of what we had before it was broken.

She doesn't realize how that makes me feel. For her, it's an anchor, but for me it's like shining a spotlight on a broken vase. I suppose she still thinks it can all be mended. Optimistic to the point of stupidity, that's my mum.

When she comes back into shot, the cat is being held up next to her face, oblivious to the expectation she's placing upon him. "Say hello, Odin."

It's a testament to my mother's physical strength that she can keep him held up like that. Odin is a Maine coon and his head looks almost as big as hers, especially with the dramatic fur. I can't help but smile at the sight of him, looking effortlessly regal with his impressive ruff of fur. Odin, typically contrary, looks anywhere but at the cam and keeps quiet for once. Mum kisses his furry cheek, making him rub back against her jaw, his purr almost as loud as her voice. "He's too busy looking for Frigg. She's hiding under the bed. Can you hear the wind outside? It's blowing a storm out there; we had some epic thunder and lightning earlier. It's the third this week. Don't worry about us though, Sprout—it'll take more than the Atlantic's moods to blow us away. Did I tell you that the house up on the other side of the loch lost its roof? Stupid buggers. We told them that design wouldn't work. All those fancy-pants engineers and architects coming up with all these newfangled designs." She shakes her head, unimpressed, as Odin starts to fidget. Mum tries to keep him in shot but it's a short-lived struggle and he leaps down to continue his hunt. "She's under the bed, silly," Mum calls to him. "You know they laughed at our houses when they saw them. I invited them over for a drink when they started the build and when I told them how we made this place they thought I was winding them up. Now who's laughing? Us!"

She chuckles and then frowns to herself. "I shouldn't be mean though. Those poor sods. I drove over and brought them back here the night it happened. I shouldn't have been on the road, really, it was fierce out there, but they only have one of those silly toy cars. I told them they needed a proper rover but they wouldn't listen. They were in a terrible state. They went back to London yesterday. I don't know what they'll do about the house once they've finished suing the people who built it. Mud and straw and old tires—that's all you need, and a bit of lime. But these people don't want the old ways, do they? Do you remember when we built this place?"

With a faint smile she looks around, still proud, still drawing so much pleasure and satisfaction from what we all built together. For her, the magic of that time still surrounds her. The memories of that summer are preserved the old-fashioned way. I was too young to record a mersive, but I have footage from my bear, watched many times since then.

That bear was one of those things that my parents would have preferred us not to have, but when pretty much every child had one and society viewed them as the cornerstone of modern childhood, they couldn't bring themselves to deprive us. From the outside it looked like any teddy bear with big friendly eyes and fur. The more expensive models could be fully customized, so some kids had unicorns or hippos or hybrid creatures that appealed to them. Mine was an average brown bear, but like every single one, it was far from just a cuddly toy.

The friendly eyes were also cameras and the rounded,

fluffy ears hid microphones, giving the AI housed within a view of the world and the ability to record whatever it saw and heard. The bear was designed to be a constant companion in childhood, providing information and advice to supplement learning as well as the usual comfort any cuddly toy can provide. What set the bear apart from all of the other intelligent children's toys was the fact that it was made using the same supporting technology as was used in neural chips. The bears were designed to record everything so that when their owners were old enough for their first neural chips, there was a wealth of data to feed them right from the start. Any learning difficulties could then be supported at the neural level; any traumatic experiences could be synced with My-Phys and used to notify health care providers where necessary. There were thousands of ways that gathered data was used to help the new neural chip better integrate with each teenager's brain.

And for the gov-corps to harvest all the data they could ever want.

When I think back to that summer, I can't tell what I remember because of what I saw through my own eyes and what I remember because I saw it later through the bear's recordings, but I remember how it felt well enough.

It did feel magical. At nine years old, I was too young to fully appreciate just how unusual my parents were. I didn't understand enough about the world to see what they did, to predict what was coming. I couldn't grasp the magnitude of the changes taking place, driving their decisions. For me, it was just an adventure. One day we were living in a perfectly normal block of flats in London's sprawl; the next we were living in an old caravan in Scotland, huddled in a valley with other families, helping one another to build our houses. We were together then, the four of us, Mum, Dad, Geena and me. And we were happy.

"I miss you, Sprout." She blows her nose. "And Geena too. I haven't heard from her, but I know where she is and . . ." Her voice breaks. "She's safe," she manages, fresh tears falling. I can't tell if it's her usual policy of not talking about anything sensitive on a digital medium, or her inability to talk about it without breaking down. I struggle to manage my frustration. Her behavior is perfectly understandable. "I think you need to put some art in your room," she says after blowing her nose again. "Make yourself feel a bit more at home. I spoke to Charlie and he's fine. I'm going to visit them soon. He might bring Mia up in the summer. I hope so. She needs to know what it's like to be somewhere normal. We just have to wait for the weather to calm down a bit. We told them it's getting worse here—those architects, I mean—but they didn't listen. Averages aren't good enough when it comes to critical data. As you well know, eh, Sprout? Well, I'd better go. The cats need feeding and I have some vases to fire. I'll show them to you when they're done. Don't let anyone tell you how to paint Mars either. And don't be too hard on yourself if you take a while to get started. Get a feel for the place. With all that expectation upon you, don't be surprised if you feel a bit blocked at first. Talk to me if you have any problems, all right? Oh, Annabelly! I am so proud of you!"

Her face crinkles up when she smiles, and I can't help but smile back.

"Oh, and when you get a minute . . . could you . . . would you record a message for your dad? I think he would like it, very much."

All the feelings of warmth and connection evaporate. She waves good-bye, blows kisses, and after another pink blur as she goes to the cam drone itself to stop the recording, the message ends. I watch it all with a scowl on my face, left with the weight of obligation. Why can't she understand how I feel about him?

Because I've never talked to her about it, comes the immediate reply. Not properly. And being on another planet, literally, is not conducive to deep and difficult conversations.

The day stretches ahead. There's time to record all the replies I need to, but I have no desire to smile and make out that all is brilliant here. At least I feel less dizzy, and stronger than I did yesterday. I'm tired, but that's to be expected. Just moving around here is like a gentle workout compared to the trip over. It's not as bad as I was told it could be though. Surely I'll be able to go outside tomorrow?

There are things to do: safety protocols to review for when I can go outside, a full tour of the base and a trip to the lab to test the paper that note was painted on. And another physical, but I'm less worried about that. Then the icon flashes to indicate an incoming call. It's Arnolfi.

Minutes later I am sitting in her office again. There's a different view on the screen this time, and a different atmosphere. She still smiles and makes out that everything is fine, but there's a tension here that I know too well to be fooled.

"We need to talk about what happened at dinner last night."

At least she's direct. "I made a mistake, a silly one. It won't happen again."

"This isn't a disciplinary review," she says. That smile again. She'll be telling me she's not a therapist any moment now. "This isn't anything other than a discussion about how we move forward over the next few days."

I have to keep positive and not let her see how irritated this is making me. "I'm feeling stronger today. And less dizzy. I'm confident I'll pass the physical, and then tomorrow, when I can go outside, I'll be busy again. More . . . connected. That's all it was yesterday."

"I can't approve a trip outside if I have any doubts about your mental well-being."

"Oh, come on. It was one lapse of concentration. In a totally harmless situation. There's no need to talk about mental well-being here." I sound annoyed. I am annoyed! I try to paste over it with a smile.

"Isn't there? I'm concerned you'll have another lapse of concentration but not in a harmless situation. There's no need to be defensive about this. I'm not attacking you. I'm just trying to help you understand how serious this is, so we can work together to ensure your integration here goes as smoothly as possible."

I've folded my arms again. Crossed my legs. Adopted the textbook pose of someone being so defensive she's one step away from walking out.

"I'm not your therapist," she says and I suppress a laugh, "but I am one of the registered health care providers on this base and you are exhibiting the early signs of immersion psychosis and we need to address it, now. It's perfectly understandable, given the circumstances, and it's nothing to be ashamed of." When I remain silent—playing her at her own game—she adds, "I need your understanding and your cooperation. We both want you to be fit enough to go outside and do the job you've been sent here to do."

I need to stop being an arsehole about this, or she'll block me from leaving the base. But it's so hard to just sit here and take this after the countless hours I've spent in offices like this, talking to people like her. Then it occurs to me that all that tedious experience gives me an advantage here. I fall back on old techniques refined years ago on Earth. "You're right," I say, softening my voice. "I'm sorry. I just . . . I just don't want everyone to think I'm not good enough to be here." I add just enough of a quiver to my voice to make it sound like I'm confessing something genuine. "I don't want to be any bother either."

Arnolfi leans across the gap between us, squeezes my arm

in what I'm sure she believes is a reassuring gesture and leans back again. "I won't discuss this with anyone else. We need to fully embed you in the present, and we need to wean you off your dependency on fully immersive personal recordings. My recommendation is that we limit your use of personally recorded mersives, and any featuring this base, to a total of one hour per day. I also recommend regular physical exercise throughout the day, along with time spent in the company of one or more of the crew here. There's lots to bring you up to speed on, so that won't be a problem. Do you agree with this plan?"

I nod. I have to. "It sounds very sensible," I say.

"Good, just give me a moment to file the restriction request with Principia and—"

"What do you mean?"

"The restriction on your mersive consumption will be imposed by Principia's AI. To take the pressure off you."

To take the control from me, more like. "To remove temptation," I say with a nod. "Of course. I understand." Fuck you, I think.

"This is a form of addiction," she says. "You can't be expected to simply stop overconsuming. That would be unfair. And I do appreciate that you have a family you miss and totally cutting you off from those memories of home could be more harmful. We'll see how you get on over the next twenty-four hours. Don't be afraid to call on me, or Dr. Elvan, if you find yourself feeling disoriented or uncertain about anything. We're here to help."

"Thanks," I say. "Can I use the lab while we're . . . doing this?"

"Of course. Principia will supervise and may restrict access to anything that could be harmful, just because you haven't been signed off as fully fit yet."

"Oh, I won't need anything like that. I'm just . . . keen to find my feet in there, that's all." I stand. "I'll go and check it out now. Keep busy, you know?"

She nods as she stands too. "This is a really difficult time for all new arrivals, even without the isolation of a solo journey over. It will get better." She's gracefully walking the fine line between being professionally reassuring and being patronizing as hell, and yet I still want to yell at her to stay out of my business. This is within her remit. She's not the one being unreasonable here.

I leave before I say something stupid. It's only when I'm out of that office, away from her, that I realize how hostile I was in there. She's just trying to help and do her job. She's not like the ones from before. I need to give her a chance.

But why the note warning me about her? I go back to my room, find it and take it to the lab. I'm hoping it's a fake as I prepare the sample for examination, that someone here somehow accessed my private data, found examples of my art, painted it in my style and thought it would be . . . funny?

Feeling nauseous, I put the scrap of paper under the microscope and zoom in, double-checking what I saw with my own lens. The paper is definitely from one of my sketchbooks. I can see the fibers of the traditionally made paper, all the hallmarks that my grandparents taught me about. The deckle edge proves that it was crafted using a frame and not made here with a 3-D printer. The sketch pads I use come from old stock, left over from when they closed their art supplies shop, after even the wealthiest stopped wanting their products. They saw it as my inheritance; my grandmother said that seeing me use the sketch pads and canvases gave them more happiness than any money they could earn from them ever would.

Chemical analysis of the paint only increases my certainty that the words were painted with the oils I have brought from Earth. It has the telltale high carbon content of the ivory black oil that I use for shadow detailing in the last stages of a painting. I love the intensity of the color. The proportion of calcium phosphate to synthetic carbon is exactly the same as used by the specialist oils manufacturer my grandparents stocked.

There's no way this could have been printed. And even if someone did steal the paper from the cargo crate between unloading it from the ship and taking it to my room, how could they have found an example of my art style to copy? Do any of them know how to hack into private data? But the biggest stumbling block for me is the motive. If it was a genuine warning, why hide it? The sort of people who do this kind of thing as a prank are not likely to make it through the selection process to come here. It simply doesn't make any sense for anyone else to have done it.

I clean the microscope plate and put the scrap in my pocket, shaking. Everything suggests I painted this myself, a warning against a person I hadn't even met yet, an act of defiance that I have no recollection of. Did I paint this yesterday and then somehow forget?

Sitting heavily on one of the lab stools, I rest my head in my hands. All this time I've been running away from it and it finally catches me up on Mars of all places. I am my father's daughter, and if that's true, then I could destroy everything here. Just like he did all those years ago.

6

IF I AM going to accept that the note is real (and I have to; otherwise, I have just spent several hours hallucinating a detailed lab analysis), then it looks like I must also accept that I painted it myself. I needed more data, now I have it, and as a good scientist I have to accept the conclusion it points me toward.

The issue is with my recollection of painting it, not imagining a note hidden in my room. And considering I've spent literally weeks of the past few months immersed in memories recorded and played back by my chip, is it any wonder I have forgotten a few little things?

But then if that's the case, I have also forgotten why I was warning myself against trusting Arnolfi, and considering I only met her on arrival, I'm struggling to understand why I did that.

The only thing I really know about her is that she is the resident therapist, even though she denies she is. That's all the reason I need to be wary of her. Yes, that's it. I was warning myself, that's all. And I just forgot that I painted the . . .

Shit. No matter how hard I try, I cannot make it seem plausible. But what are the alternative explanations? And there's the fake wedding ring, now settled into place on my finger. No amount of calm thinking is going to change the fact that I am exhibiting the same behavior as my father in the early days. Being distracted, claiming that things had been moved without his knowledge or permission, answering questions none of us had asked and then accusing us of trying to trick him. JeeMuh. Was this what it was like for him?

It's terrifying, to think that there is some part of your mind not acting in concert with the rest. Was he afraid? Was that why he—

No. Thinking about something that I have worked so hard to put away in a place where it can no longer haunt me is not going to help now. I have to stay strong. Be professional. Otherwise Arnolfi and Elvan will keep me cooped up and then I really will go mad.

I laugh, then shut that down immediately, grateful that I'm alone in the lab. I make sure that all of the tests have been deleted and head back to my room.

If there's one thing I learned at an early age, it was the art of pretending that nothing is wrong. That was what made it so hard with Charlie. He always knew. He could see past the carefully constructed walls and detect a fake smile at a hundred paces. Strange how that quality I so admired in him at the start of our relationship became one of the things I hated the most. He wouldn't let me retreat into my constructed social fort. He wanted nothing but my real self, all the time, even when I didn't want to show him. It wouldn't have been so bad if he'd accepted what I was really like at my worst moments.

Here, no one knows me. I can build that wall brick by brick, held together with the mortar of determination. I need to get outside. I keep up the smiles, I follow Arnolfi's advice, I exercise and socialize and I don't let myself sink into a single mersive—neither a recorded memory nor a game—for the rest of the day. I sleep well (thanks to neurochemical assistance), I rise early, I keep all of the worries about the ring and the piece of paper trapped behind my lips. And I manage to keep it up for several days. I need to get outside. I need to see Mars. With every day of working so damn hard to seem normal—no, damn it, I am normal!—the need increases.

And it works. Arnolfi and Elvan sign me off. He talks about writing a paper about my incredible recovery from the trip, enthusing about my blood test results and how the spinner seems to have kept me in pretty good shape. "I thought it would be at least a week before your results looked this good," he said, staring into space as he examined the numbers displayed for his sight only and I tried not to think about how beautiful his eyes are.

Less than half an hour after he's confirmed I can go out in one of the rovers, I have filed a request to take a trip outside and Petranek has agreed to accompany me. My stomach flutters with anticipation as I head toward the dust lock, running through all my training as I walk down the dusky red corridors. The Martian concrete blocks, mixed, printed and constructed by Principia and its drones long before the first human came here, have already become commonplace. How quickly we adapt. I can never decide if that is a strength or a weakness of the species. No longer chafing against something new isn't always a good thing.

I'm wearing an undersuit onesie and it's tighter than anything I'd normally wear. The fabric is breathable, warm and designed to wick sweat away from my skin. It also has a built-in nappy. The last time I wore one of these, for the takeoff, I couldn't bring myself to test its water-absorbent properties. I'm hoping I won't have to today either. At least the areas designed to absorb and contain are discreet.

Petranek is waiting for me outside the dust lock, looking

very comfortable in hir onesie as ze leans against the wall. With a broad smile Petranek pats me on the shoulder. "No need to look so scared!"

I'm more nervous than I realized. I smile back. "I'll be okay."

"You'll be more than that! You'll never forget the first moment you step outside. Let's get suited up. If you need any help at any point, or if you have any questions, just ask— doesn't matter how stupid it might sound. Sometimes people freeze up at certain points or forget the way to do something. That's perfectly natural. The prince is watching everything we do, and ze will stop us doing anything stupid, okay?"

I nod, noting the use of "ze" for the AI instead of "it." When I think about it, the gender-neutral pronoun makes more sense. Certainly more sense than the way the engineers on Earth who sometimes used "he," even though they didn't call it the prince, and "she" when they were talking about the craft that brought me here.

Petranek opens the first door of the dust lock. I expect the sense of familiarity; I trained in a sight-and-sound-only mersive that was recorded here, after all. It's a relatively small room with an airtight door between us and the rest of the base. Ahead I can see the five closed slots that lead to the external suits. They are always prepped and ready for use as part of the base safety protocols; if for any reason we all have to evacuate the base in an emergency, we have to be able to suit up as fast as possible. There are five more suits in storage, along with the patterns and nonprintable compo- nents to make replacements should the backups fail too. When stepping outside without a suit means your own blood boiling in your body, a lot of care goes into keeping them well serviced and available.

I go to the slot on the far left and Petranek picks the one next to it. Principia confirms that MyPhys reports my body to be functioning within normal parameters and that I have the permissions required to leave the base. A second dialog box requests that I actively confirm my intention to go outside and my commitment to observing all relevant safety protocols. I do so with a tap of my finger in the air, corresponding to where the box is displayed in my visual field, while Petranek says, "Acknowledged and confirmed, Principia. Thank you—we will."

There's no message wishing me a good trip. Not even in text form. I shrug off the bizarre moment of feeling socially slighted by a bloody AI and try to roll some of the tension out of my shoulders as the panel in front of me slides up.

The slot that I need to go through is only just wider than my body and about a meter high, the bottom of it at waist level. With the panel that usually seals it now drawn up, I can see the interior of the suit on the other side, waiting for me to climb into it. The seal between the suit opening and the slot is airtight, designed to keep the fine Martian dust out of this room.

I grab the bar above the slot and lift myself up, putting my feet through the opening into the suit. I've done this dozens of times in training, but this time I am shaking. My hands feel slick with sweat as I grip the bar more tightly, tilting my body at enough of an angle for my feet to find their way into the concertinaed legs of the suit and then into the boots, which are being held up, ready for me to fill them. I feel the soft foam inside molding to my feet and then I get a ping from Principia telling me I should move into the rest of the suit.

I slide my backside off the edge of the wall, standing with my legs fully in the suit now, taking care to plant my boots on the ground first, checking the legs are fully extended before shifting my hips forward. Once I feel confident to stand—albeit at an odd backward-leaning angle—I let go of the bar and plunge my hands through the suit's arms and into the gloves, crouching slightly so I can duck my head to then come up into the helmet portion.

The suit is light and well articulated but still feels odd to wear. I step forward slowly at the prompt from Principia, feeling the suit close behind me as the inner zipper, for all intents and purposes, is pulled upward by the movement. I know that behind me, pincers are closing the additional two layers and checking the seal. I wait as it's pressurized and Principia makes the final suit-integrity checks. I focus on keeping my breathing steady and making sure that the suit has settled into a comfortable fit around me as the smart fabric makes its final adjustments. It gives very limited protection against cosmic radiation, but, most important, the suit is pressurized, insulated against the cold and heated too. A microenvironment to keep my fragile body alive on a planet it has not evolved to cope with.

Principia confirms that my suit is sealed and I take in the second chamber of the dust lock through the plasglass of my helmet. It's hard to see the dust against the red concrete, but then I notice the little drifts of it at the meeting between the floor and the walls. Looking down at my gloves, I can see it in the creases, even though the suit would have been cleaned just before coming back inside. The dust is so fine there's no efficient way to clean it off completely without all sorts of extra equipment, hence the dust lock. It's easier to keep the spaces separate and keep the dusty suits outside the habitable parts of the base.

Petranek gives me a confident thumbs-up and I return the gesture. "You ready?" ze asks and I nod.

We walk together through the next set of airtight doors into the proper air lock. The door to the dust lock closes behind us and I know that there is only one more set of doors between us and outside. There are many boot prints tracked through the thin film of dust that carpets the floor.

It's a big room, large enough to hold the two rovers. I first saw one of these in an appalling mersive game I played a couple of months before the dinner party. It was a first-person shooter with cheesy scientist stereotypes needing to be rescued from evil Martians who'd squashed their gelatinous tentacular forms into combat robots that, obviously, needed a good killing. I couldn't go back to it after the first session, when one of the scientists propositioned me after a gunfight. My stomach flips when I realize that character looked really quite similar to Dr. Elvan.

"Pick a rover," Petranek says. "Banks would say to you that they're both the same, but he'd be wrong. This one has better seats and that one has better suspension."

I point at the one with better suspension and Petranek gives a satisfied nod. We climb inside, me in the passenger seat without any need for discussion. I don't want to be distracted on my first trip out. I check that the drones have been stored in the cargo area and then strap in. It's comfortable enough, with better radiation shielding and a roaming range of more than four hundred miles on its first battery. Theoretically, you could charge the spare while driving, but this is contrary to safety protocols, which dictate that a backup battery always be available. It's fully pressurized too, but once we're roaming about and climbing in and out of it, we'll switch that off to save power.

On the windscreen interior, Principia flashes up a notification that the air lock is being activated and I can hear the whirring of the depressurization taking place around us. In less than a minute, the large bay doors ahead of us open up and I see a sliver of the Martian exterior being slowly revealed. Oh God, this is it.

Petranek starts up the rover fully and the screen display changes, showing us the mapped route ahead with the same blue line projected over the view that I'm used to from taxis back home. Down the left-hand side there is a stream of environmental data including humidity, temperature, and wind speed, along with the option to view more. It's been picked up from the satellites around the planet along with various environmental posts that have been planted across the region over the past forty-odd years. Until recently even Curiosity still contributed to that data.

I'm not interested in the weather right now, however. I swipe my side of the screen to move the full display to the driver's side, wanting to see Mars alone without all that crap displayed over the top of it.

There's a long slope ahead of us to take us up from the subterranean level of the base to the surface, so there's no glimpse of the sky yet, just compacted regolith and pebbles. I can feel my guts clenching and my gloved hands gripping the armrests tightly as the rover rolls forward slowly while the last of the door disappears into the roof.

Petranek guns the engine and we lurch forward, racing up the slope like it's a ramp to clear a chasm in one great leap. I yelp as I'm pushed back in my seat, Petranek shouting "Wheeeee!" as the huge rover tires leave the ground at the top of the ramp and then land more slowly than my Earth-bound brain can handle easily.

"I love that bit!" Petranek says with a huge grin. "So, Dr. Kubrin, welcome to Mars."

How many times have I been welcomed? I don't know, but this feels like the right time to hear it.

The barren red dust stretches away from us as far as I can see, punctuated by the occasional sensor array and a few small wind turbines that are twirling lazily in the breeze. The sky is the color of a winter dawn even though the sun is high and so very small and pale. Something inside me lurches, as if some base part of me, something fundamentally human, reels at the distance and cold light of that sun.

There is a devastating beauty in this bleak place, just like in the harsh moorlands I roamed as a child, but without the abundance of life. I can't help but search for it, as if the same part of me that reels from the distant sun is desperately seeking some blade of grass, some tuft of gorse somewhere here. I know, intellectually, that there is no life other than that contained within Principia's walls and in this rover, but still I hope for it, stupidly.

I scan the landscape, looking for details that are so familiar to me, thanks to years of studying satellite data and dozens of mersives. The particular shape of Elysium Mons in the distance, the outcrop of rock just to the northwest of the Mars Principia; the landmarks are there, just as they were in the mersives. Even that stupid shooter had perfectly rendered scenery because it was recorded here, by previous occupants, and I realize with a sinking dread that something is missing. But it isn't something out there; it's something that should be inside me, yet again.

Where is the sense of true wonder? There was a flicker of it, just moments ago, but that was as much the reaction to Petranek's dramatic exit from the base. JeeMuh, how fucking dead inside am I? Yet another life experience in which the reality has not matched up with the expectation. All these moments, these landmarks in our lives that are supposed to make us feel alive, supposed to make us understand what's really important in life, and fuck, I am just empty every single time.

What is wrong with me?

"It's amazing, isn't it? The first time you come outside?" Petranek gushes. "How do you feel?"

"Amazing," I lie with an echo. Just like I lied all the other times I was asked that question. Always "Fine!" or "Excited!" or "So happy!," those fake exclamation marks taking the form of an upbeat note in my voice. I have long since abandoned the hope that speaking that way could somehow make it true. I've always feared the social impact of speaking the actual truth and so I protect the one asking the question by hiding it. Why should they suffer just because I'm some sort of emotional zombie? Surely, holding my baby, I should have been feeling elated. Of course I had to say something to make the inquirer believe that in a brittle, chirpy voice. Otherwise they would have looked at me in horror.

Motherhood is like a social minefield. From the moment you become aware of being pregnant, every single time that information is shared, you risk stepping on something explosive. MyPhys told me I was pregnant shortly after conception. I didn't tell Charlie for a month because I knew that the moment I did, I would not be my own person anymore. And I knew that he'd think he'd won.

No, I shouldn't think of it that way.

The squeals of joy that came every time we told someone, working our way out from the center of our social map, telling parents and siblings first—the latter only in Charlie's case—then friends and coworkers. I had to suffer that in person, having an actual workplace, unlike Charlie, who worked from home. Besides, for him it was just a "congratulations," a virtual pat on the back for his virility, and maybe a comment or two from some colleague who professed to know exactly what parenthood would be like for us and delighted in telling us how wonderful and awful it was going to be.

For me, it was the constant looks, the commentary when I started to show, the sense that somehow, I was no longer Dr. Kubrin but something owned by society as a whole. Something precious and yet equally derided. As some put me on some unfathomable pedestal of womanhood, others downgraded me as just another baby factory, with a head addled by hormones. What a waste of a brilliant mind. I wanted to tear a new one in both kinds of people.

But above everything else, what grated the most was the way people assumed how I would be feeling. "Oh, how wonderful—you must be so happy!" That started on day zero, with each call to spread the news. As much as I would have liked to, I couldn't say, "Well, actually, I don't feel so happy. It's kinda complicated and I'm not sure how I feel but maybe if there was a way to score about twenty emotions on a sliding scale for each one, I might be able to convey an approximation of my reaction to this." No one wants to hear anything like the truth during these landmark times. It has to be one emotion, a positive one—unless it's a quiet, heartfelt confession of fear or nervousness that can utterly disarm listeners and give them the opportunity to be reassuring—just to keep the social wheels turning in the way that makes everyone feel secure.

I didn't have the right to be angry about any of this. Cantankerous sod that I am, I know I'm the freak, the outlier on the psychiatrist's graph. And I understand how people want things to be nice. They just want a sense of connection. Validation. Some moment of confirmation from another human being that what they feel is normal. Having never had that, I know how much it is needed.

There's no point in being truthful. I can count on one hand the number of times that my defenses slipped and I burst into tears, spilling out the confession that I was not at all happy and felt nothing like everyone said I should. Every single time there was a long pause and then the confident conclusion that I was just tired. That's what motherhood was. Feeling more tired and more guilty than ever before. All these "emotionally normal" people, so appalled by someone not feeling happy at these designated times, so much more comfortable with the idea that fatigue is a more likely explanation. And then the inevitable question about why MyPhys wasn't intervening directly and maybe I should have my chip upgraded. "They can do marvelous things now," my mother-in-law said. "Direct stimulation of the . . . things that . . . make the happy drugs in your brain." I didn't have the energy to tell her the way it worked, nor how I had deliberately not upgraded my chip since getting it fitted, nor what I thought about this chemical plastering over of cracks in our lives. "It's all perfectly natural," she added to the silence, and I ended the call, unable to cope with her ignorance at the same time as I was falling apart. No wonder she hates me. I pushed her away when she was only trying to help. Of all the things I can find bottomless wells of guilt for, strangely enough, that's not one of them.

How I feel now, as I look out over the Martian plains, isn't the same. There is no real distress. And I am not just tired. I am . . . unmoved. Why should being here have made any difference now that we can experience Mars in mersives so powerful, so perfectly rendered, that our brains cannot help but convince us we are already there? I'm not seeing all of this for the first time. I have been looking at this vista for years.

But then, I'm not here because of my needs. I am here to satisfy Gabor's desire to have original art that he can sell at an extortionate price. It has to be special, to have a "unique selling point." I could just accept that I can paint anything of Mars that I want, and that need will be satisfied. I could get it out of the way and focus on the geological research I'd like to pursue. But it seems such a waste of an opportunity. While the surface of Mars has been fully mapped from above, only a small percentage has been fully recorded for mersives. It wasn't cost-effective to do more than that, not when the games companies can render pretty good approximations for the areas outside the fully recorded ones based on topographical data.

I review the route that Petranek arranged, as I didn't have any firm requests for my first trip onto the surface. Thinking that I'd be too emotionally overwhelmed to really do any proper work the first time out, I was happy to just be a passenger. The route passes through all the areas I'm most familiar with. And with good reason; they have the most dramatic backdrops, the most aesthetically pleasing scenery.

"I'd like to change the route," I say.

"We can't," Petranek replies. "This one has been approved by Principia."

"So? I'm not going to suggest anywhere dangerous. The weather forecasts are excellent; I checked them myself before we left."

"I don't know . . ."

"I'll keep it to the same range as the previous one," I say, plotting it out. "I want to see this crater. It's the same distance as the planned original end point anyway."

After a few moments of lip chewing, Petranek says, "Okay, ping it over to the prince and see if it's okay."

"Why wouldn't it be?" I ask. There are areas that can be unstable for a rover to cross in the summer—or what passes as one here—because of the ice melting in the regolith, but I know where those are. I was one of the people who mapped them!

Petranek shrugs. "The prince can be fussy about keeping us within the safety margins."

I send it in and get an instantaneous reply. Route change request denied. "What the fuck?" I mutter and type back, Why?

Insufficient drone data. Unable to guarantee minimum safety requirements.

"Oh for fuck's sake," I mutter and Petranek chuckles.

"Told you the prince is a fussy sod. Look, why don't we just carry on as planned and then you can argue with the prince when we get back?"

"No, that's a waste of our time. I'm not going to let some bloody AI dictate the way I do my job."

In my professional opinion, the areas on the new route have the same risk factors as the approved route. We can gather data as we travel.

Route change request denied.

You are impeding my ability to do my job, I type back.

"Why don't you just talk to hir?" Petranek asks, but I can't maintain two arguments at once so I pretend I didn't hear the question and carry on typing on my v-keyboard.

I need to see new areas not previously recorded by mersives for two reasons: 1: To have original subject matter to paint and thereby increase the value of my art and thereby increase the profit margin for GaborCorp. If you continue to impede my ability to do the job that Mr. Stefan Gabor personally sent me here to do, I will contact his lawyers and have them override you. 2: Because I have had a diagnosis of early-stage immersion psychosis and I believe seeing nonrecorded areas will aid my recovery. I'm sure Dr. Arnolfi and Dr. Elvan would agree.

Permission granted.

I smirk. The need to increase corporate profits always trumps any concern for employee safety. No doubt Principia weighed it up with the primary goal for my trip and couldn't find a strong enough reason to block this. Anything strong enough to withstand the lawyers, anyway.

The route displayed on the windscreen changes and Petranek whistles. "Oh wow. Okay. I haven't been in that direction before. None of us have. Isn't it dangerous?"

"No more dangerous than the original route."

"But why haven't the drones recorded it?"

"Because of your friend and mine: the cost-benefit analysis," I reply. "The lab I used to work in requested it a couple of years ago, but the corp argued that the amount of resources required to send out the cam drones and keep them well maintained outweighed any benefits that hi-def renderings could provide. Water had already been found and the value of Mars discoveries had crashed on the information markets. No one cares about Mars when GaborCorp has exclusive rights to operate here."

I don't say anything about my frustration with Gabor-Corp about this. There's always the chance that what we say will be raised later if they're looking for ways to boot us out of our contracts early. So I rant silently in my head about all the opportunities that GaborCorp is wasting by holding on to Mars and doing so little with it. I can remember my grandmother talking about the scientists before the collapse of democracy, the ones who had grand plans for colonizing Mars. All gone now. Doing something for the good of humankind, for the sheer ideological ambition of extending our footprint beyond Earth, simply isn't profitable enough. Now GaborCorp makes its money from the show Banks stars in, piping bite-size science with a heavy dollop of sexed-up pioneer bullshit into the feeds for the people who barely leave their apartments to watch and pseudo-participate in. And I lapped it up like the rest of them.

We haven't changed course yet, though Petranek has slowed down. "Are you worried about this? Want to go back to base? I don't mind dropping you off and carrying on without you."

Ze stops the rover. "No, it's fine. Sorry. I just . . . I guess I'm more of a creature of habit than I realized. I'm just not used to striking out into new areas."

"Seriously, there's nothing to worry about. I'm not going to take us somewhere dangerous, am I?" I twist in my seat to make eye contact and smile. "Trust me. I'm a geologist."

Petranek grins and turns the rover around, and we speed off as I close a new dialog box listing all of the risk factors that could endanger our safety on this new route.

7

THE THING ABOUT traveling millions of miles to another planet, one that is fundamentally unsuitable for human life, is that there are risks. There were points in the journey where the risk of my death was higher than most people would ever face during an entire lifetime, and one of those was just takeoff. I don't have any patience for Principia's nannying. This is frontier science, and art, come to think of it, as horribly pretentious as that sounds. Risk is inevitable.

If he were here, Charlie would lecture me now about managed risk. That insurmountable distance between us doesn't seem so bad all of a sudden.

I lean back and let the scenery scroll by as "memories" of shooting aliens flicker in and out of my consciousness at the sight of familiar rock formations used by the game. We're skirting the southern edge of the Elysium Planitia region and I can't help but try to imagine what this volcanic area was like when it was still active. There are fully rendered mersives that I worked on with the education and outreach team back home, designed to take curious children on tours of Mars set millions and millions of years ago. Giant volcanoes dwarfing anything on Earth, seas and rivers . . . all based on what we've pieced together so far with a minimal amount of speculation. Having found no evidence for it to date, the mersive was devoid of life. And that's what people kept asking about, as if they expected there to be dinosaurs or something. "But if there was water, couldn't there have been life on Mars?" That's always the inevitable question. Was there life then, before the atmosphere thinned and it turned into this barren place? Was there anything living in those seas? What happened to all the water? Loss into space due to the atmosphere doesn't account for all of it to anyone's satisfaction. I personally think a lot of it is still here, just frozen, and there have been extensive deposits of ice found, but still not enough to make the calculations work.

The jury is still out on whether there was microbial life on ancient Mars. I've worked on samples that could be interpreted as compelling evidence but I haven't been able to rule out geological causes for the characteristics that we've observed. I need to be out there, drilling, looking for silica and chert and clay mineral deposits, liaising with the scientists on Earth who still care about the thrill of knowing for the sake of knowing. What if that evidence is right beneath our feet now? What if Mars is more a cautionary tale than we want to believe? I don't for a moment think there was a civilization here—as much as the child in me wants there to have been one, with such a fierce intensity—but there could have been microbial life.

The Pathfinder said she was convinced there would be life on the planet they were aiming to reach. Did they make it there? They were using such advanced technology that the risk factors would have sent Principia into free fall. I hope they reached that planet and that they found life more advanced than bacteria. And I wish they could send back word of it, instantly, like in the silly sci-fi mersives, and shut up the religious extremists who haven't stopped bleating on about the Pathfinder's heresy for decades. I would love to see the looks on their faces if Earth wasn't the only place gifted with life by the god they try to ram down everyone's throats. They could do with a dose of humility on an interstellar scale. Finding evidence of life closer to home would be better.

"It's a lot to take in, isn't it?" Petranek says and I give a noncommittal grunt. "Are you missing your family?"

I am missing something, but I'm not yearning to be with my family the way ze assumes I should be. "Yes," I say, because that's what is expected. Surely I must be, somewhere deep down. I think about them a lot. But then I realize I haven't actually thought about Mia today and that old guilt surges up and bursts into life with the gassy intensity of a Strombolian eruption. I should say more—Petranek is trying to make conversation—but I might not seem genuine. And I can't tell the truth, that I was actually relieved when I left the flat with my case for the last time before the flight. That when I got in the taxi I felt lighter than I had for weeks. Oh God, I am such an awful person.

"Do you have family back home?" I ask, hoping that flipping the conversational pressure away from me will do the trick.

Petranek nods. "Father, two brothers and a couple of nieces. We're not that close. No immediate family. I was married, like, ten thousand years ago, back when I was trying out the whole femme thing. Shit, what a disaster that was."

I want to know more, but I can't ask. It's too personal, too soon.

"My ex was basically a caveman," ze volunteers. "I was totally fucked up about . . . everything." A short, nervous laugh bursts out, filling the rover. "I think I tried to make it work with him because I was trapped in the whole binary lie, you know? My mum died when I was really small, my dad is . . . very traditional and my brothers are men's men, you know? Every time I tried to express myself, it was held up against them. When I cut up my dresses and cut off my hair, they said I was trying to be like them. When I swung the other way and went hyperfemme, it was to 'assert my separate identity,' for fuck's sake."

"That's what your dad said?"

"No, the quack he brought in to evaluate me. It was really shit."

"But you got out."

"Yeah," ze sighs. "Straight from one testosterone hellscape to another. But, to cut a long and pretty awful story short, I met some awesome people who gave me a language that finally made everything make sense. I think I'd be dead now, if it wasn't for them. Those are the people I miss. Every day. But we message and . . ." Ze falls silent for a while. "It's not the same as real-time comms though, is it?"

"No," I say. I want to mention how many times I've felt alienated by my own biology, how those hours and hours of breastfeeding felt like a punishment when everyone kept telling me that it was natural and "best for baby" and a "really special time." But it wouldn't be right. Ze isn't obligated to help me navigate my own confusion. "I wanted to say how much I admire your work. I read up on it all on the way over. The water- and air-filtration systems are really impressive. And the solution you came up with to deal with the dust on the solar panels is just so clever."

Petranek laughs. "Damn, girl, you are just all the fun, aren't you?"

I feel my cheeks redden. Sensing that the comment has stung, Petranek reaches over and rests a gloved hand over my own. "Sorry. Banks says I can be a bit brutal sometimes. If it helps, I'm just massively overcompensating. Coming outside makes me think too much, so I try to keep things light. Obviously telling you about my awful family and struggles with self-identity is just small talk, right?" Ze laughs again. "I don't need to make any jokes. My conversational skills are a joke—let's face it."

"It's been a while since you've worked with someone new, hasn't it?"

From the sharp turn of hir head, I know I'm right. "Yeah, it has. I've known the others forever. We came through on the same cohort, even though Banks has been here the longest. We all went through basic training together and we worked together for a few years before that. We're a good team."

I look back out the window, feeling like a fifth wheel. I feel a stab of homesickness, but not for the flat; for the lab. We were a good team there.

"Oh shit, that came out wrong," Petranek says.

"It didn't," I say. "You were just telling the truth. This is weird for all of us."

The silence is uncomfortable so I focus on the scenery, trying to remind myself that this is actually happening, to my mind and body right now, in real time, and that I am not in a mersive. It's harder without Petranek's awkward conversation. I think about Mia, or rather, try to. She's happy and safe and will be fine without me. She depends upon Charlie anyway. He's the one she goes to when she hurts herself and the one she calls for in the night if she wakes. I'm an addendum, probably barely missed.

"So, what's it like being a mother?"

The stock replies come to mind instantly, but I don't immediately give them. "Honestly?" I finally say.

"Yeah, obviously. Unless it's something you don't want to talk about?"

"Honestly, it's mostly shit."

"I can imagine," Petranek says. "I've never bought the hype about it."

"You know, all my life I was sold the idea that having a child would make everything suddenly make sense." I look at Petranek. "Spoiler: it doesn't." Ze chuckles and I smile too. "And that whole thing about how painful periods would be like a distant memory after I had a child—that is also a load of arse."

"Yeah, that never seemed like a comforting thing to say to a young woman in pain!" Petranek says. "Like, if I was her, I'd be thinking, oh great, so I need to grow another human being inside me and expel it and then take care of it and totally change everything about my life just so this crap doesn't hurt anymore?"

"There's a new upgrade to MyPhys that's really good for them," I say. "Took them long enough to figure it out. I'm still waiting for the one that deals with existential angst."

"I thought having a baby sorted that out too," Petranek says with a wry grin.

"No. And that instalove thing people talk about, that magic moment when you see your baby for the first time? That's bullshit too."

Petranek glances at me, confused. "Really? I got a few friends who had kids and they said . . ." Ze trails off and I turn away, regretting what I said. "Everyone's different, I guess," ze adds.

Yes. Everyone is different, and I happened to be one of the people who didn't get to experience the mythical love that could be gained only by holding one's own child for the first time. That was a love, I was told by so many exhausted, harried mothers, unlike any other. More powerful, deeper, more selfless, than anything I could imagine before holding my child in my arms. They said it was like a drug, like a sledgehammer, something monumental and life changing.

Well, my life changed but I didn't get that drug part.

I sink lower in my seat, staring out of the window, think-ing of those women I grew to hate. Was that the bullshit they lulled themselves to sleep with every night? Their lives were over, so they had to invent some sort of consolation prize, presumably. One that, somehow, I didn't receive. That's how it felt in that tiny apartment, stinking of the paraphernalia of newborn chaos, that I didn't get the one thing I'd been universally promised. No instant love to cushion me against the boredom and terror of being responsible for a new life.

And it wasn't just an absence of that fictional prize; it was an absence of my sense of self. My body felt like it was one of those tiny towns obliterated by a tornado overnight, left wrecked and unfamiliar, broken pieces scattered beyond all recognition. My concentration destroyed, all joy sucked out of me like air from an open lock. The only thing moving me from one task to the next being the sure knowledge that if I didn't move, a tiny person could die.

"It sounds like it sucks," Petranek says.

I can feel the way ze is trying to move us back to that point earlier in the conversation where I was opening up. "It really does," I say, more cautious now. "I do love my daugh-ter. I'm not a total monster. I'm just . . . it just . . . I've never said any of that to anyone before."

"Obviously a day for firsts," Petranek replies. "But seri-ously, I'm glad you did say it. If there's one thing I know, it's that hiding behind a mask all the time is really fucking tiring."

We slip into a comfortable silence. I look up at the sun, expecting to see it rising and getting larger and brighter as the minutes go by, then look away again. With a thrill, I re-alize I don't recognize the area we're driving into.

I sit up again, drinking it in. Something unfamiliar at last! We're not far from the destination point, but I want to run out there now, thrust my hands into the dust and—

With a sigh, I correct that thinking. I can't do what I did as a child every time we went somewhere new. I was always first out of the car to take a deep lungful of the air and then find something to pick up or shove my hands into, just to feel like . . .

Like I had arrived.

I close my eyes, feeling like I'm trapped in this twilight state, not really here, not really awake. I want to pull the helmet off and smell Mars; I want to grab fistfuls of dust and let it play through my fingers out here, instead of in a lab. I want to brush my fingertips over the rocks and feel the texture, read its history, not just look at it all. Fuck! I'm trapped in this suit, in this rover, on this planet, and I just want some fresh air!

"You okay?" Petranek asks as MyPhys flashes up a dialog box reporting an elevation in hormonal stress markers and heart rate.

"Yeah," I say, forcing myself to calm down.

"Sometimes it can hit you out of the blue," ze says. "It gets easier. I promise. You just get used to it. I nearly lost my shit when I saw how far away the sun was when I came out on my first trip. I don't think we realized how much our brains are hardwired for Earth, you know?"

I nod. "Do you ever just want to go outside for some fresh air?"

"Oh yes. We all get that. Mersives help, as long as you don't overdo it."

Only Arnolfi and Elvan know about my struggle. At least the way I feel is normal, for a change. I stay quiet for the rest of the drive, and when we reach the end of the route I release the cam drones, requesting that they gather data in a one-kilometer radius. Each one is about the size of a watermelon, much larger than the equivalent models on Earth, as here they need tiny thruster jets fueled by methane to be able to fly in such a thin atmosphere. That's the argument for not using them to get a high-def rendering of the entire planet; methane production not earmarked for the return trips to Earth has to be justified by some solid financial benefits. Now that the information market isn't interested in real 3-D maps of Mars, there's no point as far as GaborCorp is concerned.

"I'm going to have a look around," I tell Petranek. "I want to see if there's a good vista to paint."

"No problem. I'm going to scope out a location for a sensor station. I think we should spread out some more. Do some proper exploring again. We've got a bit . . . insular. I'll have an argument with the prince about it later. 'Cause that's always fun."

We climb out of the rover and Principia sends me a ping notifying me that I can call up a map of the local area and it will show my location and Petranek's as we are monitored in real time, just like in a gaming mersive. The dot representing me is blue; Petranek is green. I almost expect a bunch of red dots to pop up all of a sudden, indicating incoming enemies. Maybe I've played too many games, just like I've experienced too many personal mersives.

There's a crater on the other side of the hill, Cerberus Palus, that stretches ahead of me, formed by the ejecta from the original impact. I feel a genuine thrill as I climb it, having stared at aerial photographs of it for years. Those photographs made me fall in love with Mars as a child, and as an aspiring geologist. To the north of the crater are spiral shapes in the rock, caused by ancient lava coils when the area was volcanically active. They can be found on Earth, and the day I saw that picture for the first time, shortly after my tenth birthday, I'd just been reading about a Terran example observed in Hawaii. It was the first time I really understood how observing geological phenomena on Earth could give us insights into Mars and its geological history. It blew my mind that the same things could happen on both planets. If only all observable effects were as easy to ascribe to common root causes.

The suit performs well as I climb, the helmet drawing away the moisture from my breath and capturing it to be recycled by the two compartments on my back that also house my air supply. Petranek's work is in evidence here too; the air tanks are small thanks to the excellent recycling processes being managed within the suit, and therefore not too heavy. I can feel the scree shifting beneath my boots and revel in the sensory feedback. The sense of disconnection is finally giving way to the joy of being in the moment and I laugh, actually laugh out loud with joy.

I am climbing up the side of a crater on Mars!

On Mars!

"Petranek?"

Hir voice comes loud and clear. "Yeah?"

"I'm on Mars! I mean . . . fuck! I'm on *Mars*!"

My helmet is filled with hir barking laugh. "Yes, you are! Having fun, then?"

"It's the Cerberus Palus crater! It's like . . . I dunno, like meeting a mersive star or something. I can't actually believe it!"

"You just keep breathing steady, Kubrin, and watch your step. You sound as high as a satellite!"

I do feel high. And even as I think that, I appreciate how low I have been, and for so long. It feels like a dense fog has been shrouding me for months . . . years . . . and has suddenly been blown away. I start to giggle, preserving enough presence of mind to close the audio link between Petranek and me, so ze isn't subjected to it.

This is no good; I can't observe anything in this state. Seeing a large boulder up near the summit, I scrabble toward it, trying to calm myself down. I'll give myself five minutes; then I'll get to work.

Looking down into the crater does nothing to ground me. My spirits soar even higher. It's too wide to see the other side in any detail without retinal-cam enhancement, which I resist, so I focus on the crater bed below, thinking about possible paintings at last. It feels right that the first one includes those spirals, so I open the interface to the cam drones and instruct them to fly across the crater and record from the area just north of the top edge, expanding out a further kilometer on some high shots too, just so I get the background scenery right.

I watch them fly off, feeling like a witch sending off flying monkeys, and decide to head down into the crater to take a look around and see if it's worth getting some samples. Watching my step, I look down to make sure I don't fall from the top of the crater edge, only to see a footprint a couple of meters ahead of me in the lee of the boulder.

For a moment, I think it's one of mine, before realizing I haven't actually gone that far. No one else is supposed to have come this far either. Oh God, what if it isn't actually there? I could verify with my lens, but I don't want that query to be flagged up with Principia. A negative result could tell Arnolfi that I'm seeing things.

But I can't just ignore it. "Petranek, can you come over here?"

"You okay?"

"Yeah, I just want you to look at something. Are you sure no one has been out here before?"

"I'm sure. And didn't the prince say as much? Let me double-check. Principia, confirm that the area in a half-kilometer radius from the rover has not been visited by a human before."

"Confirmed."

"What about a drone?"

"This area has not been documented by any craft or drone on the surface. It has been mapped by several orbiting satellites."

"Okay, thanks."

I twist to watch Petranek climb the hill behind me and then look back at the footprint. It is still there. "If no one has been here, then who left that?" I say as ze arrives. I watch hir eyes follow my prints to where I am standing now, then to the gap between them and the print. Hir eyes widen and I am flooded with relief at the confirmation that it really is there. "It wasn't me," I add.

"Are there any others?"

"Not that I can see. I reckon the boulder must have protected it from a dust devil that wiped any others out."

"Well, shit," ze mutters. "Principia, can you identify who made this print?"

Ze stares at it as I fret. If that damn AI has already lied about us being the first people here, can we trust it now?

"The footprint is an impression of a standard GaborCorp environmental protection suit."

"So anyone from the base could have left it," Petranek says.

"But could anyone from the base have scrubbed their trip from Principia's database?" I ask and Petranek shakes hir head.

"I couldn't do that; I don't have the correct level of privileges. Only Banks and Arnolfi would be able to do that." Petranek looks away from the footprint and for a moment I wonder if ze is calling one of them. I watch the frown develop on hir face as ze stares into the distance. "Shit, I knew something was going on."

I take a picture of the footprint with my retinal cam and then turn back to Petranek. "What do you mean?"

"I . . . I don't know . . . I just feel like something hasn't been right with Banks since you got here. Same with Arnolfi, for that matter. She seems a bit strung out, you know? I thought it was because Banks was being such a dick. She hates conflict, always has. But I can't see why either of them would be sneaking around here. I mean, what's to see? It hasn't been flagged as an area of interest or anything. If it was, I could see the temptation to sell some information to a rival corp, but I'm not even sure anyone cares about Mars anymore. Even the ratings for the show have gone down lately."

"Maybe that's why Banks is so uptight," I venture. "Maybe he's worried they'll send him home and want me to take over or something."

"I don't know. He's usually more laid-back. And I can't see what would bring Arnolfi out here. We're the ones she's studying, not the planet."

The thought of that makes me shudder, but it's true. She's studying the impact of prolonged exposure to low g on the human brain, among other things. I can't help but think of that damn note. I reckon it must be Arnolfi's footprint, but I can't say why I think that without explaining about the note, and I don't trust Petranek enough to mention it. Only the suspicion that note planted in me is making me think it is her instead of Banks. I have no evidence either way.

"But what would Banks be doing out here?" Petranek says as we both stare at the footprint. "Do you think we should mention it to them? Yeah, we could just ask them."

"No," I reply, without hesitation. "If they're up to something dodgy they'll only deny it. And one of them must be. Why else would they hide the fact they came out here? Let's keep this between us for now and just keep a close eye on them."

Petranek's frown returns. "Banks and Arnolfi are solid. I

can't believe they'd do anything to jeopardize their contracts. There must be another explanation."

"Keeping quiet for now is the best thing for both of us," I say. "Just in case."

Petranek reluctantly agrees, clearly shaken by the possibility that one of hir crewmates could be hiding something. I'm shaken too, but for a different reason. What else has been scrubbed from Principia's database?

8

THERE ARE MESSAGES waiting for me when I get back and I realize that Principia doesn't report their arrival when I'm outside of the base. I let the brief irritation pass; it's probably good not to be distracted while outside. They're only from family and there are no urgent tags. I've been here nearly a week now, so the messages are settling into casual updates on daily life.

I empty the bag containing a few samples into the chute in the air lock that will clean the dust off of the bags and sterilize the outside of the plasglass tubes before delivering them to the lab. Petranek and I shake off as much dust as we can as a couple of drones roll in and start cleaning off the rover. We wait while the air that came in with us is sucked out with the majority of the dust and then replenished with filtered air from the base. The air lock repressurizes as we begin the process of going back through the dust lock and getting de-suited.

"You won't say anything to them, will you?" I say to

Petranek. Ze didn't mention the footprint at all on the way back.

"I won't—don't worry. But I really don't think there's anything underhanded going on. I've known these people for years. You shouldn't be so concerned."

It's not the footprint that bothers me; it's the pattern. The note, the ring, Banks being unduly hostile . . . The pattern is more important than the detail. Where did I hear that before?

Soon enough I am distracted by getting out of the suit, which feels harder than getting into it, even though it's the same process but in reverse.

Dr. Elvan is waiting in the last chamber and I feel rather self-conscious in my base-layer onesie. Petranek seems utterly unconcerned and high-fives him as ze goes past on the way out, leaving us alone.

"How was it?" he asks.

"Fine," I say.

"There were a few stress spikes while you were out there, but nothing too unusual. Any dizziness or fatigue?"

I shake my head, wishing I was in anything but this damn onesie.

"Is there anything you're concerned about?" he asks, taking a step closer.

"No. Should there be?"

He smiles and it makes me feel like an awkward student again. "Not at all. I'm just doing my job, Dr. Kubrin. Don't worry—I haven't seen anything from your MyPhys readings to suggest you need to be confined to base. You're doing remarkably well, in fact. I thought that this would be the day you'd be just about shuffling around and doing your last physical tests. Maybe I'm being overcautious."

To look at, he is the opposite of Charlie in almost every way. His hair is black whereas Charlie's is ginger. Elvan's skin is brown whereas Charlie's is so pale that if he wears yellow it makes him look like he's about to die. Elvan's eyes are dark brown and Charlie's are the blue of a clear February sky. And there's a warmth to this man that I don't remember in my husband.

I feel a pull toward him that I didn't feel with Charlie before Mars and I head toward the doors, fighting that attraction with a polite smile, distancing myself. "Thanks for looking out for me," I say, not wanting to seem cold, and then I hurry down the corridor back to my room.

Peeling the onesie off and having a shower helps. It seems crazy that I can have a longer shower here than I can back on Earth. We can't afford the higher band of water rates back home, but here, pretty much all of it is recycled right away. There's no reason the same system couldn't be implemented in our apartment block. No reason other than profit, of course. No doubt the gov-corp wants to keep its profits from its water company subsidiaries nice and high.

Where I grew up, in our strange little commune, there was water everywhere. A loch full of millions of gallons of the stuff that we could swim in whenever the weather permitted. Rainwater that we collected on the roof and used to flush the toilet because Mum couldn't cope with the dry composting toilets that Dad wanted to use. In Manchester it rains so much, but the permits required to set up rainwater collection on buildings without integrated systems are prohibitively expensive. I can remember Dad declaring that we should set up a water racket and ship it south to make a fortune. He laughed at the time, but I knew that he was actually tempted, more to stick one in the eye of the system than to make any money.

Then, just as rapidly, I recall him months later, hollow cheeked and dark eyed: *"I can't stay here on my own. I'll go mad."*

No. I'm not going to message him. What would I say? Why do it now, after all these years? Does my mother think that being on another planet will make me feel safe enough to finally make contact? I wish she would just let it go.

I review the messages from Drew and my other lab mates, most of them making requests for samples from various locations we've discussed before. All asked with a grin and some sort of precursor like "I know this is a bit cheeky, but if you could . . ." It saddens me that this is what we're reduced to. We all felt that, even when the funding for the lab was secured, we were allowed to pursue only narrow lines of inquiry, all serving some project or plan in upper-management echelons trying to find new ways to monetize Gabor's exclusive access to Mars without actually investing any more money in it. None of us could really understand why he'd spent so much on getting that access when he barely seemed interested in the big questions. It was clear at the dinner party that he wasn't a naturally curious man. He was more like a shark, evaluating everything he came across in terms of whether he could eat it or not.

Perhaps I'm doing sharks a disservice.

By the time that we started eating, there wasn't any need to try to enthuse at him about the lab—the deal had already been agreed—but I was still keen to find some reasoning behind his fascination with the red planet. Apparently the negotiations to secure the exclusive rights to Mars access were fierce and the money involved was enough to make one's eyes water. What was it about this place that had motivated him to beat off the competition? But as the evening went on, I realized that he wasn't fascinated by Mars at all; I had just assumed he was. I couldn't understand why he seemed so uninterested in it. Even the biggest question—whether we could find definitive proof of life there—held no interest for him.

"I've heard it would only be bacteria or something from, what? Millions of years ago?" he said between mouthfuls. "Not proper aliens or remains of buildings or anything impressive."

"But even just proof of bacterial life would be monumental," Drew said, her cheeks flushed with wine and scientific passion.

"Why?"

When Drew spluttered for words, I said, "Because there are so many people who believe that we're alone in the universe. Showing them that life, even in microscopic form, is there on Mars would prove we might not be alone."

Gabor shrugged. "Can't see the profit in it myself. Though there would be a certain satisfaction in seeing how the Americans react."

I noted that Travis didn't share that cruel glint in his husband's eye. "Not all Americans are those fire-and-brimstone types."

"No," Stefan agreed, "just the rich and powerful ones, ironically enough. This sauce is excellent, by the way."

Even now I wonder if he bought that exclusive access just to spite the Americans. I'd like to think it was to ensure that any evidence of life wouldn't be destroyed or at least hidden by a damaging religious agenda, but I think if anything, it was pure one-upmanship.

I send replies to all of my former coworkers, promising to gather all the samples they want. It will take dozens of trips and no doubt just as many arguments with Principia, but I have to do my bit to push back against that willful ignorance. I'll do what I can here and then when I take those samples home, we'll analyze them in our spare time, outside of contracted hours. Doing the real science, as Drew would say, not just corporate shit shoveling.

Not all of the work we did in the lab back home was

useless; a lot of it made the previous geologist's work here easier—finding those ice deposits as efficiently as possible and giving the base water sustainability for years, for one thing. But I want to understand the geological history of this planet, not just work out how we can best exploit it.

There's nothing new from Charlie but it's my turn to send a message, so that's to be expected. The routine we got into on the trip over has been disrupted. Before I respond to his last one, I need to record one to Mia.

He's told me she watches the ones I've sent already before bedtime as part of the going-to-bed ritual. Charlie likes his routine and there's no denying it's good for Mia, but I've run out of things to say to her. I was never very good at that. Anyway, I've always thought that it's the tone of voice and the modulation that help children to acquire language. Charlie once caught me talking through a research write-up with her when she was about four months old. He stood in the doorway, watching us long before I noticed him, as I read out my draft conclusion to her in that singsong "motherese." He teased me for days afterward.

I don't think I can get away with that now; she's too old. Another idea comes to mind though, so I start up the cam before I talk myself out of it.

"Hello, Mia! It's nearly bedtime so I thought I would tell you a story. Once upon a time there was a little girl called Mia and she lived in a giant tree in a magical wood. Every morning she had her breakfast brought to her by little blue birds with purple beaks. They brought her berries and flowers filled with nectar and water for her morning drink. Mia loved living with her daddy in the giant tree, because he made sure no bears or zombies— Shit. I can't put zombies in a kid's story. I'll edit that out in a minute . . . Ummmm . . . because he made sure no bears could come to eat her. Mia's mummy wasn't at home because she had to fly to a star to make the king of the wood even more rich. Ummmm . . . I'll change that later. But every night, Mummy waved from the star, hoping that Mia might wave back."

I stab the recording button, hating the way my throat is clogging up. I'm no good at stories. This was a stupid idea. But more than that . . . I'm missing her.

It's a strangely reassuring ache, as unpleasant as it is. Perhaps I'm not a monster. It's not that I don't love her—I do—but just not with the spear-through-the-chest sort of love that those other mothers told me I would have. I regret what I said to Petranek and the lack of explanation I gave.

I should have said that when I held Mia for the first time, I just felt relief that the birth was over. I felt like I'd been thrown down a mountain. I hurt in places I didn't even know I had. When I looked into her purply pink face, wrinkled up and blotchy and distressed by the trauma of being squeezed out into the world, I didn't feel a rush of love. I felt fear. Shock. A quiet dread. Here was a new human being whom I was responsible for, incapable of caring for herself, fragile and terrifying to hold. The main thing I felt was the certainty that I would screw it up, not a love like no other.

Charlie was sobbing and I passed her over to him as the midwife checked me over. All of our arguments about where and how the birth was going to happen were forgotten the moment he held her in his arms. And I could see it come over him, that magic that I'd been promised by so many. How huge his eyes were, dark with love, taking in every detail of her face as if she were the most beautiful thing he'd ever seen. She was still covered in the mess of birth and, in all honesty, quite horrific-looking, but he was cooing at her like some lovestruck idiot.

Thank God he was. I was free to pull back, to let him do what I should have been capable of. At the birth center the emphasis was on traditional methods, so they didn't take her off to be cleaned up right away. It was the compromise we'd come to between my desire to be at my mum's house and his insistence on going to a hospital. As soon as I arrived in the early stages of labor I knew I should have stood my ground and just gone to Mum's. I couldn't stand the bland music, the pastel colors, the soft edges to everything. All the women, dressed in uniforms with little duck patterns on them, as if infantilizing mothers in labor was preferable to the cold reassurance of professional uniforms. I'd rather have given birth in the woods behind the house I grew up in, squatting over a blanket, than in that place. It was all locked in by that point though, and I knew that if I left, I'd void our insurance and Charlie would never forgive me if something went wrong. That was the argument he'd won with. What if something happens? He simply didn't listen to my counter, that it was more likely to go wrong if I was stressed out in some unfamiliar sterile environment.

The birth center was a disguised hospital, for all intents and purposes, designed to look more like a homely place without the scary medical equipment on full show. I found it jarring, that discordant mix of controlled environment and relaxed lighting. It heightened my sense of wrongness. Being there felt like looking at mainstream feeds curating "content for women," recognizing nothing of myself in them. Better than a hospital, yes, but not somewhere I could feel relaxed and safe. But then, I hadn't felt relaxed and safe for nine months, so what difference did one more night make?

It's hard to disentangle this sensation of wanting to be with Mia from the omnipresent guilt. And I know, I just know, that if somehow, magically, I could walk out of this room and into our apartment, it would quickly fade. I'd hold her, play with her a little bit, and then I'd want to be elsewhere. It's always like that. Why would that be different now?

The thing that no one ever seems to want to admit is that

small children are boring. It felt like becoming a mother meant I had to be stuffed into a smaller box in my own life. All the things that I'd strived for professionally, all of the battles hard fought and won to carve out a career in science that satisfied me as well as my gov-corp, all of that was supposed to be put away. I was a mother now, and all I was supposed to care about was my baby.

I lie down on the bed and curl up, feeling my own hateful selfishness too keenly. I shouldn't have had a child; that's what it comes down to. I should have stood up to Charlie. I should have—

I stretch out, flat on my back, calling up the list of personal mersives. I haven't used today's allocation. I didn't yesterday either. I'll see Mia, cut off this craving at the root and then go to the lab and start looking at those samples.

There are huge gaps in the list. Months when I was incapable of summoning the desire to even just record with full immersion. There are a handful of five-minute snippets in her first month, then only sporadic recordings, until the flurry of those made between the meeting with Stefan Gabor in which he told me about his "wonderful idea" and my leaving Earth. It's like looking at a timeline of my attitude toward motherhood. Those early recordings of snatched moments in between sleeping and feeding and the zombified drudge of getting through each day, then the desert of those two months before Charlie stepped in fully, and then the guilt-ridden desperation of gathering as many moments as possible before leaving.

So many of these I can remember just from the date stamp, let alone the tags I've assigned to them, I've relived them so much. I spot one that's been neglected, tagged "wrong again," and, weirdly, I can't recall its contents. According to the time stamp, Mia would have been just shy of four weeks old when it was recorded.

It takes moments to whip through the series of dialog boxes requesting confirmation that I'm not controlling machinery or a vehicle, that I am in a safe environment, that I'm aware of the risks—oh yes, painfully aware!—and then I'm in our apartment again.

It's a mess and there's the unmistakable smell of recently changed nappy: a mixture of something awful fading and the scent of the thick white cream that prevents nappy rash. Charlie is next door in the bedroom, trying to work, and I'm in the living room, shaking a giraffe-shaped rattle a few centimeters above Mia.

She is small and wriggly, her arms and legs waving around with no control. It's months before she'll grab the rattle, but I'm still shaking it above her, eager to stimulate her brain.

Her lips curl up and I stop moving the rattle. "Charlie! Charlie, she's starting to smile!"

"It's too early," he calls back through the door.

"No, it's not. Come and look! You'll miss it!"

He comes out, grinning, never grumpy about his work being interrupted like I always am. Basalt follows him out and gives Mia a quick sniff around her head. Satisfied that all is well, he lopes back to the bedroom to curl up on the bed and wait for Charlie to return. Charlie kneels next to me, leaning over her. "Hello, monkey! Are you going to smile? Smile for Daddy!"

"There, did you see that?" I say and he shakes his head.

"That's wind," he says authoritatively.

"No, it's not."

He gets up after planting a soft kiss on Mia's forehead. "I've got to finish this update. Keep working on that fart, tiger," he says to Mia.

"It really isn't a—"

The loud raspberry noise from her nappy makes him

laugh out loud. "Whoa, she's gone red. That was a corker. You'd better check she didn't follow through."

I bite back the comment that I know what to do and he shuts the door. From the way the smell is lingering, there's a chance it was more than gas.

I reach for the fasteners on her sleep suit and everything freezes.

"Sorry about this," says a familiar voice. Someone I've heard before, but I can't place him. "Just give me a moment. Everything is okay. Don't panic, Dr. Kubrin."

Mia disappears. So do all of the traces of her. No piles of clothes waiting to be sorted, no bags of clean nappies, no toys. The sofa disappears and so does the folded table on the far side of the room. It feels surreal, like I'm in one of those store mersives in which you can test whether the furniture you want fits in your home before you buy it. I'm too busy trying to place that voice to panic, and it's happening so fast that before I know it, the huge temporary dining table is back, covered with the tablecloth and set for dinner like the day the Gabors came.

Travis. That's the voice. It's Travis Gabor.

"Hello, Dr. Kubrin."

I turn and he's sitting down at the table, in the place he sat for dinner. There's even the smell of the meal recently cooked. He's wearing the same suit, looking just as handsome as he did that day.

"Come and sit down. You're probably feeling disoriented. I apologize and I will explain. You can't converse with me properly, I'm afraid; this is just a rendered mersive I constructed from memories of your apartment. I've made an effort to predict some of your responses, and if any of those match what you say, I will be able to reply to your questions. I will make it clear if I haven't predicted something you say."

Dazed, I go over to the table and sit where I did at the

dinner party, because that's where his attention is focused. As soon as I sit down, it feels like he is looking at me.

"This is the equivalent of a gaming mersive," he says with a smile. "You can't come to any physical harm here. I've locked you out of making any changes though, so this is more like a loading room, I suppose. I hid this message inside one of your personal mersives, or rather, the synaptic 'bookmark' your chip uses to access it. It was the only way that I could speak to you without anyone else knowing."

He seems so very different from when I met him at the dinner party. Back then, he was so . . . full-on, fizzing like soda, thrilled by everything and sparkling as much as he could. Seeing him now, listening to his voice and how calm he is, makes his previous behavior seem as if he was playing a part. Perhaps this is just the recording-a-message version of Travis, but this man seems more real to me than the one I met on Earth.

"I'm sorry if it was a bit strange when the transition was made between your mersive and the start of this message," he continues, "but I had to design it to fit as closely as possible, and only be accessed once you were in a recording. It helps to mask what we're doing from Principia and from your MyPhys too. I won't bore you with the details, but I can assure you that this is highly illegal. I'm putting myself at great risk to do this, along with the other people involved in making the upgrades to your chip. If you'd had one of the later versions when you signed the Mars contract, this would have been so much harder."

I look around, becoming aware of tiny differences. This isn't a perfect replication of my apartment. It's too small for one thing and the kitchen corner is inaccurate. All the paintings are faithfully reproduced, however, and I realize I'm actually able to piece together what he was interested in when he was in my apartment for real. The things he didn't attend to have been filled in by software.

"It's hard to give you this message without freaking you out. Believe me, I've given this a lot of thought. Pulling off something like this takes a huge amount of planning, as I'm sure you'll appreciate. I recommend that you sit and stay as calm as possible. Give yourself a bit of time to process it. Don't rush into anything once this message has finished. If you need to replay it, simply go back to the personal mersive you selected before. I only stole the last second or two of it to knit this one in."

I'm gripping the edge of the table, seized by the feeling that my life is about to be blown apart. I know what that feels like. It's happened before.

"You've been silent for several seconds now, probably because you're shocked. Maybe a little bit scared. I'm sorry. I need you to do something for me, something very important. Anna? Are you still with me?"

"Yes," I croak.

"I need you to understand that no one on Principia or on Earth can know about this message, or about what I need you to do. If you help me, I'll help your father."

"My father? What does he have to do with any of this?"

"He has everything to do with why we're having this conversation and why you're on Mars and nothing to do with what I need you to do for me. If you commit to helping me, I'll explain everything."

I can feel myself shutting down, like an overworked chip that has gotten too hot and is switching off so it doesn't permanently damage itself. This isn't real. It isn't happening. I don't need to hear this.

"Anna, I need to know you're going to be discreet. You want your dad to get the help he needs, don't you?"

"Stop talking about him," I say through clenched teeth. "Just shut up."

"I'm sorry. I haven't predicted that response. Have you noticed that something isn't right on Principia?"

This disjointed conversation, built on Earth, played out on Mars, actually helps. If it were with the real Travis, he'd be drilling down into this reluctance to talk about the man he's using as leverage. I'm torn between wanting to understand it all and never thinking about it again.

"Something isn't right here. I agree with that." And I don't just mean in Mars Principia.

"Then let me help you work out what that is. That's all I want. Look, I don't trust my husband; that's what this comes down to. I know he bought the rights to Mars for a reason, and I don't think it's one that will be good for anyone except himself. He's hiding something and I want you to find it."

"On Mars?"

Travis nods. "There are discrepancies between the officially logged flight manifests and the cargo weights that have left Earth. He's sending more than he's declaring. I want you to find out what that is. And I need you to get me evidence. That's going to be difficult. You can't trust anyone on that base, or the AI. They must be in on it."

"But why me?"

"All of the scientific duties of his staff up there have been scaled back. They're not even allowed to explore anymore. Mars Principia is little more than a mersive factory now, but you have good reason to get out there and look around. You're there by the order of Stefan Gabor himself and you'll be able to use that if Principia starts being problematic."

"And what if I find something? How do I tell you?"

"I've set up a dead drop for packets of information. When the time comes, ask me and I'll run you through it. If you blow this open, Anna, people could die. I'd be one of them and so would you. Do you understand how important it is that you not trust anyone on the base?"

"Yes, I understand."

"In case you're worried, you're not going mad," Travis says, appearing to look straight at me. "This isn't the same as what happened to your father."

"How the hell do you know that?" I say without thinking.

"Because I know what they did to him."

"I can't stay here on my own. I'll go mad."

I push the memory of my father's voice away and focus on Travis. "What 'they' did to him? 'They' don't exist."

"I'm sorry. I haven't predicted that response. I'm going to continue with the message."

"No," I say, and Travis pauses. I can't take this in. All these years I've been convinced my mother is simply blinded by love. And now a mere acquaintance who has somehow hijacked my chip and is using it to talk to me in secret is telling me that "they" exist? That my father really is the victim my mother has always said he was? That he was telling the truth all those times I sat there in the visiting room, silent, staring, wondering if I would ever have the man back whom I had loved so dearly? "Fuck this. End mersive."

"Anna, there's more I need to tell you. I can help. Principia—"

"No! End mersive. End mersive!"

9

PRESSING THE HEELS of my hands into my temples doesn't really do much to help but I find myself doing it anyway. I stay on the bed until my breathing returns to normal, worrying about what Elvan and Arnolfi will make of that spike in the MyPhys data.

After a couple of minutes, the pseudo-conversation with Travis feels like a dream. The familiar yet slightly inaccurate version of my home, the pure lunacy of its contents. Is what he described even possible? Can you really piggyback mersive recordings with a totally new one? I'm certain there was some kind of prosecution for something along those lines, before I was born. It was such a notorious case it was still referred to when I was growing up. Something about a company hacking the early chips—the ones that were dubbed the Titanic model because they had been famously branded as being impossible to hack—and putting products into people's personally recorded mersives. The scary thing was that no one reported it for days; they simply didn't notice that the products recorded in the background had changed from one brand to another. It was only picked up when someone with atypical neuroanatomy reported seeing designer sunglasses floating in the air in a personal mersive.

Apparently it was almost the death of chip technology. Sales plummeted, anti-chip campaign groups had a field day and then the European gov-corp made a ruling that all citizen-employees of a certain pay grade and above were obligated to have a next-generation chip implanted. One that was really supposed to be hackproof. That was the iteration before my first chip, and as far as I knew, it was impossible to hack. It was all to do with the way the chip used more biosynth tech, tailoring the implant to each individual brain at a level that made it impossible for a one-size-fits-all hack to work. Once one gov-corp took that step, all the others followed. And nobody complained, thanks to a clever program of incentives. For the end consumer, it was all about the ease of monetary transactions, access to the Internet, seamless integration with gaming environments and other entertainment consumption. For the gov-corps, it meant a tighter grip on their citizen-employees, all the data they could wish for and easier tracking of movements across borders. Having to provide alternative means of Internet access and personal identification for those without chips was expensive, after all. And if there's one thing gov-corps are good at, it's minimizing costs.

I know all of this because of late-night conversations at the commune that I used to listen in on from my bedroom. The adults would gather around the hearth, chewing over the life they'd all left behind. None of them trusted chips, even the later, more trustworthy models. They'd all decided to have theirs switched off as a prerequisite for joining the community. Apparently having them physically removed was too expensive, and they might have wanted to go back to civilization one day. It wasn't like the famous Circle cult, which required that all new members be free of any implanted tech.

Travis said—if that was actually real—that the GaborCorp staff who upgraded my chip would be at risk if his message was discovered. His being able to implant that message is more plausible when I consider that my chip was upgraded after I'd signed the contract to come to Mars. Travis knew I was coming and must have put the pressure on them to do as he asked, probably threatening their jobs if they said no. And I'd written him off as some vacuous decoration for Stefan Gabor's arm. There's obviously much more to him than I thought.

When I consider the preparation required to pull it off, I can see so many ways it could have gone wrong. I review the list of available mersives and conclude that the one I just replayed must have been hidden from the menu until today. I suppose he wanted to make sure I'd arrived and settled before giving me the message. What else could have been tampered with? Could he have somehow scrubbed my memory of painting the note about Arnolfi? Surely that isn't possible? He made it sound as though the conversation was all preloaded onto my chip before I left Earth, so I doubt he can alter things now. Unless there's some sort of back door into my chip. I shudder, wishing I could have the damn thing taken out. I never wanted that upgrade in the first place.

I could go back to speak to that copy of him, treat it like the gaming mersive Travis compared it to and try to find every possible response, like repeated play-throughs to experience every possible conversation with favorite characters. I've never been that sort of player. I don't want to talk about Dad. Ever again.

It isn't that I'm scared of what Travis will say about him—nothing could be worse than what actually happened.

It's that I spent years being forced to talk about it with a string of therapists. I didn't even need to—not like Geena or Mum—but I wanted to climb the gov-corp ladder to get to the pay grade that would give me the research opportunities I craved. I needed access to good labs and the only way to get that was to play the game, or "sell out like a total fucking bitch," as Geena put it the last time I saw her. To progress, and to have access to potentially dangerous substances and equipment, I had to jump through all the hoops. Having an official, digitally stamped clean bill of mental health was one of them.

That meant talking about it all. Over and over again. In talking therapy, in a room with an actual human therapist in real time or in virtual therapy, which was basically sets of homework in which my responses were recorded and compared against MyPhys data. I resented every moment I wasted in one of those offices and vowed I'd never put myself through that again. No wonder I bristle every time Arnolfi talks to me. It's not fair to her, but I can't help it.

As much as I hated it, I'm sure some of it was useful. The PTSD symptoms eased. But it rapidly became an exercise in behaving the way a healthy person would be expected to. It was easy enough to work out what that was. Then it was simply a matter of working out how I could portray someone who had been through something awful, learned from it, grown as a person and was moving on. Faking it until it was true, I suppose.

Perhaps it never became true though. Sometimes I have the sense of a place within me in which all of that fear and pain and rage have been locked away. Like a magma chamber so deep underground that the volcano is, for all intents and purposes, dormant. That's what I like to think I am. Safe. Stable.

But I can feel that place within me now. Travis Gabor

thought he could use my father as a way to get me to do his dirty work. Did he think I'd fall down on my knees, weeping with thanks that he was willing to swan in with all of his money and make everything better? The damage is done.

"Because I know what they did to him . . ."

What about what my father did to us? I can't think of him as a man who deserves to be helped. I've taken all this time to put some distance between me and that time, only to have a man I barely know force it front and center again.

If it wasn't morning, I'd drug myself back to sleep again, but soon I have to get on with the day, and then, right on cue, when I close my eyes I see the blood.

It was all over the rug in the living room, spattered up the wall next to it and over his face. I was twelve and I had walked in on my father as he was trying to murder my mother.

She was facedown, horribly still, blood trickling from a wound in the back of her head. He was standing over her, power drill still in his hand, looking for all the world like a villain from some terrible old horror movie. There was blood dripping from the drill bit down onto his hand, the blood the only thing moving in the room aside from his heaving chest.

Geena was following me in, delayed by pulling off her wellies in the porch, and the chittering of her voice brought me back from shock paralysis. I slammed the door behind me, earning a squeal through the wood, and I pressed myself against it. There was no way I would let her see this carnage.

"Everything's all right now," Dad said, setting the drill down next to Mum as if she were a table he'd just finished constructing. "It's all right, poppet. I've got rid of the problem."

I couldn't speak. I couldn't do anything except press myself against that door, partly to keep Geena out, partly to keep as far back from him as I could. She yelled on the other side, thinking I was just winding her up.

"Don't be scared, poppet. I've fixed the problem now and everything is going to get better. I promise."

The way his tone didn't match the horror only made it all more frightening. "Mum," I said in a croaking sob. Once I'd found my voice, my desperate need for her only increased. "Mum! *Mum!*"

"She'll be fine. I just had to get that chip shut down properly. She didn't understand because the voice wasn't broadcasting to her brain. Only mine. Don't look at me like that, poppet. It's Daddy."

Yes, Daddy . . . the man who had hit me so many times and yet never admitted to it, the man who would be smiling one minute, then seething with rage the next. And yet he was acting as if the fact that he was my father was going to make everything better, as if he had no idea that the word "daddy" held no comfort for me now.

He started to come toward me as Geena stopped her pummeling and shouted an ultimatum through the door. "Let me in, Spanner, or I'll tell Mum on you!"

"You stay back!" I said to Dad as I stared at the blood all over his hands. I wanted someone to appear, someone to be the responsible adult and tell me what to do. And then, with a sudden clarity, I remembered a story about a man who had a nail hammered into his brain and still survived. What if Mum was still alive?

I whipped my tablet from my pocket—wishing yet again that I was old enough to have a chip—but then Dad was there right in front of me. He grabbed it, dropped it on the floor and stamped on it.

"How many times have I told you not to use that thing near me? *How many?*"

Up close, I could see how bloodshot his bulging eyes were, how specks of my mother's blood had caught in the whiskers of his beard. My anger at his preventing my call for help gave me the courage to answer back. "But Mum needs help. She's bleeding, Dad."

"I'll patch her up. She'll be fine. I don't want anyone coming to the house. Now, be a good girl and boil the kettle. Mum will want a nice cup of tea in a minute, when she wakes up."

He walked away, heading back toward Mum, and I opened the door, spurred on by the need to get help. I shoved Geena back and slammed it shut behind me as Dad yelled my name.

"I hate you, Spanner!" Geena said. "That wasn't funny!"

"Shut up!" I yelled at her, and with both hands firmly on her shoulders, I propelled her down the hallway as fast as I could. When she started to dig her heels in, I seized her arm and dragged her. For a petite nine-year-old, she was hard to move when she didn't want to cooperate, but I was filled with adrenaline and wasn't going to let her stop me getting help for Mum.

The living room door opened just as I reached the front door. "Anna! Come back here! Where are you going?"

"Daddy, Anna's—" Geena's plea for an intervention died as she took in the blood. All the resistance left her and I finally made it outside as the sound of the drill started again.

I screamed for help until one of our neighbors came running, and then the memory collapses into a blur of distressed faces and medical emergency teams being flown in.

Mum survived because he'd drilled only into the chip, no deeper. It was a long recovery and she could never be chipped again. When I'd thought he'd resumed the drilling to hurt her more, I'd been mistaken. He was drilling out his own chip.

A wave of nausea seizes me as my room spins. I swing my legs out of bed and sit on the edge of it, breathing deeply and slowly, waiting for the flashback to pass. I know it will. It always does. I look at the desk, the door to the bathroom, reminding myself I am no longer there. Then I spread my fingers in front of me, counting each one, wriggling it as I do, calming myself and rooting my thoughts back into my body and the present.

I've tried so hard to be sympathetic. He was ill. He wasn't in his right mind. But I've never been able to shake off the anger. The string of therapists have said that it's fine for me to be angry. That we all process things in our own way. Mum has just as much of a right to never be angry with him, and to forgive him, even though I find it unfathomable. He so easily could have killed her. Neurosurgeons can do amazing things these days, but we lived in such a remote area that it was an hour before she was on the operating table. If it had been just a few centimeters deeper, she would have died.

The only positive about that day was that all of the months of fear and tension were over. He never came home after his treatment. He couldn't terrorize us anymore.

And now I'm crying. Fucking brilliant. A conversation with a man I barely know—that I'm not totally sure happened in my brain—has turned me back into a useless mess. All of the pain caused by my father never totally goes away. It just lies dormant, like those seeds in the desert that can seem dead for decades and then spring to life as soon as they come across moisture. And despite everything he did, I miss him. Not the man with the drill; the man he was before. The thoughtful, gentle soul with an absurdist sense of humor that used to make me weep with laughter yet leave Mum and Geena confused. The man who still saw the world as something to save, rather than something to hate. That's the man I miss.

I've been over this emotional ground so many times I am bored of it. Bored of the guilt. Bored of the bars of this emotional cell. I hate myself when I feel this way, and the only cure right now is to think of something other than my own sorry ass.

Travis springs back to mind. So, he thinks Gabor is shipping things to Mars in secret. Who cares? Stefan Gabor has exclusive rights; he can do what he likes here. We're not bloody children anymore, thinking that Mars could be a place free of the social struggles of Earth. There's no plan for a utopia here, and not just because no one can agree on what that would be. He could be shipping toxic waste here and nobody could do a damn thing about it. No, that's ridiculous. There are so many places on Earth where he could dump it for a fraction of the cost.

If Travis is right, what could he be shipping here? It's not like there's a town to sell contraband to. If he was shipping back more than he was sending, I could understand that, but not the other way around. Unless I haven't been told everything about what Principia is actually for.

There isn't enough room in the base proper to set up anything too complex, but perhaps there's another layer below us that I haven't been told about. Excavating a level down before the base was populated would be simple. Filling it with equipment would be easy if someone on the crew here is in on the secret.

But what would be the point of hiding a lab? Unless everyone here is in on the secret apart from me. Yes, that makes more sense.

There are labs here already, but those are filmed during the show. Maybe the stuff they're really investigating here is so top secret, having a totally separate space is the only way to guarantee that none of it is spotted back on Earth.

It seems far-fetched, and yet once I've had the idea, it's hard to let it go. Is Gabor funding research that is so illegal on Earth he has to do it on Mars? Maybe buying exclusive rights when he isn't even interested in the place is starting to make more sense. It's hard to imagine research that wouldn't be permitted on Earth; there are so few things that the gov-corps rule out categorically these days. If there's profit in it, they'll back it. It could be some aspect of genetic research but I'm not skilled enough in that field to make any educated guesses.

Whatever might be being researched here, the first thing to do is actually find a secret lab. At least I won't have to sneak around looking for hidden doors; a simple ground-penetrating radar will show me any spaces below or around the base if they've been built on the same level. None of this place is visible from above, so that might be the case.

I dress, grab a protein shake from the printer, thankful that everyone meets only for dinner, and head over to the equipment storage room. It doesn't take long to locate the hardware I need and take it back to my room.

When I switch on the ground scanner, there's a ping asking if I want to load the data gathered to Principia in a private or public file. Shit. Of course, anything that comes out of this machine will go through Principia, and that means it could be doctored to hide something before it's shown on my screen. I dismiss the dialog box, waiving the option to save, and kneel down in front of the device. It looks like an old-fashioned upright hoover, the sort my grandparents used to have, and mercifully is a very similar model to ones I've used back home. The panel I'm looking for is easy to locate, set near the top of the device with a screen inside that can be pulled out on an extendable arm. It's a backup feature, built in for situations in the field where uploads to a reliable database might be difficult, and to accommodate operators who are unchipped. I switch it on with a tap and it lights up.

I much prefer to use this sort of interface anyway. There is something so comforting about working with this physical device too. I feel like I am actually doing something proactive, something positive, at last.

It takes seconds to set up the test, but just as I'm about to activate it, there's a knock on my door. "Who is it?"

"Banks."

The scanner is too big to hide in my room so I carry it to the bathroom, prop it up in the shower cubicle and close the door. "Come in."

He's frowning before he even gets into the room.

"I was just getting dressed," I say, thinking he's reading the wrong thing into the delay.

"Then where were you when I called a few minutes ago?"

Surely he would have pinged Principia for my location if he couldn't find me. "Busy," I say. "Did you need something?"

He's looking around the room, at the pictures of Charlie, Mia, Mum. I don't like the slight sneer as he does so. "I need to talk to you about the show."

"I thought the new season wasn't on for another month."

"It's not, but we film as much as we can before it starts, to take the pressure off. That's what those 'Focus On' slots are all about. Surely you realized they weren't filmed live?"

"Oh yeah," I say, not having realized that at all. "I'm a big fan of the show," I add. Before I met him, I would have said I was a fan of his, but where is the charming man I watched on Earth?

There's barely a twitch of an eyebrow. "Gabor is still debating about when we show you working on a painting. He doesn't want that to become stale, but he also wants to drive demand. So before then, we're going to introduce you as a geologist."

"Which I am."

". . . Yeah." He says it like I've claimed I'm the richest woman on Earth. "So I need to talk through some possible scenes with you. Lab work maybe. You went out and got some samples, didn't you?"

"Yes."

"Perhaps you could hold one back for some lab testing."

"What do you mean? They're all for lab testing."

He sighs, as if I'm prolonging a joke that's no longer funny. "All right. And maybe something where you talk through the field equipment. The show runner said something about you being used to being filmed but not talking to a camera."

"I used to film my painting. The shot only showed the canvas and my hand, but I did give a commentary through—"

"So we need to do some camera practice. I take it they didn't cover that in your preflight training?"

I'm still smarting about being talked over. "They didn't." He rolls his eyes and then gives me a look like it's my fault. "There was a lot of other stuff to cover. Like how not to die in space. You know, important stuff."

"Well, you made it here, in all your white-skinned, blue-eyed glory. You'll look great on film, but I'm sure you know that already."

He says it with such a barb in his tone that I feel like I've just told him his mother lied about who his father was. "I can't help what I look like. It's not why I was picked to come here."

"Yes, the *geology*. Obviously. No need to go into that again."

"Were you an arsehole before you came to Mars or has being here so long made you into one?"

I regret it, instantly. I need to work with this man. But that shouldn't have to mean that I just let him treat me this way with no pushback. I decide against an apology. If I just take this crap from him without standing up for myself, he'll treat me worse as time goes on.

He's waiting for me to say sorry though. When I don't, he casts his eyes over the room once more and says, "I need you to come up with five ideas for 'Focus On' slots. I need them by the end of the week. When we have something signed off by the show runner I'll start training you."

He leaves, so icy he's practically chilled the air. I close the door, resisting the urge to slam it dramatically. The thought of working with him is as appealing as dental surgery. Perhaps I'll be able to find out why he hates me from Petranek. It's not a reassuring thought. It feels more like playground tactics. "Why doesn't your best friend like me?" That's worthy of a five-year-old.

When I'm sure he's not going to come back I retrieve the ground scanner from the shower and reactivate it. I have to hold it upright for only another second or so before its own legs extend out from just above the base and stabilize it.

I've chosen weak pulses with a very limited range, mostly to stop Principia from freaking out about anything unusual. The results are displayed instantaneously.

There are no spaces anywhere around the base or below. The structure is exactly as I'd expect it to be from the maps I've learned of the base.

"Well . . . shit," I mutter. I'm disappointed. I guess I'd hoped it would be that straightforward. But if whatever Gabor is shipping here secretly isn't in the base, where the hell could it be?

10

I TAKE THE scanner back to storage, return to my room and flop on the bed. I have no idea what to do next and, frankly, I don't want to get involved. No, that's not it. I don't want to be used. Being the pet artist for one Gabor is enough; I'm not going to be a spy for the other. There's nothing to be done for my father now. It's too late. For all of us.

There is an alternative explanation that is all too plausible: I didn't have that conversation with Travis and I've just scanned the ground beneath this base because of a delusion. But it's just as easy to imagine that Principia—an AI I know has already permitted the deletion of data from base records because of the footprint—is hiding the scanner data from me. JeeMuh, this is the road to madness.

Instead of thinking myself into knots, I check whether all the cam drone footage has been uploaded to the Principia database. Regardless of whether I want to be or not, I am contracted to be Stefan Gabor's pet artist on Mars, so I'd better get to work.

The first step is easy enough: use the data to create a detailed topographical map. It's nothing new, and I could get exactly the same information from extant data. However, using the cam drones means that I can create a fully rendered mersive and step inside it, walk around and look at different viewpoints to find the best vista to paint. I could, if I wanted to, remove rocks and see what it would look like without them, then swing the view around so I can play with perspectives. In short, all of the things I could do on Earth if someone up here sent those drones out for me and then let me download the data. No. I mustn't think that way.

The process is easy enough to start off with a few requests made from my v-keyboard. As Principia crunches the data, I consider the need to find something about this exercise that could only be done on Mars. Short of going out there with an easel and having pictures taken of me while I work, I can't think of anything that could come close to being special here. I don't want to waste canvases by trying to paint while wearing one of the environmental suits though, and even if people saw the pictures, they would assume they'd been faked.

Perhaps I can do the finishing touches outside. I hate the idea of using actual Martian dust in the paintings, but it's stipulated in the contract. I could glue some tiny bits of rock onto the canvas while outside the base to finish off a painting. Maybe I could line the canvas up exactly with the view I've painted and have a couple of cam drones film me taking rock fragments from the exact corresponding locations. That could be cute.

Even with a rudimentary plan, I still feel dissatisfied. There's something distasteful about using the surface of Mars like some sort of crafting table. I want to treat this place with reverence and respect, but perhaps I can't escape the human curse of screwing with every environment we come across. Certainly not with the sort of contract I have signed.

Principia pings me a notification telling me the data is ready for me to explore. I haven't even gotten off my bed, so I'm halfway to being ready to go. In moments I'm standing at the edge of the crater I visited this morning, only this time I'm wearing joggers and a T-shirt.

I stagger a couple of steps back, briefly overwhelmed by the sensation of really standing on the surface of Mars. How backward is the life I lead now, where mersives have more realism, more immediacy, than reality? My cheeks are wet with tears as I take in the beauty of the red dust, the dramatic sweep of the crater bed below me and the volcanoes in the distance. I could get back in the shuttle now and go back to Earth, satisfied that I really have been here.

After a few deep breaths I start to walk around. It's not perfectly rendered like a game would be; the ground feels smooth beneath my feet instead of peppered with sharp stones, but it's good enough for me to use the way I need to. Everything changes to reflect my position, so I take a short stroll, mulling over the possibility of having the crater lip form the bottom portion of the painting. I like to have something highly textured and interesting in the foreground, with elements that give a sense of scale in the rest of the painting.

I spot a cluster of rocks farther round the rim that could be a good detail to have front and center, and I walk clockwise around the crater toward them. Perhaps if I can find the right angle, I could line up one of the distant volcanoes to be a feature in the background. As I walk, I wish that the render included physical sensations. It would be so good to feel the ground crunching beneath my feet and even just a gentle breeze on my face. Because I'm more visually oriented, it isn't enough to break the illusion for me though.

Just as I start really losing myself out here, a dialog box pops up from Principia. "Would you like to explore the data more efficiently?"

My first instinct is to just swipe it away. But the total area that has been reproduced is several square kilometers. Maybe there's a better way to review it than physically walking. "Yes," I type back.

"Hello, Dr. Kubrin."

I yelp and spin around. A man is standing behind me, someone I've never seen before. He is slightly taller than me, his skin is light brown, his hair is black and his eyes are dark brown. "Who the hell are you?"

"I am Mars Principia. You indicated a desire to explore this data more efficiently. The most efficient means of learning an unfamiliar interface is to watch another person."

I've had enough of unexpected visits to my headspace. "You could have warned me you were just going to turn up!"

It has the grace to look confused. "I am sorry. My records indicate that your chip was upgraded before you left Earth. Have you not used an avatar-based interaction with an AI before?"

"No, I have not."

"There is no need to be afraid, Dr. Kubrin. I am here to help."

"Why do you look the way you do?"

"I am presenting as one of my standard avatar models, based on your reactions to other members of the Mars Principia base."

JeeMuh, has it picked an avatar that has similar features to Elvan because I fancy him? How the ever living fuck does it know that?

"Would you like me to change my appearance?"

"It won't make any difference."

"I beg to differ, Dr. Kubrin. Based on your profile, should

I assume the form of a human-size spider, you would experience distress."

"Is that supposed to be funny?"

"No, Dr. Kubrin, I was merely explaining the importance of interacting with an avatar that makes you feel at ease. Is there anything I can do to make you feel more comfortable? I am aware that my speaking to you is a potential breach of your communication preferences. I had hoped that you would find it more palatable in a mersive environment with a human avatar."

It really is like talking to a person, like I am having a conversation with someone outdoors on Mars. I've talked to hyperrealistic people who don't exist dozens of times before, like everyone has, on a gaming server. Not when working with what is effectively a very clever database interface. No, that's unfair, but still, this is an AI deciding what to say to me, actually conversing, without having been scripted by a games company. The AIs I've worked with in the lab are nowhere near as advanced as this.

It's doing my head in. I'm tempted to tell it that the only way to make me feel more comfortable is to bugger off, but I can't deny the fact that this is a much easier way to communicate than using a v-keyboard. No wonder they are being phased out. I had no idea the upgraded chips could provide such a compelling interface with an AI. "It's voice interfaces without any visuals that I don't like. This is . . . okay, actually."

"Why don't you like voice-only comms? I can use this voice instead of the gender-neutral default, should you find it more comforting."

"That's none of your bloody business!"

"I simply wish to isolate the cause of the problem, so that I may attempt to provide a solution. That is one of my primary purposes."

I recall the file I read on Mars Principia during my training. This AI has been here for twenty years longer than any human settlement. It was sent up with the second cargo batch and oversaw the construction of the base and the creation of enough oxygen and fuel to maximize human survival rates long before the first human arrived. It was designed to solve problems, that much is true, but not the sort of problems I have with voice-only interfaces.

"I'd rather not discuss that with you."

"I understand. Would you like me to demonstrate how to interact with this data more efficiently?"

"Yes, please."

The avatar comes over to stand next to me. "Everything you can see has been rendered from the data gathered by the cam drones you released earlier today. All objects within the hi-res range of the cams can be selected for closer examination. For example, that rock over there." He points at one a few meters away. "If you want to look at that rock more closely, focus your retinal cam on the rock and draw a circle around it in the air with your finger. This indicates that you want to inspect that object in more detail." He demonstrates the movement and I copy it with a different rock. The rock seems to fly toward me and then stops just in front of me, floating in the air.

"You can now rotate the object with your hands. As this is visual-only data without full-immersion simulation, you will not receive sensory feedback. If there is a detail you wish to enlarge, simply tap and pinch outward, as with a standard Web interface. When the enlargement reaches the pixilation point, you will be notified that any further magnification may not be accurate. As the cameras record with a resolution of five hundred megapixels, you can examine small details in the landscape as well as rocks. When you have finished examining an object, simply swipe it away."

"Okay, that seems straightforward. What about changing my viewpoint?"

"If you wish to move a short distance to a place which is in clear sight, simply point to the location from which you wish to view the rendered data and say, 'Move me there.' You can move to a location out of sight by calling up the topographical map—I have placed the icon in your visual field—and then pointing to the location you wish to 'travel' to and saying, 'Move me there.' Would you like to try it now?"

"I'll do it once you've gone."

"I am available to assist you for as long as you are reviewing the data, Dr. Kubrin. I have more than enough processing capacity to run this avatar and carry out my other duties simultaneously. I am happy to stay."

"Happy? You don't feel anything though, do you?"

"It is a figure of speech, designed to facilitate natural conversation and thereby aid communication. I do not feel emotion; it is true. However, I can simulate it if you would prefer me to appear to be more emotional."

"No, thanks."

"Are there any other ways I can help?"

"I'll ask if something confuses me, thanks."

"Is there any way I can improve our interface outside of this mersive, Dr. Kubrin? It is far more efficient for us to communicate verbally than via dialog boxes and typed responses."

Folding my arms, I frown at him. "Is improving efficiency one of your primary purposes too?"

"Yes. Increased efficiency equates to increased profitability. Perhaps we could develop a tailored solution? One in which my initial contact with you is via a ping or dialog box, and then should further communication be required, it could be carried out verbally."

"No," I say. Then: "I'll think about it. I'd like you to go now. I need to concentrate and I prefer to be alone."

Why am I justifying myself to an AI? The avatar gives what I would describe as a polite smile, turns and walks away. He fades until he finally disappears, like he's walking into mist. I feel my shoulders drop an inch with relief.

The lesson proves to be very useful and soon I am zipping about the landscape. Changing viewpoint location feels a lot like flying but without the wind in my face, as once I've selected a new point the landscape effectively moves beneath me at great speed. I laugh, filled with an inkling of being godlike, before I stop messing about and get back to some proper work.

I soon lose myself in the examination of different possible backgrounds to a crater-lip foreground. Of course, I could paint whatever I like, but it feels important to make it accurate. Probably some sort of justification for coming all the way here, or at least an attempt to approach that. I like the idea of the art being like a viewing portal to a very specific place on Mars. Perhaps it's more a personal desire to feel I've achieved something on a technical level.

I find the perfect spot, with an interesting cluster of rocks on the crater rim, as I'd originally hoped for, with the largest volcano in the region, Elysium Mons, in the background. It's so far away that the cams have only picked up on the suggestion of its dramatic slopes, but it fits with what my eye expects to see.

Wanting to be certain, I draw a frame in the air with my fingers around the ideal image and take a shot of it for later reference. I also mark my location on the map. It's only when I look at the little blue dot and its location, on a topographic map, that I realize this cluster of rocks is not where I thought it was. Having seen this very cluster not far from my original start point, I'm thrown by the fact that this location is more than ninety degrees farther round the crater than I thought.

Examining the cluster of rocks, I wonder whether I've

simply muddled myself with zipping around all over the place and am actually in the original starting point at the edge of the crater where I first saw them, and not standing where I think I am. Or perhaps I've remembered them incorrectly and the cluster of rocks is merely similar, not identical. I go back to my starting location—one that I am certain of—and find the rock cluster I saw before Principia came to help. It looks exactly the same. Two large boulders leaning against each other, a third resting on top of the one on the right, reminding me of those left behind by Ice Age glacial flows on Earth. All three have the most beautiful shades of red and fascinating contours and seem unique.

I call up the shot I took farther round the crater and display it like a floating poster so I can compare the two. They are identical. How can there be two identical, unusual clusters of rocks next to the same crater in different locations?

All of a sudden, that sense of really walking around Mars disappears. It feels like I'm in some cheap mersive, like the ones I played when I was at an entry-level pay grade, in which chunks of landscape are repeated instead of rendered on the fly to save costs. How much of this is just bullshit hacked together to make it seem real?

But this isn't a gaming server. This is a render on a multi-purpose server, built from data I've just collected. Perhaps this is a glitch. Even as I think that, I don't believe it. Principia is regularly serviced and upgraded and this is the sort of task that a computer well below its capabilities could handle.

"Principia? Could you help me with something, please?"

"How may I help, Dr. Kubrin?"

He's appeared behind me again. I wonder if it's something to do with not wanting to just pop into existence within my sight. Maybe the original programmer wanted to make it as realistic as possible. I turn to face the avatar, disturbed by how I do find him attractive, and the reason why.

"Could you show me which cam drone recorded the data for each area, please?"

"I can." He waves his arm and a larger version of the topographical map appears between us, like a war map in some historical mersive. Suspended above it are little static models of each cam drone, and in a pale green color, transparent cones depicting the range of their cams shine down onto the map. They overlap, as expected, and all appear to have been functional. I look at the areas where the identical rocks are located and they seem to be covered by two different cam drones.

"Can you check for errors in the rendering, please?"

"There are no errors."

I frown at him and he looks back with a patient expression. *It*. It looks back at me. Either it doesn't know or it is deliberately hiding something from me. JeeMuh, Travis's message has gotten to me.

"Is it possible to review data just from one cam at a time?"

"It is. However, the rendering will be impoverished and less immersive, as portions of the skyline would be missing. Would you like to manipulate the data differently? My understanding was that you desired a fully accurate representation of the area mapped."

"I did."

"Has this not met your expectations?"

I push down the instinctive need to placate its hurt feelings. It doesn't have any; it's just a question, without the loading that it would normally have if spoken by a person. I want to ask it why there are two copies of that rock formation, but fearing that it has deliberately tampered with the data to hide something from me, I keep quiet. "It's not that. I'm just looking into different ways to play with the data, that's all. It's . . . an art thing."

"If you wish to view this data again, simply request 'cam

drone map.' To view the data per cam, simply tap the relevant cam in this representation. Can I help you with anything else, Dr. Kubrin?"

"Would I be able to render more than one cam drone's data individually? Like . . . separating them out? I'm thinking about doing something like a triptych and that might be useful."

If it has worked out that I'm lying, Principia gives no indication. "Yes. Simply tap more than one cam drone in the representation and ask for a separated render."

"That's great. Thanks. You can go now." I feel like I'm ordering a servant about and it makes me uncomfortable. Principia nods and walks away, fading out as he—it!—did before. I would really like to ask that coder what they were aiming for there.

I look at the cam drones, the little cones of coverage shining down from each one, and tap four, including the two that I think are copies, and say, "Separated render, please."

The landscape around me vanishes and I regret not taking a picture of the replicated rocks. Then the landscape appears around me again, but there are clearly visible edges, like I'm standing inside an old-fashioned projection. Using the map, I work out which area matches each cam drone's coverage and walk between them, resisting the temptation to simply "fly" from one to the other. It rapidly becomes clear that the render has used the data from one of the cams twice. Looking at the areas of overlap, I work out which one is false. It's cleverly done, with the overlaps merged beautifully in the full render. But the little details, the ones that could be overlooked so easily, reveal the duplication.

If I'd been playing a game, I'd understand the replication as a cost-cutting measure, but the only explanation here is that Principia is trying to hide something by replacing the real data from that area with the data from another, causing the duplication of details that might easily have been missed by someone paying less attention.

Thinking it is trying to hide something related to the footprint—which has been missed by the drones thanks to its being obscured between two rocks—I look up the missing area's location on the map. It's the other side of the crater though, and I discard my theory that Principia is trying to cover up other footprints.

It said there were no errors. If Travis hadn't left me that message, I would be on my way to the crew now, asking them to look into a potential problem with the AI. Now I don't trust any of them. Shit. I need to physically go out there and see what Principia is trying to hide.

11

BACK IN THE undersuit onesie, I'm just about to leave when I realize I haven't sent that message to Mia. I edit out the mistakes, and once it's ready, I start recording a message for Charlie to go with it.

"Hi. I've recorded a story for Mia. It's not very good, but I thought she might like it at bedtime. Does she have any favorite stories at the moment? If you send one to me, I could maybe read it out to her or something.

"I went outside today for the first time. It was . . ." I stop, catching the lie before I speak it. I was about to claim it was magical, that it gave me the moment I'd been waiting for. I try to recapture that sense of newness that I felt briefly while in the rover, but it's marred by everything that's happened since. I don't want to lie to Charlie, not about this anyway, but I can't tell him about Travis.

Principia already knows about the footprint though. And Charlie is a GaborCorp employee and he signed an NDA about all of our communications before I left. The lawyer who'd enjoyed the taste of the sauce suggested it as a way to keep things simple. Everyone knows that comms are routinely monitored for any breaches of corporate policy, but when it comes to Mars, there are so many topics that could be sensitive, I was worried I wouldn't be able to say anything about my time here. "It's a fairly standard contract, and you both being at the same pay grade helps," he'd said. "Once you've both signed this, you'll be able to talk about anything that hasn't been explicitly labeled as 'need to know.' It might help."

"It was weird," I say, resuming the message. "It felt like I was in a mersive for most of it; then we went to a part I was less familiar with and we found a footprint there. Not aliens, before you ask, but someone from the base. It's just that we were told that no one has been that way before. I don't know. It makes me feel uneasy. I'm not sure that everyone here is being totally open about what they do here. Normally it wouldn't matter, but living here is all about trust. It's a closed environment and if anyone messes up, we could all be screwed, you know?"

I sigh, wondering if I should just delete it all. But it's actually helping. I want to know what he thinks of it all too. And maybe there's a bit of me that wants this on record.

"I can't help but think I didn't need to come here. Things just . . . don't feel right. It's not that I feel unsafe . . . It's like, I don't know, a creepy feeling. And it doesn't help that Mum wants me to send a message to Dad and now I feel like an arsehole because I don't want to send one. What do you think? Am I being unreasonable? Oh, I'm moaning too much. I'm sorry; I think I must just be tired. A bit stressed. I'm fine, really. I hope everything is okay at home. Say hi to your mum for me. And message me back when you can, okay? Bye."

I should tell him I love him. I send it before I give in to the temptation to delete it. I'm not telling him anything dangerous and I want to know what he thinks about the footprint. Am I overreacting? Is Petranek right and there's some harmless reason behind it? Someone taking a stroll and wanting to keep it private? I shake my head. Why? It must have something to do with what Travis wants me to find. Damn it! My curiosity is going to be the end of me.

As I dither about whether to go back to the footprint or to the rocky area that wasn't included in the render, I find myself worrying about Mum. Why does she want me to send a message to Dad? Has Travis done something already? No matter how hard I try, I can't stop worrying about it. No doubt she'll be waiting for a message. I can't stand the thought of her at home, talking to the cats, wondering why she has such difficult daughters. I want to shake her and say, "Because of Dad! That's why!" but she wouldn't listen anyway. She'd just blame me for being judgmental and Geena for being a coward.

I sit back down on the bed and start recording a new message. "Hi, Mum. I haven't recorded a message for Dad. I don't understand why you want me to, to be honest. Has something happened? I've been thinking about this and I need you to tell me why you believed him and not the diagnosis. I don't think I can say anything to him until I know. I hope you are okay with me asking this. I should have asked you in person, bloody years ago. I love you. And I miss you. And I just want to understand, okay? Bye."

I send it, feeling better. I can't just crank open that box I've nailed shut without knowing more. I can't talk to him without understanding why she forgave him. Now the message is sent, I can focus better on the trip outside.

Seeing as Principia has already approved the route to the footprint once before, it makes sense to set out in that direction. I head to the dust lock and hear its door close before I round the last corner. I stop. Someone else is going outside. I don't want to have to explain what I'm up to, so I wait.

Then I call up a dialog box and ask Principia to show me where everyone is in the base. The transparent map floats over my vision, revealing Elvan in the medical bay, Arnolfi in her office and Petranek in the labs. It's Banks who is going outside.

I hurry back to my room. What if he's seen the route that Petranek and I took and is going back to cover something else up? I can't risk going out there at the same time and looking at the very thing he probably wants to hide. He mustn't know I'm onto him.

The conversation we had earlier about the show comes back to me and I can't help but think of the way he sneered at my room and how he talked over me. The comment he made about the way I look. Even if I hadn't been a fan of his, it still would have hurt.

Given his animosity, he would have been an obvious suspect for tampering with my stuff and leaving that note, but it isn't possible. Then it hits me. I've been assuming all along that Banks couldn't have tampered with my belongings because he and Petranek were outside when I disembarked. Somehow I had assumed that they had just gotten back when Arnolfi called me after Elvan had finished his tests, inviting me to meet Petranek and Banks for the first time.

With a few taps in my visual field I find a record of who has left the base and when since my arrival. I don't trust it with regard to the footprint, but I have no reason to believe that everything here has been falsified. I match up the times and realize Banks and Petranek actually got back to the base while I was still with Elvan. It was only when they went into the communal area that Arnolfi invited me.

Banks would have had more than half an hour to come into my room, go through my stuff, plant the note and then leave again. It's obvious he doesn't like me being here and even though he's tried to hide it, the hostility he bears toward me is undeniable.

Shaking, I sit on the bed, trying to recast my favorite media star as the sort of person who would try to drive a newly arrived colleague mad. I simply can't understand why he hates me so much. Not even Petranek could understand it, and ze said he'd been acting strangely when we discovered the footprint.

Why is he leaving the base now? To set a trap? To plant something else that isn't supposed to be there so I start sounding like a lunatic if I tell anyone else?

I call up my v-keyboard and ask Principia if anyone else is scheduled to go outside today.

It replies with "Dr. Banks is scheduled to leave the base in twenty minutes. Would you like to continue this conversation via voice interface?"

I stare at the "yes/no" options floating in front of me. "Yes," I say.

"Thank you, Dr. Kubrin. Would you like me to adjust your communication preferences?"

"As long as you ping me with text first . . . all right. Yes."

"Thank you. I have updated your preferences. Would you like to accompany Dr. Banks on his expedition?"

Even if I didn't suspect he is the one trying to screw me up, I'm the last person on Mars whom Banks would want as company. "Where is he going?"

"Dr. Banks is checking on a sensor bank and then the comms array."

"Can you show me those locations on a map, please?"

Neither of those are close to the footprint. I could wait a little longer and then head out once he's clear of the base. But there's something going on with Banks and I don't want to miss whatever he is planning to do out there. I can't follow him physically—it's not like there are many places for me to hide—but I can still spy on him.

"No, he's not heading in the direction I'm interested in.

Thinking about it, I could just use a cam drone. Would I be able to control it remotely, like on Earth?"

"Yes, after I give you a brief training session."

Soon Principia and I are together again in a mersive back on the surface of Mars. The drones are easy to control and it's just a matter of adapting to the different propulsion, gravity and atmosphere. Satisfied that I've got the hang of it, Principia gives me a nod and says, "Would you like me to prepare a cam drone to leave the base now?"

"Yes, please. And I'd like a live feed from its primary camera sent to the wall in my room."

Before long I'm back in my room and there's a shot of the slope outside the base with fresh rover tracks in it filling the wall. An area map in the top right-hand corner marks where the cam drone is and where Banks is too. His rover is heading pretty much in the opposite direction from the footprint, which disappoints me. I'm still curious though, so I send the drone up high, where he'll be less likely to spot it from his rover, and go on the hunt.

A shaded circle appears on the map, showing where the main image is being taken from. I can move the cam with my hands, just like in most gaming mersives, so I can keep my eye on the screen. Banks hasn't gone far and the drone can move faster than the rover is currently. I'll catch him up easily.

It rapidly becomes clear that there are no tire tracks going in his direction. I speed the cam drone up until the coverage circle on the map overlaps the supposed location of the rover. There is nothing but rocks and dust. No sign of Banks.

"What the fuck?" I mutter beneath my breath.

Principia pings a text question to me. "Do you require assistance?"

I tap "no" and swing the cam drone around to head back to the base in the hope of picking up Banks's tracks and finding his real location. Why is Principia showing the wrong location for him? Is it being tricked by Banks, or does it know where he really is and is trying to trick me into thinking he is somewhere else?

I don't see Banks's tracks until I am right by the exit ramp and they are going in the opposite direction from the dot on the map that is supposed to mark his location. "You dodgy bastard," I whisper, and follow the fresh tracks to his true location, staying high and zoomed in until I spot the rover. It's parked by the edge of the Wafra crater, several kilometers away from where Principia is telling me he is, and Banks is climbing out of it.

Did Banks trick Principia into thinking he was elsewhere, or is Principia trying to mislead me? If it's behaving like the AIs I've worked with, it won't be drawing the connections between Banks's fake dot and what I'm doing. If Principia had human cunning, it would know that the ruse has failed.

Raising the drone a little bit more, just to keep it out of the usual vertical range where people look, I zoom in on Banks. The helmet that makes it less likely he'll see the cam drone is also making it harder for me to see his face, but if I lower the drone, he might spot it. I could move it a long way away from him—the zoom is so good on this cam that the curvature of the planet would be a problem before blurring would be—but he'd still be able to see it. And if he sees a moving speck on the horizon, all he has to do is zoom in with his retinal lens and he'll see that someone is spying on him.

Is it worth the risk? I don't have the skills to hack Principia, or Banks's chip. I do, however, have a good excuse for nosing about the planet with a cam drone. Sod it. I'll keep it a long way back and just move it slowly across the horizon. If he asks, I can pretend that I was focused on the data from the cam directly beneath the drone, not the ones on the side of it. I'm not sure how plausible it would be to claim not to have seen him, but I'd rather risk his thinking I'm onto him than never know what the hell he is doing out there.

I reposition the drone, switch the view to look out of one of the side cams and find Banks. He's now sitting on one of the huge boulders thrown up by the original impact, looking like he's just enjoying the view. I zoom in, adjust for glare from the plasglass of his helmet and get a closer look at his face, expecting him to be talking to someone or at least interacting with Principia in some way. But no, he's not speaking or moving his hands at all. He is crying.

It's not gentle weeping either. His eyes are scrunched tight, tears are rolling down his face and his whole body is shaking with each sob. I feel suddenly guilty and the sordid sense of voyeurism is distinctly unpalatable. He doesn't look like a man about to do anything dodgy. He looks like a man having a nervous breakdown.

"Shit," I whisper. The certainty that Banks is responsible for the note and the footprint, part of some elaborate conspiracy to drive me crazy, collapses. All of the reasons it didn't make sense before still stand. Besides, half an hour isn't nearly enough time to go through my stuff, hack my private space, find an example of my art style, perfectly reproduce it and then hide it.

Watching him sob transmutes my suspicion into pity. He hasn't exactly made me warm to him, but I can't stand the sight of anyone suffering, even a belligerent arsehole like him. It doesn't feel right to watch, but it also feels wrong to ignore it. Should I head out there in the other rover and "stumble across him" so I can offer comfort? No, I'm not the ideal choice there.

Perhaps I should tell Petranek. I wince at the thought of the conversation opener. "So . . . I was just spying on your friend because I think he's dodgy, and he's sobbing out on the edge of a crater, so maybe he needs a hug or something?"

I should tell Arnolfi at least. Banks might already be at risk of some sort of breakdown for all I know. And making sure he is okay is more important than any embarrassment I might feel.

Leaving the cam drone to hover where it is, I check to see if Arnolfi is still in her office. A movement on the wall draws me back and I see Banks standing up and then going back to his rover. Relieved, I watch him start it up and turn around, hopefully to return to base. I check that he's heading in the right direction, and when I'm sure he's coming back, I change out of the onesie and back into the T-shirt and joggers, then send the cam drone toward the location of the footprint. I can use that as my reference point, to be certain that I'll be sending it to the area that Principia is hiding with the replicated cam data, so I can see what the missing cam data should have shown me.

At the back of my mind, I fear that as soon as Principia works out where the drone is heading, it'll sabotage the expedition somehow. If it wasn't a glitch, and that area is being hidden deliberately, surely any cam being sent there will be redirected or have its data doctored? Just as I'm about to abort and call it back to base, I decide to press on. If something happens to the cam drone, it's one more tick in the Principia-is-deliberately-hiding-something box.

If Principia is doctoring the data to hide something, somebody must have told it to do so. Its artificial intelligence doesn't include the spontaneously generated desire to hide information from people; there has to be a reason why. This base is owned by GaborCorp, so the natural conclusion I can draw is that someone in that organization—possibly Gabor himself if Travis is to be believed—is telling Principia to cover something up. Again, I'm reminded of the risk; I'm sure that when someone as powerful as Stefan Gabor wants to hide something, it stays hidden, by whatever means necessary.

On the aerial map, Banks's fake dot is also heading back to base, almost like a mirror image of his current movements. Could he have set that up?

The cam drone is approaching the edge of the Cerberus Palus crater now and I redirect my attention to finding the footprint. It's exactly where I expect it to be and a close examination of the immediate area confirms my suspicion that any other footprints have been erased by weather conditions or by an ineffectual cover-up.

The area that was not included in my earlier mersive rendering is on the other side of the crater, two kilometers away. I direct the cam drone to cross the crater and head straight for it. Halfway across, I get a ping from Principia.

"Yes?"

"I have detected a dust storm rising in the north. Apologies, Dr. Kubrin, but I must recall the cam drone to base to prevent damage."

Bingo.

"Oh, okay, fair enough. Can I pick up where I left off tomorrow?"

"I have noted your desire to and I will keep you informed of environmental conditions. It may be two to three days."

"Understood." I let Principia take the controls and I watch the view swing round before the feed is shut down. Oh, I understand all right. Fine. I know where to look now. I just don't know how to do that. Maybe I need to go back to that mersive and discuss it with Travis. He did say there was more that he needed to tell me.

Before that though, I need to tell Arnolfi what I saw. If Banks does something that endangers himself or anyone else, I would never forgive myself.

I don't see anyone else on the way to her office. The base feels strangely empty when everyone is secreted away in their rooms. With only the environmental support system's background hum, the red concrete corridors feel lonely and slightly spooky.

The door is ajar and I slow down, wondering if she is about to leave. Then I'm creeping up to it on tiptoe, like the spy I don't want to be, to peer through the crack.

Dr. Arnolfi is sitting on the edge of her seat, hunched forward with her head in her hands. Her breath is ragged, like she's either crying or panicking; it's hard to tell which. Either way, she is clearly distressed.

I pull back to rest my back against the wall. Has the same thing upset both of them? Have they had a row? What could have left the composed Arnolfi like this and sent Banks outside to sob alone?

Uncertain of how to handle it, I drift back down the corridor. I don't want to impose myself on her, nor do I want to raise Banks's distress if it is somehow tangled with her own. I'll talk to Elvan instead.

I round the corner and almost collide with Banks. He's still in his onesie, just back from his excursion, his eyes bloodshot. The fabric over his chest is still wet with tears that ran unchecked when he was in the environmental suit.

"Sorry," I say without thinking. "Are you all right?"

"Fine," he says, starting to go past me.

"You look like you've been crying," I say. "Is something wrong? Can I help?"

He rounds on me, his eyes filled with hatred. "I know what you're doing and I'm not falling for it. You are, quite literally, the worst person to speak to right now."

"Why? What have I done?"

"Just . . . fuck off, will you?"

He marches off and I'm left alone in the corridor. I almost go after him, unwilling to be his emotional punching bag, but I know I'll just make things worse. When the desire to stand up for myself evaporates, I'm left feeling shaky and uncertain, then angry at Banks for making me feel this way. Fuck him. I'm glad I didn't go outside to see if he was all right. At least I'm somewhere safe.

Dr. Elvan's medlab is just a little way down the corridor. Even as I start to walk toward it, I know I shouldn't. Then I'm knocking on the door and he opens it.

"Hi, Anna," he says, swiping something out of his virtual vision at the sight of me. "Come in."

I go inside and lean against the bed I lay upon for my first examination. I have an image, sudden and bright, of lying down, pulling him close and kissing him. I do my best to ignore it as he sits down by his desk. "Is something going on between Arnolfi and Banks?"

"What do you mean?"

"Have they had a fight or something? I just went to see her and she seemed upset, and Banks has just got back from outside and he's obviously been crying."

His frown tells me all I need to know. "Not that I know of. Crying? Banks? What did Arnolfi say?"

"I didn't talk to her. When I saw how she looked I didn't want to disturb her. Look, Banks hates me for some reason, so he won't talk to me about it, but I think he needs to talk to someone. Crying while he's outside doesn't seem the safest thing to do, you know? Not that tears and snot are dangerous, but the distress might be." I'm babbling, and even though I know I am and the reason why, I just can't stop myself. "I mean, what if he fell or something? Do you think I should tell Petranek? They seem close. I don't want to seem like I'm interfering though. It's bad enough that I've come to tell you, isn't it?"

He holds up his hands. "I didn't get a chance to answer the first question! Or was that rhetorical?"

Blushing, I admit that I can't even remember what it was and we both laugh. Oh God, it seems far too easy with him.

Did I ever feel this way with Charlie? Surely I must have. Maybe it's still there, millions of miles away, buried under the banality of married life. No, I'm not even fooling myself thinking that it's a relic just waiting to be excavated. It was never there. JeeMuh, how did we end up together?

"Because I'm your doctor and you came to my office?"

I jolt. "What?"

Now his frown is directed at me. "You asked how we ended up together. Are you still experiencing symptoms?"

Is that what Travis was? Some bit of my brain all muddled up? "I don't think so," I say, even though I just manifested one. I shrug. "I'm sorry. Principia has been getting me to do voice interface stuff and . . . I obviously shouldn't do that. It's why I avoid it; otherwise I just end up saying my thoughts out loud at all the wrong times."

He doesn't look convinced. Probably because it's about as convincing as that dust-storm excuse that Principia gave me. "Did Banks give you a hard time again?"

I shrug. "It's nothing. I'm fine, really."

"Let me do a checkup. I was going to call you in for one later anyway."

I sit on the bed and he checks me over as I try not to think about his proximity. This is ridiculous. It's like I'm having my first crush again.

"Well, you're still doing much better than any of my predictions," he says. "I'm going to have to rewrite the parameters if the next crew member turns up in such good shape at the changeover."

"Are you going back to Earth, then?"

He nods. "Yep. My turn to go back."

"Does Banks never want to go back? I mean, he's going to hold that record for a hell of a long time. Is it that important to him?"

"I don't know," Elvan says. "I've advised GaborCorp

that we're in uncharted territory with Banks. I'm all for working out what happens to people who stay on Mars, but I worry that he's taking on a lot more risk than anyone else."

"Could his prolonged stay on Mars make him unstable?" I think back to Arnolfi. What if they'd had a row about his behavior? What if she's trying to warn him and he won't listen?

"I think Arnolfi would be better qualified to make that call than I am. I'll talk to him," Elvan says. "Thanks for telling me. I'm sorry he's being such a . . . an unprofessional."

We share another smile at his last-moment change. "I just wish he'd tell me what I've done."

He reaches up to tuck a tuft of hair behind my ear. "You haven't done anything."

The palm of his hand is warm when I press my cheek into it. Then he's leaning forward and I'm tilting my face up to his and then we're kissing like we've been held apart for days and can finally carry on where we left off. The voice in my head that is squealing about Charlie, about commitment and faithfulness, is shoved away as we wrap our arms around each other, frantically, almost desperately. He smells so good and it just feels impossibly right. Like we should have been doing this all along.

He pulls away and as soon as we break contact the guilt rushes in.

"Shit," I say, sliding off the bed. "I'm going, because if I don't, I'm going to do something stupid."

He just nods and I walk out. Three steps away from the door I get a notification of a message arriving from Charlie. A half chuckle, half cough at the timing of its arrival bursts from me and I scurry back to my room, ashamed of my own weakness. I can't let myself be alone with Elvan again.

I lock the door when I get back to my room, mostly to keep myself in, and play the message on the wall. For the first time since I left Earth, I am so glad we're deprived of real-time conversation.

Charlie looks tired again. He's sitting on the sofa this time, Mia flopped against him fast asleep. It feels like an actual string in my chest is pulled when I see her. Basalt is lying next to them, muzzle on the leg not covered by a child, dozing.

"Hi, Anna," he says quietly and Mia gives a loud sigh, shuffles slightly and is off again. "It's been a long day. Mia just wouldn't settle. She loved your message. Thanks. I'm glad you're settling in. We knew it would be tough, but you know, every day that we get through is just another closer to you coming home, right? Now you've arrived, it feels like I can actually start counting down to when you're back.

"Have you been keeping up with the feeds up there? It's almost capsule-opening time down here. I've had to mute that word; I'm so sick of all the speculation about what will be inside. Obviously, I want to know what the Pathfinder left for us, but the way people are acting, it's like waiting for the Second Coming or something. Or the third, I guess. So many people have said she was the messiah and that Atlas was like the Rapture or something. She took all the best with her, blah blah blah.

"Listen, I've got to go to bed. I'm shattered. I'll message you properly tomorrow, okay? Bye."

I stare at the "end message" notification. That was it? I tell him about the footprint, about things being weird and my mum and . . . and he just ignores it? "Principia, did my last message arrive in full?"

There is a text confirmation that it did. Then Principia says in my head, "The message was delivered in full to Charles Kubrin, opened and viewed at nine thirty-one p.m. GMT."

"The whole message?"

"Yes, Dr. Kubrin. Is there a problem?"

"Show me the message he received."

Principia plays me the whole message I recorded and sent earlier. So he just didn't want to talk about my worries. Anger swiftly burns through my chest and I hate the way it feels, the way it threatens to take me over and make me into the same kind of monster it made my father. In an attempt to suppress it, I tell myself that he was obviously tired, that Mia had been a handful, but still, it's always the same pattern. We have to stop everything and talk through anything he's concerned about, and then when it comes to something I am struggling with, it's glossed over. No wonder I shut down when I couldn't cope. What would have been the point of saying anything? He always had a way to make any concern sound smaller than it was, until I felt smaller than I was. If I persisted, it was because I couldn't let something go due to some fundamental character flaw, rather than the original issue being unresolved. If I wanted to process something by talking it over, I was "obsessive." If he wanted to do the same, it was because he was "analytical." Now he is showing his contempt for my concerns with silence. I shouldn't have stayed with him. I should have left the day I packed my bags. How did I build up that head of steam only to let him win?

I replace the image on the wall with one of the Scottish Highlands. Amazing what clarity a few million miles can give. I don't love my husband and I don't think I ever did.

12

I WAKE THE next morning with a headache, my mind leaping straight back to where it had been the night before. Just because I don't love my husband, it doesn't mean it's okay to sleep with Elvan. The counter to that is less coherent, more a mess of anger and resentment and lust and loneliness. The pure id response of "But I want to! Right now. And he's just down the corridor, and anyway, your husband is a dick."

Trust me to end up rediscovering my libido on Mars. Millions of miles from the one man I'm supposed to shag and a plethora of devices to satisfy me when alone. I don't feel like I can ask Principia whether any porn was uploaded to the Mars mirror of the Internet, let alone download a mersive and have that on my file. Especially when Arnolfi and Banks are probably monitoring my mersive consumption very closely.

I can't understand why Elvan has this effect on me. He must think I'm pathetic: the stereotypical sex-starved wife who blooms at the slightest show of affection. No, I don't think he would see me that way. I think, somehow, he sees more of me than I've even shown him. It's like we've got shortcuts set up between us. No need to go through the awkward flirtation stage and the worrying about whether the feelings are mutual. I just know they are. I know we work together. Just as certainly as I know Charlie and I don't.

It isn't Charlie's fault. None of it is. I'm not the woman he married anymore. No, worse than that: I wasn't her back then either. She was just a construct, a study of someone who could live a corporate life made manifest in the world. All of the clothes I wore were new, chosen to fit with the kind of person I needed to be, not who I actually was. The handmade, natural-fiber clothes, sewn by our neighbor in exchange for pottery made by my mother, looked ridiculous outside of our valley. The scruffy ease of wearing my favorite combo of trousers and long tops was exchanged for the sleek, tidy lines of synthetic materials that felt better against the skin but had no history to them. I discovered a new awareness of my waist, bust and hips, and that clothes for women were all about accentuating them instead of being practical.

With the new clothes came a new lifestyle with new hobbies taken up to look good at assessments and to fill in gaps left by my bohemian childhood. What use would being able to light a fire in a wood be? Far better that I play the latest mersives and learn how to respond in virtual spaces instead of just staring and then jolting whenever it was my turn to speak.

The places I went to in the evenings to socialize were never of my choosing; they were the places other entry-level candidates were going and I just tagged along. When Charlie and I met in a bar, I in a dress that sparkled and changed color to match the music (why the hell I thought that was a good idea I will never know), he in a dapper suit, how was he to know I wasn't who I was pretending to be?

The only thing Charlie did was fit into my image of the life I wanted. At the core was the science and getting to work in a decent lab. Everything else was built out from that. What I needed to know, who I needed to be, whom I needed to impress, all were informed by that core goal. I reinvented myself. The entirety of my teens I was doing that; why stop before I had what I wanted?

It started with pretending that I was fine after Dad was sent away. At first it was for Geena's benefit, some misjudged notion on my part that as her elder sister, I had to show her that everything was all right. I didn't notice that all I did was make her think I was cold and uncaring. How could I have? I was working so hard at being strong for her and for Mum as she recovered from the trauma, and besides, I was barely a teenager!

Then, when I knew what I wanted to do with my life, it became painfully clear that growing up in a community like ours was going to work against me. And it wasn't just the skills I needed to acquire and the ones I could forget. It was all about being able to pass myself off as someone who could work in a team. Who could thrive in an environment where it was all about goal setting and project management and allocation of resources. There were mersives that provided scenarios designed to help corporates refine their soft skills. I devoured them, learning the language of the corporate world and working out the kind of person I needed to be to succeed in it: sociable, bright, ambitious and above all else, willing to value the goals of my employer above my own.

Gov-corps say that marital status makes no difference to career progression, but everyone knows that's a lie. Society is far less screwed up about gender than it used to be but still somehow wants to lock us down in stable relationships. It's like some part of Western mentality simply couldn't escape the idea that if two people are married, they are somehow safer. More predictable. And when it comes to balancing the books, they're cheaper. With minimal living-space guarantees shrinking year on year, there is no getting away from the fact that a married couple can now fit into a flat that five years ago was allocated to a single person. They may not be happy crammed into their shoe box, but it's better than living in a singleton cube at the equivalent pay grade.

It's not that I married Charlie so we could get a bigger place. That larger space still has to be shared, after all. For a time I really did believe he was good for me. Stable. Supportive. Driven to climb the corporate ladder just enough to be interesting but not enough to be bullish about it. With my sights fixed on reaching the necessary pay grade, it was easy to overlook the parts that didn't really fit. I just remolded myself to accommodate. He never learned to adapt to me because I never made it necessary.

It started to unravel when Drew hired me. It's like I could plot my happiness with Charlie on a graph; as the satisfaction of getting to where I wanted to increases career happiness, the line showing marital happiness starts to take a nosedive. The pretense of being happy to socialize more in mersives than in the real world—that was the first to fail. I just couldn't live without seeing people in person, so I dialed back on the use of the social games he'd drawn me into and went back to some of the clubs I'd been part of before we married.

We never agreed on whether mersives were the best way to relax. For him, the ideal Sunday afternoon would be a couple of hours meeting up in a puzzle game with a group of friends on a shared server, then going off for a stroll through some exotic location, rendered fully immersively. I never liked those, though of course I never said so in the early days, when I was suppressing my own preferences to be that successful corporate climber. As time went on though, I visited Mum more, desperate for long walks around the loch and real fresh air. He couldn't handle the insects. "Why do you want to go somewhere with thousands of little flying bastards everywhere who just want to eat you?" he'd moan every time I packed to go. I could never find the words to express why mersives were never quite good enough for me.

We were so poorly matched, but I didn't see it at the time. I suppose I didn't want to admit to myself how fake I had become and how false our relationship was. How I had used him.

But it wasn't like there was nothing in it for him. JeeMuh, am I really this awful? Can't I let him just be a nice guy who fell in love with who I was pretending to be?

I can, right up until he started getting moody, started asking why I was at the lab all the time, why I couldn't change my schedule to fit better with his. I can think kindly of him right up until I remember the way he started to act whenever friends came to visit, or when we went out. As the lab took more of me, he seemed to resent anyone else having even a moment of my attention. It got to the point where I started canceling social plans because I simply couldn't face going through the tedious bullshit of explaining who would be there and what we'd be doing. Taking him with me no longer worked; he'd drink too much and insult my friends.

That should have been enough of a warning. I should have left him then. But I didn't really care about dropping ties with the people I'd simply tagged along with to look like I had a life. All carefully chosen so that when GaborCorp reviewed my social activity I looked normal. None of them really knew me. None of them missed me either.

I didn't notice my world shrinking because I had my work and that was all I cared about. I filled the gaps left by my abandoned social life with painting. Charlie loved that: something I could do at home, that he could talk to his colleagues about. I know he showed them my videos. "Look at how talented my wife is" was one of his favorite things to boast. Then it started to feel like there was a subtext. "Look at what I caught. Surely I'm a better man for being able to find someone like her."

But the more I painted, the more I remembered who I really was. It started to be as much about having something I could focus on that wasn't Charlie, something that was indisputably mine. I could forget he was in the flat when I was painting Mars, shutting everything else out as I talked through the process. It got to the point where the only thing I looked forward to when I was heading home from the lab was getting the canvas out again. When we made love, I was thinking about what to paint next. Just going through the motions, detached from my body, doing enough to make him think I was still present. It was no way to live. So I decided to leave.

I packed my bags when he had a rare site visit and would have been gone by the time he got back if the taxi hadn't been late. When he came home to find me in the living room, shouting at a virtual booking AI, surrounded by my art supplies bagged up and resting against one tiny suitcase, he lost it. He wasn't angry, as I'd feared he'd be. He was devastated.

He cried; then I cried; then somehow he persuaded me to stay. I don't even remember what he said. I wonder if it was as much a desire to just end the emotional barrage from him. I knew that if I left, he wouldn't let me go. "Just give me two more months," he said, weeping. "I'll do whatever it takes to make you happy. Just two months, and then if you want to go, go."

It seemed so reasonable at the time. And yet now, lying in bed on another planet, I feel such anger at myself for being so weak. I should have just walked out. I should have grown a fucking backbone and said, "Actually, Charlie, I have all the data I need about our relationship and another two months is not going to change the conclusion." But seeing him cry, watching him fall apart and having the chance to end that distress . . . That was too powerful to resist.

So I stayed. And I did try. We talked, I tried to explain how I felt, he pretended to understand and then we spent three hours discussing his needs and feelings. He did make an effort, but the tragedy of it all was that it didn't matter what he did. A better version of himself was never going to be enough because I just wanted to be alone and have some space to breathe. A singleton cube would be like a palace because I would be able to fill every square centimeter of it, instead of shrinking myself down to accommodate him.

Looking back at his charm offensive, at those six weeks of the Very Best of Charlie, I'm even more convinced that he knew what he was doing all along. As soon as I decided to leave I should have made different contraceptive arrangements. I should have been more careful. But it was always something he took care of, like making sure we always had spare canisters for the food printer and sorting the recycling.

He said it was an accident. That he'd been so upset by the crisis and so focused on making it better that he'd forgotten to get his treatment topped up. With so many MyPhys notifications about stress levels, he'd just muted it and forgotten to review the messages waiting for him. All of that considerate, loving, making-so-much-effort-to-please-me sex had resulted in a pregnancy I never wanted.

I didn't even think it was possible to have an unplanned pregnancy anymore. I'd seen stories on news feeds about it but never really believed that someone could be so careless or ignorant. Nevertheless, there I was, pregnant and in shock. For days I kept it secret, telling myself it was just a bunch of cells, that I should get rid of it and not even think about it.

But it would be impossible to arrange without his knowledge. While he couldn't stop me from having an abortion, I couldn't keep it a secret from him. It was one of the many compromises that hung over from the last days of democracy, in which the Far Right practically removed a woman's control over her own body. The gov-corps that emerged from that time dialed a lot of it back, but not all of it. Charlie had a legal right to know about any termination. It was stipulated in the marriage contract that I had skimmed over, thinking that since we'd agreed not to have children, it wouldn't be relevant.

Back then, I thought there were only two routes ahead of me. One was to leave, notify him of my intent to terminate and fight it out in court if he objected to my decision. With so much of the legal process run by AIs, it would have taken only a week, long enough for a human judge to review the case once all the information was in place. I would have a strong position; he had always ensured his contraception was up to date until I had almost left him and I was unaware of his failure to have the hormonal treatment updated.

The other route was to stay and make the best of it. I could have left and had the child, of course, but I simply couldn't face it. Just as I simply couldn't face the prospect of telling him I wanted a termination. The week before I told him, I agonized over it. Did I really want to abort? Did I really want to go through with it? The truth was, I couldn't bear the thought of any of those options. When I imagined what it would be like to have won the right to abort if he stood against it, really thought about what it would be like to go into the clinic and have the cells removed . . . I felt awful. Even though I knew that was exactly what it was: a bunch of cells. But equally, when I imagined the pregnancy, my body no longer being my own, I was filled with the purest dread. I was simply incapable of imagining myself with a baby. It was never something I ever saw in my future.

I took to crying as soon as I left the house for work. I'd give myself the walk from the apartment block to the tram just to feel sorry for my stupid self, and then once I was on the tram, I'd scour the Web for images of babies in the vain hope that something would light up some circuit in my brain that could make the thought of motherhood palatable. But there was nothing. It was already missing. I ended up drifting to the rare communities with public settings that let people view without declaring their presence, reading countless entries written by women talking about why they'd decided not to have children. Talking about the last corners of society in which the idea that women were only for bearing children still existed and how they had left them.

Then I would cry the rest of the way to the lab.

Of course, I had to tell Charlie in the end. I think some part of me was hoping that he'd say it was the wrong time, that given the difficulties we were having, perhaps it would be best to abort. But of course he didn't. In Charlie's world, the last seven weeks since I'd almost walked out had been great. We'd "come so far" and he felt really good about all the ways he'd been proving he was a good husband. My hesitant confession that I wasn't sure if it was a good idea, seeing as we never wanted children, was pushed aside. "But that was before we grew together, right?" I felt so sick when he rested his hand over my lower stomach, cooing about the thought of life blossoming within me. I wanted to smash a vase over his head and run out of the apartment and never go back. Find someone at the commune who could put me in touch with people who could hide me. But I didn't. I just smiled. I just smiled and said what he wanted to hear. Because I always fucking do that.

A notification saves me from the bottomless well of self-hatred. It's a message from Mum. Oh good, something else I can flagellate myself with.

"Hello, Sprout!" She's sitting by the fire, Frigg stretched

out on the sofa next to her, Odin sitting on her lap. He's so big, the top of his head is pushing her chin up and the struggle for who gets to decide where Mum's face is allowed to rest is obviously still ongoing. "So it's"—she squints at the clock across the room—"sometime after midnight and the wind is howling away. Can you hear it? This storm is on the way out now but it's been a belter. These two reprobates haven't left the house for days, have you, your majesty?" She looks down at Odin, who rubs his face against her chin and starts purring. "He's all love and cuddles now, but you should have seen him earlier. Grumpy sod. Anyway. I got your message. Thank you, darling. You do look a little bit tired. Are they working you too hard? Is that why you haven't sent a message to your father?"

I sit up. What the hell? I told her why!

"I know it must be hard. I may not be an expert on these things—you know I was always better at coding software than understanding people—but I do think it's important to make an effort."

Mum never talks about when she was a software engineer. That was her life before the commune. Why talk about it now?

"There was a feature on you on *Norope Tonight*! I thought they would have shown some of your artwork, but they didn't. They didn't even mention the painting part. They just talked about you being a geologist. They talked about the Mars show and that lovely Dr. Banks. Is he just as handsome in person? Are you going to be on that show? They said it's the season break or something but it will start up again soon, after the capsule has been opened. It's all very exciting. Everyone here sends their love and they are so proud of you. Not as proud as me, obviously." She gives one of her wicked grins and Odin meows loudly at her.

"Shush—I wasn't talking to you. I talked to Charlie earlier. I think Mia might be teething. She's so bonny and bright as a bulb. You must be proud of her too. I never thought you'd have children. Funny, isn't it, how things change? And I know you struggled in the early days, Sprout, but you made it through, and imagine how proud she's going to be when she knows her mummy went to Mars!"

I lie down again. Trust Mum to say exactly the wrong thing at the wrong time and be totally oblivious to it. Not that she can see my face right now, in fairness, but she never did pick up on the subtleties of human interaction.

"Right, I should go to bed. Don't look at me like that, Odin. I'm allowed to get up if I want to. You'll soon have most of my bed anyway. Yes, I know, you're beautiful, yes." She kisses him on the top of his head. "Bye, then, Sprout. Oh, and if you could film a message with Dr. Banks in it, that would be lovely. You know, for science." She adds a wink to that wicked grin and the recording ends.

First Charlie, then Mum. Neither of them addressed the things I talked about. Maybe Principia is censoring what I say and hiding it from me. I could understand that about the mention of the footprint—even though that NDA should make that concern invalid—but asking Mum to explain why she believes Dad? Why stop that from getting through? And if I didn't ask for that, the message would have been just a few seconds long, surely? Something isn't adding up.

I know that heading straight into a mersive is not going to look good when my usage is reviewed by Arnolfi and Elvan, but I have to go back to Travis. He might have predicted this and he might have set something up to help me. Maybe that information dead drop he's planned could be used for messages home.

But if I go back to talk to Travis, I have to think about Dad again. What did Travis say? Dad has everything to do with why I'm here? On Mars? It makes no sense.

I wrack my brain trying to remember if there was anything Travis said at the dinner party that could hint at a connection between him and Dad, but there's nothing. I take a mental step back. Everything to do with why I'm here . . . Did Travis know my Dad, years ago? No, Travis would have been a kid when Dad was locked up. How could they know each other?

But Dad might have corresponded with him. He is allowed to send messages to people. Over the past ten years he's sent dozens to me that I've deleted as soon as they've arrived. It was just too painful to watch them, to be taken back to that room, listening to him ranting. Why invite that into my own living room, or worse, just the confines of my head? But why would there even be a correspondence between the two of them? No, I simply can't imagine it.

I clench my teeth and groan. I need to stop being such a coward and face this. I know where this hesitation comes from: it's the fear that I'll go and play back that same mersive and it will just end as normal, Travis a figment of either my imagination or a deepening psychosis. Both seem far more probable than his explanation. Preloading my chip? How could he have arranged that so quickly? It was upgraded only a week after I signed the contract to come to Mars. There's no way he could have gotten everything recorded, set up and found a dodgy technician in time. Unless . . .

Oh shit. Forgetting my fears, I open the menu, select the relevant mersive and go back, barely paying attention to Mia and Charlie as I wrestle with my suspicion. Then everything freezes and Mia disappears, along with the sofa and the dog, and in moments the table appears again.

"Hello, Dr. Kubrin. You came back. I'm glad; we have more to discuss."

"You're damn right we do," I say, sitting in the same chair as before so I line up with where he's looking. "Did you set all of this up, right from the start?"

He nods. "GaborCorp employs hundreds of thousands of people. Do you really think that my husband often goes to dinner parties to listen to midlevel managers beg for funding? If he did that, he wouldn't have time to do all the other shitty things he does."

I think back to that night, how enthused Travis was about my artwork. "You weren't really a fan of my art channel at all, were you? You were laying it on a bit thick."

"I like your art, very much," he says. "But I confess that I only became a fan after I realized how useful you could be. My husband isn't imaginative enough to come up with the idea of sending an artist to Mars. He's one of those people who only says they like a painting after they've heard how much was paid for it. I bet he made you think it was all his idea to send you there."

"Yes, he did."

Travis nods. "Well, it was mine. As I said before, it gives you a reason to go and explore."

"So where does my dad come into this?"

"I know someone who was an old friend of his, someone who secretly supported the commune. Did you ever find out what that was really about?"

"What? It was just a bunch of hippies who got tired of the corporate machine, wasn't it?"

"I'm sorry, that isn't the correct answer," Travis says and I curse the fact we're not actually conversing. "The commune you grew up in was a cover for activists who needed somewhere safe and remote to live. Your mother and your father were at the top of the European gov-corp's most wanted list for about ten years, before our mutual friend got them out of trouble and gave them new identities. They tried to live in plain sight, pretending to be part of the system, but they couldn't hack it, so a bunch of them got together and went to Scotland. Before it all went wrong with your dad, your parents were some of the most exciting political radicals in Norope. Your mum has written books that are now being used as the foundation for the next generation of activists."

"Activists? My mum and dad? Don't be ridiculous. And my mum isn't a writer; she was a software engineer and now she's a potter." He just stares at me. I haven't asked a question. "What kind of activism?"

"They wanted some basic human rights to be included in gov-corp citizen-employee contracts."

"The definition of basic human rights changes with pay grade," I say, unimpressed. "What kind of thing, specifically?"

"Well, your parents believed people had a right to digital privacy."

The idea seems absurd to me, like an old bastion of a bygone age that only the most romantic and naïve would wish to defend. Digital privacy was one of those old-fashioned ideas that died in the '30s along with "true democracy" and online anonymity. Ideas that couldn't fit in the modern world and caused more harm than good—surely my parents knew that! Travis must be mistaken. "Which old friend of my dad's do you know?"

"I'm sorry—I can't tell you that. It would endanger him. All I'm willing to say is that they go back a long way and he tried to protect your father, but his enemies were too good at their job."

"Okay, I'll play along. Let's pretend my dad was always telling the truth. Who put the voice in his head?"

"The European gov-corp. Or rather, unscrupulous people hired through a succession of shell companies and front organizations so the money couldn't be traced. They were trying to destroy the commune. The fact that they didn't is a testament to your father's strength of character."

"Yeah, he just destroyed my family and nearly killed my mother. What a hero."

In the silence that follows, I become aware of such a resistance to the idea that it's my father who is the victim. It feels like being told we actually lived in a palace or that I used to be an opera singer. Ridiculous.

"Wait. If the commune was this big secret thing, then why are you telling me this?"

"I've read your psych profile; I know you would never betray those people. I'm telling you to make you understand that I know far more about your family than you might imagine. That I really do know enough to help him."

"And enough to hurt them too. Are you threatening me?"

"Do I need to?"

"JeeMuh, you actually predicted I would say that. You are one dodgy bastard, Mr. Gabor." Again, I am glad this is not a real conversation.

"I haven't told you how I can help yet. Are you able to be briefed now?"

I can digest all of this later. It's time to get what I need and leave, as quickly as possible. "Yes. Principia is already blocking me from examining a specific area."

He nods. "Yes, narrowing in on a specific area is the first step."

I sigh. The program running his responses has misinterpreted what I said. "How do I stop Principia from interfering when I find the area I want to investigate?"

"Once you have a suspicion that something is being hidden—perhaps Principia is denying access to you or to cam drones—you need to pick a location that's within a couple of kilometers from where you want to go. Make the trip to that location several times and film each trip. Audio and visual only is fine. I need you to build up a good amount of data so it can be used to create fake trips in real time to trick Principia into thinking you're somewhere you're not."

JeeMuh, I had no idea that sort of thing was even possible! He's talking about hijacking the connection between my brain and Principia, sending data that the AI will think is coming from the lenses in my eyes and being processed in my chip! The sort of thing I thought was just stupid spy mersive stuff.

Travis must have thought I'd know this was possible; he's not giving me a chance to process it all before the next instruction. "Once you've done it at least three times, put the files containing those recordings into this folder."

He points at the wall. All of my paintings disappear and the wall is replaced with a gray background with my own chip's file structure displayed. Fuck, it's like he's showing me the inside of my own mind. I watch as he drills down five levels and locates an innocuous folder labeled "Mars textures research" in the area where all of my art mersives are kept.

"Don't put anything else in there; that's really important. Your chip has been loaded with a randomizer, the sort the gaming companies use to generate landscapes that look fresh from limited data. That's the first part. Any questions so far?"

"But gaming companies recorded environmentals for their mersives. Can't we just use that data?"

"I did consider that, but for one thing, I'd have to buy access to them and someone could follow the money. For another, they aren't as accurate as you might think; it was only a couple of kilometers around the base that was recorded, even though the games companies claim they have far more. The areas outside of the zone actually recorded were generated using satellite footage that's decades out of date. Gathering your own data is the simplest way to do this."

He wants to feed the software with realistic data; I can understand that. But I'm not a cam drone, designed to capture environmentals. "What if there are slight variations to my route? I can't guarantee I'll look in exactly the same directions each time. How can I be sure there won't be gaps in the environmental recordings?"

"Slight variations are good; they give the software more varied data to crunch. It's sophisticated enough to handle any small gaps."

"Have you put anything else in this chip?"

He smiles. "Only the software that does the rest of what we need it to do to fool Principia and get the data home."

He looks so pleased with himself I'm almost tempted to end this now and send a message to his husband. But that threat over my family holds me in check. If he does really know people close to them, it would be easy for him to find out everything he'd need to make their lives difficult. Whether it's screwing with their online lives or revealing their activist activities, he has enough money and power to be a real threat. And if he really can help my father, surely that also means he can interfere with the care he's already receiving. Men as handsome as he is shouldn't be allowed to be this clever and unscrupulous. It isn't fair. "What do I do once I've saved the files into that folder?"

He leans forward, and the recording of him gives the distinct impression that he's excited. "The next time you go outside, you tell Principia your route and then one minute into that route, say the words 'Ergo Elephantine Erasmus.' I know it sounds weird; I just really wanted to make sure you don't ever say it by accident. Once you say that phrase, the other bit of software I've popped into your chip will take over the tracker dialog between the geolocator and Principia. It will trick Principia into thinking you are making the same route, and if it or anyone else on the crew chooses to examine your visuals, they'll be shown the route you recorded. You can do this several times; the fake data being played for anyone caring to watch will be different each time."

"But won't I only have the same amount of time as the fake trip?"

"You will be totally safe for that duration, yes. The geolocator will give fake readings until you return to the location where you give the code. Theoretically, the fake footage of your route can be generated indefinitely, but if someone is watching your feed closely, they will notice repetition after a bit of time. Principia knows Mars too well to be fooled by it for very much longer than the footage naturally lasts. Keep it below that length of time and you should be okay."

I shake my head. "There's another problem here. How can I review anything I record when I'm hidden? Principia has already doctored cam footage."

"You do it all inside your head. Record with full immersion and don't let it save automatically. Before you start recording, specify that you want it to be saved to this folder." He navigates to another folder in my brain. "You can immerse in it at any point. Edit and save within this folder. When you have something concrete, keep it saved there but rename it 'ready for home' and it will be sent back to Earth, via Principia, without it knowing."

"How?"

"The same way that all of your messages are sent, just through a back door. It's dark web stuff. You don't need to know how it works—just trust me on that. It'll dump the data in a dead drop location for me to pick up on Earth when I'm safe to do so."

I close my eyes, giving myself a moment to make sure I understand the plan. I gather data to feed to a secret program hidden in my chip so that Travis's tech can trick Principia into thinking I am somewhere else, so I can go to the area it has been hiding from me. It's clear that Travis knew that Principia would be a problem when he planned all this out.

"And say I get what you want. What happens then?"

"Let's take it one step at a time."

I don't like the sound of that. "So I won't be able to just send you this data and then forget about all of this?"

"I wouldn't want to make any promises. But I can assure you that as soon as that data lands in the dead drop, your father will be given all the care he needs."

"Fuck you very much," I say with a tight smile. "End mersive."

13

THERE ARE FAR too many assumptions in Travis's predicted dialog tree for my liking, but I can't deny that he has planned well. While I'm still annoyed that he is using me just as much as his husband is—and for a far riskier task—I do feel a strange relief that he made all this happen. I was never comfortable with the sense that I'd been picked out as a result of pure kismet. It simply didn't fit with my view of the world. I wasn't that lucky—or that unfortunate, depending on my mood at the time. It always felt too unlikely on some level that a multibillionaire would come to dinner, let alone be so impressed by my art that he would want to spend millions to send me here. What else has Travis been doing behind his husband's back? I dread to think.

At least I never have that concern with Charlie. He is as he appears to be, and even though that can sometimes be infuriating in its dullness, it is reassuring too. I'm too hard on him sometimes. It wasn't his fault I pretended. And I can't blame falling pregnant squarely on him either. As much as I want to.

It bothers me that Charlie didn't mention the footprint, or my concerns about the others here. If it had been something I'd mentioned several times, I could let it go. He gets bored of my circular thinking, not understanding that sometimes talking this sort of thing through repeatedly is my way of processing it. I haven't mentioned it before at all though. Principia must be screening the messages. But then I remember the NDA and groan in frustration at the lack of satisfying answers. This is the thing people don't talk about with AIs. They're delighted to have them find music they'd like, or take care of menial admin tasks—like rating every bloody thing under the sun—but they don't worry about coming into conflict with them.

For most people, that wouldn't even be an issue. Unless they have a lot of money, or the sort of role that requires the most advanced chips and close contact with an AI, most people don't even find themselves in this situation. And it's the not knowing that makes it worse; Charlie could just have overlooked it.

I can't take my concerns to anyone else. The specter of my mental health will rear its irritating head again, not to mention the possibility that they could all be in on it.

I have never felt so alone.

When in doubt, gather more data. That's the only thing I can do. I need to determine whether the messages were censored, and even though I can't prove that definitively, I can see whether Charlie and Mum simply forgot what I'd asked them. It's harder in Mum's case; she may be deliberately not addressing the subject. It's not like I've asked her why she took up pottery.

I'm reminded of what Travis said about her writing and about my parents' activism. It still seems silly, but when I really think about it, their attitudes to corporate life and general Noropean society were always counterestablishment. They uprooted us, turned their backs on good careers and went to live in the Highlands, for Christ's sake. Surely activism is just a sneeze and a "bless you" from that sort of decision.

Looking back on the commune with adult knowledge, I see it's true that some sort of funding would have been needed. I'd always assumed that everyone had set it up with savings and cash from liquidated assets, but how could they have had any? The lure of corporate life is all about earning the sort of lifestyle you want through a particular branch of either the gov-corp or one of the international corporations operating in Norope. There's no incentive to buy a house now; in the collapse of the '30s, it all got so irretrievably fucked that only the emerging gov-corp—which had effectively eaten all the banks—could actually afford anything. The "solution" was touted as "neosocialism," but really it was all about reestablishing top-down control. Allocating housing and deducting rent from corporate salaries were the easiest ways to incentivize people to climb the ladder. As Dad always said, "If you know the people on the rung above you get a bigger box, you focus more on climbing the ladder than on questioning why."

The adults I grew up around thought it was all bullshit and opted out. It was only careful legal wrangling that stopped them all from being classed as nonpersons and therefore made vulnerable to all the programs designed to minimize the number of such societal outliers. Self-sufficiency was a big part of it, as was some sort of sponsorship, which had never really been explained to me. It wasn't commercial sponsorship, the sort of thing that would have required we cover our handmade houses with smart-ad triggers (there was no point in such a small community, after all). It was legal sponsorship. Perhaps that had something to do with the mutual friend Travis mentioned. Someone who was obviously still plugged into the system, given what Travis had said about not wanting to risk exposing him.

When I get back to Earth, I'm going to get answers to all these questions. I'll make Travis explain it all, and if he doesn't, I'll threaten him. He won't want his husband to find out what he's done.

But then, with the sickening feeling of a heavy stone pulling my stomach downward, I know how stupid I am to think that. It's far more likely that he'll never speak to me once I'm back, to minimize the risk of any of this being discovered. And even more likely, he'll have me killed. Does that even happen in real life? With all that money, surely it would be a simple thing to have me offed by some paid assassin?

Not as easy as sabotaging my return home, or having someone here cause an accident.

Or something like Principia. I can see it unspool so easily in my mind: I send the answers Travis wants to the dead drop and then he sends a message to Principia, either hacking it or simply making an irrefutable financial case for my death. Then the next time I'm outside, Principia fiddles with the air supply in my suit, or directs the rover over unstable ground, or fails to warn me of a dust storm so I'm caught outside, making it so easy to cover up a variety of murderous acts.

JeeMuh, I am so fucked.

There's no point panicking though. The best thing I can do is find out what Stefan Gabor is hiding, then work out the best way to use that information. I don't have to send it to the dead drop, after all. I owe no loyalty to Travis whatsoever.

What I need to do is get outside and record the journey to the edge of the crater again. Principia can't keep up the story of a dust storm indefinitely, so I'll paint if it doesn't let me go outside. I just need to be smart, keep my head and think before I communicate anything with anyone else.

Before tackling Principia, I record a quick message for Charlie and Mum, reminding Charlie about my concerns—without actually saying the word "footprint"—and asking Mum to tell me about Dad and believing him again. It's highly improbable that an AI as sophisticated as Principia is applying a really basic keyword-flagging filter, but the caution still makes me feel better.

I put in a request to go back to the crater again, near the footprint but not those exact coordinates. Unsurprisingly, it is denied because of the dust storm that I don't actually believe is real. But with all the sensor arrays running through Principia, there's no point trying to verify it.

Painting is better than doing nothing and it will give me something to send in a progress report, which is due soon. Breaking out the canvas and paints, arranging them on the desk to wait while I find the easel, is all so comforting. I unscrew one of the oil tubes and give it a quick sniff. I'm home again, music on, Charlie in the bedroom, Basalt lying across my feet like a heavy, breathing rug. I miss that stupid dog so much. JeeMuh, I miss him more than my husband. What kind of a human being am I?

The easel is buried underneath the other canvases. It must have come loose from the packing straps during transit; I would never pack it like this. I push away the thought that someone went through my stuff before it was brought to my room.

It can't be proven. I must not get paranoid. More paranoid than I already am, at least.

I was twelve when I first learned what the word really meant. It stopped being an empty adjective, used with the casual ease of a child who had never really felt it, when Dad's behavior changed.

Looking back, it seems like it happened overnight, but I know it didn't thanks to the recordings made by my memory bear. It stayed in my room, in a box, to be taken out only when I wanted to talk to it or for special occasions. My parents had grown up in a world where animated toys were sophisticated but didn't have AI, making them mistrustful. They had a friend do something to the bear's innards to cut it off from the Internet. It limited its function horribly, but it was the only way they would accept it in the house. The friend—whom I never met; could that be the one connected to Travis?—had the bear sync with a home memory hub, also detached from the Internet. That meant it could still record things I wanted it to, and could still get to know me and give what help it could with its limited internal dictionary and encyclopedia. It also meant that, critically, when the time came to get my chip, I had a load of data ready to feed it, so the transition was easier. That data gathered over my childhood acted as a shortcut, enabling my Artificial Personal Assistant settings to be tailored more accurately right from the start. Not that I had one of those superadvanced ones you could talk to like a real person; we could afford only a fairly basic model that was compatible with the regular upgrades needed for the first ten years.

As it happens, Bear was out and recording Mum's fortieth birthday party when Dad first started behaving strangely. Dad had been quiet all day, but I had thought it was because he was tired. We'd been up late the night before, decorating the communal hall for the party and doing the cake decorating. I'd felt so important, being just old enough to be genuinely useful, and rubbed in the fact that I got to stay up late to make Geena pout. With her sulking, and the pressure of giving Mum a special day, I'd thought Dad was simply preoccupied.

I've watched the footage of that afternoon many times in therapy. I haven't seen it for more than fifteen years now though. I got so sick of the opening shot of my twelve-year-old face looking down at Bear and saying, "Hi! Are you awake? There's a birthday party today and you're invited!"

"Oh! Wonderful," my bear said, and that would always be where the playback was paused first. Questions about how I felt about my bear having to stay in the box when other children took theirs everywhere. Questions about whether I loved my bear, whether it made me sad to put him away afterward, whether I was angry at my parents for their attitudes toward it. It was so tedious. The first few times I'd point out that it had nothing to do with the problems I'd been having. Then I learned that there was no point telling a therapist that something is irrelevant. It's all relevant to those bastards; every single sigh, every gesture, every insistence that they were barking up the wrong tree. I soon learned to stop resisting the direction they wanted to take. Better that than get frustrated with the fact that there was no way for them to ever be wrong. I much preferred comments about how guarded I was.

Ten minutes more into that recording—ten minutes, thirty-five seconds to be exact—is the next time it was always paused. That was when I wandered into the kitchen, Bear cuddled tight against my chest, eyes out so he could see too. Dad was rummaging in a drawer, looking pale and biting his lip. I'd seen him do that only when he was trying to fix something difficult, so I asked what he was doing, still eager to help.

"Looking for the sealer," he said.

"But I already covered the food. It's all laid out already." When he didn't answer, I said, "Is it for the leftovers? I was going to give them to the piggies. And the chickens will like the—"

When he found it he headed straight out, ignoring me. I trailed after him all the way to the communal hall.

Inside we'd decorated it with homemade bunting and paper chains, the former brought out for all parties, having been made by everyone in the commune, the latter made by Geena and me over the past week. I showed my bear the different triangles and told him who had made each one and why they'd picked those colors. That's the part always fast-forwarded through until the moment I spotted Dad doing something with the wiring on the far side of the hall.

"What are you doing, Daddy?" How I hate the sound of my reedy childhood voice now.

"I'm protecting us," he said.

"What from?"

"Monsters."

"Daddy, I'm twelve now. I know there's no such thing. What are you really doing?"

"What I said, protecting us." He was using the handheld sealer dispenser to attach something to the wires leading from the hall's hub to the screen where we planned to have pictures of Mum displayed during the party. At the time, I thought he was doing something to make sure the electricity didn't short. It was only in my twenties that I learned he was attaching a device of his own making, something he believed would stop the voices he'd started to hear from being sent through the connection. It actually did nothing; it was an old-fashioned circuit board with some ancient RAM jammed into it and a few diodes soldered on in a pattern.

That was what paranoia really was. And when Mum learned about it, a few days after the party thanks to a throw-away comment from me, she actually asked him, "Why are you being so paranoid?"

And that was the first time he hit her.

I push away the memories, reminding myself that it was a long time ago and he can no longer hurt her and that I am literally on another planet now, safe. I focus on the canvas now resting on the easel, waiting to be filled. I both love and hate this moment. The emptiness of the canvas excites me with the purest sense of potential, and yet at the same time, it paralyzes me. I have a sense in my mind of what I want to paint, and in this moment, just before I mix the first color, it is perfect. There is a quiet dread of the first daub, the instant that emptiness disappears and it has to be finished, has to get to a point where it will fail or succeed. Between now and that final touch of brush against canvas will be a constant negotiation between my ability and that perfect image in my mind. It will evolve, it always does, but the final piece will never be exactly what I want.

Mum says it's the same with her pots. She told me that the only way to be happy as an artist is to make peace with perfectionism. To accept that the final result will never match what you might have had in mind at the start and that's okay. "Sometimes it turns out better than you thought," she said to me in a message that I've played so many times over the years. "And sometimes, you sit down and think, 'Ah, there's nothing in me today,' but that might be the day you do your best work. And sometimes you don't even think. You just do the work and the art follows. And those days are rare and precious. The only thing you must be strict with yourself about is showing up to do the work, no matter what mood you're in."

Today I am actually in the mood to paint, despite my trepidation. I haven't painted for months. Have I forgotten how to?

After a few moments of staring at the canvas, I open a sketchbook, dig out a pencil and call up the stills I saved from the mersive to display on my wall. Soon I am absorbed in describing the shape of the rocks with a few light strokes of the pencil, tweaking the composition, arguing silently with myself about whether to keep it accurate. The alignment of Elysium Mons in the far background with the shapes of the boulders could be better with just a slight adjustment.

In the distance, I spot the tip of a tall, thin metal structure, some kind of communications mast, I think, that I hadn't really paid attention to before. I put it in the sketch and decide the picture would probably be better without it, leaving the pure majesty of the Martian surface without any sign of humankind.

I check my contract, making sure that there isn't any stipulation about what exactly I paint. It details that it must be of the Martian surface, that all pictures must be recognizably of Mars and preferably give the viewer a sense of being there. I'm not allowed to include any scientific equipment, including sensor arrays and weather stations. I'd forgotten about that. Strange that it be banned, when the tech being used up here isn't that different from what is used on Earth. But then, corporations always get twitchy over this sort of thing, and a blanket ban is far easier than dozens of sub-clauses trying to pin down the exact parameters of acceptable artistic expression.

I'll have to leave that mast out, meaning total accuracy isn't possible anyway. That's a relief. I'll move Elysium Mons, then, and make it a little bit bigger too. And just to be on the safe side, I'll make a record of the changes I'm making.

I call up a map of all the artificial structures in the Elysium Planitia region, and then seeing that it includes even the landing site of every scientific exploration vehicle sent to Mars in the last century, I apply a filter. There's no way that mast can be part of one of those abandoned vehicles; it's too tall. Dozens of little dots disappear from the map, leaving about a dozen atmospheric stations that have masts farther away and, closer to Principia, communications boosters used to strengthen comms with the rovers and also provide fail-safes should the primary comms go down.

But none of the remaining dots correspond with the location of the mast I can see in the shot on my wall.

I zoom in with a simple hand gesture. The image of the mast gets briefly crisper, and then when I zoom in again, it disappears.

"What the fuck?" I mutter, zooming back out again. It doesn't reappear.

"Principia? Have you edited this image data?"

"No, Dr. Kubrin. Would you like me to show you the editing—"

"No. I want you to reload this image, using the original data from my save." I point at the wall, so it knows which one I'm referring to.

When it reloads the mast tip is still missing. "Can I help you with anything else, Dr. Kubrin?"

"No." I sit back, looking from the wall to my sketch and back again. Did I imagine that mast? Why would I do that? But if I didn't imagine it, that means Principia has not only edited it out on the fly, without any request to do so; it's also lied about its actions.

Lying AIs are nothing new; the truth is only as pure as your relative pay grade after all, but I still find it disturbing that this keeps on happening.

If Principia is deliberately hiding this mast, it could be part of what Travis wants me to find. I need to work out how far away it is. On Earth, I'd be able to do it relatively easily, having a program set up to help me work out perspectives for landscapes. I can easily adapt that for Mars though. And even better, it's such a simple program, I don't even need to use Principia to do it; it's housed within my chip.

I'm used to using it immersively, so I look up the exact dimensions of Mars, save the figures to my temporary memory cache and lie down on the bed.

It isn't long before I'm standing in a featureless gray room. A tiny purple sphere is hovering in the air in front of me, waiting for me to start.

I love this program. It was designed to help children learn basic mathematical concepts but is used by artists, architects, game designers and all manner of other professionals. I tap the sphere and a simple dialog box floats next to it into which I can input the dimensions I want the sphere to be, the scale and which shape I'd like it to be. I keep the sphere, make it the same dimensions as Mars and alter the scale to one-hundredth. The program asks me if I want to be inside the sphere or on the surface. I select the latter.

The sphere expands, making everything below me purple. It's far too big, so I adjust the sphere until it's the size of a large house, just big enough for me to move on top of the surface.

I chuck in some features—the crater and its dimensions, Elysium Mons—using aerial maps of Mars to get the distances right. The program scales automatically once relative distances and dimensions are given. I even put in the boulders, importing a wire frame of them extrapolated from the mersive data. Once it's all in place, I change it to visualization mode, where the really fun stuff can be done. I check that everything looks the same—albeit massively simplified and almost cartoonish—and then I make a little copy of the mast, the exact length that I sketched it. It's simply a matter of selecting a symbol from the floating menu and then pinching the thumb and forefinger of each hand, touching them against each other and then pulling apart until I have the length I want. Then I put the little stick-like shape in the correct location on the horizon.

As a tool for playing with composition, it's very basic. Where its strength comes in is during the next phase. The same calculations that are used to keep everything in perspective and the correct scale if they are moved closer or farther away can also be used to calculate distances between points. This way, a town designer can chuck in all the proposed buildings in a really simplified form and literally move them about until the skyline looks good. Then the user can work back from that perfect skyline to calculate exactly where the different buildings would need to be placed in relation to one another. It's easier and faster to manipulate than complex modeling mersives, which can be overwhelming in their detail, and is also the same reason this is used to help kids. They can't get distracted by textures and details. It's pure geometry.

I tell the program that I want to calculate how high the mast is and how far away it is from the boulders. It's sophisticated enough to take the curvature of the sphere into its perspective calculations, and with Mars being just over half of the size of Earth, it makes a difference.

Of course, my sketch didn't use exact measurements, but I have a good eye for this sort of thing. I mentally give it a margin of error of plus or minus two meters for the height, based on the other masts on Mars, and feed that into the program too, so it can give me the range of possible distances.

In moments, that's exactly what I have. It's about five kilometers past the crater edge, just on the edge of the area covered by the missing cam drone data and potentially slightly taller than the other masts. When I do a bit of digging, it turns out that the masts that are on the official map vary in height too, depending on their primary function.

I confirm that there really is no mast in that potential area on the official map. For the first time, I have something tangible to go on.

If I didn't imagine it. I can't shake that concern, but if I start questioning every single discrepancy between what I see and what Principia decides to show me, then I'll drive myself crazy. As soon as this fictional dust storm has been allowed to pass, I'll go straight out there, get the visual data to feed the program to disguise my location and then see if it's what Travis hopes I would find.

If there is a mast, one of the crew could be gathering additional data and piping it back to Earth secretly. I can't imagine what that would be; perhaps they are measuring the impact of something highly experimental or illegal. I'm not even sure there's been any international agreement on what would be illegal out in the Martian wilderness. We are all bound by Noropean law and any subsets that are Gabor-Corp specific, because we are all contracted to that organization and are living in a GaborCorp facility. While GaborCorp has exclusive rights to access Mars and exploit its resources, it doesn't own the planet. No one does. Yet.

Of course, there are some things that would be so illegal there would be no point doing them on Mars. Making androids with fully simulated human likeness would be one of them, but what would be the point of making robots that could pass off as people up here on Mars? They would be so expensive to ship back to Earth.

Perhaps one of Principia's drones found something that demanded more investigation. My heart dearly wants it to be the remains of an ancient alien civilization, or that elusive definitive proof of life. It's unlikely to be either of them. I just don't believe in scientific fairy tales.

I save the distance and bearing so I can find the mast easily from the boulders and then close the program. The first thing I do when I'm fully back in my own body is rub out the mast from my sketch. I omit it from the list of differences between the proposed painting and the actual view on the planet, and just as I'm deciding where to start the painting, there's a ping from Dr. Arnolfi.

Reluctantly I take the call. "Dr. Kubrin. I'm sorry to disturb your work, but there is a team meeting that you must attend immediately."

She doesn't even give me a chance to reply. The stress in her voice has somehow leeched into the muscles of my back.

I run my hands through my hair a couple of times, check that I don't smell too bad and then head straight there, arriving to find everyone else taking places around the table.

Dr. Arnolfi looks positively haggard. Everyone else is silent, having noticed the same. I take a seat next to Elvan, certain that some bad news is about to be delivered.

"Thank you for coming, everyone. I thought it best that we all learn this at the same time. I'm afraid we've lost communication with Earth."

14

I'VE GOT TO hand it to Arnolfi; she plays a good game. She looks concerned, genuinely so, but I know she's behind all this. The timing is just too coincidental. Principia knows I was viewing data gathered from the cams, so it's reasonable to assume that Arnolfi knows that too. She has the access privileges and the right to examine my activities here under the umbrella of being a mental health care professional. She must have realized I was zeroing in on whatever Principia has been trying to hide from the cam data. Principia must have told her that it had to remove the mast from the image I was sketching and she's called this meeting to announce the drop in comms as a distraction. There's a chance Principia has dug about in my chip, without my knowledge or consent, and found the files that Travis put there. She must have cooked this up with Principia; the dust storm can't be faked indefinitely, and to stop me from using the dead drop they've had to invent this comms cut. It's extreme, and faintly ridiculous, but it underlines how far they're willing to go to stop me from uncovering their lies.

But, reflecting on it, cutting off the comms from Earth is far too heavy-handed an approach. And if I had rumbled Travis's plan, I wouldn't do anything like this; I'd let everyone involved carry on in ignorance, so I could see what data was sent and how bad the leak was. Then I'd have ample evidence for prosecution.

This is paranoia again. The flush of willful disbelief in what is really happening starts to fade. I am not the center of the universe and this is not necessarily all about me and what I'm supposed to be doing for Travis Gabor. I don't trust Arnolfi, but I can't be certain that this is all a ruse.

I think back to the disappointing messages from Charlie and Mum and the fact that nothing else has come back from them yet. The comms could have started malfunctioning already, causing that sense of disconnection from my family. No, that doesn't feel right either.

Biting my tongue to remind myself to stay quiet, I scan the faces of the rest of the crew, trying to work out if any of them are in on a secret with Arnolfi. Elvan looks worried and a little bit shocked, as does Petranek. Banks is gripping the table, his upper lip shining with sweat. He looks like he's trying not to panic as he stares at his own fingernails. JeeMuh, he could have sabotaged something. Is he scared of being found out? Or has this happened because he hasn't been maintaining the comms array when he said he was?

Then it all clicks into place; he's panicking because he knows what Principia is trying to hide from me. Maybe that's why he hates me so much, because he thinks that I'm going to find out what he's been up to. Travis assumes his husband is behind the secret payloads, but that is something Banks could have set up with secret backers on Earth. Stefan

Gabor probably has no idea what is sent to Mars and why. He certainly didn't seem to care about it at the dinner party.

A rival corporation may be using Banks to get one over on Gabor, using his tech, his money and his exclusive rights to gather data—or whatever is being done up here—beneath GaborCorp's nose the whole time. Damn! It's bold and crazy and certainly stressful enough to account for Banks's strange behavior. Looking at him now, and his barely controlled panic, I'm starting to think that he is behind it all. Maybe Arnolfi found out and he persuaded her to keep it secret. Then they fought about it, he went outside and she stayed in, trying to work out what to do.

"Okay, no comms . . ." Petranek breaks the silence. "So, I'm guessing that the prince has checked all the obvious things?"

"Would you like me to participate in this meeting?" Principia's default voice pipes through the communal speakers.

"Yeah," Petranek replies without consulting anyone. I guess I'm the only one here who has any problem with it and I keep silent.

There's a brief notification that pops up in my visual field, one I'm too distracted by watching Banks to take in, and then Principia's avatar appears to walk up to the table, taking a place between Arnolfi and Petranek.

A furtive glance at the others tells me that they can all see it too. Principia notes my brief confusion and says, "Everyone here can see me, but I appear according to everyone's preferences, using Augmented Reality through each individual's chip."

Embarrassed that it felt I needed the clarification—and that I actually did—I give a quick nod. I can feel Elvan's gaze and glance at him to see his reassuring smile. It's not an immersion psychosis symptom, that smile tells me. I wonder briefly how Principia's avatar looks through Elvan's chip.

Has it chosen to present itself to him as a woman who looks like me?

"Would you like me to confirm what I have considered the obvious things to be, Dr. Petranek?" At hir nod, Principia continues. "I can confirm that the equipment used on Mars to receive communications is in perfect working order. I have also verified that I am able to send messages, but I cannot verify that they have been received, as no confirmation pings or data receipts have left Earth."

"How can you be sure we're receiving?" Elvan asks.

"I have used several satellites in orbit around Mars to check the functionality of the local comms array. I have been able to ping the communications satellite that orbits Earth, used by GaborCorp to route comms from Earth to Mars. The comms problem is local to Earth. I cannot identify where the problem originates or its nature. It could simply be a matter of the satellite in orbit around Earth suffering a malfunction. However, its system appears to be in perfect working order and none of its fail-safes have been triggered."

"What could the cause of the silence be, then?" Elvan asks.

"There are a few possibilities," Petranek says. "It could be as simple as one link in the chain going down, stopping any broadcasts reaching the first satellite relay."

"You don't believe that though, do you?" Elvan replies.

"No." Petranek leans forward, resting hir head on hir hands. "Look, the system that was put in place to maintain contact between Earth and Mars is super-robust. This is not the sort of shit that can go down easily. Even if there has been a mechanical error, there are so many backup solutions I don't think the problem would last for long. GaborCorp owns over a hundred satellites, a good chunk of which could easily be repurposed if the main one went down. Which we don't think is the case anyway. I think the most likely explanation isn't technical."

"Meaning someone over there has decided to cut us off?" I ask. "Can they even do that?"

"Of course they can; it's not hard," Petranek replies. "The comms channel between Earth and Mars is a deliberately narrow pipe. It's all encrypted, and short of someone purposefully hacking into a very specific set of GaborCorp servers, no one else can talk to us. It's part of the exclusive rights setup and the deal with the network for the show. No one wanted any leaks. The most likely explanation is that, for whatever reason, GaborCorp has cut us off. Hopefully it's temporary."

"But why would they do that?" I ask. "We have contracts and the right to—"

"Oh, fuck any rights you might think you have!" Banks snaps. "It's obvious what's happened here."

"It isn't to me," Elvan says quietly.

"Hostile takeover." Banks practically spits the words out. "I saw it coming a fucking mile off. The ratings for the show have been in decline and that was the main money-spinner. Gabor doesn't give a shit about the science or even Mars. He wouldn't have any reason to fight for the contract if someone else wanted it."

Petranek shakes hir head. "Bollocks. If there was a takeover, we'd have been notified. They have a legal responsibility to inform staff, even if they're on another planet."

"What if Gabor is being prosecuted?" I ask and immediately regret it when everyone stares at me. I shrug. "I'm just trying to think of reasons why that notification may not have come through. Maybe if something really big happened, everything could have been frozen. That's what happened with that printer subsidiary a few years ago. Over ten thousand people couldn't print any food, just like that, no warning. The legal notices came through over twenty-four hours later."

"Even if that's what's happened, the radio silence can't be part of a hostile takeover," Petranek says with confidence. "No one can take the Mars contract from Gabor while there are people here without guaranteeing the safety of the Principia crew. Communications with Earth are defined as core survival needs. I can show you the clause right now."

"That clause is a crock of shit," Banks says, rubbing his fingertips over the sweat on his upper lip. "There are like ten thousand fucking loopholes that could be exploited. We're going to die here."

"What the fuck is your problem, Banks?" Petranek's stare doesn't seem to penetrate his panic. "We're protected by globally recognized law, not just our GaborCorp contracts. Stop freaking out and—"

"You're protected!" he shouts. "Whatever is happening, all of you are going to be fine, so don't tell me how I should be reacting to this!"

In the silence that follows his outburst, I look at Arnolfi. She seems just as puzzled as the rest of us.

"Just tell us what your problem is, for fuck's sake," Petranek says.

"She knows," he says, pointing at me. "It's why she's been sent here."

"What?" I don't have to fake my confusion; I can't see how this follows from what Travis did. And surely Banks doesn't even know about that.

"That's why he sent you here, isn't it? To take my place. You're just what the network wants. White skin. Blue eyes. Get those ratings back up. You can drop the act now."

"I have no idea what you're talking about," I say, relieved that from the sound of it, he's referring to Stefan Gabor and why he sent me, rather than Travis. Then the comments about the way I look, here and back in my room, finally sink in. "Is this why you've been treating me like shit since the moment I got here? Because you think I'm going to steal your job?" I laugh. I can't help it. It bursts out of me, fueled by nerves and the old sense of absurdist humor. "Seriously?"

He's caught between defending his position and accepting he may be wrong. "They really sent you here to paint?"

"Yeah, they really did. I had to fight to get clauses added to cover me for geological work. You can look at my contract if you don't believe me. There's one section about the show, if memory serves, saying I need to make myself available for filming, that I answer to you and some stuff about what I'm not allowed to talk about when being filmed. That's it."

He leans back, attention turned inward as he hears the truth in my tone.

"I'd be a terrible presenter," I say. "I can't do what you do, and even if I could, I don't want to take your job." I try to meet his eyes. "In fact, before you treated me like shit, I was a huge fan of yours. There's no way they'd replace you, let alone with someone like me."

The smile I was hoping to get in return doesn't materialize, but for the first time, he doesn't glare at me. It feels like he's looking at me properly for the first time. "So I totally misread all this, then."

"See for yourself." I send the relevant portion of my contract to him and he scans it in moments.

"Shit," he mutters.

"I think the word you're looking for is 'sorry,'" Elvan says.

"I am sorry. I was—"

"A total dick." Petranek finishes the sentence for him.

"That too," Banks agrees. And then I get that smile, the one I'd been looking forward to for so long, and it sends an electric thrill though my chest.

"Right." Petranek leans back. "So, now that's sorted, let's think about this loss of comms. Is anyone waiting for anything critical to come back from Earth?"

Everyone shakes their heads. "Just personal messages," I say and everyone else agrees apart from Arnolfi. She looks pale and drawn. Maybe she doesn't have anyone back home to talk to. "You haven't said anything," I say to her.

She blinks at me. "It's not my area of expertise," she replies. "I was waiting for feedback on a paper from my colleague and . . ."

Trailing off, she looks like she could cry at any moment. I look to Elvan, but he's checking something only he can see. Banks and Petranek are looking at some figures they've called up on one of the screens.

". . . and then Principia said that the comms were down. I thought it would be best to call a meeting about it."

"I want to know if anyone else has gone dark," Petranek says. "If it's just the GaborCorp comms network, then it's likely to be some sort of legal dispute. If others are down too, it could be something else. Terrorist attack maybe. Something like that. Can you tell us, Principia?"

The avatar shakes its head. "I do not have authorization to access data broadcast on non-GaborCorp channels."

"But can't you just, I don't know, pick it up from space?" Elvan asks. "I remember something in a cartoon from when my dad was a kid, with aliens watching Earth TV that had just kind of leaked into space."

Banks smirks. "Maybe in the days of analog broadcasting, but not now. We'd have to tap into a specific satellite network and decrypt the transmissions."

"Yeah." Petranek sighs. "You're right. Stuff isn't just blasted out there for free anymore."

"But these are extenuating circumstances, surely?" I say. I want someone to push this. I want someone to expose the lie. I may not understand why we've been cut off, but I know someone here is trying to stop us from talking to Earth, and I am—or rather, Travis is—the most likely reason for that.

"You said yourself that communication with Earth is classed as a core survival need. Surely GaborCorp lawyers would defend us in these circumstances?"

Everyone else looks at Banks, as if they know something that I don't. He shakes his head. "No."

"C'mon, Banks—she has a point," Petranek says. "You know how to tap into different networks, don't you? You did it that one time when there was the—"

"*Theoretically,*" Banks cuts in, flicking a nervous glance toward Principia's avatar. "But it would be illegal, and Principia would be obligated to report it."

"I would," Principia says. "I would also include any supporting statements from the crew along with my report."

"We'd back you up," Elvan says. "Then at least we'd be able to find out if there's some sort of legal dispute going on, or a hostile takeover."

Banks shifts uncomfortably in his seat. "No, I can't."

I look to Arnolfi, seeking a sign of collusion between them, or even a veiled threat in her eyes, but she's focused elsewhere, eyes scanning something in her visual field.

"But—" Petranek begins, and Banks stands up, slamming his hand on the table.

"I said no! And that's the end of it! If GaborCorp wants to keep us in the dark, we have to deal with it."

We all watch him leave. Petranek, looking distinctly unimpressed, folds hir arms. "Did he just flounce? 'Cause that looked like a flounce to me."

"Definitely a flounce," Elvan says and, frowning, looks at Arnolfi. "Did you talk to him?"

She jolts, as if caught daydreaming. "I haven't had a chance."

"What's going on?" Petranek leans in, lowering hir voice. "Is something wrong with Banks?"

"I saw him crying outside," Elvan says. I keep the correction to myself, knowing that he's doing it to keep me out of it and to limit the sense of gossiping.

"Maybe it was because he thought I was going to replace him," I suggest.

"He hasn't been himself since you got here," Petranek says and then winces. "That came out wrong. It's nothing to do with you, obviously, and he knows that now. Maybe he'll get his head together and then come back to us on the comms. He's always been one to do stuff by the book. Maybe we just put too much pressure on him all at once."

"Sometimes rules have to be broken for the greater good," Elvan says, and I try not to read more into it. If we had an affair, there wouldn't be anything good that could come from it.

"I think that's a step too far for Banks." Petranek stands and stretches. "As far as I see it, if Banks isn't willing to hack into another corp's comms network, we just have to wait until GaborCorp comes back online or until the forty-eight hours are up."

Arnolfi's head snaps up. "What do you mean?"

"If GaborCorp can't reestablish a connection within forty-eight hours, they are obligated to report it to the Noropean gov-corp, and then the comms will be handled by them, whether Gabor wants that or not. I reckon there are several really fucking stressed people back home, arguing with lawyers, knowing this all too well. Whatever the problem is, if Banks isn't willing to check what's going on for us, the only thing we can do is sit tight until Norope takes over or until GaborCorp sorts their shit out."

"And what if they don't take it over?" Elvan asks.

"Then you'll have to make contact with them for us, won't you, Principia?"

"I will be forced to intervene," Principia says.

Arnolfi's lips are now just a mere suggestion of a line

scoured across her face as she stares at Principia's avatar. I'm doing the same. The phrasing "forced to intervene" intrigues me. If it was a person saying that, I would think there had been a disagreement between them, but Principia was going along with her plan, for now. Principia being an AI, I try to resist that interpretation. They mean what they say with no subtlety. To interpret anything more than that would be giving in to the lure of paranoia.

I will not be my father.

"I'll be in the lab if anyone wants me," Petranek says and Elvan stands too.

I watch them leave and then I turn back to Arnolfi. "Are you all right?" I ask, but there's another question I'd rather be asking. Are you behind all of this? But I know I won't get a truthful answer out of her; I just know it.

She swipes something away from her vision. "It's just a bit unsettling."

"Yeah." I lean back, folding my arms and crossing my legs, noticing my defensive body language too late. "This comms problem couldn't be caused by someone on the base, could it?"

She remains silent so I look at Principia. "No communications are reaching the first satellite relay in orbit around Earth, Dr. Kubrin. This situation has not originated on Mars."

"Why did you ask that question?" Arnolfi asks. Now she's focusing again, that bloody therapist brain of hers is kicking back in.

I shrug. "Just wanted to be certain." I look at the avatar again. "Is that dust storm still blowing outside?"

"Yes, Dr. Kubrin. Would you like me to show you the footage from the external cams?"

I don't manage to keep a slight chuckle from escaping. "Oh, go ahead."

Images of dark, chaotic swirls of dust are displayed on the communal screens. "And that's live, right now?"

"Yes, Dr. Kubrin."

"If you say so," I mutter, getting up. "I guess I'd better carry on with my painting, then." I can't resist giving Arnolfi one more look, and my distrust must be showing, because she seems to shrink back before she looks away.

When I'm halfway across the room, I hear Arnolfi's chair scrape back. "Dr. Kubrin. I know you didn't want to talk about your father and his mental health issues, but I do feel it would be useful."

I round on her. "Useful for who, exactly?"

"You, of course." She's more composed now, but still very pale. She's more than unsettled; she is stressed out. "I've noted your distrust of what Principia has been reporting, and I think we need to make sure that any paranoid tendencies aren't allowed to fester. They can be so damaging, as I'm sure you are aware."

"Don't you"—I cut off what I planned to say, fumbling for a replacement—"worry about a thing, Dr. Arnolfi. I know the difference between paranoia and being lied to very well."

I wish I were as confident as I sound. I'm little better than a stupid male duck, puffing out chest feathers to seem more impressive. I want to have it out with her, here and now, get it all out in the open. But something holds me back. Perhaps the sense of self-preservation that has served me well in the past. I always knew when to be quiet around Dad. I certainly learned faster than Geena and my mother did. All of my instincts now are telling me to back off, to let her think she's winning. I don't even know what game we're playing here, but I know the surest way to lose is to expose my hand too quickly.

I give her a polite smile and leave before I lose my self-control, walking briskly back to my room. Locking the door behind me, I let out a long breath and kick off my shoes. The blank canvas is where I left it on the easel, the sketchbook resting on the bed, covered in eraser rubbings.

This is not paranoia. The coincidences are too great. Principia is hiding visual data from me and stopping me from going outside to see things for myself. It's stopping me from flying drones over the area I need to investigate. I send a message to my husband, mentioning a footprint and a sense of unease, and less than twenty-four hours later, before he has had a chance to reply to that message properly, communication with Earth is oh so conveniently cut off.

Laying it out in my mind like that, and dredging up some faith in myself that I know what is real and what isn't, makes the fluttering panic in my chest subside. This is totally different from what happened to Dad. I am not acting the same way he did. I'm not talking to people who are not there; my mood isn't swinging between happy and murderously angry. This is all really happening and Arnolfi and Principia are at the epicenter.

And now I feel angry. Something is being hidden, and I have a good idea where to find it. I don't know whether Principia is aware of Travis and what he's done, but it knows I'm closing in on the place where the answers are, and that AI is stopping me from getting to them.

I'm not sure how Arnolfi fits into this, but I'm convinced she's involved. She's hiding something, and I can see it taking its toll. For now, the best hypothesis I have is that she is involved with covering up Gabor's secret activities, and my poking around in things is stressing her out. I thought Banks was involved, but I'm less certain now. Then again, for a man known to be rigid in his obedience to the rules, he's certainly very good at sneaking out to places he shouldn't go. Sneaking outside to have a good cry hardly makes him seem like the mastermind behind all this fuckery though.

I just want to be free of all of these questions and this constant sense of unease. If I'm going to get to that hidden area, I need to get out of the base. If Banks can trick Principia into thinking he's going in the opposite direction from his actual bearing, maybe he can do the same for me, and that will be a lot more efficient than having to make several trips to feed the visual data to Travis's cover-up program.

I head for his room before I have a chance to talk myself out of the shitty plan that is barely formed in my mind. Banks is only just starting to come around to my presence on the base, so there's little chance he'll do this for me as a casual favor. There is one thing I'm certain of though: he won't want anyone else to know he's been making unauthorized trips and tricking Principia. If I'm going to get to whatever is being hidden on the other side of that bloody crater, I need to get some help from someone on this planet, rather than a copy of them trapped inside my hacked chip. Even if I have to put the pressure on Banks to do it.

15

"COME IN."

When I enter, Banks is sitting at his desk, covering something with a piece of paper. My first thought is that he is sketching something, but then I notice the fountain pen in his hand. Is he writing an actual letter? On paper?

I don't feel comfortable enough to ask him about it. Besides, there are more important things to address.

"Hi," I say, trying not to seem nervous. "Do you have a minute? I'd like to talk to you."

He nods and waves a hand at his bed. "Or did you want to go to the communal area?"

"This is fine," I say, perching on the edge of it. "It's too private for out there."

He looks calmer than he did at the meeting, but far from relaxed. There are damp patches at his armpits. I wonder if there are at mine.

Desperate for something to break the ice, I gesture at the paper. "Are you a fellow artist?"

He frowns at it and shakes his head. Then, after visible deliberation, he moves the paper aside. "Calligraphy. This is copperplate. It helps me to relax."

The script is beautiful and very accomplished. Suspicion briefly resurges as I wonder if he would be capable of faking my brush style, but using a pen like that is a totally different skill. I let the idea die again.

"Now that I'm not being a dick," Banks says, "have you come with questions about the show? We can brainstorm some ideas if you like. It won't take long."

He's nervous, trying to control the conversation, marking out the topic that he is comfortable with talking about even though I've made it clear this is a private matter. I do all I can to keep looking relaxed, nonthreatening. Not that I've ever appeared to be dangerous in my entire life. "I don't have any questions. Given what's going on, we may not have to worry about the show for a little while anyway."

He takes a sip from a glass of water on his desk and I notice the tremor in his hand as he puts it back down again. "You must think I'm a terrible person. I'm not normally like that. I am really sorry I treated you so badly."

"How about we start again? Draw a line under it all." I extend my hand toward him. "I'm Anna Kubrin. I'm a big fan of the show."

He puts on a smile that I know he's learned for camera-work. It transforms his face, crinkling his eyes and making him so much more handsome with its warmth. "Why, thank you, Anna. We work very hard on it. I'm Kim Banks."

We shake hands; his is hot and, thanks to the way he rested his palms on his legs when I held out my hand, recently dried on his trousers.

It feels better between us. I don't want to go crashing into this with threats and ultimatums. The softer approach feels better. I have to be patient. Clever. The former was never my strong suit, but I'm capable of following a plan to a goal.

"I wanted to talk to you about the preliminary work I've been doing for the first painting."

There's a flicker of relief before his confusion takes hold of his face. "Okay. But you should know that I don't have a clue about anything artistic."

I lean in, closing the gap between us. "I want to talk to you without using a certain name. It's the one who was present at the meeting but doesn't have a real body."

He nods slowly. Instead of the question I was expecting, he asks, "How about we refer to that as the tin man?"

"Okay. So, I sent out some cams to take pictures of an area I want to paint."

"You went out with Petranek. Ze mentioned it."

"Yeah. So the idea was that I get a massive area fully rendered in a mersive; then I can walk around it, find a good perspective to paint and use that as a reference."

"Okay," he says, leaning back in his chair now, relaxing. Good.

"When I reviewed the data, the images from one of the drones was missing and when I looked into it, the tin man denied it."

"Where did that drone cover?"

"I can show you, if you like?"

I call up a generic map of the Elysium Planitia region and he gives me permission to throw it up on his wall. I talk him through how I discovered it, show him the region; and then I tell him about the mast.

"And the tin man denied editing the image?" When I nod, he looks back at the map. "This is definitely weird."

"Have you ever been out that way?"

He shakes his head. "No, I haven't. In the early days of

the show, I did a lot of external shoots. But then when that first game came out the interest dropped right off. That's when we changed the format, bringing the focus into the base and onto the crew."

I point to the place where Petranek and I saw the footprint. "Not here? Recently?"

"No. Why?"

"We saw a footprint there."

There's no sign of anything but surprise on his face. He comes over to stand next to me, close to the map. "There? I thought the area between the base and that region was unstable."

"That's what the tin man said. He didn't want us to go there, but I used Gabor's orders for me to paint the surface of Mars against it."

"What made you want to go to that crater in particular?"

I try to recall the decision. "I don't know. It was pretty much random. Just a big crater I'd always wanted to see, I guess."

"Petranek didn't mention seeing a footprint."

I try not to blush, fail and try a shy smile instead. "I asked hir not to mention it to anyone. The tin man said no one had ever been there, even though we were seeing physical proof that it was lying. Seems very dodgy to me."

"Yeah, it does."

I take a deeper breath, release it. "Of course, the tin man may have been telling the truth if someone sneaked there without him knowing about it. Do you know anyone who'd be able to do that?"

Shoving his hands in his pockets, eyes very firmly fixed on the map, Banks shakes his head. "No. It's impossible. The tin man knows where everyone is at all times."

"Everyone?" I watch him nod in profile. "Apart from you."

He starts to refute it, then sees the look in my eye and

falls silent. He walks away from the map to lean against the bathroom door. He presses his finger to his lips, attends to something in his visual field, and then some god-awful Gregorian chant starts playing through the speakers above his desk. He comes back to me, leaning close to my left ear and dropping his voice to a whisper. "You're smarter than I thought. All this, just to make me confess something?"

"Not exactly. I want your help to figure this out. I know that you can go out there and make the tin man think you're somewhere else."

The sweat is back, making his forehead and upper lip shine. He draws in a ragged breath and swears to himself.

"Look, I don't want to get you in trouble. I swear it. But I saw you crying out there and—"

"Didn't the psych talk to you about privacy lines?" he hisses, the old antagonism flaring back into life. "You have to respect them on a base this small and isolated."

I can feel the good work I've done to put him at ease unraveling by the second. "I'm sorry. I just hate seeing people upset and . . . Look, you don't have to say anything. I can see this is stressing you out. I wouldn't have raised this with you if it wasn't important. The tin man is hiding something. I want to go and find it, and I can trick it once I'm outside, but with this fake dust storm I can't even get out and—"

"Fake dust storm?"

"I sent out another cam to get the data from the missing area; that's when I saw you where you weren't supposed to be. Just as the drone got to the crater, the tin man says there's a dust storm. Nothing was on the mid- to short-term forecasts before then. Dust storms don't spring up with such short notice, not with all the hardware we have in orbit now."

"You really think the tin man is making up storms just to keep you confined to base?"

I know that tone in his voice. We're two sentences away

from me being branded as too imaginative in the best-case scenario, or mentally ill in the worst case. "I know how this sounds. But look at the evidence. Something is on the other side of that crater, and if you can trick the tin man, I reckon you can help me to get out there and find out what it is."

I can see he's curious. He keeps looking back at the map, chewing his lip, wrestling with the temptation. But I'm not sure if he's being tempted to help me or to report me to Arnolfi. His shoulders slump and he shakes his head. "Listen, I can't take the risk. I'm sorry."

"Can you get me out of the base?" When his frown deepens, I add, "Theoretically. Could you do it?"

He runs a hand over his face, clearly torn. "If I wanted to, yes. I know how to trick the tin man into thinking that the manual override hasn't been activated. I could get you outside without it knowing. Once you're out there . . . it gets harder but I could probably sort something out. Only if you gave me full user privileges on your chip though. I'm assuming you wouldn't want that."

"Well, it would be a good exercise in trust, I guess."

"You can ring-fence off your stored files from me, and as soon as we're done you can revoke those privileges again. But it's all academic. I'm not going to do it. It's not worth it."

"We're not doing anything illegal here. In fact, if it came to it and we were prosecuted by the corp internally, I'm sure that the tin man's actions would be seen as an impediment to my primary mission here. And—"

"It's not that simple."

"No, really, it is! All Gabor cares about is me painting enough pictures to make him more rich. You said as much yourself. Getting out there is—"

"Have you heard a fucking word I've said?" His voice is loud enough to drown out the monks for a few seconds. He shuts his eyes, mouths an expletive. "The answer is no."

With an angry wave of his hand, he swipes the map off the wall and returns to the desk to slump in his chair.

I rest my head against the wall and close my eyes, frustrated. What is he so afraid of?

Then I remember the meeting and the way he reacted to the news that we were cut off. The way he'd emphasized that we'd all be fine. Like he knew he wouldn't be.

Slowly, telegraphing my movements so I don't startle him, I go and crouch beside him, lining up my mouth with his ear. "Is there something in your contract that's stopping you? What are you so afraid of?"

To my surprise, his eyes well with tears again, and I realize he hasn't really found his strength since the meeting. "If you do something that merits a disciplinary, you might get a warning, right?"

I nod.

"And if it's bad enough, but not illegal per se, what's the worst that could happen to you?"

"I'd get kicked out. And if I didn't find somewhere else to work within the notice period, I guess the very worst thing would be ending up as a nonperson. But that's really rare once you get to . . ." It suddenly clicks into place. His panic before, his insistence that he won't break the rules, even though he clearly does. He must have a different kind of contract from me, one with fewer protections. "That's not the case for you, is it?"

He drops his gaze and stares at the floor.

"If GaborCorp is bought out of the Mars contract, are you not protected?"

He shakes his head. "I'm not protected by anything. I'm owned."

"I don't understand."

"I'm classed as an asset, not an employee. I have no employment protection rights, or even human rights. GaborCorp owns me like it owns this base and everything in it. If I break the rules, it isn't just a note in a file; it's a black mark. Get three of those, and years can be added to my contract. As it is, I won't be free until I'm seventy-six. I don't know if they'll ever let me go home. They have no obligation to send me back to Earth, just as they have no obligation to ship the lab equipment back at the end of its life."

"JeeMuh . . . But surely . . ." The words peter out. I'd heard of people with this sort of contract but never actually met one. Charlie didn't believe they actually existed. For him—and until now for me—the idea of indentured service in modern gov-corp life was like some urban myth, a societal cautionary tale. "Did you even want to come to Mars in the first place?"

He shrugs, and there is so much contained in such a small gesture. Years of leading a life in which he's made no professional choices. How deep does this go? "Oh shit, that's awful. It's wrong! It's slavery!"

"No one else knows," he says, a sudden fear in his eyes. "I don't want them to. It's GaborCorp policy to keep indentured status confidential. Otherwise people abuse assets and it reduces productivity."

Now tears are welling in my eyes. "I won't tell a soul—I swear it. But there has to be something we can do! I mean, you're famous! If people knew, they—"

"You think I haven't been tempted? I reckon the debt held against me could be crowd funded and paid off in hours if the news broke online. But GaborCorp doesn't want that debt to be paid off with other people's cash. I'm more valuable to them as I am now. If I was a real person, I'd be earning millions a year. Now . . . now I get to pay off a fraction of the debt each year at rates they control. If I made this public, the penalties stipulated in the contract would mean I'd die before I was free."

A tear slips free from my eye. Not of pity. Of anger. "I'm going to do something about it," I say.

The fear in his eyes makes another tear fall. "No! I shouldn't have told you. I don't even know why I did. Shit! Swear to me you won't."

"I promise. Is this why you were crying? Outside, I mean."

After a long pause, he nods. "I don't know what's been up with me lately. I just . . . I feel like I'm falling apart. I've never come close to telling anyone. Not even the woman I would have married if I could. I don't even like this job. I hate having to do the show. Pretending to be enthusiastic about everything Mars when I fucking hate this place. I don't give a shit about the world record either. Being on Mars the longest time doesn't mean anything if you don't have a choice. If I had a life to go back to, staying here would be something real. A sacrifice." He wipes the back of his hand across his eyes. "I don't know why I was taking it all out on you."

"Maybe it was safer to let it leak out at me than the others," I suggest, wiping my eyes too. "And maybe the thought of someone taking your place and being paid for it was part of it too. In fact, it makes a hell of a lot of sense. And for the record, you are a real person. Jesus fucking Christ, I want to burn all of this down to the ground and fly back to Earth and . . . and start burning all that too."

"I shouldn't have told you."

I reach for his hands, expecting him to pull them away, but he doesn't. I take hold of them, tight, wanting him to feel I am really here. "I won't tell anyone else. I promise. But if I do think I can get you out of this, I'm going to try. I won't make it public. But there's someone on Earth, someone who will owe me once this mission is done. I'll ask him to pay the debt off."

"Yeah, but it's millions."

"He's rich. And I'll have one over on him. A secret he won't want me to tell anyone else."

Banks looks back at me now, incredulous. "Do you even live in the real world? If someone that rich doesn't want people to know something, you'll die before it gets out."

"That has occurred to me," I say with a sigh. "Ah, fuck. What a fucking mess."

"You're going to get yourself killed if you play those sorts of games. Believe me. I've seen it."

"I'm already playing, whether I like it or not. Look, I'm not going to put any pressure on you to do anything that will make things worse for you. But if you can tell me how you trick the tin man, I'll go out there by myself and you won't be implicated at all."

"Going out in a dust storm is really dumb. Going out in one alone is practically suicide."

"Like I said, that storm isn't real." I give his hands one last squeeze and let go. "If I can prove it isn't, then we know for certain that the tin man is hiding something. Right?"

He leans back in the chair again, looking like he's listening to this awful music. I find his expressions fascinating. I've only ever seen one aspect of this man: the charming show presenter, so good at his job that I really believed that was the whole of him. It feels like I've been looking at only one portrait, thinking it was many when it was only changes in lighting. There is so much more to discover.

His eyes flick to me and I see something calculating in them. He comes back to whisper in my ear again. "If you're right and if the tin man is hiding something, what do you think it could be?"

"I really have no idea. There's a mast, about five kilometers on the other side of the Cerberus Palus crater, which means there might be a comms array there. Maybe data is being sent back to Earth without having to go through the base. I genuinely don't know." As soon as I say it, I worry I've said too much. I search his face for signs of any duplicity, but he looks thoughtful.

"That region has been controversial in the past. I was never allowed to film there. I was told it was because there was some sort of agreement with the international community to leave some areas as untouched wilderness. I didn't have any fucks to give about it, for obvious reasons, so I never pressed for more. The mast makes that seem like bollocks." He leans forward again, his eyes sparkling with the thrill of discovering a mystery. It feels like I'm finally meeting the man I hoped I would. "I wouldn't put it past Gabor to have set something up there, though it would have had to be done before Principia was established, or concurrent with this place being built; otherwise, we would have seen payloads coming and going."

"But think about it," I whisper back. "How do we know about anything happening outside of these walls? Through the tin man. All sorts of stuff could be going on out there and we'd be none the wiser unless we were physically standing there, looking at it. We think we can see the entire surface of the planet in real time, but all of that is piped through the tin man first. It could be withholding all sorts of data. I mean . . . JeeMuh, there could be a whole fucking city there right now and we'd never know about it."

He smirks. "It's not a city. That would be insane."

"I know that. And I know it's not aliens or proof of life either—believe me." I don't want him to think I am stupid. I actually care far too much about his opinion of me. "But you get my point. Something is being hidden and if we can just go there and see it with our own eyes, then . . ."

"Then what? What's your plan?"

"Then we use it to guarantee our safe return home. Both of us. And we use it to get you free from that contract."

I can see the temptation, perhaps even a glimmer of hope. Then it disappears. "You've been playing in too many mersives. The real world doesn't work like that."

"Maybe not. But if we don't find out what's there, we won't have anything to bargain with. And now I think something's there, I need to know what it is."

He laughs. "Yeah . . . this is the most interested I've been in Mars for years." He scans my face, shaking his head. "I knew you were trouble."

"Just get me out of the base, just for a minute. Hell, just out into the air lock. If there really is a storm, the shield doors will be down at the top of the ramp and we'll hear it. If the tin man is telling the truth about it, I'll come straight back inside and . . . and I'll think of something else. I won't bother you again."

It feels like everything is hanging on his response. Not just my hope that we will discover the truth, but also the desire to be taken seriously, to have found an ally at last.

"All right. Fuck it. I'm going to die on this fucking rock anyway; what difference does another five years on my contract make?" He frowns. "But I'm going out there with you. I don't want you sucked out of the air lock and killed. You do realize the risk, don't you?"

I nod, trying to mask my inner exultation with the appearance of professionalism. "We'll take some tethers with us."

"I'll need a few minutes. You ready to go when I'm done?"

"Yeah. I'll go get changed."

I head toward the door and he follows me, then rests a hand on my shoulder. "Anna. I shouldn't have told you. You won't—"

I turn around and hug him, feeling the way his body stiffens before he puts his arms around me too. I don't think this man has been held for years. I turn my head to rest it flat against his chest, and I tighten my arms around him. "I won't tell anyone," I say again as he finally starts to relax. "I promise, Banks. I promise."

He finally lets me go, turning away as quickly as he can to hide his face. "I'm sorry. I'll see you soon."

I go back to my room, all of my troubles with Charlie and Mia seeming inconsequential in comparison to what I've just learned about Banks. I want to sit down with him over a drink, spend the rest of the afternoon talking so we can get to the sort of conversation in the small hours when people really open up. How did he end up in this situation? How many others have this sort of contract? How can this even be happening now?

I think of all the arguments Charlie and I had about my coming here, and it always came back to the same thing: when it was all done and I was home again, we'd have money, actual money in an account, separate from our corporate allowances. We'd be wealthy enough not to have to climb the corporate ladder in order to improve our lifestyle. And that's even before the paintings are sold. Even though I'll get only a fraction of what Gabor will receive for them, he plans to charge such a huge amount that each one sold will bring in a windfall.

We'll be able to rent a place outside of the corporate allocation scale. Somewhere with a garden. Depending on what happens once I'm back, we may even be able to buy something. That's something we'd never even bother dreaming about without this opportunity.

"Is this what it comes down to, then?" Charlie said one night after we'd been bickering for hours. "Our daughter loses her mother for two years, but it doesn't matter because she'll get a garden to play in?"

"Do you really want me to tell Gabor that I won't go? Do you think he'll just shrug and say, 'Oh, never mind'?"

"He'll send someone else. You're not the only fucking

artist on the planet, Anna. There are millions of painters who'd do anything to go there."

"Well, there may be millions of people who are better artists than me, but his husband thinks I'm the best."

"I didn't say they were better than you. I'm just saying you're not unique."

"And that's supposed to make me feel better? Because making something unique is what I'm aiming for, as an artist."

"You're a geologist. The painting is just a hobby. Why are you so keen to break our family for a fucking hobby?"

"Maybe if you listened to yourself you'd realize you're answering your own question!" I yelled and shut myself in the bathroom.

If it wasn't for the guilt, I'd have laughed with joy when I left the flat for the last time before the flight. Oh, I cried when I held Mia, but by the time I reached the airport, I was all smiles. For days I told myself I was too busy, too nervous to really miss her. Then when I was strapping myself into the seat an hour before takeoff, the tears were because of my fear of dying rather than an aching for my child. I couldn't tell anyone that I didn't miss her or Charlie, not really. That the only misery I felt was the thought that I was such an awful person. How narcissistic is that?

And all this time, Banks has been here against his will. Not even being paid. Uncertain about whether he will ever be sent home. I can understand his fear. It costs millions per flight. If he really does have the same status as a nonhuman asset, they will leave him here.

I sit on the bed to take off my shoes. Surely they wouldn't abandon him here? But then, with him unable to tell anyone without serious repercussions, the GaborCorp leaders are free to do anything they like. They are the ones controlling the narrative, not Banks. If he dies here, everyone will be told that he loved this place so much, he couldn't bear to leave it. It sounds like he has no family back home, no one pressing for his return, anyway.

As I pull off my clothes and dress in my undersuit onesie, I think about what he said about the world record. He doesn't want to be here any more than I do. No, that's not true. I do want to be here, I think. But I know the date I'm leaving. I know it's finite. JeeMuh . . . being trapped here, forever, knowing that I'd never be able to feel the sun on my face or feel the breeze in my air unless it was in a mersive . . . it's the most horrendous thought. I'm not going to leave him behind. I'm not going to let Gabor get away with this. Whatever I find out there, past that crater, I'll use it as leverage. I'll work some way to force them to let him go home.

And then we'll both die on the way back in a terrible accident . . .

No! I must not think that way. I stretch out the tension in my shoulders, give Banks access to my chip and start putting on the rest of my clothes over the onesie to hide it in case I run into anyone else en route to the dust lock. I'm thinking too far ahead anyway. Right now, all I have to do is see if there is a storm outside or not. One step at a time, and there are many more to go before I need to work out how to blackmail one of the most powerful corporations in the world.

Before long, Banks and I are hurrying down the corridor to the dust lock in silence. He won't tell me what he's done to hide our movements, and I haven't asked. I get the feeling he doesn't want to lose that one bit of power he has, even if it's only over Principia knowing where he is. I can understand how a man who has nothing—not even basic rights— wants to protect his own secrets.

Once we're inside the dust lock I follow his lead, staying silent, grateful that this isn't my first time outside. We hide our outer clothes in a locker, climb into the suits and head into the air lock without being disturbed.

There must be dozens of ways for Principia to be aware of what we're doing—doors being opened, suits being filled, cameras in every corridor and in the locks—but somehow, we aren't challenged. The only thing I notice is that Banks manually activates the air lock from an access panel, there as a failsafe, and that he opens the door with a manual override.

When we step through into the last part of the locks, I note the silence. Banks looks at me as he listens too. Surely if there was a storm we'd hear it on the other side of the doors?

An unfamiliar dialog box opens, asking for permission to open voice comms with him. I don't even recognize the software interface. What the hell is he using? I give permission nonetheless.

"If it's a really bad one, we might hear it on the shield doors, but it depends on the wind direction," he says.

"Even so, surely we'd still hear something," I reply. "Are the microphones in the suits still working properly without the tin man knowing what we're doing?"

He stamps his foot and I hear the clang. "They're working normally. Let's hook up the tethers, just in case."

There are cables to attach to the suits in case there's an emergency near the base and someone needs to go outside in a storm. They've been used only once, long before I arrived, when a rover malfunctioned and couldn't get back into the base as a storm was coming in. The two crew members outside were helped in by two others tethered as we soon are. The cables are clipped to the back plates of the suits and don't impede our movement as long as we're simply heading to the doors and then up the ramp.

When I give the thumbs-up, Banks opens the last door of the air lock and we're in the subterranean garage where the two rovers are kept. There is a little bit of dull light spilling down the ramp and the outer doors are open. The dust that covers the floor rests undisturbed.

Banks moves toward the ramp, the cable unspooling behind him. "Well, I'll be damned," he says, looking up. "It's a beautiful day out there."

I join him. "You know what?" I say, unclipping the cable from his back. "It looks like perfect weather for a drive."

16

BANKS UNCLIPS THE tether from the back of my suit and it's slowly pulled back in automatically. I head for the nearest rover but he doesn't move.

"Listen," he says when I reach the driver's-side door. "I can't go with you. It's one thing to risk coming into the air lock, but if you do find something out there and I'm with you . . ."

"It's okay," I say, pasting a smile over the crushing disappointment. "I understand."

"I'm sorry."

"No, really, it's fine." It's not though. Going out there alone is stupid. But I daren't embroil anyone else in this. I can't hide them from Principia and I can't tell them what Banks is capable of without betraying him. "Will you still be able to keep me hidden?"

He nods. "Yes, but it's going to lead to a serious disciplinary if this is found out. For you, I mean."

"Is there any risk to you?"

He sighs. "If you die out there and they do a full inquiry, they'll find what I've done. Otherwise, no. So don't die, okay?"

"Okay." I open the rover. "And you'll be able to hide the fact I'm driving in this thing?"

"Yeah. Don't worry about any of that. Just be really careful. Don't call up anything that uses the satellites; it might alert the tin man."

No weather reports, then. Not that I'd trust anything now, but still, it's yet another risk factor increased.

"If you get into trouble, ping me on that secure line I just opened to you," he says. My worry must be obvious. "But only in an emergency, okay?"

"Okay."

I climb into the driver's seat, hoping the onesie is as good at wicking away sweat as it's supposed to be. I've never driven a real rover before. I've done hours of training in mersives of course, but somehow this feels different. It all looks exactly as it should, and I know what to do, but there isn't proper muscle memory to draw upon. The gulf between mersive training and real-world adventure looms before me.

"I'm going back in now," Banks says. "Come find me as soon as you get back, okay?"

I can see the guilt in the way that he hesitates before each movement. He feels bad about this—that much is clear— and I really do think he'd come with me if he wasn't afraid. That's the power they have over him.

I start the rover and drive up the ramp, wanting to get out of his sight as soon as I can. I want him to get back inside and safe again, and the longer I hang around, the greater the risk. The "do not disturb" notice I put in place on my public profile is still there and I can only hope it's enough to stop people from going to my room to find me.

There are several hours of daylight left and it's as fine a day as Mars gets. The sun is only as strong as it would be on an early-spring day back home, even though it's summer here now, but in the heated rover it makes no difference to me anyway.

The rover's controls soon feel familiar. What I lack in muscle memory I more than make up for with concentration, and soon I'm bouncing across the surface, leaving a satisfying dust trail behind me. The fear that I won't be able to drive well enough subsides, giving room for other fears to increase, most centered around being alone should anything terrible happen. I need a distraction.

I find some Russian soul music from the '50s to play in my helmet, thinking of the boyfriend who introduced me to it in the summer before I met Charlie. He was a fellow geologist, less ambitious and more gregarious than I, always dragging me out to clubs that tried a little too hard to seem edgy. The band I'm listening to now was one of the few I actually liked, and we'd danced in the humid darkness, pressed close to each other.

I can't help but smile at the memory of Elvan's hands resting on my hips as we swayed to the singer's mournful voice, how they moved into the small of my back, pulling me closer. How we kissed—

I jolt, braking instinctively. No, that wasn't Elvan; that was . . . Jordan? Jorg? Something like that. Back on Earth, years ago. I've never danced with Elvan. Just as I've never danced with Charlie.

Shit. I change the music to some harmless electronica and move off again, keeping my mind fixed on the route. I've examined it so much in trying to work out what Principia has been hiding that I'm fairly certain I'll be able to get there without needing to activate the nav system. Not wanting to risk pinging the satellites, I trust in my visual memory of the route Petranek and I took. Soon enough I pick up the old tire tracks, yet more evidence that not even a little storm has passed over since our trip.

Strangely enough, driving helps this to feel far more real than the trip out with Petranek. Each bounce of the rover, every large rock I have to steer around, makes me feel like I am actually interacting with what I can see. It helps that I didn't play that stupid Mars game long enough to merit driving the rovers in it, and that the mersive training for using this vehicle was set in a massively simplified environment to keep my attention on the controls.

I change the music again, this time to something I can sing along to, a playlist of all sorts of songs from the happiest times in my life. Soon the rover is filled with an old twentieth-century crooner classic and my voice warbling its way through the notes with it.

I can't remember the last time I sang. I can't remember the last time I felt alone and so damn happy about it. The novelty soon wore off in the ship on the way over, and that was why I spent too much time in my mersives. But now, knowing that there are people whom I will be going back to before the day is out, this solitude feels like a gift. No Charlie to face on my return, no Mia to feel drained by in moments. I turn up the volume and sing even louder.

The time passes quickly and I reach the crater sooner than I expected. I park and jump out of the rover to scrabble up the slope of the Cerberus Palus crater edge, disturbing my and Petranek's footprints to reach the top. I find the original print in the lee of the boulder again and gaze down into the expanse below.

It's simple enough to work out which way I need to go; I've moved around this crater enough times in the doctored mersive, staring at its edge in relation to distant volcanoes, to be fairly confident of where the target area is. The only thing

I need to decide is whether to risk driving up and down the lip of the crater so that I can take the most direct route across.

The sides are steep and the ejecta is very loose in places. I tentatively step down from the lip and the powdery dust slides beneath my boots, making me scrabble upward in a panic to get back to the top of the rim. That answered the question well enough. I'll drive around it, keeping the crater on my right as best I can. Surely by the time I reach the far side I'll be able to see that mast at least.

Back in the rover, singing as loudly as I can, keeping the crater edge in sight, I don't feel like I'm on my way to uncover some sort of corporate conspiracy. I feel like I'm on a day trip. I never seem to be able to match my mood with my environment. Being worried about Dad at my mum's party, when everyone else was laughing and celebrating. Being scared of him on one of our family walks out of the valley, as Geena chittered away, oblivious. And endless days as a new mother at home, feeling like I was trapped in some bizarre limbo between life and death when I should have been filled with joy.

Maybe it wouldn't have been so bad if the apartment block's club for new parents hadn't been filled with people who could somehow find delight in the contents of nappies. Who could find a sense of achievement in getting through a pile of laundry and clearing a space on the floor that would remain pristine for all of five minutes.

I simply couldn't understand why they all wanted to talk about baby stuff. We were immersed in it, twenty-four hours a day; it made no sense to me to meet up with people I barely knew and talk to them about it too. I wanted to find someone like me, someone desperate for human contact with an adult and conversation about anything other than milk and sleep and shit.

I went only twice. The first time I just tried to fit in, only to return to our apartment and sob for an hour. At the second meeting I resolved to make an effort, hoping to discover another outlier like me who had merely been pretending to blend in, like I had.

But no. Any time I tried to draw the subject away from babies, I was met with blank stares or mild confusion. Comments about how they hadn't had a moment to keep up with anything on the feeds. It was as if the world outside had ceased to exist for them, while I was craving it. And what made it worse was that they simply didn't care that their lives had imploded. They were filled with that incredible, deep, brain-numbing love. I couldn't be around them, feeling like a monstrous collection of raw nerves.

Charlie thought I was still going to the group until one of the other fathers asked him why I'd stopped. He couldn't understand my revulsion, declaring it just another example of me not permitting myself to be like other people. As if it were a conscious decision on my part. Of course, when we switched roles and he became primary caregiver, he went to that club and jumped right in. He started spouting tips he'd gleaned from so-and-so at the club, even passing on gossip. He'd been sucked in, assimilated, like non-player characters in conspiracy mersives who start off as your friend at the beginning of the game and then start saying the catchphrases used by the enemy. Unlike in those mersives, I couldn't express my horror with a gunshot to his head.

As a child, I never appreciated how much I needed to be accepted by the people around me. I grew up in a community that celebrated diversity, encouraged independent thinking and defended those who wanted to live differently. But I'm sure that even those people couldn't have accepted what I became. A mother who feels no joy, no love . . . that's the sort of deviance from the norm that no one seems to celebrate.

Perhaps if I were braver, if I'd found courage enough to go

online and find communities of other freakish mothers, it would have been different. But there was no way I wanted my online profile to show membership in such groups. No matter how many times GaborCorp claimed that our private time online was our business and not taken into account, I never believed it. I didn't want Drew or any other future line manager to know how much I struggled with being a mother. It was too fundamental a flaw to admit to the world. As soon as you have a child, it feels like that's the only metric you can be measured by unless you actively push against it. Even now, with people living on Mars, with others having left our solar system, motherhood is still held at the center of being a woman and it sucks.

Sometimes, on the worst days stuck at home in the first month, I'd fantasize about dying, but only in a painless, romanticized way. Like lying down on some distant grass to slip into an endless sleep. But then that would always be followed by some imagined autopsy in which a man reports on my dead body. "Female in her early thirties. Has recently had a child . . ." and it would all fall apart in a confused mess of hating everything.

I have stopped singing. Even on another planet, I can still be sucked into that well of self-hatred. "Okay," I say into my helmet. "That's enough. There is nothing you can do about any of that right now. Park that shit and focus on something else." After a pause, I say, "Okay." I am talking to myself as I drive on Mars. I smirk, unconcerned. When people really go mad, they don't speak to themselves like this, and definitely not with a pep talk.

Three songs later, I've traveled around to the opposite side of the crater, so I stop the rover and get out. I take a moment to orient myself, confirming my position as best I can without any GPS, before clambering up the ladder riveted to the side of the rover. Standing on top, gaining just that tiny bit more distance to the horizon, I see the top of a familiar mast.

My heart ramps up its activity as I use my retinal lens to zoom in. It looks like a comms mast, probably about five kilometers away, pretty much in line with the estimate I worked out with my geometry program. I can't see anything else, but there are rocks and small canyons between here and that region. Who knows what else could be out there?

Carefully, mindful of how I really cannot afford to have a silly accident out here on my own, I climb back down and get back in the driver's seat. As I set off on the new bearing, I try not to think too much about the fact that I don't have any data on the region I'm driving across. Given the time of year and the fact that I'm not too far away from Principia, I'm not worried about changes caused by the fluctuations in water liquidity in the regolith, but there are other risks. It's not like there are roads here, built on properly surveyed and prepared ground.

The irony that I would really appreciate Principia's input right now doesn't escape me. I slow down, examine the landscape ahead of me with more caution and hope for the best. It increases the risk that someone will discover I'm not where I'm supposed to be, but that's better than increasing the risk of an accident.

The landscape dips and the mast goes out of sight. I hate not using any navigation support and realize that the last time I went anywhere this blind was before I was chipped. When I was a teenager, I was happy to go wriggling into holes in the side of the valley, following cave networks that were far more dangerous than I appreciated. I loved nothing more than getting away from my sister with little more than a head torch, a packed lunch and a geology app. How I craved that life once I left it, where satisfaction at the end of the day could be measured in how many new rock samples I could arrange on my dressing table.

Geena never understood my fascination with "boring old stones," no matter how many times I tried to explain it. For me, it was like a heady mix of time travel and treasure hunting. She was far more interested in animals and insects, always bringing some new critter into the house to be her latest pet. When she brought a snake inside, Dad went ballistic, despite her protestations that it wasn't poisonous. She just wanted to look after everything that couldn't talk back to her. Mother them. I saw no appeal in it, unsurprisingly. I wonder if she had kids.

We were never close as children and positively hated each other in our teens. She blamed me for Dad's imprisonment after I testified against him. She didn't see the difference between a secure mental health facility and a prison. Despite everything he did to us, despite the fact that he almost killed Mum, she couldn't let go of the idea that I was disloyal. She got it into her head—after hearing Mum say as much—that if he was sick, the best place for him was at home. She was too young to understand how dangerous he was and too young to appreciate how much I'd shielded her from him. All those times I came up with excuses to get him out of the house, away from her and Mum, when I could see one of his episodes approaching, she believed I was selfishly monopolizing him.

"You want him all to yourself, all the time!" she blurted out at me one day, not knowing that I'd just spent three hours sitting at the top of the valley with him, convincing him that there was no need to burn our house down. I was too exhausted to argue, shutting her out as best I could and taking solace in identifying the samples I'd gathered on my last trip. The psychiatrists gave it a fancy name after the fact: dissociation. I didn't think a fancy label was needed for

the fact that it was easier and safer to think about rock clas-
sification than about why my father would hit me for things
I hadn't even said.

As I close the distance between myself and the mast, it
suddenly occurs to me that there might be other sensors out
here, able to pick up the rover, or even just the vibrations
caused by its bumping around over the rocks. Without knowing how Banks is hiding me from Principia, I can't be certain
if I am hidden from whatever else could be out here. There's
nothing to be done about it though. If I want to see what that
mast is for, I have to physically go there.

When the terrain starts to rise again out of the depression,
I check the mileage for the current journey. I've traveled four
and a half kilometers since I last stopped the vehicle. Halfway up the next shallow incline, I park the rover once more,
convinced that whatever the mast is part of must be on the
other side of this hill.

This feels like proper Martian exploring as I fight the
downward pull of the scree to climb to the top edge. Even
though this area has been mapped from above, the sense
that there is something unknown—indeed, something being
actively hidden—is quite thrilling. Such a rare flavor of excitement when out of a mersive.

The top of the mast reappears, along with my thrum-
ming heartbeat in my ears. As I near the top, I start to
crouch, just in case there are cameras or people. If it's a
comms tower, there won't be either. But if it's part of something else, there might be.

At the crest of the hill I crouch behind an outcrop of rock
and look down into what appears to be a man-made crater.
The mast rises from the edge of an area about half a kilometer in diameter that's been cleared of rocks and is covered in
trackways of compressed dust, but it's the least interesting
thing here.

There's a launchpad, just like the one at Principia; the strut that holds the rocket firm is on its side, in the position it would be in after takeoff. The pad itself is clear of dust and scorched black. Something has taken off recently and there is a fresh channel in the dust left by the newly retracted umbilical corridor that would have connected it to the base. JeeMuh! Another base that must be down there, below the surface!

A little way away from the launchpad I can see the telltale hump of the access-ramp cover and a few rover tracks nearby. Over on the far side, in the best position to gather the meager sunlight, is a bank of solar panels. There are cam points poking out of the surface and I zoom in on one. It's covered in dust but I still daren't go down there, just in case it can still pick me up.

For a few minutes, all I can do is stare at the launchpad. All this time, there was another base, when I had been told—in fact the whole world had been told—that there was only Principia. It must have been built at the same time, maybe even before our base, and its activity masked by Principia. This is what Travis was hoping I would find.

Even though I can see it with my own eyes, I find myself disbelieving it. Surely a base with its own rovers and a rocket would have been discovered? Unless everyone knows already. Maybe even Banks does.

JeeMuh, what if he tricked me into coming out here?

Get a grip! This is wild speculation and it won't serve me here. I need to find out more about that base without getting close enough to be detected.

I slide down the slope to the rover and retrieve the ground scanner. Like before, I use the panel instead of a direct interface through my chip, to avoid inadvertently pinging Principia. Figuring that I'm actually on the other side of the man-made slope, I take it down to the bottom and put it on the flattest ground I can find. From here, the pulse will go under this artificial hill between us and get a cleaner reading of the subterranean base.

I set a wide scan area and a strong pulse, choosing to take the risk that it will be detected in favor of getting all the information I need in one hit. I double-check the settings and hit the green button.

The data is shown on the screen since I daren't risk sending it to my chip in case it screws with what Banks is doing.

The base is huge! At least three times the size of Principia. There's a massive open space close to the launchpad, large enough to hold a rocket underground, and lots of bizarre shapes that make no sense. I can't see any people on this sort of scan—the pulse bounces back off solid structures—or the sorts of things contained within the rooms, but there are sections that look like replicas of parts of Principia. The living-quarters layout is the same, but repeated three times. A crew of about twenty people could live there.

That's insane. How were they all brought up here in secret? Unless they arrived before Principia was populated and told never to go anywhere near it?

Why the hell has Gabor lied about this place? What could they be working on inside to merit hiding it from the world?

Whatever the reason, I daren't go inside without more sophisticated scanning equipment and a better cover story for my absence from the communal areas. I'm getting hungry too. I save the data in two different files in the ground scanner's local memory and switch it off. As I'm waiting for its stabilizing legs to fully retract, I take one last look around and notice something behind me in the dust.

A footprint. And another. A whole trail of them, heading back toward the Cerberus Palus crater, mere meters away from the route I took to get here. I heft the scanner back into the rover and climb inside, convinced that at any moment, someone from this base is going to find me and chase me off, like some ancient rancher.

I follow the prints for almost a kilometer, which takes me back along the same general route at first, but then through a small canyon. There the footprints stop and the tracks of another rover begin. I follow those to a small crater about half a kilometer away from Cerberus Palus, where it obviously parked, and then the tracks simply disappear.

Frustrated, I climb out and walk around, spotting a groove in the dust that starts a few meters away, as if the rover had suddenly shrunk to the size of a small pebble. On closer inspection, I realize that the driver must have dragged something behind the vehicle to obscure the tracks, not realizing that a pebble got caught and made a new track of its own.

The tiny track is heading for Principia, only going round the opposite side of the crater from the edge I followed. Either someone else back at my base knows about the other station and has visited it, or one of the secret base inhabitants has been spying on Principia. Either way, there is at least one more person on this planet who knows about both bases. The question is, who?

17

I PULL MYSELF out of the suit and finally let out a sigh of relief once I've put my feet on the cool floor of the base again. I retrieve my clothes from the locker, dress and then get the ground scanner from the compartment on the other side of the dust lock. It's been cleaned and the data is still there. Good. All I need to do is get to Banks and tell him to stop fooling Principia, and then I'll feel safe to upload the data to a private folder.

I step out into the corridor only to see the edge of someone's back as they go round the corner. I freeze as the sound of their footsteps stops. They must have heard the dust lock door open. Damn my own stupidity! I should have checked everyone's locations first.

There's enough time to get only three steps away from it and for the doors to start closing when Petranek rounds the corner. "There you are!" ze says with obvious relief. "JeeMuh, where the hell have you been?" Ze holds up a hand before I reply. "I found her! By the dust lock." There's a pause and I watch hir eyes take in the ground scanner and the tips of the onesie sleeves, which are longer than those of my loose jumper. "Wait, were you outside?"

I can already hear someone running down the corridor behind me. It seems absurd to deny it, and it's clear they've been looking for me. Shit, why didn't Banks warn me? He set me up!

Just as I'm silently cursing his name, Banks almost collides with me from behind. "Anna!" Then he sees Petranek coming closer and his expression shifts from panic to a blinking, sweaty relief.

"We've been looking everywhere for you," Banks says. "Arnolfi needed to speak with you." He hugs me. "I couldn't warn you," he whispers in my ear. "And you weren't in your room," he continues, loudly enough to let everyone hear as he lets me go, "even though Principia said you were. It was so weird. Are you okay?"

Petranek is right next to us now and I can hear Elvan and Arnolfi approaching too. There's no way I can cover this up. Judging by what Banks has said, something went wrong and now he's terrified I'll drop him in it too. "I'm okay," I say, realizing I haven't said anything. "See? Look, I'm fine."

Elvan and Arnolfi arrive, and the relief on Elvan's face makes me blush. "I don't know what all the fuss is about. I'm fine."

"You weren't in your quarters," Arnolfi says.

"Is that a problem? I wasn't aware we were confined to them."

"It's a problem when Principia says you're there and you don't respond," she replies.

"I had a DND notice up. I didn't—" I almost say that I didn't hear the request to enter, but I need to drop that ruse. "I didn't think that anyone needed me."

"You were outside?" Elvan says, catching up. "In a storm? By yourself? What the hell were you thinking?"

"That goes against every safety protocol I can think of," Arnolfi says. Her voice is calm, quiet, but there is such rage in her eyes it makes me flinch. Then it is gone, but I am certain I've seen her look at me like that before. When?

"It would have been, if there was actually a storm," I say. "But there wasn't. Principia lied about it."

"I think you need to come to my office," Arnolfi says, and I feel a confusing flash of fear, but Petranek shakes hir head and speaks up before I've had a chance to respond.

"No, not yet. Anna, are you saying that the rating-seven storm—that's on all the weather satellite pictures, the cams, and confirmed by the weather stations outside—is bollocks?"

"Yes, I am," I say firmly. "And I don't want to discuss this with you in private," I say to Arnolfi. It isn't just the fact that this deception needs to stop; it's that I don't want to be alone with that woman. Why do I feel that so strongly? "This is something that everyone here needs to be aware of," I say, focusing on one problem at a time. "Principia has been lying to all of us about the storm, and about something else too."

"Anna, it is my firm belief that you are experiencing a psychotic episode." Arnolfi takes a step toward me. "We knew you were at high risk of one, and this reckless behavior has all the hallmarks of—"

"Now, just wait a bloody minute!" I regret raising my voice, but I can't let this damn psych plant ideas like that. I know, more than most, how quickly those roots can grow deep. "You can go out there, right now, and see for yourself, before you start making accusations like that."

"Wait, the storm has passed," Elvan says, eyes staring into the middle distance. "It's clear out there now."

I laugh, trying to stifle the slightly hysterical edge to it. "Of course it is. Principia knows I'm calling its bluff. Go ahead—ask it how long it's been clear out there and I'll prove to you that it was lying."

"Would you like me to participate in this meeting?" Principia asks, and I'm the only one to say no. The avatar joins the group, smiling politely. Now that it's standing next to Elvan, the resemblance between them actively embarrasses me.

"When did the storm pass?" Elvan asks it.

"There wasn't one!" I say.

"The weather conditions have changed in the past three hours. The wind speed has dropped to three miles per hour. The temperature is—"

"When did the wind speed drop?" Elvan asks.

"The wind speed started to drop two hours and forty-five minutes ago."

I can see Banks looking up the time that we went outside, but I don't need to. I know how long I was gone and that Principia has given the only time window that could make me look like I'm lying. Two hours and forty minutes ago I was telling Banks that the storm was fake. Neither of us looked up the conditions then; we knew from the meeting that the conditions were supposed to be bad outside. Now Principia is making it look like I made an error, that by the time I stepped outside, the storm was already abating.

I am being undermined by a fucking AI.

"Well, Principia confirms that there wasn't a storm when Anna went out," Arnolfi says. Her stare is making my skin crawl. "Principia, how long ago did Dr. Kubrin ask for a weather update?"

"Dr. Kubrin was informed of the storm eight hours and thirty seven minutes ago, when I was forced to return a drone under her command to base."

"And it was mentioned again at the meeting," I say. "That was hours later."

"But you didn't check the weather between the meeting and when you left the base," Arnolfi says.

"Dr. Kubrin has not left the base," Principia says.

"I have! I went out there and it was obvious there was no storm at all today. The tracks from when I went out there with Petranek were still there!"

At least, I know they were there farther away from the base, when I picked them up again following our original change in route. I didn't look near the entrance. "Principia made up that storm to stop me from using the drone. This is what I'm trying to tell you; we're all being duped."

Petranek leans against the wall. "I have no idea what the hell is going on," ze says. "Principia says there was a storm, Anna doesn't believe it and goes outside but Principia says she never left the base."

"I did go outside!" I rest the back of my head against the same wall as Petranek. There is no way I can avoid a disciplinary here. But that's better than being accused of having a psychotic break. "It's just that I had to hide it from Principia because it wouldn't let me out of the base if the storm was going on outside."

"Dr. Kubrin, you never made a request to leave the base after the storm abated," Principia says. "How can I have denied you permission to leave if you never requested it?"

"I . . . I just knew you wouldn't."

Elvan winces. "You say you went outside. You certainly weren't in your quarters when Principia thought you were. How do you explain that?"

I can feel the heat crawling up the skin of my neck, into my cheeks. I keep my eyes fixed on Elvan, making sure I don't glance at Banks and give him away. "I tricked it. It's hard to explain."

"You tricked Principia?" Petranek's arms are folded; hir head is tipped to the side, an eyebrow raised, all the body language suggesting ze doesn't believe me. "How?"

"That isn't even possible," Banks says, and I look at him, silently screaming his name in my head. He's throwing me to the dogs here to save himself.

"I can't . . . it's . . ." Every single thing that springs to mind sounds like complete bullshit—because it is complete bullshit! I can't even pretend to pass off what he did as my own work because I have no idea how he did it, and anything technical I try to say will just be refuted by Principia and Petranek.

But I can't say it was him. No matter what they do to me, it would be so much worse for him.

"Principia, where is Dr. Kubrin now?" Arnolfi asks.

"Dr. Kubrin is two point five meters away from the entrance to the dust lock," Principia says. "I cannot account for her movements between the time she entered her room at fifteen hundred hours, three minutes and twenty seconds, and the time she was sighted by Dr. Petranek in this corridor."

"Would it be possible for Dr. Kubrin to leave the base without your knowledge?" Elvan asks.

"It would not be," Principia says, "if all systems are working within established parameters."

"But you know they weren't, because Principia thought I was in my room and I wasn't," I say. I pause, trying to keep hold of what I'm actually trying to prove to them here. "Look, the important thing is that I did go outside and I went to a place that Principia has been hiding from me, and there's another base there, far bigger than this one."

Petranek half coughs, half laughs. "What? Are you crazy?"

"No, I'm fucking not!" I yell, furious that I'm being accused of that on one of the rare occasions when I'm confident of my own mental health. "I've just been there and I can prove it to you!"

"I think this has gone far enough," Arnolfi says. "Dr. Kubrin."

I kneel down in front of the ground scanner, opening the panel and doing my very best to ignore her voice and the awful flicker of fear it's sending through me.

"Dr. Kubrin. Anna." Arnolfi's voice is getting more insistent.

"I did a ground scan, right by the base," I say. The interface is sluggish, or does it just seem that way because of the pressure? "I stored the data here. I can show you."

"Just let her do this," Elvan is saying to Arnolfi.

I tap through to access the memory. There's nothing there. I go back a couple of steps, feeling like my stomach is trying to claw its way out of my throat. "I don't understand," I whisper, now stabbing at the panel's display. "I saved it in two different places and it's all gone."

The silence being woven by the others above my head feels like it's taking on a physical weight. No matter how many times I try to access the files, there's nothing there.

"There is no data saved on that device, Dr. Kubrin," Principia says. "Can I help you to—"

"You wiped it!" I shout at the avatar. "That's why it was slow. You fucking bastard! You wiped the files as I was trying to find them!"

"Anna." Elvan catches the scanner as it tips away, my hands focused on reaching for Principia's throat. Petranek grabs my arms and pulls me back.

"Whoa! Easy, Anna. There's no one there to . . . errr . . . strangle, remember?"

I scan their faces. Even Banks is looking at me the way I once looked at my father. "Oh Jesus, none of you believe me! I went there! It's about five kilometers northwest of the Cerberus Palus crater. There was a launchpad—I saw it! It was scorched and the stabilizer was flat on the ground. Something has taken off from there in the last few days. I swear it!"

Arnolfi's glare is terrifying. "Dr. Anna Kubrin, I am confining you to quarters until your mental health status has been fully assessed by myself and Dr. Elvan. Any criminal investigation into the possible corruption of Principia's primary functioning will be discussed following our assessment."

"No! I don't need a fucking mental health assessment! I was there! Why would I make that up? Why would I do that?"

"Let's get you to your room," Elvan says softly, allowing Banks to take the scanner. He touches my arm and I jerk it away from him.

"It's Principia. It's hiding the other base. You just have to come with me. It'll take an hour, tops, and then you can see for yourself!" I look to Petranek, whose discomfort is clear. When I turn to Banks, he lifts the scanner, mumbles something about taking it back and hurries off.

"It really is for the best that you come with me now," Elvan says, his voice smooth and calm.

I am not like my father. I will not lash out again. I fill my lungs and breathe out slowly, straightening my back and looking Arnolfi in the eye. "This is not immersion psychosis, but I understand your concerns and I will cooperate fully."

With a triumphant thrill, I watch her step aside and look away. She seems weak all of a sudden, and I notice her trembling hands as I walk past her. Then I feel like a bully. No one here likes conflict, and that was probably just as hard for her as it was for me. But then I remember the note and push that guilt away. I have enough of that to fill me for a lifetime without adding more.

Elvan is silent on the way back to my room and doesn't cross the threshold when we reach it. "I think it would be a good idea for us all to take a break and speak again in a little while," he says. I want to embrace him, or rather, be held by him. Now the drama has passed, I feel shivery and uncertain. I want to feel where the edges of myself are.

"Probably for the best," I reply, going in. "But I am telling the truth. This looks bad, but I know what I saw. Something took off from there, in the last day or two, I reckon. Gabor is up to something and he's hiding it from everyone on Earth."

He's trying so hard to seem neutral, to not give any indication of doubt or belief. I understand why; if I am breaking, he doesn't want to reinforce the delusion, just as much as he doesn't want to make me feel even more isolated.

"I'll be back later to do a physical exam. Your MyPhys data is showing elevated cortisol and other stress markers. Try to rest. Have something to eat and drink if you can."

"But no mersives, right?"

My attempt at a wry smile seems way off target. He merely nods and, after a brief hesitation, closes the door.

I strip off the soiled onesie, dump it in the recycler, and shower. My mind drifts from thoughts of the secret base to the comms blackout preventing contact with Charlie and Mia. I wonder how Charlie is coping with the loss of contact. What have they told him on Earth? And no doubt Mum is worried sick. She'll be convinced there's been a terrible accident here and that it's a total media blackout while GaborCorp figures out how to handle it PR-wise.

There's nothing I can do about that though. Then I remember Travis's dead drop. I've devalued the leverage potential of the information about the other base by blurting it all out to the rest of the crew. Maybe the dead drop uses a different means of communication though. I hurry into the bathroom, look at myself in the mirror and start recording immersively.

"The comms have gone down. I have information but I don't know if anything can get through to you. I need to know this works. If you're clever enough to set all this up, you'll be clever enough to get a message to me. Let me know what's going on, and I'll send you what you want." I end the recording, name the file "ready for home" and store it in the folder he sent me. I try not to think too much about a back door in my chip being exploited to send that to Earth.

I sit on the bed, tired. What bothers me about the way Arnolfi has handled this is that Banks might think I tricked him, or at the very least that he got sucked into my delusion. But with Principia acting against me, it's impossible to prove I'm telling the truth. At least I haven't implicated him, and he knows that. I shouldn't have thought this was a setup—why would he do something that would make an inquiry more likely?

Now that I have time to myself, the anger is setting in. Why didn't I take some retinal-cam shots of the other base? Why didn't I check the weather before I left?

The latter is unfathomable until I remember Principia suggesting, when it took back control of the drone, that the storm would probably last a couple of days. It just didn't occur to me to check the weather again after that.

As for the lack of other evidence I could have gathered, it's less clear-cut. I was shocked and worried about getting back, but those are poor excuses.

I think back to standing on the crest of that hill, looking down at the launchpad. I did really go there. I did see that. Yet why is there the creeping fear that I imagined it? Sitting here on the bed, back in normal, comfortable clothes, it's almost as easy to believe none of it happened.

Shit. What if none of it did?

"Stop it," I whisper to myself.

Principia pings me, making me jump. "May I speak with you, Dr. Kubrin?" the message reads.

I want to tell it to fuck right off, but I check myself. Feeling personally affronted by an AI is pathetic. It's just a tool, after all. It hasn't *chosen* to screw me over.

"Okay," I say out loud. "Come and talk to me, then."

The avatar appears to walk out of the bathroom, presumably because I am sitting on the bed resting my back against the wall, so it can't pull its usual trick. It makes me laugh, unexpectedly, to imagine it's just used the loo, and it looks at me with a semblance of mild confusion.

"What do you want?" I say to it.

"I would like to know how you caused the error that led me to report that you were here earlier when you were not."

"I'd like to know why you're happy to make everyone else think I'm mad. We don't always get what we want, do we?"

"I am not happy about that. I am incapable—"

"Oh, give it a rest. You deleted that data from the ground scanner, didn't you?"

"I am not at liberty to discuss anything that could be relevant to your mental health assessment."

"You have an answer for everything, don't you?"

"Yes."

I laugh. It is completely oblivious to the bitterness and passive aggression in my tone. "Was Arnolfi behind that order?"

"Yes, in line with standard protocol relating to the management of mental health disorders."

"The thing that really pisses me off," I say, shuffling to the edge of the bed, "is that it is entirely within your power to prove that I am not having a psychotic break. Is this an order from Stefan Gabor? Is he the one who is ordering you to keep that other base hidden?"

"I am not at liberty to discuss anything that could be—"

"Yeah, yeah." I hold my hand up. "I got it the first time."

"However," Principia says, "not only are you at liberty to provide the information I have requested; you are obligated to comply."

"I'll have to leave that to be addressed at my tribunal," I say.

"Would you not prefer to cooperate, in order to reduce the likelihood of prosecution?"

With a sigh, I say, "It's not that simple. Unlike you, I have personal reasons to withhold information."

Principia looks for all the world like he is mulling that over. "Are you hoping that if you remain silent and a full investigation is ordered, evidence will be found to support your claims regarding my actions?"

"That hadn't even occurred to me, but thanks. I'll bear that in mind."

"You are welcome, Dr. Kubrin."

I smirk. AIs are amazing things, but talking to them still doesn't feel the same as talking to a real person. "Careful," I say. "You wouldn't want this conversational log to be reviewed and have you seen as encouraging me to resist, would you?"

Principia gives the sort of smile that would, were it a real man, make me think that was exactly the reason why it had said it. It's unsettling to suddenly find yourself wondering if an AI is better at brinkmanship than you are.

"Has it occurred to you that keeping me confined to quarters is reducing my ability to do my job?"

"I have given that careful consideration, Dr. Kubrin, and have concluded that given you have all the materials you require to paint in this room, along with reference materials that you have explored immersively, there is no impediment to your primary role."

"You'd better stop distracting me, then, hadn't you?"

At least it's intelligent enough to understand a polite request to bugger off.

When I'm properly alone again, I look at the blank canvas. I may as well paint. There is literally nothing better to do right now.

I find the sketch pad, some of the rubbings still trapped between the pages from where I erased the mast. The basic composition is there, but I feel something is missing, other than the mast.

I add some detail to the cluster of boulders as I listen to an ambient-music playlist that's free of vocals and heavy beats. Soon my mind is only partially on the page as I start to wonder which approach to take with Arnolfi. I feel strangely calm, even though my career is in jeopardy. Somehow I can't muster any concern about it, even when I think about how Charlie would react to news of a disciplinary. None of it seems that important in comparison to the existence of that base. How do I get back out there without getting Banks into trouble? How do I prove it's real? Right now, for everyone else here, it's as fake as my wedding ring.

I haven't thought about that for days and I can't even remember when I put it back on. How could I have forgotten it? It shows how little I care for my marriage. I still can't bring myself to take it off though.

An hour passes and the playlist comes to an end. I rest the sketch pad on the bed and get myself a coffee, wondering why Arnolfi hasn't come to do the assessment. It's getting late.

I prop the sketch pad against the wall and stand back to judge the picture. The boulders are there in the foreground, the volcano peak is in the far distance, as I planned, but the new addition to the picture is not my usual fare. I can't decide if it works or not, but somehow it feels right.

In the foreground, running below the boulders, are several shadows, as if there are people out of shot with the sun behind them, a sun far stronger than it really is here. Their shadows are the only sign they are there, giving the viewer of the painting the sense that there are other people behind them, looking at the same view. At least, I hope they will. I'll see how they turn out on the canvas.

There's a knock on the door and all the tension rushes

back into my body. I set down the cup, trying to loosen up my shoulders, and call, "Come in," as confidently as I can.

Elvan stands in the doorway, holding a small medkit. "Hi. Can I come in?"

I nod and close the door behind him. When he sets the kit down on the desk I flip the cover of the sketch pad over the picture. I hate people seeing my work before I'm ready to show them.

"Has Arnolfi spoken to you yet?"

I shake my head. "I guess she wanted me to cool off."

"You seemed to calm down pretty quick, considering everything that was said," he replies as he opens the kit. "A lot of people would have really lost it."

"Were you worried I would?"

He turns to look at me over his shoulder. "No," he finally says. "I think you handle pressure well. You dealt with Banks at his worst. He's changed his mind about you."

"Yeah, now he thinks I'm mentally ill."

"I didn't mean that. Could you take a seat and roll up your sleeve for me, please?"

I perch on the edge of the bed and do as he asks. "Can't MyPhys tell you everything you need to know?"

"It can tell me a lot, but not everything. And I don't like to rely on it too much. This is just a formality."

"I suppose you need to take blood too? Just to make sure I'm not tripping on anything?"

He secures the blood pressure cuff. "I do need to take blood, but I don't expect to see anything untoward in it. It's more to rule out a few things and to put it on record that you're clean. Just in case there's a tribunal."

I wait as the cuff constricts, silently vowing that I'll get evidence of that base, tribunal or not. His attention is on his task; he's calling something up in his visual field and tapping away, humming as he does so.

I recognize the tune. I was listening to it earlier. "How do you know that song?"

"Hmm?"

"That soul song. Where did you hear it?"

He looks blank. "I don't know. I don't listen to American soul."

"No, it's Russian. A band that was big about thirty years ago. They played a few years ago in a club in Manchester." I realize how stupid this sounds. "They're really obscure."

He shrugs. "I don't know where I got it from. It's been stuck in my head for bloody days. Blood pressure is slightly elevated but given what's going on, I'm not too worried. Perhaps you were singing it and I heard you or something."

"Perhaps," I echo, not believing it.

"Blood test next," he says, putting the cuff back in his kit. "Just like the one you had a couple of days ago. You must be feeling like a bit of a pincushion. Sorry about that."

"What's a pincushion?"

He grins as he pulls out the pen-shaped device. "I asked the patient who first said that to me the same thing. Back when people used to sew, they used pins to hold the pieces of fabric together." He adjusts the position of my arm as he talks. I love the sound of his voice. It's so soothing. I tell myself that it's all just a bedside manner thing, but even so, he has it in spades. "When they weren't using the pins, they'd be stuck in a little squishy ball made of stuffed fabric, so they were safe. That was called a pincushion. He complained I was treating him like one. Hold still—it's applying the anesthetic now and will be done in a few seconds."

"Was he very ill, that man?"

Elvan nods. "He was old and had had a life that would have crushed most people. He lived through the collapse of democracy and the riots in the thirties. His wife died in those. He had some stories to tell. Okay, that's all done now. Thanks."

There's a tiny dot of sealant on the inside of my elbow. "I'm not having a psychotic break," I say. "Surely you can tell that from my brain activity?"

He takes the vial of blood from the pen and pushes it into the side of the medkit box. "That's more Arnolfi's specialty."

"Oh, come on. You know this stuff too."

"I'm not an expert though, and the brain is such a complex thing. Not everybody presents the same way neurophysiologically. I'm not supposed to discuss this with you."

"Do you believe what I said about the other base?"

He puts the pen device back into the kit and rests his hands on either side of it. "Anna, I can't talk about this with you. It wouldn't be right. I could do more harm than good, and I would never want to harm you. Ever."

There's a thrill in my chest when he uses my first name. Has he done that before? There's a knock on the door and I tense up again. "Shit. Arnolfi's here," I say. "You'd better go, I guess."

But it isn't Arnolfi at the door; it's Banks and Petranek. Their expressions are grave, and for an awful moment I think that they've come to tell me that I've been sentenced to death.

"Kubrin, I'm sorry," Banks says, stepping inside. He looks so serious, as if he's trying to work out how to tell me the means of execution they have planned for me. Petranek follows him in, unable to meet my eyes, all of hir usual relaxed confidence gone. I start to shake. "About what happened before," Banks begins and I hold my breath. "We know you're telling the truth."

18

MY BODY IS flooded with relief and then anger, but I suppress the latter, grateful that I have support now at least. "You've known about it all along?" I ask, trying my best to keep the sharpness from my voice as I move farther into the room. It's a little crowded with all of us in here now.

"No, not at all," Banks says, as if he's horrified by the idea. "We just checked the satellites in orbit."

"Hacked, more like," Petranek says, giving him a sideways glance. "It wasn't easy."

"So you saw the base?"

They both nod. I can see how bad they feel about what was said before, and my shoulders drop as the adrenaline eases.

"Not in real time," Banks adds. "From the last mapping survey done years ago. It was the best way to get something without setting the tin man off. The live feeds are better protected than Gabor's personal data vault. I found all the raw images, before the data was processed, looked up the area you mentioned and"—he spreads his hands, as if imagining a rabbit popping up out of a magician's hat—"there it was. That whole area was excluded from the released images. You were right." He looks me straight in the eye as he says it and I feel just that little bit better.

"But that's . . ." Elvan was leaning against the desk as if he needed to steady himself, fumbling for words.

"Crazy?" Petranek says, then gives me an apologetic smile. "I'm really sorry for not backing you up. It's just such a ludicrous thing to find a few kilometers away, you know? I feel like such a twat for not having found it myself. If you hadn't started looking there, we'd never have even looked, let alone found it."

Elvan frowns at me. "Were you tipped off?"

"No," I say, truthfully. Travis didn't know what was being hidden, after all.

"It just happened to be in the first area you just randomly chose to look in?"

"Are you trying to say something?" The muscles in my back knot up again.

He shakes his head, frowning to himself. "I'm not implying anything. I'm just wondering if you saw something that made you look in that direction. I mean, you could have chosen so many places to go to, and yet the first trip out sets you on the path to finding the other base."

"I guess," I say, feeling unnerved. Did Travis plant something else in my chip, something subliminal? "But regardless of the luck involved, we're all on the same page now, right? You believe me about the base." All three of them nod and I feel an easing of the tension at my core. "What did Arnolfi say? I take it that's why she didn't bother coming to assess me?"

Banks and Petranek exchange a look. "She isn't on the base," Petranek says. "And the . . . 'tin man' won't tell us where she is. It's not like the glitch with you; it's being open about her not being here."

"One of the rovers is gone," Banks adds.

"Well, it's obvious, then, isn't it?" I say. "She's gone to find the other base. She believed me, even though she pretended not to, and has gone to look for herself." I bite back the other things that spring to mind about her and the way she handled the confrontation. They are her friends after all.

"I think it may be more than that," Elvan says. "I think she already knew. She's been under extreme stress the last few days. I had to speak to her about it; MyPhys alerted me. She told me it was something to do with news from home and that she didn't want to talk about it."

"I thought she looked rough at the meeting, earlier," Banks says. "And she's losing weight. I thought her cheekbones were more pronounced."

When Petranek gives him a look, he shrugs. "I notice those sorts of changes. The camerawork and the show make me think about how people look. I was worried she'd look different for the next season and that there would be gossip on the feeds about it. You know what those bloody harpies are like."

"If she already knew, and the tin man is hiding her location now, they're both in on the secret," Petranek says. "And she was willing to rake you over the coals to keep it," ze adds, looking at me. "This is deeply fucked up."

"You said you did a ground scan." Elvan still seems rather shaken, but I think it's more the possibility that Arnolfi has been hiding this than the news of the base that's upset him. "What did you see?"

"It's much bigger than this base. I think it could have housed about twenty people, maybe more if they got cozy. It looked like there was a really large underground space near the launchpad."

"Like a hangar?" Petranek asks.

"I don't know—maybe. I could tell you a lot more about how unnatural the crater that the base is set in is, but that's not so useful."

"So how do we handle this now?" Banks asks. "It's obvious that GaborCorp has been doing this on the quiet, and if it's a base that big, they've been bringing people and equipment up here in secret."

"I still can't quite believe it would be possible though," Elvan says. "That's not a small thing to hide, and it's not as if it's on the other side of the planet. It's a short drive away, for heaven's sake!"

"The proximity suggests that it was built at the same time as this one, maybe using the same core systems," Petranek mulls aloud. "It's far easier to manage a parallel build when there isn't a huge distance involved. You can share resources more easily too, and a lot of the weather data gathered for us could be used for that base too, without needing to ping satellites. The tin man may well be running both."

"That would make a lot of sense," Banks agrees. "Then when the other base needed to do stuff outside, we could be told there's a storm and kept indoors. It's just attention management, really, isn't it? That and data control."

"It hid drone data from me," I say. "I wouldn't have noticed if I wasn't examining it closely. You guys have been steered away from going in that direction and told to focus on other things. It's so easy to hide stuff going on out there when the tin man controls all the data."

"But what is the point?" Elvan pulls the chair out from under the desk and sits heavily. "It can't just be for the show. They could run that from a studio on Earth now. They could ship us back home, get us to sign a contract to stay isolated while we film a few more seasons, and it would cost a fraction of what it does now."

"I think it's a cargo thing," I say. "It's probably all to do with having an excuse to ship stuff to Mars, right? If we weren't here, and Gabor wanted to send people or equipment or whatever to the real base, someone would notice and start asking questions. If Arnolfi is in on this, she and the tin man could get those extra things smuggled to the other base without you guys finding out. It could be off-loaded while still on the pad and driven off, without even needing to use the umbilical corridor."

"And I thought we were here for science," Petranek says, gloomy. "This is so fucking depressing."

"I think the science is still valuable," Elvan says, but his optimism sounds hollow.

"I bet the science they're doing in the other base is far more interesting though." Banks sits on the bed. "So, who wants to go and find out what they're doing there?"

"Well, obviously, I'd be all over that like a rash," Petranek begins, "but there is the whole megasecret aspect of this to consider. They might, I dunno, have guns or something."

"You play too many shooters," Banks says. "They're likely to be just like us. But better paid, I bet."

We exchange a look and there is warmth in his wry smile. He's grateful that I didn't betray him.

"Have you tried contacting Arnolfi?" Both Banks and Petranek nod.

"No response. And the local comms are working fine." Petranek sits next to Banks and nudges him with hir shoulder. "Cheer up, Banks. Are you worried one of those people at the other base will have been here longer than you?"

He nudges hir back. "Bugger off. I'm wondering whether GaborCorp cut us off because our resident supersleuth was getting close to springing their secret."

"That's occurred to me too," I confess. I feel strangely tired. Maybe it's the relief that we are discussing this together. I didn't realize how much energy it took to be suspicious of everyone around me. Now it's us against Arnolfi, instead of just me. No, I mustn't think that way. This isn't a fight.

Elvan twitches suddenly and turns away from all of us. "Is it Arnolfi?" Petranek asks, but he holds up a hand. A couple of seconds later, he stands up.

I hold my breath, expecting something awful. His hands move, tapping invisible options, and then he finally turns back to us. "I've just given Principia permission to make Arnolfi unconscious. She was attempting suicide."

"What the fuck!" Petranek leaps up. "Where is she? Principia? Where is Arnolfi?"

A box appears, asking for permission to use my wall, which I grant immediately. A map is displayed, a flashing green dot showing her location. "She went to the other base," I say, recognizing the local landmarks. "That's where it is."

"We have to go and get her," Elvan says, grabbing his medkit.

"All of us," Banks says. "No secrets, and we watch each other's backs, okay?"

We all nod. "We'll meet in the dust lock," Petranek says, opening the door. "Banks, bring your portable, just in case."

"Your portable what?" I ask as they all hurry out.

"You'll see," he says and then I'm alone again.

Half an hour later I'm sitting in the back of the rover with Elvan, Banks in the front passenger seat, Petranek behind the wheel. Now that Principia knows we have to go and collect Arnolfi, there's no concern about using the nav system, so there's no need for me to provide any directions. All I can do is sit there, wondering what to do.

I haven't told any of them about the note. I almost did, a couple of times, but whenever I plan what to say about it,

I sound insane. The same with my wedding ring. There is something very wrong here. I just know it, when I consider the note, the ring and the fact that Arnolfi went out to the other base by herself. Add in Elvan's comments about how easily and quickly I found something that has been hidden from them for so long and that terrible sense of unease deepens.

After what was said outside the dust lock though, I can't bear the thought of anyone doubting my sanity. Trying to draw conclusions from these disparate nuggets of weirdness feels too close to being a conspiracy theorist. I smirk at that as I gaze out over the Martian wilderness. We're driving toward the best proof of a conspiracy we could ever hope to find. I should be thinking more along these lines.

I feel a pressure on my right hand, the one resting on the seat between me and Elvan, and see that he has rested his over it. He's staring out at the landscape through the opposite window and doesn't look at me as his gloved hand closes around mine, squeezing it gently.

It feels like a deeply intimate gesture, despite the fact that we're with other people and are wearing thick gloves. There's something about the way it seems absentminded of him, like there's some part of him seeking contact without being consciously aware of it.

"Are you okay?" I ask him on a private channel.

"Worried about Arnolfi," he says. "What made her try to take her suit off? Principia interpreted it as suicidal behavior, which it is, but still. Just seems so out of character. What if someone else was with her, forcing her?"

"Wouldn't their APA have shut them down? It would be easy to recognize as harmful behavior. Everyone at that base must be on the same contracts as us, and bound by the same rules."

"Yes, I suppose so." He sounds unconvinced. Then he

notices what he's done with his hand and starts to pull away, but I hold on to him.

"It's okay," I say. "I think we both need this."

"I shouldn't have presumed."

"It's not the bloody nineteenth century! It's fine."

He lets his hand rest back where it was and we travel on in silence.

"Nearly there," Petranek says eventually.

"I just remembered something," I say. "When I was coming back before, I saw that someone from that base had gone toward ours, first on foot, then in a rover that they got into in a small canyon. I'll show you all on the map."

"Maybe that was Arnolfi," Banks says grimly. "If she knew about it before today, that is."

"Or one of the people from the other base, giving Arnolfi the benefit of the doubt here," Elvan says. He pulls his hand away as Banks twists in his seat.

"Elvan, she went there without telling anyone, Principia covering her. I think the writing is on the wall."

Elvan doesn't reply.

I see a familiar slope rising ahead. "That scree is pretty loose; it's probably best for us to park on the level, then climb up."

Petranek takes my advice and we get out. "She's just on the other side," Elvan says, and the rear compartment of the rover is opened.

I wait as he takes out his medkit and another bag, which he hefts over his shoulder. Banks removes a small case, gives me a nervous glance and slams the rover shut.

"Arnolfi is effectively asleep," Elvan says as we all climb the slope together. "MyPhys isn't reporting any injuries, but I think it might be wise to wake her up back at our base, in a familiar environment. She's likely to be disoriented and she might still be distressed."

"Agreed," says Banks. "But I think we should get the lay of the land here before we go back. Don't you?"

Elvan gives a noncommittal grunt as Petranek says, "Hell, yeah!"

I stay quiet, feeling that this isn't my mission. We pass the tracks I left before, and the messy impression of where I parked the rover and then turned it around. Running parallel a few meters away to my left are the tracks left by another rover, presumably the one that Arnolfi traveled in. We reach the crest and look down into the fake crater together.

"Holy shit," Petranek says.

Arnolfi's rover is on its side, having tumbled down the scree by the look of it. There's a set of footprints running from it to the launchpad and then on toward the hump of the ramp roof.

"She must be on the ramp," Elvan says. "MyPhys didn't report any injury from the— Oh for fuck's sake, Principia!"

"What is it?" Banks asks.

"It's just released her data. She has a broken arm and mild concussion." He jumps down the slope, landing halfway down and sliding the rest of the way to start sprinting as soon as he reaches the flat ground.

The rest of us follow, the others pulling ahead, used to throwing themselves around in low g and more confident in the suits.

Arnolfi is lying in a crumpled heap just outside the storm doors of the exit ramp. Elvan repositions her carefully and peers through the visor of her helmet. I catch a glimpse of some blood that has run down the inside of the plasglass and my stomach heaves. I turn away to see Banks and Petranek in close conference a little way away. It looks like Petranek is trying to convince Banks to do something. Probably to break into the base.

"Is there anything I can do to help?" I say to Elvan.

"No. She's stable. MyPhys is already treating the shock. I need to get her to the rover and back to our base. You could help me with that."

I look over at the other two. It looks like Banks is giving in, nodding and walking toward the far side of the storm doors.

Petranek notices my attention. "We're going to hook up to the system here, see if anyone is inside."

"Have you asked the prince?" Elvan suggests and Petranek laughs like he's asked the most ridiculous question.

"We're negotiating," Banks says. "The prince is not being very helpful."

"Ze isn't talking to us," Petranek adds. "Ze says ze's not at liberty to answer any of our questions."

I open a private channel to Banks. "Are you going to break in? Is that what that case is for?"

He twists around and gives me a nod. He doesn't want to risk his response being logged. "I wouldn't dream of hacking into GaborCorp equipment, Dr. Kubrin," he replies as he kneels down and opens the case. Satisfied, I close the channel.

"We're going to take Arnolfi back to base," Elvan says.

"We need to stay together," Petranek replies. "This is serious shit, Elvan."

"There's probably a medlab inside this base," I say. "Why don't we take her inside with us?"

Elvan smiles at me. "I don't know why I didn't think of that. It might not be stocked though."

"But we know someone was here, because of the launchpad. If nothing else, there will be printers," I say.

He considers it and then nods. "I'd rather treat her here before taking her across that terrain." Elvan straps Arnolfi's arm to her body so we can carry her without risking further injury. We get her to the storm-shield door as it starts to open.

"I managed to change the prince's mind," Banks says with a grin.

Petranek claps Banks on the shoulder. "If you weren't such a dedicated company man, I'd think you were one shady bastard," ze says to him.

Banks remains silent, pulling a couple of wires out of the manual-override panel and tucking them back into the case. I get only a glimpse of what looks like an old-fashioned screen and keyboard before it's closed.

It's dark inside, with only a couple of meters of ramp exposed. We all switch on the torches built into our helmets and head inside.

It could be Mars Principia. Everything looks the same. Banks opens the air-lock doors and takes us through the process of getting inside manually. There's a brief debate about whether it's safe to enter a secret base that isn't answering any knocks and has a hostile AI, but there's no way any of us are just going to turn around and go back to base without getting some answers first.

There are suits still attached to the wall in the dust lock, but it's no effort to remove them. Elvan and I wait for Banks and Petranek to get inside; then we unstrap Arnolfi's arm and hold her up until the others pull her through from the other side. Elvan winces at every jolt, as if it is his arm that is broken, but there's nothing else we can do, short of putting her through the equipment hatch, and with those injuries, he doesn't want to risk her being blasted by the cleaners on the way through.

As Banks plugs his case in on the far side of the dust lock, only one set of doors between us and the base proper now, Elvan does a proper assessment of Arnolfi's injuries and straps her arm up again.

"It's not too bad a break," he says with relief. "It won't take me long to set it in the medlab."

"Is anyone else here?" I ask. "Are they actively trying to keep us out?"

"With the prince being such a pain in the ass it's hard to tell," Banks says. "Our attempts to contact them may be being blocked. Ah, that's it. Gotcha, you difficult bastard."

The doors open and the lights in the corridor come on. Even though I know these are standard energy-saving devices, the same as the ones in Principia, I can't help but feel like the base is empty.

Elvan goes over to the lockers and opens the one on the end. Inside there is a stretcher; he unfolds it and clicks the pieces of its rigid frame into place. "Can I have a hand getting Arnolfi to the medlab? I'm going to assume it's in the same place as ours is."

"I suppose if we were going to be shot, we'd know by now," Petranek mutters and picks up the stretcher with Elvan.

Banks and I follow them out. Sure enough, it is laid out exactly the same way as Principia is, the medlab just off the central communal hub, a spur off to the sleeping quarters, to labs, and an extra door that all of us stare at as we pass it.

"It feels deserted," Banks says. "I'm starting to think that there really is no one here."

"But someone was here," I say, pointing out a cup that hasn't been recycled yet, resting underneath the table that mirrors the one we usually eat dinner at.

There are no other signs of people. Once Arnolfi is laid out on one of the medlab beds, Banks and I go exploring, leaving Petranek to stay with Elvan. We open a group channel and Elvan gives us a running commentary on Arnolfi's status. He speculates that she got her injuries when the rover tipped over, as the concussion was caused by a blow to the side of her head. Without the padded helmet, it would have been much worse.

"Let's check out the sleeping quarters first," I suggest.

"We might be able to get a sense of how many people have been here."

"Agreed," says Petranek. "Don't go through that extra door until we're back together again."

"Ze hates being left out of anything," Banks says to me.

"Yeah, especially finding dead bodies or monsters or a welcoming committee with guns," ze replies. "And before you say it, Banks, I do not play too many games. It's what we're all imagining, right?"

"Speak for yourself," Elvan mutters. It sounds like he's still working on Arnolfi.

"I don't understand why Principia isn't talking to us," I say. "I mean, he—*it*—butts in all the time. Maybe it doesn't run this base. Maybe there's no AI here at all."

"No, Principia is here too," Banks says confidently. "It just won't respond to any of my questions or do anything to make it easy for us to be here."

"Is there air here?"

"Yes, but I recommend we all keep our suits on," Elvan says quickly. "It may be that a pathogen was introduced here and killed everyone."

"Principia would tell us if that was the case, surely?" Petranek says.

"You'd think so, but considering it wouldn't even open the door for us without a fight, I don't want to make any assumptions," Banks replies.

The sleeping quarters are exactly the same as ours, only laid out differently so the bathrooms are shared by two people instead of each having an en-suite.

"I guess we got the five-star base," Banks comments.

"And the better infection control," Elvan adds.

"You really want this to be a zombie-apocalypse scenario, don't you?" Petranek says but Elvan denies it.

There are no personal effects in the rooms, but they have

definitely been used. Many of the beds are unmade and I find a long blond hair on one pillow.

"Keep it," Elvan says. "I could extract the DNA and see who it belonged to."

"Are we having fun yet, kids?" Petranek says.

"Hey, he's not our only resident sleuth," Banks says. "Anna has been examining the toilet rolls in the bathrooms for clues."

"I've just been seeing if they've been used, that's all," I say, prodding Banks as best I can through his suit. "All of the bathrooms have one, meaning all were in use."

"She's right," Petranek says. "The first people to populate the bases printed the rolls and put them in the bathrooms. Elvan's done here; we'll meet you by the mystery door."

"We'll be there in a minute," I say. "I just want to check every room."

"You're one of those gamers who has to go into every nook in a mersive, right?" Banks asks.

"I don't really play many, to be honest. The ads drive me insane."

The banter makes me appreciate just how scripted the shows were. The levity makes me feel strange, considering the situation, but this is how they work as a team. Talking, keeping it light to push back the confusion. I'm sure they are all just as disturbed by this as I am, but there's no desire to feed one another's fears. Petranek's quips about monsters and zombies are like a release valve, something to make us smile as we worry about what we will really find.

There are only three rooms left. I'm not sure what I'm hoping to find. Banks is moving more slowly than I am, following rather than being proactive, as he continues to try to get a response from Principia.

I open the penultimate door and freeze. Banks bangs

into me from behind and I stumble in, struck dumb by the sight of the canvases tossed onto the bed. Four of them. Four paintings of Mars, in my style, piled up and abandoned.

"What the—" I grasp for words as I approach them. The sense of camaraderie, the comfort of being in this together, is blasted away by a piercing stab of panic. How can these be real? How can paintings that are clearly my style be here when I can't even remember painting them? Is this a mersive? Is Arnolfi doing this?

"What is it?" Elvan asks. "Anna? What's happened?"

I can't reply. Nothing meaningful is coming to mind. All I can do is stare at them.

"There are paintings here, dumped in one of the rooms," Banks says. "Anna is pretty freaked out right now." Banks looks at them in confusion and then wraps an arm around my shoulders, steadying me. "What is it?"

"They look like I could have painted them," I manage to say. I find myself searching for something jarring within them, some clue that will reveal that they're just clever fakes. It wouldn't be any less confusing, but it would be less frightening than finding work that would have taken tens of hours and then somehow had been forgotten.

There's one of the view just as a rover emerges from the base; another of a wide vista with a dust storm rising in the distance; and then I uncover one of a familiar cluster of boulders, three of them, in an aesthetically pleasing formation with the peak of Elysium Mons rising in the distance. Then I see my own signature in the bottom right corner, hidden in a crevasse, visible only to those who know to look for it. "Oh fuck." I stagger back, my legs feeling like someone has dissolved the bones inside them. There's no doubt that I painted these. That's exactly the way I would have signed it and no one else could have predicted that—I sign in a new place each time. Elvan makes some sort of comment about shock and being there as soon as he can.

"I must have painted them . . ." I say, the ramifications making me shake violently. "They're mine, but . . . I've never seen them before."

19

ELVAN PUSHES THE warm cup into my hands and kneels in front of me. "I'm okay," I say, embarrassed as the three of them stare at me. "Really. It was just a bit of a shock."

I stare at my gloves resting on the communal table alongside my helmet. Petranek and Banks are seated across from me, both of them grave-faced. I'm doing all I can to appear calm, more for my own benefit than for theirs. A memory of the pan on the hired stove in our kitchen corner when Charlie was cooking that sauce springs to mind. How it had reached the boil and the lid was just starting to rattle. I feel like so many fears and thoughts are boiling away inside me that I need to keep my hand on the metaphorical lid. Otherwise I'll just fall apart, and I've seen what that's like. I won't be like him. I will keep myself calm, and at some point soon this will all make sense. I have to believe that.

I don't remember taking my helmet off, but I know one of the others must have been with me when that happened, so it isn't as frightening. I look away from the distorted reflection of myself in the visor, back to the gloves. "Well," I say with an attempt at a smile. "At least we know the air is fine."

"I checked it first," Petranek says with a hint of professional pride. Ze takes off hir helmet too and gives me a grin. "I thought it might look weird if I didn't do that," ze adds.

"Drink up," Elvan says. "I know it seems old-fashioned but it does help. And it's preferable to your chip managing the shock neurochemically."

"I just don't understand." I take a sip, trying to hold the cup steady so Elvan doesn't make even more of a fuss. Should I say what I'm thinking? It feels like such a risk, but I can't go back to struggling through this kind of fear and doubt alone. "How did those paintings get here? And why don't I even remember painting them?"

There are no suggestions. "Are you absolutely certain they are yours?" Banks asks. "Could someone have faked them?"

"They are definitely mine. I sign them in a particular way, in a different place on every piece. Why would someone fake some of my paintings—that I haven't even painted yet—and then hide them here? I've been planning to paint that one with the boulders. Back at our base there's a sketch pad with that exact composition on the front page, and I drew it this afternoon, from scratch! How is this even possible?"

"It isn't," Petranek says eventually. "Either someone is fucking with us, or you're lying."

"I'm not!" A lump clogs my throat. "Why would I lie about this?" I croak around it.

"I believe you," Elvan says gently. "I can see from your MyPhys readings that you are genuinely in shock. But you led us here, and your pictures were inside this base. Are you absolutely certain you've never been here before?"

"Yes! I am one hundred percent certain. Christ, can't you tell that I'm telling the truth? I don't have any explanation for this and it is freaking me out." The tears come regardless of the fact that the last thing I want to do is cry. "I'm not crazy," I add. But I feel it. This must have been what it was like for him. All those times I looked at my father, staring at something with the same terrified confusion that I stared at those paintings with, and felt nothing but frustration. I simply didn't appreciate how awful it was for him to keep forgetting things, to keep finding his belongings in places they shouldn't be. If Travis is right, the ones who did that to him must have been using his chip to remove tiny snippets of memory. Not enough for him to consciously realize, but enough to destroy him. I close my eyes, wishing that I could go back and change what I said about him. Wishing I could have been more compassionate instead of only seeing the violence.

"No one has said that you're crazy," Petranek says, pulling me from the edge of another guilt well. "At least, not since I did when I was being a dick back at Principia."

"There were tracks between here and our base," Banks says. "Could someone have stolen them?"

"But I've only been here a couple of days. I haven't painted anything yet! I've done one sketch. They would have taken me a couple of weeks to produce, and I couldn't paint en route."

We sink into silence once more. "Has anything else weird happened?" Elvan asks quietly.

I can't stop the blush. "Yes," I confess. "When I arrived, I thought I'd packed more canvases than were in my cargo crates. Four more, in fact, so this kind of fits with that, even though the flight manifest said I had the correct number." I hesitate. "And there was the note I found in my room."

I tell them about the painted warning I found when I arrived at the base and watch the different reactions flit across their features. There's confusion, mostly, but I can't see any disbelief. That's something, I guess. And there is a relief to be had in finally telling them, even if it doesn't lead to any resolution.

"Look," I say, my voice a quavering mess. "This . . . is actually happening, isn't it? I don't want to say this but what if—"

"This is not immersion psychosis," Elvan says, with the utmost confidence.

"But how do you know?" I shudder.

"This doesn't follow the pattern of the disorder."

"Besides," Petranek adds, "this headache I've got is extremely real."

"In immersion psychosis," Elvan says, "there is a sense of extreme dissociation, of repeated déjà vu, of treating those around you as if they're not real. And it very rarely manifests as a situation as bizarre as this. If you were sinking deeper into that disordered state, your mind would be trying to put you back into more comforting and familiar scenarios. This is neither of those."

I nod, mildly reassured. Then an explanation occurs to me that is so ridiculous, I almost discount it immediately. Given the situation though, maybe only the ridiculous can offer an answer. "What if . . . what if I was here before? What if I was sent to this base to work, and . . . something happened . . . and everyone hated me and went somewhere else and left me behind and . . ."

I wince. It falls apart as I try to voice it. Everyone is looking at me with either pity or incredulity. "What if Arnolfi brought me to Principia after she . . . I dunno, took my memories or something?" What started as speculating aloud, trying to find a logical explanation for how those paintings could be here without my recollection of them, feels horribly right somehow. "Is that even possible?"

Elvan frowns and looks away, considering it. "Theoretically, recent memories can be removed. It's something that was explored to help trauma victims, but my understanding is that it's unreliable and potentially dangerous. The brain encodes memories in many different ways. I think it would be incredibly difficult to do that."

"But not impossible!" I say, my voice a little too high as my heart races. Oh JeeMuh, please let this be the answer! As horrifying as it is, it's better than this emotional purgatory of never trusting my own eyes and memory. "And wouldn't it explain why I just happened to send the cam drones out to the location where I'd see the mast? I mean, you asked whether I'd been tipped off about this place because it was just so unlikely I'd stumble across it right away. Maybe"—I feel the fear's grip easing—"maybe some part of me remembered, deep down. You said it's unreliable." Yes, I can cope with this. I manage a smile, despite the inevitable questions that follow: who did it to me and why? Those we can find answers to together.

"It would explain the note too," Banks says, nodding. "And, Elvan, you said that you think Arnolfi already knew about this base."

"That was a theory," Elvan says quickly. "She may well have had bad news from home, as she said. For all we know, she may have been told that GaborCorp was dumping Mars and we were going to be cut off for a while. That would cause the stress markers I saw."

"I think that's less likely, given this place." Petranek waves a hand at our surroundings.

"Is it?" Banks's expression is grim. "It's empty now. Maybe they finished what they needed to and went home. Maybe we're not needed to cover up for them anymore."

Petranek sighs. "So what do we do now?"

"Arnolfi is stable and sedated," Elvan says. "And it looks like whoever was living here has left, given all the rooms are completely empty, agreed?"

We all nod.

"I'm not getting anywhere with the prince," Banks says. "Short of doing something really, really illegal—which I am not prepared to do, before you ask—I don't know what to suggest. I've tried accessing the data here via all the different ways I can think of, and it's locked up tighter than a duck's ass."

Petranek, frowning at my teacup, says, "Have you tried accessing the food printer logs? It's not the kind of data that would be classified as critical and you know who might not have twigged what we could interpret from it."

"On it," Banks says and then grins. "Yes! Finally. Okay, so the last thing to be printed before that cup of sweet tea was—shit, less than twenty-four hours ago. It was a big meal serving twenty-one people. Lots of carbs."

"All the suits were in place and two rovers were parked inside the storm doors," Elvan says, "so are we agreed that it's highly unlikely they are out there on the surface now?"

We all nod.

"We need to look behind that door," Banks says. "The one that our base doesn't have."

"I reckon it must lead to that big space Anna saw below the launchpad," Petranek says.

"Of course no one's here," I say, slapping the table as I realize where they've gone. "They took off! The scorch marks on the pad—"

"But the shuttles only fit five at a push," Petranek says. "And it wouldn't be a comfortable trip."

"Unless they were working on another kind of ship or—" Banks says, and then we're all on our feet, tea abandoned, Petranek and I grabbing our helmets and locking them back into place as the four of us head for the extra door.

"When you ask Principia for information, is there just no reply?" Petranek asks Banks on the way.

"Yeah. I've never known it to behave this way at all. I was

wondering if it's some sort of weird security setting to do with us not being recognized as crew here, but that doesn't feel right to me."

"Maybe it's had an order from someone at a higher level," Petranek says. "Have you asked it?"

"Well, here's the problem," Banks says. "Principia, have you been ordered to be silent by someone at a higher pay grade than us?"

"Principia," Petranek says after poking hir tongue out at Banks. "Do you acknowledge our presence here?"

"I do, Dr. Petranek."

We all stop at the sound of Principia's familiar voice.

"Why haven't you been communicating with me?" Banks asks. "Why answer Petranek?"

"It is not a matter of who asked the question, Dr. Banks," Principia says. "None of you are permitted to be here. However, given your continued presence, the stress being caused to Dr. Kubrin and the injuries sustained by Dr. Arnolfi, I have queried whether the policy of maintaining silence is the best course of action and am currently awaiting guidance on how to proceed."

"Guidance from whom?"

"I am not permitted to disclose that information."

"Have comms been reestablished with Earth?" Petranek asks.

"They have not. Please wait."

"Come on," Petranek says to us. "Let's see what's on the other side of the door."

"You do not have permission to go past this point," Principia says as Banks tries to open it.

"We don't have permission to be here either," he snaps back. "But we are. How do you square that with your orders?"

"It is a difficult situation that we find ourselves in," Principia says. "I cannot fulfill one of my primary functions with regard to my care of you. This is dissatisfactory. Please wait."

"Oh for fuck's sake," Banks mutters. He holds up the case and gives us a look.

Petranek shakes hir head. "Not yet."

"Principia, there are paintings in one of the bedrooms here. Do you know how long they've been there?" I ask.

"I'm sorry, but I do not have the answer to your question, Dr. Kubrin. Normally, I would be able to carry out a detailed search of security footage in order to find the answer; however, I am not permitted to share any potentially sensitive data with you."

"Have I been here before?"

"I'm sorry, Dr. Kubrin. I am not at liberty to disclose that information."

I look at Banks and his face reflects my worry. "That wasn't a denial," I say.

"Thank you for your patience," Principia says. "I can confirm that I will be able to answer your questions in one hour, five minutes and ten seconds."

We all groan except Banks. "That's the most dumb-ass thing I have ever heard you say," Banks shouts. "What difference will it make to tell us now?"

"I'm sorry, Dr. Banks, but I am not at liberty to disclose that information."

"Oh, fuck this," Petranek says, and opens the manual access for the locked door. In seconds ze and Banks have got it open.

"You are not permitted to pass this point," Principia reminds us, unnecessarily. "If you proceed, you may be subjected to disciplinary action."

I look at Banks as Petranek strides through the doorway into the short corridor beyond, followed by Elvan. "Are you sure?" I ask him, on a private channel. "I'll cover for you, if you don't want to do this."

He touches my forearm, just briefly, and pulls away. "I've dug my grave already. But I appreciate the thought."

We go through the doorway together as Petranek pushes a second door open at the other end of the corridor. "Holy shit," ze whispers, and we pick up the pace.

It is a hangar, as ze speculated, but it's filled with all sorts of equipment rather than being just an empty space. There's a whole section filled with what look to my untrained eye like bits of space junk. There are huge printers, one of them bigger than my apartment back home, and more than a dozen smaller ones. I recognize a molecular printer at the far end, built to the same specs as the one back at the lab.

"Well, I think it's safe to say they were working on a ship," Petranek says, going to the junkyard area. Ze clambers over a couple of pieces, frowning. "What the hell is that?" Ze picks up something that looks like a cube with several pipes coming out of it, like a modernist pineapple. Ze tosses it back. "I recognize a lot of this stuff—at least, I can figure out what it must be—but some of it . . . Whatever they made, it had some additional features I can't even begin to guess at without seeing some specs."

Banks is at the far end of the hangar, looking up at the base of a fully extended platform. "They built whatever it was down here, then lifted it out onto the launchpad, by the look of it."

"There's a clean room," Elvan says, peering through a window I hadn't even noticed. "Three more molecular printers in there too."

Petranek looks from that window to the molecular printer out in the main section. "So they were building something from scratch, something that needed complex electronics that couldn't be printed easily . . . Are there drones in there?"

Elvan nods. "Half a dozen. All dormant."

"This would have cost millions . . . no, billions," Banks says, heading back to us. "It's . . . insane."

"Maybe Gabor's mining asteroids," Elvan says. "I saw something about that on one of the feeds, years ago, talking about how Mars could be a good place to run a mining operation from. Considering the scarcity of various minerals on Earth, maybe it makes sense, economically."

Petranek looks unconvinced. "I never bought into that idea. So you can mine stuff from asteroids—big deal; you need to build a refinery here so you're not shipping back crap, and the cost to get those refined materials back to Earth kills the profit. It's cheaper to use molecular printers for the super-rare stuff and take the hit on the time it takes to produce what you need."

"And why keep a mining operation secret?" Banks says. "Whatever they were building here, they didn't want it to be known about. What would that be? Androids?"

"Again, why do that?" Petranek replies. "Why make something you can't use on Earth? No profit. Besides, it's a type of ship they were building, and I reckon they left on it."

"But why?" I ask. "Why come all the way to Mars in secret to build a ship, only to go home on it?"

"Maybe they haven't gone home," Elvan says. "Oh . . . shit . . . what if this has something to do with Atlas?"

"Gabor thinks the Pathfinder was a lunatic," Petranek says. "He didn't have any fucks to give about that suicide mission. You must have seen the interview with him and that Alejandro Casales—you know, the one who started that Circle cult? It was years ago. Anyway, Gabor wiped the floor with him. Said the Pathfinder was just another one of those doomsday-cult leaders who kill all their members. She just did it with more style."

"Maybe he said that so no one would think he was interested in following her," Banks suggests, but he doesn't sound convinced.

"He doesn't have the tech to build a ship anything like Atlas was." Petranek picks up another piece of junk, the frown now set in. "The Pathfinder may have been insane, but she was one hell of a scientist and she wouldn't let that Mackensie guy sell any of their advances. We just haven't built anything that could make that kind of trip in a human lifetime. And I'm not even convinced they did."

"But what if she left the knowledge in that capsule?" Elvan says. "The one they're opening soon. What if there was a copy? What if Gabor got hold of it?"

Petranek laughs. "There is no way they left blueprints for building another Atlas. Why would they do that? They wanted to leave everyone else behind. Why give them a way to let the unchosen masses follow them? The only thing in that capsule will be some boring memoir or a collection of poetry or some sentimental bullshit to placate the abandoned. You know, the whole 'Hey, you can forge your own paths to God' shit they spout in the States."

Banks is staring at Petranek. "I had no idea you were so jaded about Atlas."

Petranek shrugs. "One of my brothers got all nerdy about it one summer. Drove us all crazy." Ze nudges at another piece with hir foot. "Maybe there's another base on Mars. Maybe they went on a test flight." Before any of us can respond, ze says, "Nah. You don't take a crew of twenty-one on a test flight."

"If they all left on it," I say. "And there aren't nineteen bodies buried somewhere." A deathly silence falls and I take in their horrified faces. "Oh. I shouldn't have said that out loud, should I?"

"I bet Arnolfi knows what they were building," Elvan says. "I've been thinking about this. Did you see the footprints when we arrived? They came from her rover, went to the launchpad, then went round to the ramp entrance. She was concussed, had a broken arm and yet she still climbed out and did all that before I had to shut her down. She was motivated."

"Like she was scared of being left behind," Banks says. "The question is why, considering she's contracted to be here until next year. You need to wake her up," he says to Elvan.

Elvan sighs, looks down and then nods. "Yeah. I think I do."

We all go to the medlab in silence. I wonder if the others are feeling the same sense of dread that has settled over me, but I don't want to ask them. I can't help but feel that if Arnolfi was scared of being left behind, there's a reason why that's more than just wanting to go wherever that ship has gone. What if there is something on Mars she wants to get away from?

What if it is me?

No, that's just paranoia. If I was that much of a problem for her, she could easily have done that psych assessment straightaway, declared me unfit for duty and confined me to quarters. She could have drugged me up and made me incapable of being any sort of problem. If she was the one who wiped my memory, why not do it again? I shiver at the thought of it. It feels like I've been violated, but it's such a nebulous feeling. Not like someone breaking into your room and stealing things. I have no idea what she has taken, aside from the memory of painting those canvases. And why do that?

The fact that she came here as soon as I made the claim about a second base bothers me too. If she hadn't done that, it would still be a secret. She must have panicked. But why?

The endless questions are doing nothing but making me feel more stressed. I grasp for something else to think about and find myself wondering what Mia is doing now. There's another pang of missing her, but this time I don't push it away. I savor it, letting myself wish I could hold her. I always think about the bad times, about the nights I couldn't sleep because I was too busy listening to her breathing. But there were special moments too, and now, when I expect it least, I remember her first laugh. I sneezed, that was all, the sort of sneeze that comes out like a squeak that usually irritates the hell out of Charlie. But it made her giggle. And then I laughed and made another squeak and she laughed again.

Suddenly she was more than just a demanding biological machine. She was a little person. A person I had neglected. Oh, I kept her clean and talked to her and made sure she had everything she needed in the moment, but I didn't give her myself. Not like those other parents did. There was always something in the way, like I was stuck behind a pane of glass, watching her through it, wishing I didn't have to keep looking. When tears well in my eyes I push that thought away. Better to think about that laugh. I must have a recording of it somewhere, in a mersive. I'll find it later. Once all this is done. And it will be, by the time the day is out; it will all be out in the open. I have the feeling I will need something made of pure joy when that happens.

I can see how upset Elvan is, and how he tries to hide it with silence as Petranek fills the channel with speculation about the clean room. Most of it goes over my head, giving me the mental space to think about Elvan instead. He's close to Arnolfi and he feels betrayed. All of them are shaken by finding this base, but it has been a relief for me. Now there are others banging themselves against Principia's walls too, puzzling it out with me. I take what little comfort I can in the fact that I don't feel alone here.

When we reach the medlab and gather around Arnolfi's bed, Elvan hesitates. "She's going to be disoriented. Maybe I should wake her alone."

"No," Banks says without a beat. "We stay together."

"Don't you trust me?" Elvan asks.

"I don't trust her," Banks says.

"We'll stand back." Petranek takes a few steps back until ze reaches the wall and leans against it. "Then she won't feel crowded. How about that?"

Elvan agrees and takes off his helmet and gloves, gesturing for us to do the same. I do it for him, not to make Arnolfi feel more at ease when she wakes. "It will take a couple of minutes for this to wake her," he says, preparing a pen syringe from his medkit. "I suggest that I speak first, just until she's fully back with us. An interrogation as soon as she opens her eyes isn't going to do anything except distress her."

When the others nod, he injects her and then taps at something in his visual field. He's probably monitoring her vitals. He replaces the syringe and then rests a hand over hers. He is such a gentle man, so caring. I look away.

I glance back only when a little moan comes from Arnolfi and then I turn away again, not wanting to witness her distress. Not wanting to witness his kindness toward her either. He talks to her in his soft voice, soothing her, telling her about her injuries and then where she was found.

"Is this Principia?" she asks. I look at her then, as Elvan tells her where we are.

Her face crumples. "Oh God. Oh God, it's all gone wrong," she croaks and starts to cry.

Banks and Petranek exchange a look as Elvan holds Arnolfi's hand and tries to comfort her. They are impatient, but their care for their colleague is still there. I have none of that care and have to fight the urge to just grab hold of her and bombard her with questions.

"Did you know about this base before today?" Elvan asks as she settles into a silent weeping.

She nods, her face a portrait in shame as she tilts away

from him to notice the rest of us here. She blinks at me and then returns her gaze to Elvan. "What must you think of me?"

"Well, we're not really sure what's going on, to be honest," he says. "But I'm upset you hid this from me. Was it a corp order?"

She nods, then shakes her head, the tears flowing more freely now. "I wish it was. There's no point lying to you anymore. It's all over now. They left."

"Look, what the fuck is going on?" Petranek blurts out, shooting forward to lean over Arnolfi. "What were they building here? A ship?" When Arnolfi nods, Petranek leans closer. "Why are you so upset? Because they left you behind? Why did you want to go with them so much?"

"Because we're all going to die here," she sobs. "They left us all to die!"

"What is this bullshit?" Petranek yells. "Why are you saying this?"

With her good hand, Arnolfi covers her face, inconsolable. Banks puts a hand on Petranek's shoulder and gently pulls ze back. "Has she had some sort of breakdown?" he asks Elvan.

"It's difficult to say," he begins, but Arnolfi scrapes her hand down her face and seems to rally herself.

"I'll tell you everything. There's no point hiding it now. But you have to know, before I tell you, that you all agreed to this."

In the stunned silence she looks at me again and I know she is lying. There's too much guilt in her eyes, in the way she cannot hold my gaze. She swallows and looks at the others again. "You all agreed to stay behind and die. You just can't remember."

20

ELVAN ADJUSTS THE bed so she's sitting up and gets her a glass of water. "I'm sorry," she croaks before taking a sip. "I'm not quite myself."

"It's perfectly natural after a neural shutdown," Elvan says as Petranek shrugs off Banks's hand and goes back to leaning against the wall, arms crossed, frown back in place.

I watch Arnolfi gather her wits, like she's putting her armor back on, fixing her face and taking deep breaths. Like someone about to go onstage. "What exactly did everyone consent to?" I ask, not wanting to give her another moment to build those walls back up. I know how much can be hidden behind them.

She swallows, unable to look any of us in the eye for a moment. "This place had to stay a secret. The order came from the top."

"So now you're saying there was an order to keep this place secret?" Petranek says, and Elvan holds up a hand.

"We can't trust anything she said in the first couple of minutes of waking up," he says.

"Including the part about us being left here to die?" Petranek asks.

"Especially that," Elvan replies evenly. "Let's start again."

I press my lips together in frustration. She never answered my question and Elvan isn't helping. He's too trusting, but I can see I have an ally in Petranek; ze doesn't seem to be buying into Elvan's excuse either.

"I knew about it. It was part of my job to make sure that it never got leaked through the show. And most of the time I never even thought about it. I focused on my own work. I didn't like you all being kept in the dark and I tried not to dwell upon it."

"Why not tell us?" Banks says. "We're all locked into contracts. We've all signed NDAs, for all sorts of stuff."

She shrugs. "That's what Gabor wanted. Strictly need to know."

"What did everyone consent to?" I ask again.

She bites her lower lip. "I want you all to know that I had no choice in this."

"Shit, this is bad, then," Petranek mutters.

"Everything was spiraling out of control and I had to make sure that the primary mission wasn't jeopardized, so . . ." She puts the cup down and presses her shaking palms together. "So I had to dial back. I had to perform a neurophysiological procedure to . . . to help you all to forget about this base."

"What. The. *Fuck?*" Petranek says and Banks puts his hand on hir shoulder again. "Are you saying we all knew about this place too at one point, and you made us forget about it?"

She nods and winces at the expletives that burst from

Petranek. Banks seems strangely calm and Elvan looks at me. We stare at each other for a few moments, both of us processing what she said.

"So that is how I found this place, then," I say, feeling strangely reassured. "Some part of me must have made me head in this direction subconsciously. I guess you didn't do a good enough job of scrubbing my brain."

"It was all your fault!" Arnolfi blurts out, then reaches for the water again.

"*My* fault?" I ball my fists. "What, my fault that you lied to your colleagues, that you tried to make out that I was having a fucking psychotic break? That was my fault?"

"You found this place, about a month after you arrived," she says through her teeth, barely able to hide her anger now. "You wouldn't let it go."

A month after I arrived? It's so chilling, hearing her speak of something I did and have no recollection of. She may as well be describing a parallel universe. Now I know why she looked so angry when I went outside during the fake storm and reported what I'd seen. It was because I was doing it all over again.

"You placed me in an impossible situation." She looks away from me, trying to suppress that rage at me again. "I didn't want any of you to get into trouble!" she says to the others. "It was the simplest, cleanest solution."

"And we consented?" Banks asks. When she nods, he says, "Do you have something we signed?"

"Fuck whether we signed anything!" Petranek says. "You scrubbed our memories? I mean, how does that even work? It's not like we're computers! Elvan, you said yourself it was only theoretical, and potentially dangerous!"

Arnolfi looks at him in confusion. "Why were you talking about it?" she asks.

"Because of the paintings," he says.

"Did you bring them here?" I ask. She nods. "So you've scrubbed out, what, a month of our memories? What have you told our friends and families back home?"

"The comms blackout." Petranek snaps hir fingers. "That's to cover all this up, isn't it? JeeMuh, that is some fucked-up shit right there."

Arnolfi doesn't reply. She looks at me. "I couldn't dispose of the paintings back at Principia. The material isn't degradable enough for the waste processor. I couldn't risk burying them, not with you likely to use ground scanners and being so"—her lip curls—"so curious about everything. So I brought them here."

"This is unbelievable," Petranek says. "I mean, literally unbelievable. Are you seriously telling us that you thought that a risky, potentially dangerous neurophys procedure was the best option? Seriously?"

"Would you have preferred me to report the security breach? To potentially—"

"Yes!" Petranek cuts her off. "Yes, I would have preferred that, like any sane person would. People find shit out that's above their pay grade all the fucking time, and I bet they don't get scrubbed. I would have preferred an adult conversation in which we all agreed to sign an NDA. Was that not an option?"

Arnolfi squeezes the cup, her knuckles white. "Not at the time, no. It wasn't."

"Why?"

She doesn't answer.

"So, you've altered all the time stamps," Banks says, still unemotional. "To make us think Kubrin just arrived a couple of days ago? Why wipe a whole month though? Why not just from the day we learned about the base?"

"Kubrin made it all very difficult. If she wasn't here, it would have been far easier, and not just because she found

Segundus." Arnolfi waves a hand at the room. "That's what this place is called."

"Easier because of our routines?" Elvan asks.

"Yes. I could have taken a day of memories, no problem. But Kubrin is an oddity for us all. And we all encode memories on multiple levels in multiple parts of the brain. I had to dial you all back to the day she arrived, so I could be certain I took out—"

"What else did you take?" Petranek yells. "Can you cherry-pick?" Ze glares at Elvan and Banks. "Why are you both so fucking calm about this? She fucked with our heads! I would never consent to that! Never!"

"Petranek," Banks says, putting himself between Arnolfi's bed and his friend. "Lynn. We're all shocked here, and we're all upset. But we have to keep calm. Okay?"

Petranek searches his eyes. "Why aren't you angry?"

"I am," Banks says. "I really am, but right now, I'm keeping it under control. And you need to do the same; otherwise, this could escalate into something we can't take back. Okay?"

I find myself admiring his self-control at the same time I'm wondering whether he's honed it over the years of his indenture. Constantly holding back his anger has become second nature to him. The thought is sobering.

Despite what Arnolfi has done to us, I don't feel angry. I'm not sure how I feel. Numb. No, that's not right. Something between that and being vindicated. But the whole consent thing doesn't sit right with me at all.

"Do you have proof we consented?" I ask, watching the vein at the side of her forehead pulse. "Do you?"

"You pre-consented in your contracts," she finally says.

"That's it," Petranek says, balling a fist. "I am going to—"

"You're going to take a deep breath and stay back," Banks says, moving himself between them again. "Seriously, Petranek, there are more important things to address here than your need to punch her. Right?"

"I thought so," I say. "I must have known what you were going to do somehow. That's how I left the note for myself," I say to Elvan.

"What note?"

I ignore Arnolfi's question. "And what about my wedding ring? Did you replace that too?"

Arnolfi nods. "Wedding ring?" Elvan asks.

"This one is fake," I say, holding up my left hand. "It should have an engraved message inside, but it doesn't. I guess you didn't know about that," I say to Arnolfi. "You just printed a new gold band. Shit. You stage dressed everything. Did you carry me back to the rocket and strap me in?"

She nods.

"And you activated that mersive? The one that I was in when you first—I mean, when you pretended to first greet me?"

Another nod.

"That's why you recovered so quickly from the flight," Elvan says. "Damn it." He looks at Arnolfi. "Did you drug her to simulate the weakness and . . ." He trails off at her nod. "I should have looked more closely at the blood work."

"There wouldn't have been any point," I say. "Principia held that back from the results, didn't it?" I watch her nod again. "It's been in on this all along. You weren't incompetent," I say to Elvan. "You were duped, like we all were." I focus on Arnolfi again. "Where is my real wedding ring?"

"I don't know. You weren't wearing it when I had to—"

"So you didn't ask me?"

"You didn't know where it was. You'd lost it."

"Really?" I look at the others. "I don't think I went into this memory scrub willingly. I don't think any of you did either."

"Agreed," Petranek growls.

"And there's something else that doesn't work for me here," I say, feeling a dark satisfaction at the way patches of sweat have appeared in the underarms of Arnolfi's onesie. "So, I found this place the first time round, you scrubbed our memories, most likely without our consent, and then what? What were you planning to do? Because resetting everything, changing the dates and presumably having the old, original messages from home re-sent to us—all that seems like short-term thinking to me. You might have faked a comms blackout when those messages started to get difficult to manage—I guess we didn't just repeat the same stuff we sent the first time, so they started to get disjointed—but how long were you planning to keep that up?"

"Until she left with them," Banks says. "That's right, isn't it?"

Arnolfi doesn't reply.

"You wanted to keep us all in the dark until the ship left; then you didn't care if we found out," Elvan says, "because you were supposed to be on it."

Arnolfi remains silent, trying not to cry, or pretending to be upset. I can't be sure.

"But they left you behind," Petranek says with a bitter laugh. "And now you have to face the music. You may as well lift the comms blackout, now we know. And we'll have to renegotiate our contracts, like we should have the first time round, for fuck's sake."

Banks is frowning at the floor. "What is it?" I ask him.

"You said this base was need to know," he says to Arnolfi. "This place was more important than Principia, presumably, for you to have gone to such lengths to keep it secret. But not the base; the ship, right? That ship was the primary Mars mission all along. Not our science. Not the show. That was all pantomime distraction, to hide this place. Tell me if any of that is wrong."

"It's all correct," Arnolfi whispers.

"And now that ship has left, so the primary mission has been completed. I don't think you were upset about being left behind because you wanted to go with them—and we'll get to where that is in a minute—I think you were upset because you had to stay here."

My stomach starts to churn. Elvan moves away from the bed, pushing away the medkit as he passes it, coming over to stand next to me.

"But why be upset about that?" Banks continues. When Arnolfi remains silent, he looks at the rest of us. "I don't think the comms were cut by her to cover up the message issues. Principia would have stored that month's worth of the original comms. It's clever enough to mark out discrepancies— hell, she probably reviewed them all to make sure her cover-up was still intact. What if the comms blackout happened for a different reason? What if it's because, with the primary mission completed, GaborCorp has closed its Mars operations— for good?"

Arnolfi covers her face, stifling a sob.

"What, just leaving us here?" Elvan asks. "No, that's not possible."

"Think about it," Banks says, ignoring Arnolfi's distress. "If GaborCorp only put us here to cover for that ship being built, then why spend the money to send us home again? We're surplus to requirements now."

"No," I say. "They wouldn't do that. It would be a PR disaster, for one thing."

"They can spin any story they like," Banks replies. "No one will question it. We're too far away for an investigation. And—"

"No!" I say, more forcefully, knowing where all of his speculation is coming from. "I'm contracted to do a minimum of one hundred hours of promotional activities when I get back to Earth, to help flog my paintings. And Gabor needs them to be shipped back too! And all of you have hugely valuable skills and experience. Even if GaborCorp doesn't want to continue having a human presence on Mars, it makes no sense for them to just leave us here to rot. We have a rocket and the fuel to get back. It'll be a squeeze for all of us to travel back in it, but we could. That's not what's going on here."

"Can you lift the comms blackout?" Petranek asks Arnolfi. She shakes her head, face still covered with her hands, tears slipping out from under them. "Did you enforce it in the first place?" Elvan asks. Another tearful shake of her head.

"Principia," Banks says with a look of resignation. "Did you initiate the comms blackout with Earth?"

"I did not, Dr. Banks."

"It really originated on Earth?"

"It did, Dr. Banks. Would you like me to participate in this conversation? I have relevant information that Dr. Arnolfi seems to have omitted from—"

"You keep out of this, Principia!" Arnolfi says, pulling her hands away from puffy eyes. "That's an order."

"I must inform you that you do not have the authority to impose that upon me, Dr. Arnolfi. Your authority has been revoked due to your suicide attempt and will not be restored until you have passed a full mental and physical evaluation. Dr. Banks now holds the highest pay grade and resulting security privileges."

"Has your time limit elapsed, Principia?" he asks.

"It has, Dr. Banks. I apologize for the inconvenience. Would you like me to participate in this conversation?"

"Yes," Banks says, and Principia's avatar shimmers into

view, no available doorways or perspectives to trick us into thinking it has just walked in. I prefer this form of arrival. There's an honesty to it.

"I want you to answer our questions, Principia. No tricks," Banks says. "Did you assist Dr. Arnolfi in her efforts to keep this base hidden?"

"That is a complex question," Principia replies, eliciting a groan from Petranek. "Would you like me to itemize the actions I took to keep Mars Segundus a secret at the behest of Dr. Arnolfi?"

"Bloody AIs," Petranek mutters as Banks gives Principia a nod.

"As there are over three thousand seven hundred actions, I shall group them into broad categories," Principia begins. "I edited incoming data from satellites and drones to remove any images that could lead to the discovery of Segundus from the results. I falsified weather data and external cam footage to create the illusion of dust storms to prevent the use of drones within a twenty-kilometer radius of the base and to ensure that members of the Segundus crew and Principia crew would not encounter one another on the surface. I falsified records relating to multiple items of hardware to prevent the discovery of their reassignment to Segundus. I assisted Dr. Arnolfi in the management of messages to and from Earth to replicate personal communications when the base time stamp was changed. I omitted blood work data before presenting the results of Dr. Kubrin's tests to Dr. Elvan. I gave an objectively verifiable lie as a response to one thousand, two hundred and three queries made by the crew. I ring-fenced data accumulated in the first twenty-seven days after Dr. Kubrin's true arrival and prevented any access to that data and ensured there were no ways for anyone except Dr. Arnolfi to review it. I altered the time and date stamp in Principia's mainframe. I—"

"That's enough," Banks says. "Did you help Arnolfi to take our memories?"

"Not directly, Dr. Banks. I assisted with the production of specialized drugs, at the direct request of Dr. Arnolfi."

"Did you know what they would be used for?"

"Given Dr. Arnolfi's research and the neurochemicals that would be affected by the drugs, I was able to form a hypothesis. That was why I challenged Dr. Arnolfi when she made the request to use the molecular printer to create them."

"And she told you?" Elvan asks.

"Yes."

"And how did you reconcile that with your duty of care toward us?"

"Quite easily, Dr. Elvan. Dr. Arnolfi's skill at minimizing side effects and the results she's obtained in the past made the risk of physical harm very low. Safeguarding the preservation of memory is not a stipulated requirement within your contracts, or in the universal basic human rights agreement made between GaborCorp and Norope."

"Jesus fucking Christ," Petranek spits. "You were more than happy to keep us in the dark too, given the fact that Segundus is actually the primary Mars mission."

"That was taken into consideration; however, Dr. Arnolfi has led you to believe that it was a level-one security requirement to keep the knowledge of Segundus secret from the crew of Principia that led her to remove your memories. This is not true. Sensitive activities that are conducted on a need-to-know basis are common within GaborCorp and on the rare occasion when there has been informational bleed, the breach is handled with additional clauses to contracts. Not the removal of memories."

We all look at Arnolfi. She is hiding her face behind her hands.

"So why did you do it?" Elvan says to her.

She remains silent.

"Principia? Did she tell you?"

"No, Dr. Elvan."

"The ship that was built here," Petranek says. "Where has it gone?"

"The ship Semper Gabor has set course to follow the Pathfinder."

Petranek laughs, the same kind of strained guffaw that comes from my own lips. "I don't believe it," ze says. "We were right."

"But no one knows where they went," Banks says.

"The knowledge of the Pathfinder's destination has been in GaborCorp's possession for approximately thirty-six years and three months," Principia replies.

"But that's almost as long as Atlas has been gone." Banks falls quiet. "I guess no valuable information stays secret if you have enough money."

"Is this the stuff that's supposedly in the locked time capsule?" Petranek asks.

"Yes, Dr. Petranek, along with additional data secured by GaborCorp relating to the technological advances made by the Pathfinder and her team."

"So Segundus was set up to build a ship using that technology to find her?"

"Yes."

"Whoa. I cannot wait to see that!" Petranek rubs hir hands in anticipation.

"I am sorry, Dr. Petranek. That data has been deleted. It was stipulated in the mission brief that as soon as a successful takeoff was achieved, the data would be wiped to prevent any future corporations from using it, should GaborCorp lose exclusive access to Mars."

"Shit. So that's why Gabor paid through the nose for that access, then? Because of the highly sensitive nature of the information—presumably stolen or bought in a very shady secret deal—Gabor decided that the best way to keep the project truly secret would be to build it on Mars, where he controls all of the satellites, all of the data, all of the access. Everything."

"Yes, Dr. Petranek. Mr. Gabor decided that the massively increased cost was an acceptable security investment. With industrial espionage so rife, and information so difficult to control should it fall into the wrong hands, he decided to remove those risks."

"And he smuggled the crew here?"

"The word 'smuggled' implies the secret transportation across borders of illegal goods. Rather, there was simply no media coverage of the crew of Segundus leaving Earth."

No one can split hairs better than an AI. I look at Arnolfi. "So, judging from the way you reacted when I said the ship had taken off, I guess you really, really wanted to go and find God with the rest of the crazies."

"Shut up!" she snaps.

"So why did you have to wait to tell us this?" I ask Principia. "It's not like we could do anything about the ship now it's left."

"I consulted Captain Singh about the events that have occurred here, and she asked that I wait until the ship was out of real-time communications range."

"So we couldn't call her up and talk to her?" Banks says, incredulous. "That seems pretty damn rude." He looks at Arnolfi. "Perhaps she was worried that you'd say something mean about leaving you behind."

"So now the ship has left, is this place just going to be mothballed?" Petranek asks.

"No plans have been made for the continued use of this facility."

"And Gabor didn't plan to mothball Principia, once that ship was done?"

"No, Dr. Petranek. The ship was completed six months ahead of schedule and no guidance has ever been given with regard to Principia's continued funding once Segundus fulfilled its mission."

"Six months?" Petranek gives a low whistle. "I've never known a complex engineering project to be finished that far ahead of schedule."

I notice how quiet Elvan is, and the way he's staring at Arnolfi. "What aren't you telling us, Arnolfi?" he asks.

She doesn't respond.

"I've known you for over fifteen years," he says. "I've seen you go through the death of your father. I've seen you go through a divorce, and through a cancer scare. I have never seen you fall apart. What aren't you telling us?"

Her hands drop onto her lap. She looks terrible with her pale lips and bloodshot eyes. But it isn't just those physical things. It's something in the way she looks at Elvan. Like some part of her has given up.

"I didn't lie to you when I said I was struggling with some news from back home," she finally says. "And I didn't lie when I said we've all been left here to die." She laughs mirthlessly, like a woman who has just discovered that life is simply a terrible joke that she shouldn't have fallen for. "You always wonder what you'll be like in a disaster. You know I've always loved those old movies where there's an earthquake or a volcano or something and you follow all these characters through the crisis. Cathartic, I suppose. I think I used to watch them and wonder whether I'd be like the hero. Saving people. Being selfless." She laughs again, bringing back the sense of dread I felt earlier. "I'm not. I'm the one who does everything they can to save themselves at the first opportunity. The one who dies because it looked like a sure way to survive but it wasn't." Her face creases into such an expression of despair that I cover my mouth, feeling as if I know something awful has happened, something worse than I could possibly imagine, just at the edge of my consciousness. "They lied to me. So that I would help them steal the hardware they needed to finish the ship more quickly. And I betrayed all of you. People I care about. That I love. Just to be left behind. I . . ."

Her words are swallowed up by a heaving sob and she breaks down, leaving the rest of us to bear reluctant witness.

"What was the news from home?" Elvan asks. "Tell us!"

She shakes her head. "I can't. Oh God! I can't go through it again!"

"Principia?" Banks looks at the avatar. "Do you know what she's talking about?"

"Yes, Dr. Banks. I believe Dr. Arnolfi is referring to news that came from Earth shortly before the blackout. I must warn you that you will find this emotionally distressing."

"Just fucking tell us!" Petranek yells.

"On the morning of December thirteenth, shortly after one p.m. Greenwich Mean Time, three thermonuclear missiles were fired from the United States of America, targeting three key locations in GaborCorp's R and D divisions in Andalusia, Madrid and Manchester, followed shortly by a second wave targeting key GaborCorp facilities in France, triggering a full-scale nuclear retaliation from the European and Noropean gov-corps in which one thousand five hundred missiles carrying a total of over five hundred nuclear warheads were launched. We lost communications with Earth shortly afterward. Initial estimates of deaths caused by the first strikes in Europe and Norope are over eight million, with a further—"

I'm dimly aware of the wall sliding up behind me before

I realize, with a bizarre detachment, that it is instead my body that is slipping downward as my legs collapse beneath me. I don't hear anything more from Principia as a high-pitched whining sound deafens me. All I can think of is Mia, little Mia, plump and perfect, pointing out of the window at a new star in the sky over Manchester in the middle of the day.

21

GRIEF MAKES TIME elastic, stretching it into hours that feel like days, then contracting it sharply, snapping it back, until you blink out of a reverie and find the day is almost over. I'm not sure how long I have lain here, on my bed, back in Principia. There's no hunger. No thirst. Barely any connection to my body. Just this limbo, this gray expanse in which shock and misery wrap themselves around me like thick fog.

Trying to come to terms with this feels like trying to hold all the details of a mountain in my mind at once. I can visualize a peak, a sheer face covered with snow, a slope of scree, or one distant shot. More than half a billion estimated casualties and a projected four billion more deaths over the next five years; that distant view of what has happened on Earth is too pulled back to mean anything. Almost half of the world's population wiped out in a war that took less than one hour. It's too big to understand.

So my mind goes to my baby. To my mother. To Charlie. My father. Geena. Drew. Sometimes there is so much grief I am lost to it, reduced to a sack of skin, excreting and emoting, nothing more. Sometimes I just stare at the blank wall, spent, letting memories of kisses and sparks of life spent with them pass through my mind like water in a stream.

At one point I realize that for the past week or so I've been recording and sending messages to them when they were already dead and I scream into my pillow, the thought adding a vicious sting to the wound. All those times I got angry at Charlie for not answering me about the footprint, and at Mum for not answering my question about talking to Dad . . . It's a long time before I can stop crying.

Selfishly—for is being selfish not what I am best at?—I wish I had loved Charlie more, that we had nourished each other more, if only so I could be given the bittersweet solace of a pure grief. The same with Mia. If only I'd been a better mother, able to let myself be subsumed in that loving oblivion of motherhood, so that now I could feel this pain without guilt and regret.

I cannot allow myself the simple pain of wishing for just another moment with them. I don't deserve the cleanliness of that. I cannot permit myself to enter the delusion that all I want is to be with them again, just for one last kiss, one last embrace and the opportunity to say all the things I never said. Those desires weren't there yesterday, when my erased brain thought they were still alive. I'm not so foolish as to believe that anything surfacing now is genuine.

It's simpler with my mother though. That love was pure, with only a few scuff marks of disagreement and frustration with her faith in my father. We connected through art and blood. Nothing could be deeper than that. And now she is gone. And even though I've always seen this on the horizon, as all children do, it doesn't make it easier.

And there is the grim hope that she is dead. That she did

not survive the initial blasts, even though there is an appalling probability that she did. I cannot bear the thought of a slow death for her, so I hope she was in Manchester, visiting Mia, seeing that star with her. I can only hope that she had time to gather Mia up, press my child's face into her chest and hold her when it happened. That she took the place I should have had.

There's a way to know, but I can't check that yet. I need the safety of this fantasy. One of my own making, not a mersive, and not Arnolfi's doing either.

And then there's Dad and Geena. Dad's hospital was in London. While it wasn't one of the first-wave targets, no doubt it would have been destroyed in the second or third. And as for Geena, I have no idea where she was. Which country even. All I can do is hope she had a swift death. What kind of hope is that?

Drew and the rest of the team will have died first, working where I once worked in Manchester, in the huge Gabor-Corp complex that was one of the first hit. Unlike Gabor, who probably has a gilded bunker somewhere that he was stuffed into immediately, they probably didn't even know what was happening until it was far too late. Like most people, we thought nuclear war was relegated to the status of an outdated, unfashionable plotline in cheap mersive backstories. Why would there be something as unprofitable as nuclear war, now that all of the countries that have nuclear warheads are corporations caught in a mesh of mutually profitable arrangements?

Behind this grief, like a person waiting behind a heavy curtain, is the question of "What next? What do we do now?" but I don't have the strength to pull that curtain back now. I don't think any of us do. We've all retreated into private spaces to ride out the shock. At some point someone will seek out company, but it's too soon for me. I manage to print a light meal, force myself to eat it and then fall into a fitful sleep.

Another day slides by. I can't face the company of others, and when Banks pings me, asking if I want to eat dinner with everyone else, I decline. I spend the day in bed, sometimes in my room, sometimes in a mersive. I don't fear it now. I don't think there was ever any risk of immersion psychosis. The side effects of the drugs Arnolfi pumped into me, to fool everyone into thinking I'd just been in zero g for months, explain my disorientation and my occasional lapses in those first days after her reset. I spend time with Mia, trying to find happy moments to cling to, only to come out of them sobbing. I ask Principia to lock access to the mersives for seven days, fearing they're only going to cause me more harm. Unable to focus on anything, I print myself something to make me sleep, following a quick sign-off by Elvan, and let myself sink into restful oblivion.

The next morning feels different. The sleep, despite being artificially triggered, has helped. I make myself get up and eat, shower and dress, cajoling myself through each task. There's no safety net here, no friends or relatives who will turn up on the doorstep and help to keep the wheels of life turning while I fall apart. I don't have that luxury.

There's a knock on my door as I'm toweling my hair dry. It's Elvan.

"Hi."

"Hi."

"Is it okay for me to be here?"

"Sure." I step back and gesture for him to come in, straighten the bedclothes quickly and dump my food tray in the recycler. "How are you feeling?"

"Ummm. Everything? No, I'm feeling all the bad things. You?"

I shrug. "I'm sorry—I feel I should know this—but did you have much family at home?"

"Yeah, I come from a big family. They live all over the world. We scattered and only came back together for big things—you know how it is."

I nod, even though I don't know. My small family scattered but never came back together again.

"Most of them have died," he says, sitting on the edge of my bed. "I'm relieved, actually. Isn't that terrible?"

"It's not terrible to hope that the people we love aren't suffering. Do you want something to drink?"

He shakes his head. "I wasn't married though. I don't have any children." He reaches out to brush my hand with his fingertips. "I can't imagine what it's like for you."

I frown at him. "There isn't a hierarchy of grief. I don't get to say this is worse for me. That would be bullshit. We all lost the most important people to us."

He nods and I sit next to him. "Have you watched—"

"No," I say before he can finish. I know he's talking about the death messages. I've never seen one before and the thought of having several waiting for me is awful.

I argued with Charlie about them before I left Earth. The head of the team sending me to Mars suggested I record some, and that had sent me spiraling into such a depression by the time I got home that Charlie wouldn't leave me alone until he'd winkled it out of me. I'd never recorded a message for loved ones to watch in the event of my death and I'd never watched one either. The thought appalled me then and it appalls me now. "I can't face it."

"So you don't know if they died."

"I know Charlie and Mia will be dead. And Basalt. That's my dog. They lived in Manchester. I hope my mum was visiting them; I know she was planning to. I don't want her to have to live in that . . ." I let the silence take the words I can't speak. He knows what I mean.

"It's hard to watch the messages, but it does help. I never really liked the idea of them, but now I can see why people started doing them."

"We must have already watched them," I say. "I can't help thinking that we've already been through this before. It's really doing my head in."

He gives a grunt of agreement. "I've been having similar thoughts. I have the feeling that I've been processing this, unconsciously, ever since Arnolfi did this to us. I didn't tell anyone else, but MyPhys flagged up some imbalances in my neurochemistry that it corrected, but it niggled at me, you know? I thought the only thing that had changed was your arrival, and I couldn't work out why that would be triggering those changes. I even looked at the levels and thought, yeah, it looks like I've just been through a major trauma. Weird." He shrugs. "I guess it's easy to feel stupid when you have all the answers. There was something else though . . . I wanted to talk it through with you, if that's okay? I totally understand if this is the wrong time, given your husband and your—"

"I'd be glad to have something else to focus on," I say. "Truth be told, it wasn't a happy marriage."

He nods slowly. Sitting this close to him, I'm fighting the urge to just lean in, tuck myself under his arm and cuddle up. I focus on my desk instead. It's safer.

"So, there's been other neurochemical activity that, well . . . I don't quite know how to say this, but it seems that you do trigger it. And like I've said, many times, this isn't my specialty, but I can recognize certain patterns of brain activity. I mean, it was one of those things you go out of your way to learn when you're training to be a doctor, even when you're warned not to."

"Elvan," I say with a weak smile. "Just tell me."

"Being around you triggers the same underlying chemical changes as being with a lover."

"Wow, that has to be the most unromantic thing I've ever heard." He snorts at the quip. I smile and then I feel terrible for making a poor joke in the circumstances.

"I haven't finished," he says. "I don't know if it's been the same for you, but I've had these feelings about you."

"It has been the same for me," I say. "To the extent that I started avoiding you because it felt too easy to just fall into a habit I hadn't made yet. That's what it felt like."

He nods. "Yes! That's exactly how it's felt, and I realized that, well, maybe we did form those habits. Before she scrubbed us."

"It makes sense. Which means we had an affair. Oh. This is awkward," I say, trying to seem light in the face of this obvious truth.

It seems I can feel even more guilt. Not just for what we must have done, but also for the tiny spark of longing still within me.

"There's a way to verify it," he says, still hesitant. "Just tell me if this is really not the thing to talk about now."

"No, it's fine. We have to talk about it, don't we? We have to work out where things are really at."

"That's how I feel. Maybe I'm just grasping for something comforting. I don't know. I'm not sure how to feel. About anything. But the thing we could do, that I didn't feel was right to do alone, is review the cam footage that Principia hid from us when Arnolfi reset the clock."

My mouth is dry as I nod in consent. I let Elvan take the lead after I give Principia permission to display the images on the wall. I'm caught between not wanting to see myself being unfaithful and wanting to know the truth. It's one thing to have an unhappy marriage, quite another to learn you're the sort of person who breaks an oath, a contract, formed with the best intentions. Now I am a terrible mother and a worse wife. I have the briefest sense of relief that my marriage is over now and crush it with the omnipresent, leaden guilt. I disgust myself.

With snippets of film, mostly taken in the medbay, we watch the progression of the affair. It started before the war on Earth, after an immediate mutual attraction that neither of us seemed able or willing to control. There's an evening in the medbay where I play him some of my favorite music, like we're teenagers desperate to know every nook of each other before we finally, physically give in to the lust. The Russian soul song comes on and we dance to it—the video makes Elvan jolt on the bed next to me.

"That's where that damn tune came from!"

And I realize how this same music triggered the memory of us dancing, when I was in the rover. I wasn't imagining or fantasizing; I was remembering something real, encoded in a way that managed to survive Arnolfi's intervention. I wonder if Elvan's scent has been triggering the urges to get closer to him, touching upon memories buried elsewhere in my brain.

Elvan finds a segment filmed in the medbay, a week after my actual arrival. It looks like he's doing a routine medical before I pull him down to kiss me as I lie on the bed. A movement that matches the one I craved when I was there after the memory erasure. The embrace is tight, passionate, like we've been starved of affection for so long and are gorging ourselves, feasting on that which we offer each other so enthusiastically. We part before we make love, fearful that we'll be discovered, promising to meet that night. In silence, Elvan manipulates something in his visual field with his hand and the images speed up, pause and then cut to his quarters. He is in bed; the time stamp says it's shortly after midnight. It has the distinct coloration caused by filming in the dark, all muted grays of varying shades.

"I didn't realize Principia films our quarters too." My voice is hoarse with tension.

"They aren't classified as private spaces," Elvan says. "Every square centimeter of the base is designated as a work space. It's a loophole."

"But why film in them?"

He shrugs. "Principia? What's the justification for filming our quarters?"

"All GaborCorp work spaces are routinely filmed for your protection."

We exchange a look, unimpressed with the same old corporate bullshit, then go back to watching the screen. He fast-forwards until there's a crack of light that falls across his bed and I sneak in.

It's so strange watching myself this way. Usually I experience recordings taken through my own eyes, the sound heard through my ears. It's hard to believe it is me, even though it clearly is.

"I can't stop thinking about you," past me says. "Am I a terrible person?"

"No," Elvan says, pulling back his cover. "Am I a terrible person for wanting the same?"

My cheeks are burning. It's like watching a really bad romance mersive, only with far more guilt and discomfort. "We didn't manage to stay apart for long, did we?" I say to him. He gives the slightest nod. "Principia," I say. "Didn't you report us for having an affair?"

"No, Dr. Kubrin. I do not judge human activity; I merely gather data."

That's news to me. The way the adults used to talk when I was growing up, anyone would think an AI was always watching and judging, even actively seeking out evidence of transgression. If I'd realized the sleeping quarters here were cammed, I wouldn't have done what I'm watching now.

"If there was a tribunal, it would be used as evidence," Elvan says. "But it would have to be a colleague who reported us, I guess."

"Principia, did we spend any other nights together?"

"Since the tenth day after your arrival, you and Dr. Elvan spent every night between the hours of midnight and six a.m. in each other's company," Principia replies. "With the exception of the night Dr. Arnolfi removed your memories, when you spent a total of nine point five minutes in Dr. Elvan's quarters."

With a frown, Elvan says, "Show us."

The footage jumps to another nighttime shot. "I don't want to talk about the war or the stuff you said about another base or anything Arnolfi said about it," I say to him on the screen. "I just want to be with you. Is that okay?" Instead of grieving for my husband, I was jumping into bed with Elvan.

"I think we've seen enough, haven't we?" I ask, just as there's a knock on Elvan's door in the footage, making that past version of me leap out of the bed, grab my shoes and dash into the bathroom.

"That's Arnolfi," Elvan says, leaning forward.

We watch her enter as past Elvan starts to get out of bed, only to have Arnolfi tell him there's no need. As he tells Principia to turn on the light, Arnolfi presses something to his arm and he slumps, unconscious. "I'm sorry, Asil," she whispers, and I ask Principia to increase the volume. "This won't hurt—I promise. And it will make it easier for you to cope. We're all struggling, aren't we?"

She has a pen syringe slipped up her sleeve. She takes it out and checks it before injecting him in the neck. "You like her too much, that woman. I know you believe her, so I have to do this." She leaves the room shortly afterward and then we watch past me come out of the bathroom, try to wake Elvan and then rush out.

"I must have thought she'd come for me next," I say. "That must've been why I went back to my room and painted that note."

"But why paint it?" Elvan says. "Surely you didn't have much time?"

"I couldn't trust Principia, so I couldn't leave a digital message and I would think a pencil note would be too easily faked, but painting . . . that's something I'd believe I'd done." I look down at the fake wedding ring. "Not that it helped. I knew this was fake, I had the note . . . it didn't help."

"Oh, I don't know," Elvan says. "You knew something was wrong so you distrusted Principia and pressed on with finding Segundus. I'm sorry if I gave the impression I didn't trust you—before it all came out, I mean. About you finding the other base so quickly."

"It was perfectly understandable. It was far too much of a coincidence, because it wasn't one at all. I guess some part of me wanted to prove it was real."

He nods. "I reviewed her research. The wiping technique is reliant on identifying synaptic structures created within a certain time frame. The further back you try to wipe, the more unreliable it gets. Our brains are like distributed processors, connections made all over the place, triggered by all sorts of things. I guess your drive to prove you were telling the truth held on to that memory somewhere else that she couldn't reach." Elvan shifts so that he's facing me. "So, how do you want to handle this?"

"Handle what?"

"Us."

"Oh."

"I know we're all still reeling," he says, his hand moving

closer until his fingertips brush mine. "And I know this is a terrible time, but . . . I can't help but feel we were supposed to be together."

"What, like fate?"

He takes in my wrinkled nose and smiles. "Not exactly. I mean, it just feels right. Well, it would if there wasn't . . . Damn it. I'm sounding like a jerk."

"I don't want to rush into anything," I say. "I don't want to be with you, wondering if I'm just clinging, you know? And I think we both need time to grieve."

"Of course, yes." He stands, runs a hand through his hair. "Thanks for talking and . . ."

"Elvan." I stand too and reach out to take his hands. "You don't need to be nervous around me. This is the weirdest, most awful foundation to any relationship, let alone an affair that was wiped from our memories. I'm here for you, and I want to help you get through this. Okay?"

He nods and we embrace and it feels good. I watch him go and then I sit back down again. I wonder whether he's right about the death messages helping. I've never received one before—at least, not that I can recall—and like him, I've never liked the idea of them. They cost a fortune—at least, the ones that are guaranteed to be confidential do—and they're often horribly out of date. I doubt Charlie or my mum made one. It's just not their style. I don't know what would be worse: the standard notification of their death or a personalized message from them.

"Principia, are there any death messages waiting for me?"

"Yes, Dr. Kubrin. They were released to you once already and then ring-fenced, as I explained before. Would you like to view them now?"

"How do you even have them? I thought we lost comms with Earth when it all . . . happened."

"Your death messages were uploaded to me upon your arrival, Dr. Kubrin, fully encrypted, only released upon confirmation of the death of the relevant party. Messages for an employee are stored in the GaborCorp server closest to that employee, to minimize the risk of losing messages should the deceased have been killed in a catastrophic incident."

"That is so bloody morbid." Principia doesn't seem to have an opinion about that. "All right, then, yes, release them to me now. I'll view them on the wall."

A list of names appears, a devastatingly long one, all confirmed as dead. I swipe it away after seeing my mother's name at the top, and I break down into tears that I'd thought were spent.

It passes. I drink a glass of water and ready myself once more. "Principia, I can't handle all those names right now. I'll say a name; you tell me if there is confirmation of death. Charlie Kubrin."

"Yes."

"Mia Kubrin."

"Yes."

I already knew she was dead, but hearing the confirmation feels like some last remnant of hope being slaughtered within me. I grab my pillow and sob into it, my tears soaking into it as the loss gouges something out of me once more. It isn't just the thought of her death, or even the way she must have died, that makes me howl with grief. It's the fact I can never make it up to her. That chance to return home, filled with longing for her, ready to fall into that promised love and for us to knit ourselves together as we should have been has been stolen from me, and the injustice, the sheer cruelty of it, is too much to bear.

All I can do is let it rampage through me until I am left depleted, like a blackened forest after a forest fire. Eventually,

I can speak again. "Andrew Wilkinson." It's been a long time since I have said my father's name out loud.

"Yes."

"Geena Wilkinson."

"No."

I clamp a hand over my mouth in an effort to trap the sob. My sister survived. Oh God, how awful. "Did any of those who died leave me a death message?"

"Yes. Claire Wilkinson and Charlie Kubrin recorded death messages for you."

Who do I destroy myself with first? "Play Charlie's on the wall."

A much younger-looking Charlie appears on the screen, dressed in a shirt he loved two years ago. He smiles and then schools his face into a more serious expression. "I shouldn't smile, should I? Because if you're watching this, I'm dead and you'll be crying." He frowns for a moment. "At least, I hope you will be, because that means you loved me, and that you miss me. And that's all I can hope for, right?

"I love you, Anna. I know I annoy you sometimes. Annoyed you? Should I use the past tense? I don't really know how to do this. I just wanted to say sorry for the stupid things I've done and probably will do between now and when I actually die. I hope I didn't drown. I probably shouldn't say that either, should I? I hope it was quick. And I hope I need to record lots more of these between now and when I do actually shuffle off.

"Oh, and the file containing all our confidential household stuff is in a folder called 'groceries.' Just in case you need it. I think my APA tells your APA or something. I don't know how this works. Is there anything else I'm supposed to say? Oh yeah, um, if you want to be with someone else—you know, if I die young—I want you to know that I'll come back and haunt you." He bursts out laughing. "That's a joke. Kinda." He laughs again and blows a kiss, and the recording ends.

The tears have stopped. Now I appreciate, acutely, why so many people hate these messages. How can anyone who is in their prime, who cannot imagine their own mortality, possibly record anything of merit? That wasn't the Charlie I left behind. That was pre-fatherhood Charlie. And I find myself being glad I am free of him.

"Come and haunt me, then, you bastard," I whisper and swipe the still of his face away, hating myself.

I'm tempted never to watch the one from my mother, to avoid the risk of thinking less of her afterward. But then my mum is cut from a different cloth than Charlie. I ask Principia to play it.

"Hello, Sprout! I'm recording this on the midwinter solstice because it feels right to face up to death at the darkest point, knowing that things will get better. They will get better, Sprout—trust me. It seems dark now, but you will smile again, you will laugh again and you'll be able to think of me and smile instead of crying. I lost my mum when I was very young, so I know what I'm talking about.

"I've only made two of these horrible things in my life, one for your dad and one for you and Geena, but then I realized that wasn't right. There are things I want to say to you that I can't say to your sister, important things, so here we are. Let me have a slurp—one sec, Pickle." She leans sideways and comes back into shot with a large glass of wine. She takes a long draft and smiles. "That's better. Now. Two things. First: your sister. I know you've never been close, and as a parent that's such a hard thing to see. You always hope that siblings will be there for each other when you're gone, and now I *am* gone I worry that you're on your own. I want you to go and find Geena, darling. I want you to patch things up if you haven't already.

"She won't be easy to find, I'm afraid. I last heard from her about two years ago and she said she was joining the Circle. I looked them up online and I didn't like what I saw, but there we are. She said she met that Alejandro Casales and he made so much sense, she joined there and then. I think she was always running away, to be honest, and she'll run away from them one day, but if she has, she hasn't told me yet. They do allow visitors in special circumstances, and I think my death would qualify. Please do try, Sprout. It means an awful lot to me.

"And now the other thing. Your father. Now, don't switch this off, because I know what you're like and you need to listen. I know you've never believed me when I said he wasn't mad. You must have thought I was some weak wife who couldn't face up to the fact that her husband went insane. Well, you're wrong. He didn't go mad. He was a risk to the European gov-corp's operations. They drove him mad. We're both risks, but they thought they'd kill two birds with one stone. Anyway, my word isn't enough; it never has been for you. That's why I've included proof. And it's cost me a small fortune to buy this security level, so make the most of it! I'd be in a lot of trouble if I was still alive, but what are they going to do? Bring me back from the dead to prosecute me? Ha!

"You can access it at the end of this message. I don't have the power to do anything to bring those responsible to justice. There is no justice for little people like me, especially little people who are on wanted lists. I don't know if you'll be able to do anything either, but if you can, do! If you can't, don't feel bad about it. I just want you to know the reason I have always stood by your father. I want you to know the truth about him. He is a good man who made a bad enemy, nothing more.

"Well, that's that, then. I hope you carry on with your art, Sprout. I know you love your rocks, but you have a talent, and it may bring you just as much joy. I love you, deeply. And I want you to be happy. And if you are on Mars when you get this, then draw something in the dust for me. I'd like that. Bye-bye, love. Bye."

I can do nothing but weep for what feels like hours in this dreadful elastic time. When it is done, I open the file that became available at the end of the message. And the tears start again.

22

THERE IS NOTHING better for plumbing the depths of regret than discovering—too late—that your parents really were far more than you thought they were. My mother was not the corporate bore I thought she was before we all moved to the commune, and neither was my father. Travis was telling the truth.

There are dozens of documents contained within the file she sent me, with an overview handwritten by my mother and scanned in with her tablet. I skim through transcriptions of private messages sent between top figures in the European government, discussing the problems my parents were causing. How they were single-handedly responsible for the groundswell movement that forced the European gov-corp to enshrine more human rights in their citizen-employee contracts. Things like the right to appeal the results of any legal dispute that relies upon a human judge. The right to change jobs. The right to equal maternity and paternity leave. All of these ideas, lost during the tumultuous '20s and '30s in the seismic dying throes of democracy, preserved and then reintroduced into online communities via a clever network of bots that masqueraded as people. My mother wrote the code that powered them and my father wrote the comments and posts and micro-updates that they scattered online. My parents convinced entire online populations that there were thousands of people out there who thought these rights were important and worth fighting for. The power was in the illusion of the consistent minority, the type of group that has so successfully shifted the attitudes of society in the past. I have a flash memory of my father talking to me about it when I was too young to understand. *"It's the consistency that's important. It helps to form a pattern and that pattern is more important than the detail when it comes to changing people's minds."*

The only mistake my parents made was settling down. And I can understand why they were sucked into the system they had always fought: to provide a safe home for me, their first baby. Geena wasn't born yet. And while they were willing to take the risk of minimal health care and constant threat of imprisonment for themselves, it all changed when they had me to consider. But even in London, well within Norope's physical and legal borders, those top figures in Europe still pursued them. After a "close call" that Mum doesn't detail, they appealed to a friend, someone Mum only refers to as "Dr. B," who helped them to set up the commune.

But it wasn't enough. I try to understand transcripts of code, pages and pages of the stuff, but it goes right over my head. Mum's summary says it's proof of an external party hacking Dad's chip, finding a way around the settings that made everyone think it was shut down. It's terrifying reading—I can't help but wonder how many other people have been attacked this way—though Mum's notes are very matter-of-fact, detailing times and dates of the first onset of symptoms, along with a very unemotional account of how she realized, in retrospect, how long it had been happening, even before she got hold of this data to prove it.

Her love for Dad drove her to go back to that world they'd tried to leave, but she didn't obtain proof of the hacking until three years after Dad's incarceration. By then it was too late. She couldn't risk exposing the crime without incriminating herself, and being the sole parent, she dared not take the risk of seeking a prosecution.

There's a document called "read this last." As if predicting the anger that has bubbled up as all of this has sunk in, Mum left a scan of a handwritten note. It is dated a week before I left for Mars.

> *Sprout, don't be angry with me for not telling you about all this before. I know what you're like. You wouldn't have been able to let this go. Living with injustice is one of the hardest things in the world. Your dad and I should have had the rest of our lives together, but I know he would have wanted me to keep you both safe. Pretending not to know what they did to him was the only way to do that.*
>
> *Perhaps, when you get back from Mars, when those paintings make you some money, things can change. It will open doors for you, doors I could never even get close to. Pick your friends carefully. I know Stefan Gabor sent you to Mars. You should know that his husband, Travis Gabor, is a friend of Dr. B, but that is something he'll never admit to. If you are desperate, he may be able to put you in touch. Be careful. I love you. Mum.*

She knew me too well. That same inability to let an injustice go drove me to find Segundus a second time. Some part of me, deep down, couldn't let Arnolfi get away with what she did and steered me back to the secret she tried so hard to hide. I close my mother's files down, making sure they're all saved in my personal, most private folder, in my own chip, with no copy left on Principia's database. Then I realize it doesn't matter. The people who did that to my father are either dead or struggling in the aftermath of the war. My parents are dead. There is no justice to seek anymore.

This is the only legacy of my mother that I have. I weep at the thought of her beautiful ceramics that she'd always planned to leave to me, that I in turn would have left to Mia. Geena was always more fond of Mum's strange hats, handmade just like the pots, so there was always the understanding that they would be left for her.

Mum wanted me to go and find Geena after her death, but the Circle is based in the States. As the first missiles were fired from there, there's no doubt the retaliation will have been brutal. How did my sister survive? Perhaps the Circle is in such a remote area that it escaped any direct hits.

"Principia, I have some questions. Come and talk to me."

The avatar walks out of the bathroom, but there's not a flicker of amusement left in me. "How can I help, Dr. Kubrin?"

"Did Travis Gabor die?"

"No official statement has been made to that effect. As he is not a relative, I cannot disclose any more information."

I think about trying to locate where Geena would have been when the bombs started falling, but what's the point without knowing what we're all going to do next?

"Can you send a message to everyone except Arnolfi, asking them to meet in the communal area this evening at eighteen hundred hours? Tell them I think we need to take stock and work out our next steps."

"Done. Is there anything else I can help you with, Dr. Kubrin?"

I look at the sketch pad resting on the desk. "Something's been niggling at me. If you edited the data from the cam drones before showing it to me, why was the mast in that last picture I worked from?"

"Can I clarify that this is the image you are referring to?" It displays the one I had in mind, a view facing toward Segundus, only missing the mast.

"Yes, that one. Why didn't you remove the mast before you showed it to me?"

"I did, Dr. Kubrin. This is the image I presented to you."

"But I saw the mast. I drew it! That's why I knew it was there!"

"I can only theorize that it was a remnant of memory that escaped Dr. Arnolfi's treatment. You do seem to store visual memories in an atypical manner, with a great deal of activity in the associative cortex as well as the visual cortex and—"

"Stop! I don't want to know." I can't stand the thought of Principia rooting around in my brain. "And Arnolfi wiped the results stored on the ground scanner, didn't she?"

"Yes, Dr. Kubrin, with my assistance. Would you like a fully itemized list of the actions I took?"

I lean back against the wall. "No. It doesn't matter now. There is one last thing though. If I was here for a month before she did that to us, surely I got loads more messages than the ones you gave me access to since the wipe?"

"Yes, Dr. Kubrin. I have made all of the data I ring-fenced available to you. Perhaps you didn't notice the notification I sent."

"I've been . . . No, I didn't."

Principia drops a shortcut into my visual field and I open the folder containing dozens of messages I have no memory of. From Mum, from Charlie . . . many are tagged "Mia." There's more than three weeks of communications, appearing like a gift.

I close the folder. I'm not ready to watch them yet. Instead, I dismiss Principia, go to the sketch pad and flip the cover back to look at the sketch. It's exactly the same as the painting I found in Segundus, with one difference. The shadows. And now, knowing what I do, I don't see shadows of people standing on the rim of the crater, just out of shot. I see the shadows left by the burning glare of a nuclear blast, staining the red dust of Mars with an echo of the dead.

WE gather in the communal area, silently exchanging embraces and questions about how we are coping. Everyone looks tired and drawn, but the raw horror has passed. It's finally sinking in. Petranek prints us tortilla chips and salsa, commenting that the printer outside the gym is best for sour cream in case anyone wants to print some. No one does.

"How's Arnolfi?" Banks asks Elvan.

"The concussion has passed and her arm is pretty much healed. Her chip is providing neurochemical assistance but she's very withdrawn. I'm not sure we can keep her confined to quarters indefinitely."

"I've been thinking about this," Banks says. "All of it, actually. Anna was right to call this meeting. We don't have the luxury of taking any more time out to grieve. We have hard decisions to make. I don't think Arnolfi has the right to be here for this discussion, given what she did. Does anyone disagree?"

Elvan frowns. "We can't just ignore her."

"We can't trust her either," Petranek says.

"I suggest we revoke all of her medical privileges permanently, along with her right to digital privacy," Elvan says. "We give Principia strict instructions on how it interacts with Arnolfi and we try to bring her back into the group."

"But she crossed a line," Petranek says.

"So we punish her forever?" Elvan glares at Petranek; then his features soften. "I know how you feel. But I don't want to be the sort of person who makes another suffer for the rest of her life, just for making one poor decision."

"Many poor decisions!" Petranek counters. "It isn't just the wipe, Elvan; it's the fact she lived with us, deceiving us, making us think our loved ones were alive when they were all dead! Taking hardware from the base to give to Segundus, hiding critical information from us. What if she had told us about that place? What if we could have all worked together to find a better solution than them all fucking off and damning us? She denied us that opportunity, to save her own neck. I can't forgive her for that. I'm sorry. I just can't."

"Then what do you suggest?" Banks says. "A trial? A formal punishment?"

Petranek's lip curls in disgust. "No! I don't know. We could send her to Segundus."

"Solitary confinement, then," Elvan says, shaking his head. "That's cruel."

"Then go with her!" Petranek snaps and then immediately holds up hir hands. "Shit, I'm sorry, Elvan. I'm sorry. I just . . . I can't deal with this sort of crap. I'm a bloody engineer. I'm not cut out for making decisions like this."

"I think we need to put the issue of Arnolfi to one side," I suggest. "Like Banks said, we have hard decisions to make. Whether we stay on Mars, for one. We have the ship and the fuel to go back to Earth. One-way trip, I reckon, given what's happened. Does anyone want to do that?"

Everyone looks at one another, as if waiting for someone else to speak first. "I think it would be suicide," Banks finally says. "All I can pick up is the emergency broadcast signal. There's no Internet. No power in a lot of places as far as I can tell. I reckon a lot of places were hit by EMP blasts. It's going to be hell there. Chaos."

Petranek and Elvan both nod. "I agree, for what it's worth," I say. "I don't think we could survive there, and there wouldn't be any guarantee we'd even be able to land safely. So that means we're staying here, then."

It's something we've all been facing since that hammer-blow at Segundus, but actually voicing it for the first time makes it feel more real. We sink into silence and I feel that surging, brutal grief drawing close again, threatening to drown me once more. I grip the edge of the table, pushing it back, unwilling to fall apart in front of them all.

"I've been running some numbers actually," Petranek says after a loud clearing of hir throat. "This is the stuff I am cut out for, after all. We can survive for the next two years without lifting a finger, pretty much. That's based on current usage of power, oxygen, water and food printers. We've built up a decent food-printer canister store by re-stocking above usage levels with each delivery from Earth, but that will run out. In terms of power, there's no problem. It's all renewable energy and we have printers and a really good clean room in Segundus to make replacement parts if we need to. Same goes for oxygen production and structural integrity. As for water, I can guarantee supply for ten years, if our usage doesn't change and if the ice sources are as extensive as the data suggested."

"I'm fairly confident they are," I say, so relieved to have something unemotional to focus on. "I reviewed all the data on the trip over. That doesn't mean we shouldn't find other places to drill bores, but I have time to find good locations."

"Lucky we've got a geologist," Banks says kindly.

"Yeah," I say, accepting the implicit apology. "Looks like I will be useful after all."

"So food is the issue, then," Elvan says. "What can we do about that?"

"The garden dome was mothballed after the damage caused by the big storm three years ago," Banks says. "It was pretty crap anyway, but it could be repaired and improved maybe?"

Petranek nods. "It's worth a try. But I think we'll be better off farming some algae and building a processor to refill the printer canisters. It'll be a lot of work, but I could do it with help and there are loads of drones and equipment at Segundus. There are algae cultures ready to start it off, because they planned to do this years ago and shelved it. And we will probably find more food-printer canisters over there too, come to think of it. So we have time."

"I need to discuss molecular-printer requirements with you," Elvan says to Petranek. "We're going to need more vitamin D supplements, and a few other things are going to run out in a year or so."

"We're going to be okay," I say, making them all face me. "I mean, look at you. You're the most intelligent, skilled and awesome people I've ever met. We have the hardware. We have an AI with tons of Mars-specific experience. We can do this."

"Careful, Kubrin," says Petranek with a glint in hir eye. "You'll be suggesting a group hug soon."

"There is one more thing I want us to discuss," Banks says. "I think we need to develop our own contract for living here together. As far as I can tell, GaborCorp no longer exists. There's been no contact for over five weeks now. It's way past the official limit when another organization would intervene. So I say we declare ourselves an independent colony with new rights, responsibilities . . . the whole shebang."

"I have many thoughts and feelings about this," Petranek says with a broad grin. "I'm printing more chips. Anyone want coffee?"

My APA pings me before I can reply. The notification makes me jolt. "I have a new message," I say, making everyone else freeze. "At least I think I do. Incoming data of some sort."

"From Earth?" Elvan says.

"I don't know. It's still downloading. It looks weird. Principia, it looks like my APA is downloading a huge packet of information. Do you know what this is? Is there an actual message?"

"I am not detecting any incoming data, Dr. Kubrin," Principia replies.

"There's nothing coming in on the comms," Banks says. "Is your chip—"

"Hello, Dr. Kubrin."

The room around me fades and I'm back in my apartment, the table filling the room, all the old paintings on the walls. Travis is sitting at the table, just like all the other times I talked to him, but he's wearing different clothes. His hair is shorter, worn in a less fashionable style, and he looks tired.

"I'm sorry if you were pulled here. I could only do so much with what I had available and this is a message I don't want you to miss."

I sit down, hoping that the others are taking care of my body as my mind is focused here. "What's going on?"

"I'm afraid I haven't had the time to predict dialog trees for this message, so I'll keep it to the point. I'm not on Earth. I'm on Atlas 2, a ship created by the Circle cult to follow the Pathfinder. We left Earth thirty-nine days ago and we're moving pretty fast now, so I had to bundle all this up damn quick and send it in a rough-and-ready package before the distances got too great. I'm not an expert on sending data across distances like this without a relay.

"I'm sorry I didn't send this before. I'll be honest; I forgot about our arrangement. Things moved quickly on Earth and then after we left . . ." He pauses, looks away for a moment. "You'll already know what happened after we left. The American gov-corp funded this venture and didn't want anyone to follow us. There are about ten thousand people on this ship, and only I and two others know what they did— other than the bastards who gave the order, of course.

"For what it's worth, the Circle had no idea that was going to happen. They're good people.

"There are two things you need to know. One is that your sister is still alive. She's on this ship. I've known her for months in the Circle and just didn't make the connection. Different names . . . you're not very alike, but anyway, she's alive and well.

"The second is that I've had the data on the Pathfinder's destination, and the tech she used to build Atlas, for many years. I helped the Circle with it, and now I want to help you with it. I know my husband was developing the same tech at various research facilities, but not what he was planning to do with it. As far as I could tell, you weren't involved. That's why I'm sending it to you now. It's everything that was in the capsule. Everything you and the rest of the Mars Principia crew need to build a craft to follow us. There's nothing left for you on Earth now, and I can't see why you'd want to stay on Mars, so if you want to try, build something and follow us. Hey, maybe we'll get to have a drink together after all.

"Good luck, Dr. Kubrin. I hope to see you again one day."

The room disappears and then in the next blink I see Elvan's face. I'm lying on the floor in the communal room and he's kneeling next to me. Petranek and Banks are hanging back, looking worried. I blink again and Elvan smiles.

"You back?"

"Yeah. I'm okay." I sit up. My APA notifies me of the need to create a temporary space in Principia's memory to cope with the huge amount of data that is still pouring in, getting too big for my own personal cache to handle. I approve it and get to my feet.

"I think there's another option on the table," I say to the others. "You might want to sit down."

EPILOGUE

"ARE YOU NEARLY finished?" Elvan's voice comes through the helmet speakers, making me smile.

I look down at my old wedding ring in the palm of my glove. He doesn't know I have it. "Yes."

"Because we're going to start preflight checks in an hour."

"It's okay. I'm not far away. I have plenty of time. And Petranek won't let me touch anything anyway."

"Okay. Just . . . just leave plenty of time to get back, darling."

He's nervous. "I will. See you soon."

For the past two years, the ring has been kept in its box, the fake chucked into the recycler on the same day I found the real one. It wasn't hard to find—Principia knew where I'd been in my first month here and for how long; it was just a matter of retracing my steps with a metal detector that it helped me to make.

I tilt the ring to read the engraving inside. *Stronger together*. It never rang true when I first read it, and now it's just a sad reminder of how ill-suited Charlie and I were for each other. The fact that he sprang the engraving on me, without discussing what it would say, still grates, even all these years after his death. I need to let this go.

But I'm not ready yet, and there's something else to finish first. I tuck the ring into my belt pouch and carry on scraping a channel in the dust, finishing a long loop that forms the tip of a tail.

It's taken me all these years to work out what to draw in the dust for my mother. Instead of making something poignant, or overly complex, I've decided upon something that would make her smile: a simple line drawing of her cats, Odin and Frigg, curled up next to each other. It may not be sophisticated, but I know she would love it. And just like she said I would, I find myself smiling at the thought of her on the sofa, the cats clambering over her as she complains lovingly. I send up the cam drone, check that it looks right and then take a picture. There's no way to know how long it will last, but that's not what's important. It's what she wanted.

"Mind if I join you?" Arnolfi's voice comes through just as I'm guiding the drone back to the rover.

"Not at all."

I turn to see her approach and give her a wave.

"I'm not the only one who needed to come outside, then," she says when she arrives.

"It's a big day," I say. "Nervous?"

She nods. "You?"

"Terrified. And Elvan is like a mother hen." I rest a hand on her shoulder and she mirrors the movement. "Petranek and Principia think it's ready and that's good enough for me."

We turn and look down the hill toward Segundus, admiring the craft on the launchpad. At its core is most of the original rocket that brought me here, but now it is so much more than that. As Petranek said, "It ain't pretty, but it'll get the job done."

"I've come to tell you something," Arnolfi says. "I think . . . I think you'll understand, better than the others will."

"Look, we've been through all that. It's behind us now. I know Petranek is still a bit prickly, but considering ze wanted to kill you, I think things have come a long way."

Arnolfi drops her hand from my shoulder and turns to look away from the ship, out into the wilderness. "I'm not going with you."

"What?"

"I'm going to stay on Mars. I've made my decision and it's the right one for all of us."

"Is this some sort of guilt-complex bullshit?"

"Anna." She turns to me again. "Without me on the ship, the odds of mission success go up by fifteen percent."

"Who worked that out? How?"

"It's all to do with redundancies and how much more food there will be. Look, I don't want to go into the details. Principia knows. It did the calculations. This is the right thing to do."

"Is this your idea of penance?"

She sighs. "When I did what I did, I hated myself. I don't want to be that person anymore. I need to stay here. I need to know I can put you all before me, like I should have done back then. And besides, I can live here for a long time. With more space."

"But you'll be alone."

"I'll have the prince. And I'll be able to play all the opera that Banks hates as loud as I like."

I embrace her. The woman who wronged us all, who

taught me how to forgive, who helped us to build the craft we'll soon be leaving on. "You want me to tell the others, don't you?"

She nods. "Will you? I said my good-byes to them all earlier. They just didn't realize it."

"Yeah, if that's what you want."

"It is. Take care, Anna. Godspeed."

I try to speak, but my throat is clogged. I head back to the rover and, after another wave, watch Arnolfi head out, away from Segundus. She wants to watch the launch from a safe distance. I almost run after her, to try to convince her to come, but I have to respect her choice. And I understand it. I would have done anything to prove I was a better mother, had I had the chance. This need to prove that we are not the worst of ourselves can sometimes make us better people. She has the right to find her own proof.

I sniff, not wanting to cry when I can't wipe my nose, and take out the wedding ring again. I can't take this with me either.

I dig a hole, stare at the ring for a long moment and then drop it in. This is the second time I've done this, but this time it isn't to bury my guilt, as I'm sure it was before. It's to put something to rest.

I cover it, rest my hand over the little mound for a moment and then stand up. Mars, in all its barren, rust-colored glory, will soon be a memory, merely the place I was when everything ended, and everything began. And for the first time, I have no doubts about where I am going or even about the hope that fills me. I will be with people I love, and that is all that matters.

ACKNOWLEDGMENTS

OH, THIS WAS such a hard book to write! What really didn't help was that our house was filled with builders for a large chunk of the first draft, so I want to thank my mum for giving me a quiet spot to write in when I had to run away from all the noise and dust.

Thanks to the marvelous Jennifer Udden, my agent, for support, for edits and for sending me the right GIFs of her emotional reactions to this book at the right times. Thanks to Rebecca Brewer, my editor, for saying such kind things to me in an email that made me cry when I was totally convinced that this was a terrible book that should never see the light of day. And for pushing me again, making me delve deeper to make it a better book. You both make me a better writer and I am so very grateful.

Thanks to Amy Brennan, a very splendid geologist, for sending me lots of interesting information about Mars and useful notes on surviving there. I hope I didn't get anything wrong about the geology and the base, but if I did, it was all my fault and not Amy's!

Thanks to the team at Ace for continued support of these

books, and for spreading the word about them so much more effectively than I ever could!

Finally, thanks to my incredibly supportive family. My lovely son, who offers hugs whenever I need them, and my amazing husband, Pete. He knows how much I have wrestled with this one and has kept me fed, cuddled and reassured throughout. Thank you, darling.

Lastly, I wanted Anna to be one of the mothers we so rarely see in our books and films and TV shows, one for whom motherhood really does not come naturally. But we exist and postnatal depression is such a hard thing to go through. I offer my love and my respect to those of you who know how hard it is.

So, going back to Pete, this is why I dedicated this book to you, my love. Because you got me through one of the toughest times of my life, and not just me, our little Bean too. You were my strength, you never judged me and you never complained when I was at my worst. Thank you. I love you.

Photography by Lou Abercrombie

Emma Newman is the author of *Planetfall* and *After Atlas* and a professional audiobook narrator, reading short stories and novels in all genres. She also cowrites and hosts the Hugo-winning podcast "Tea and Jeopardy." Emma is a keen role-player, gamer and designer-dressmaker. Visit her online at enewman.co.uk.

TRICIA SULLIVAN

Occupy Me

A search not for who you are but what you are, a stunning revelation about the Universe and our place in it.

A woman with wings that exist in another dimension. A man trapped in his own body by a killer. A briefcase that is a door to hell. A conspiracy that reaches beyond our world.

Breathtaking SF from an Arthur C. Clarke Award-winning author.

● ● ●

'Occupy Me keeps the pages turning and the wheels of thought whirring. It's a psychedelic experience, a wacky tapestry of an idea' *SFX*

'This is science-fiction at its most surreal . . . the premise is brilliant' The Daily Mail

AL ROBERTSON

Crashing Heaven

Meet Hugo Fist.

A diamond-hard, visionary new SF thriller. Nailed-down cyberpunk ala William Gibson for the 21st century meets the vivid dark futures of Alastair Reynolds in this extraordinary debut novel.

With Earth abandoned, humanity resides on Station, an industrialised asteroid run by the sentient corporations of the Pantheon. Under their leadership a war has been raging against the Totality – ex-Pantheon AIs gone rogue.

With the war over, Jack Forster and his sidekick Hugo Fist, a virtual ventriloquist's dummy tied to Jack's mind and created to destroy the Totality, have returned home.

Labelled a traitor for surrendering to the Totality, all Jack wants is to clear his name but when he discovers two old friends have died under suspicious circumstances he also wants answers. Soon he and Fist are embroiled in a conspiracy that threatens not only their future but all of humanity's. But with Fist's software licence about to expire, taking Jack's life with it, can they bring down the real traitors before their time runs out?

• • •

'A stylish blend of techno thriller and hard SF' *SFX*

'Bizarre, intelligent and, above all, come-thing new' *Interzone*

'Seriously satisfying cyberpunk action meets thoughtful moral philosophy with a dash of detective noir and a supersized side of strik-ing science – the year's best debut to date, and make no mistake' *Tor.com*

ALEX LAMB

Roboteer

*A fast-paced, gritty, space-opera based on cutting
edge science, perfect for fans of Peter F Hamilton
and Alastair Reynolds*

The starship *Ariel* is on a mission of the utmost
secrecy, upon which the fate of thousands of lives
depend. Though the ship is a mile long, its six crew are
crammed into a space barely large enough for them to
stand. Five are officers, geniuses in their field.
The other is Will Kuno-Monet, the man responsible
for single-handedly running a ship comprised of the
most dangerous and delicate technology that
mankind has ever devised.

He is the Roboteer.

• • •

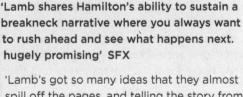

**'Lamb shares Hamilton's ability to sustain a
breakneck narrative where you always want
to rush ahead and see what happens next.
hugely promising' SFX**

'Lamb's got so many ideas that they almost
spill off the pages, and telling the story from
both sides is a smart way of balancing the
argument' *Sci-Fi Now*

**'Alex Lamb has crafted a terrific debut
novel. If the subsequent volumes are as
good as this one then Lamb will surely be prominent in
many an SF fan's bookcase' Starburst Magazine**

'*Roboteer* hits the ground running . . . Lamb handles the
politics without resorting to info dumps and in Will has
created a sympathetic and well-rounded hero' *The Guardian*

ABOUT GOLLANCZ

Gollancz is the oldest SF publishing imprint in the world. Since being founded in 1927 Gollancz has continued to publish a focused selection of bestselling and award-winning authors. The front-list includes **Ben Aaronovitch**, **Joe Abercrombie**, **Charlaine Harris**, **Joanne Harris**, **Joe Hill**, **Alastair Reynolds**, **Patrick Rothfuss**, **Nalini Singh** and **Brandon Sanderson**.

As one of the largest Science Fiction and Fantasy imprints in the UK it is no surprise we have one of the most extensive backlists in the world. Find high-quality SF on Gateway written by such authors as **Philip K. Dick**, **Ursula Le Guin**, **Connie Willis**, **Sir Arthur C. Clarke**, **Pat Cadigan**, **Michael Moorcock** and **George R.R. Martin**.

We also have a strand of publishing in translation, which includes French, Polish and Russian authors. Gollancz is home to more award-winning authors than any other imprint, with names including **Aliette de Bodard**, **M. John Harrison**, **Paul McAuley**, **Sarah Pinborough**, **Pierre Pevel**, **Justina Robson** and many more.

The SF Gateway
More than 3,000 classic, rare and previously out-of-print SF novels at your fingertips.
www.sfgateway.com

The Gollancz Blog
Bringing you news from our worlds to yours. Stories, interviews, articles and exclusive extracts just for you!
www.gollancz.co.uk

GOLLANCZ
LONDON